Praise for Joan Wickersham's

The Paper Anniversary

"THE PAPER ANNIVERSARY is told with all the compassion, affection, and wry humor of an Updike. . . . a wonderful book, a rich and satisfying story with unforgettable characters."

—Elinor Lipman, author of *Isabel's Bed*

"An astute contemporary parable, generating a surprising amount of empathy for Wickersham's characters. . . . This appealing first novel . . . has taken us through stretches of under-explored territory and down some surprising byways."

—Elaine Kendall, *Los Angeles Times*

"THE PAPER ANNIVERSARY feels like life. . . . Wickersham fashions from the mercurial, transitory feelings and words and deeds of everyday life a story rich in subtle movement and emotion. . . ."

—Mark Leccese, *The Boston Phoenix*

"THE PAPER ANNIVERSARY is witty, tender, real and sweet, and a tribute to all couples—couples who think they know what they want, couples who aren't sure, and couples who are some of each sometimes."

—Christine Crumbo, *Wichita Eagle Beacon*

"THE PAPER ANNIVERSARY is funny and tender, as if *Scenes from a Marriage* were rewritten by Margaret Drabble. A delight."

—Meg Wolitzer, author of *This Is Your Life*

"Wickersham is a thorough, honest, and quietly magnetic novelist. . . . an astute and graceful drama about the status of compassion and love in a world rich in options and ambiguity."

—Donna Seaman, *Booklist*

A Book-of-the-Month Club Alternate Selection

For orders other than by individual consumers, Washington Square Press grants a discount on the purchase of **10 or more** copies of single titles for special markets or premium use. For further details, please write to the Vice-President of Special Markets, Pocket Books, 1230 Avenue of the Americas, New York, NY 10020.

For information on how individual consumers can place orders, please write to Mail Order Department, Paramount Publishing, 200 Old Tappan Road, Old Tappan, NJ 07675.

The Paper Anniversary

Joan Wickersham

WASHINGTON SQUARE PRESS
PUBLISHED BY POCKET BOOKS
New York London Toronto Sydney Tokyo Singapore

A Washington Square Press Publication of
POCKET BOOKS, a division of Simon & Schuster Inc.
1230 Avenue of the Americas, New York, NY 10020

Published by arrangement with Viking Penguin, a division of Penguin/USA Inc.

ISBN: 0-671-89071-9

First Washington Square Press trade paperback printing March 1995

10 9 8 7 6 5 4 3 2 1

Cover design by John Gall

Printed in the U.S.A.

"Commuter Marriage," chapter one of this book, first appeared in somewhat different form in *The Hudson Review*.

"Brown Penny" by William Butler Yeats is from *Collected Poems of W. B. Yeats*, Macmillan, New York.

For Jay

*My thanks to all the friends who read the manuscript
at various stages: Nina Barrett, Rowena Barrett, Caroline Chauncey,
Sarah Ream Johnson, Christopher Milford, Holly Russell, Alexander
Stille, and Jessica Treadway. To Pamela Dorman, Hal Fessenden, and
Ann Rittenberg, for their patience, candor, and constant support.
And to Jay Wickersham, for sustaining me
through the writing, and long before.*

Part I

1

Commuter Marriage

❧

On the platform at Penn Station, at six-thirty on a Saturday morning, a young woman in a red sweater stood waiting for the Boston train to pull in. She was small and slim, with short light hair pulled back into a stubby ponytail. Two shiny pieces had slipped out to frame her face, which looked quite young, schoolgirlish, although she was twenty-seven. The childish look was heightened by the fact that she was wearing bright red lipstick and smoking a short, smelly cigarette, and doing neither with much authority. On her bony forearm was an enormous man's watch on a black leather strap; every few seconds she shook her arm until the watch flopped down around her wrist, and she frowned at it, with a crease down the center of her freckled forehead.

The train came in a little late, and very slowly, as though aware of its own charisma—a faraway circle of light moving in, growing bigger, pulsing a little in the dark air of the tunnel, and then behind it a lumbering line of coaches, big, gray, dusty, hooked together like elephants in the circus. She knew that they were full of people, but it was still a surprise when the train gave a sigh and the passengers started coming out: sudden clutter and commotion all over that still platform. I am a woman meeting her husband at a train, she thought, and it made her feel important, glamorous, like someone in a forties movie. She looked into the faces of the men surging across the floor past her. How would I feel if he were my husband? Or he? And then she saw Jack, and tried to think for one objective moment: And what about this one? But he was pressing his arms around her and bringing his face down against hers. "Ow," she said after a minute. "Your suitcase."

He let go of her instantly and stepped backward with the suitcase, which had been pressing into her legs; then he looked down at it, frowning slightly, as though it were a child he had called into his study to scold, but now he had it there he couldn't remember what it had done wrong or figure out how to punish it.

They checked the suitcase, leaving it in a dented metal locker. "Why can't we just go back to the apartment?" Jack said, his mouth against her ear.

She shrugged; he still seemed a little strange and foreign, his hair a different length from when she had seen him last: someone she had just met at a train. "Ed and Caterina are there."

"Toss 'em out," suggested Jack.

"We can't do that. It's their apartment. I thought we'd spend the day doing New York things, and then go home. They're going out to dinner tonight, Caterina said."

"That's tactful of them."

"Don't be so grouchy."

"How about if we check into a hotel for a day? Does that count as a 'New York thing'?"

She hesitated, then kissed him quickly and bent to lift the suitcase and heave it into the locker.

The sight of Maisie, as always, even after three years together, turned Jack shy. She was so pleasing to look at, so neat. When she got out of bed in the morning, the bed was made. Her small body, naked, was surprisingly voluptuous, yet neat: small brownish nipples centered on round breasts, a golden isosceles triangle suspended between small shining hips. Her clothes, folded in the drawer at home, were deceptively inanimate, like sleeping faces—stacks of black jeans, flat-folded sweaters, and T-shirts in all colors, aqua, fuchsia, lime, black. Then she put them on and they belonged to her, she inhabited them.

Marrying Maisie had surprised him, like having a strange cat come to sleep in his lap: the mystery of being singled out. Dreaming his way through graduate school, he had met her at a party one spring and walked her home, up the stairs, into a bare cool apartment, where they'd sat on the floor and talked until morning. He could not remember leaving; his life with Maisie stretched back to that dawn, a continuum, a filibuster; if one of them stopped talking, the whole thing would be over. Maisie seemed like a detour from the fate that really belonged to him, dull, safe; he felt as though he had mistakenly got on the wrong bus, to a much more thrilling destination; his sense of honor prodded him to tell the driver, but he knew that if he told, he'd be put off.

They had lived together before they were married, but not much after. When they met, Jack was in the middle of a Ph.D. in German literature. They lived in each other's apartments and then consolidated into one place, in a noisy student-filled apartment building on the Fenway in Boston. All night long the building shook with the bass notes of a hundred stereos. They had to put their clothes bureau in the living room; their bed completely filled the tiny bedroom. Maisie worked as a secretary in the Harvard natural history museum; she hadn't figured out yet what she wanted to do. She cooked dinners for friends and dragged Jack dancing every couple of months. On Sundays they went for long walks and drank wine by the river and ended up at a foreign movie. Then Jack's father died and left him a french fry factory up in Maine. That sobered them both, a bucket of cold water. Jack had to go, for a while at least, to untangle the threads of the business, until he could find someone else to run it or buy it. Of course I'm coming, said Maisie. I'll be the boss's wife, and I'll give gracious dinner parties that will intimidate the hell out of your employees. They got married and moved north, to a little cottage in a wintry deserted beach community. Two rooms upstairs and two rooms downstairs, and a fireplace that didn't work.

Something was wrong with the heat in that house. No matter how high they turned the thermostat, the rooms were still icy; at night the sheets were frozen and painful. One morning the pipes froze. Jack, swearing, put on his coat and brought in shovelfuls of snow, filling the bathtub with it, so that when it melted they would have water. Three days later the snow was still there, frozen, in the tub. Night after night Maisie sat on the couch wrapped in a blanket, watching television. She watched comedies and westerns and late-night reruns and the news, impassively. Her mother came from Virginia to visit for a few days and said she thought the house could be charming, if only Maisie would do something with it. Why didn't they take the car over to Calico Corners and pick out some nicer curtain fabric and maybe make some cushions for the living room? Maisie shook her head; this question seemed to her unanswerable. Her mother and Jack looked at each other, worried; good, thought Maisie, good.

So when she said she wanted to try working in publishing, and that the only place to do that was New York, Jack was actually relieved. It was the first time she'd wanted to do anything since they'd moved to Maine. Caterina and Ed said they'd love to have her. ("Are you kidding?" said Caterina over the phone. "A built-in baby-sitter!") Maisie had read articles about husbands and wives pursuing careers in separate states, with enormous phone bills, hopping on and off planes. She saw herself arriving back in New York after a few days in Maine with Jack: a long tanned leg (they had spent the weekend sailing) thrusting out of a taxicab, followed by a briefcase bulging with manuscripts, and glowing Maisie saying "Keep the change" and tossing her hair back and running up the stairs two at a time to her top-floor brownstone apartment. When Jack came down she would let her answering service take all the calls while she and Jack lay in bed before an enormous atelier window. Then she would get up and call in for her messages, impatiently writing them down with a silver pencil: call this agent and that agent, and this famous writer is stuck on his book and needs your advice, and can you fly out to California to discuss the movie rights for that horrible but phenomenally successful potboiler you pulled out of the slush pile last year?

When they left the station she took him to her office, which he had not seen in his two previous visits to New York. The Saturday darkness and emptiness stripped it of its importance. How could she make him see the bustle of the book-lined reception area, the flashing lights on the telephones, the sheets of paper curling out of typewriters and computer printers? On the other hand, the desertion of the place gave Maisie new power; she was free to stroll down the long halls pointing out the offices of editors, walking around conference tables and letting her hand trail along their gleaming surfaces. She stopped to show him the aquarium in her boss's office; he bent obediently to look through the glass at a tower of slow ascending bubbles, rainbow-skinned fish hanging still in greenish water. She did not tell him it was part of her job to feed them. Then on to her cubicle, where she had left the desk strewn with urgent-looking clutter: memos, three fat manuscripts, message slips, mailing envelopes stamped PRIORITY, all put there in excitement the night before, knowing that the next time she saw them, Jack would be with her, impressed. But he only glanced at the desktop. He lifted and dropped the cover of a thesaurus that lay on top of her filing cabinet, and looked at the topless walls and said, "It must be kind of distracting, working in here," and she could tell he was thinking, You left me alone up there to come work in a cubicle?

To get to the factory, you drove north, north, north. You smelled it before you saw it, an oily fried smell breathing out of the pines along the road. It was cold where the factory was, always winter, but the building gave off a feverish yellow sweat, and the snow in the parking lot was slippery with grease. When you came away, you smelled of it. Jack's hair was cold and greasy, and his clothes; the first thing he did when he got home was take a shower. He went to the factory every day and sat in his father's old office overlooking a slippery ravine behind the building: graying grass-cloth walls, cans of old paper clips and pencil ends, manila folders, their ends softened and frayed, iron tiered trays with IN and OUT written on masking tape in his father's handwriting, faded and stuck on too long ago now to come off. A diagram on the wall proclaiming the respective merits of the Maine and Idaho potatoes, and adjudging the Maine superior; hidden in the desk a research report revealing that more consumers preferred Idaho. Under the rickety swivel chair, a plastic T-shaped mat designed to protect the carpet; it was too late now for the carpet, which was filthy and beaten down, but all day Jack swiveled the chair around on the mat: his island. He was the king in a parliamentary kingdom; there was nothing for him to do. The business ran itself: the potato buyers, truckers, peelers, cutters, oilers, packagers, shippers, and distributors were all in place, doing their jobs. At home in the first few months, he and Maisie had talked brightly about changes that would make the company more profitable and more attractive to a prospective buyer: new cuts, new packaging, new advertising, new incentives to make supermarkets carry the brand. But every day, when he came into the office, the heavy oily air sucked the ideas right out of him; he fell into the chair and swiveled, looking out the window, until it was time to go home. The things on the desk acquired the cachet of heirlooms, things his father had wanted him to have.

They walked around on broad, mica-specked sidewalks. They stopped for brunch at a deli. They went to museums, where Maisie stopped intently in front of everything and Jack circled with his hands in his pockets and his jaw tight, willing the day to move along. They had coffee in a coffee shop, their elbows drooping on the scarred Formica tabletop. Being alone this way, in public, was exhausting; they had things to talk about, and the longer the things went unsaid, the bigger they loomed. The afternoon grew cooler; the sun went behind the buildings; Fifth Avenue was suddenly, miraculously, navigable, cleared of shoppers and people with cameras. "Can we go to the apartment yet?" said Jack, his feet dragging like a little boy's.

"Not yet," said Maisie, looking at her watch.

"It's not as though I don't know Caterina and Ed, or don't like them," said Jack. "I have no objection to sitting around and talking to them for a while."

"I want to be alone with you," Maisie said, and took him to walk around Tudor City.

Finally she let them get on a subway. There were free seats in the car, but someone had thrown up on one of them, and there was kitty litter sprinkled on top of it and around it. Maisie and Jack stood at the other end, hanging on to metal loops, with Jack's suitcase wedged between them. The trip took an hour. Jack said, "I can't believe you do this every day." Brooklyn, when they got there, was a dark, misty orange sky hanging over squat buildings packed with lamplit windows. "I guess all those kitchens are full of people having Saturday night supper," Jack said. He imagined kids in pajamas, after their baths, and a grandmother reading to them or playing War with them while the mother scrambled eggs. But Maisie said no, she thought the apartments were full of people taking showers and putting on makeup and getting dressed for dates.

Caterina and Ed's apartment was in a row of brownstones, some of which had carved wooden doors with beveled glass panes and chandeliers inside and glimpses of living rooms painted dark green; and some of which had iron doors with metal grilles on them, and bedsheets over the windows instead of curtains. They lived in a bedsheet building, two flights up. Maisie turned keys in a series of locks, and at the last minute the door was pulled open by Ed, who had wet hair and a faint mentholated shaving-cream smell. "Caterina's getting dressed," he said, shaking hands with Jack. "How've you been?"

Maisie kept Jack and his suitcase in the kitchen until after Ed and Caterina left, leaving the phone number of the restaurant where they would be. She wanted him to walk through the apartment not as a guest, but as a possessor. Yet following him through it, down the hall to her bedroom, she felt a bit embarrassed, the way she had when her mother had come to visit her at college: two worlds, both loved, but best kept apart.

His suitcase lay in the middle of her immaculate floor, filled with a jumble of clothes he hadn't bothered to fold. She thought of him in the little house in Maine last night, bachelorlike, just throwing things in. And now it was as though the pressure of some pent-up desire had burst the suitcase open; socks and shirts had exploded all over the room. The very messiness of it made her nervous. She'd had a stately plan for this reunion: some wine, dinner in the kitchen with Caterina's linen napkins, a talk over coffee and cigarettes, and then a procession down the dark hall to bed. The sound of Jack splashing in the bathroom, the implacable hiss of the shower, filled her with dread; she felt as though something irreversible had been set in motion, a clock ticking steadily toward an hour. When he came out, red and shiny and scrubbed, she barely looked at him, ducked past him into the steamy bathroom, where she wiped off the mirror to look at her pale reflection and tried to remember how much she had missed him. His wet towel, crowding Caterina's on the towel rack, made the bathroom look sloppy; she took it and hung it on the back of the door. When she came out, she realized she had stayed in the bathroom too long; there was Jack, lying naked with the shades down. She wished he would not do that, take off his own clothes; it seemed so businesslike. But she could hardly ask him to get dressed again so that she could undress him. She untied her shoes and put them side by side next to the bed, and she lay down beside him.

Afterward she was relieved: a responsibility discharged, the library books renewed and now you didn't have to worry about them for another two weeks. Relief made her lively; she threw back the covers and kissed him and told him not to move, she'd check on the baby and throw together some dinner. But he came after her anyway, slowly belting himself into his bathrobe. The baby was sleeping on her stomach, her head turned to the side, her mouth sucking softly and her tiny fists curling and uncurling. They stood on either side of her crib, looking down at her and then at each other, but neither of them said anything.

They had the dinner Maisie had planned: linguine with shrimp and vegetables. A salad. Raspberry sherbet. Jack ate and ate, plowing through what Maisie considered delicate food. She lit a cigarette and thought how this enthusiasm, which should have gratified her, instead irritated her. Didn't he understand how carefully she'd chosen the tomatoes and zucchini at the farmers' market? How her hands had itched after deveining the shrimp? How long it had taken to julienne everything?

"So," said Jack. "What do you think?"

"What do I think?"

"How's this going?"

"What do you mean?" said Maisie, putting out her cigarette in her plate.

"We said we'd try it for a while, and see how it worked."

"It's only been four months."

"So—"

"I can't exactly leave the job now. I mean, I like it, it's going well, and I've really only just started to learn. If I came back to Maine, we'd be right back where we started."

"I guess we could try living halfway in between. Boston—"

"Now that's crazy," said Maisie, pushing her chair back and carrying plates to the sink. "I'm not going to commute from Boston to New York every day."

"A couple of times a week."

"You'd be the first to tell me we can't afford it. Plane fares—"

"And what about Caterina and Ed?" said Jack. He was still sitting at the table, twisting to face her as she moved around, putting the food away.

"What about them?"

"You can't stay here forever, you know."

"Who said anything about forever? It's just temporary. Until I can afford my own apartment."

"Your own apartment? But that's so—"

"So what?"

"Definite."

She sighed, squirting dishwashing soap into the sink. Dennis, she thought, yes Dennis, the murder-and-crime editor at her publishing house, he would know how to handle this. They went out for drinks sometimes after work, to a little bar off First Avenue filled with solitary men and women in leather jackets. The tough look of the place at first thrilled Maisie, but nothing ever happened there. No one talked; they just wanted to drink. She and Dennis sat at a tippy little table in the back, Formica made to look like wood, and he told her about his marriage, made so his wife could get out of Russia. His wife was a painter, who slept and drank when she was with him and went away for weeks at a time. It sounded very sophisticated to Maisie, this relationship that swung between politics and passion. She imagined their home, Dennis's Village apartment, as sunlit and messy, empty glasses and vodka bottles, flattened paint tubes, old photographs of Russians stuck into the dusty mirror frame, a rumpled bed, a half-eaten sandwich. Dennis, she was sure, would not get entangled in the logistics of separate households; he would not go trundling back and forth in a sleeping car; he would not ask her in a timid little-boy voice how long this might go on. He would accept the arrangement grandly, or reject it grandly. But Jack—in these discussions with him she always knew what he should say, but he never said it; and so, although she knew better, she was forced to proceed on what was explicit between them, like a minister who, knowing perfectly well why two people should not be married but receiving no answer to his "speak now or forever hold your peace," had no choice but to go on with the ceremony.

Caterina was sitting in a white wicker rocking chair, holding the baby on her lap. "Trot trot to Boston," she said to it. "Trot trot to Lynn. Be careful, be careful, Ellie doesn't fall"—and here she opened her eyes very wide, and her mouth, and the baby looked blandly back—*"in!"* and opened her knees so that the baby dipped briefly between them and came up again, looking surprised. Maisie stood at the window, pulling apart a begonia leaf along its veins. It came apart very neatly, as though the veins were deliberate perforations, put there by some considerate manufacturer. It had rained twice already this morning, but now the sun had come out, outlining the raindrops on the windowpanes in white. A strange overexcited brightness was in the room. "Doesn't it make you feel weird to know that no matter what you do with the baby today, she won't remember it?" she said.

"I don't think of it that way," said Caterina, hoisting the baby straight up in the air so its baggy yellow pajama feet dangled. "Because, all right, maybe she won't remember this specific moment, but she's got to store up all these good days in her subconscious somewhere. And anyway, you never know when things really start to count."

Maisie dropped the pieces of the leaf she was holding and plucked off another one. "I read in a magazine that kids who are treated badly at an early age remember it."

Caterina gazed into the baby's face. "How could anyone treat that badly?" she asked. "Look at those little cheeks. Don't you just want to bite them?"

Maisie looked at the baby. She was its godmother; so far this had produced nothing in her but an uncomfortable sense that she was letting the baby down. She had known Caterina for years; they had lived together at boarding school and at college and seen each other through exams, lovers, jobs, and weddings; but seeing Caterina with the baby made her want to back away, as though she had come too close to the fire. She wanted to ask Caterina sometimes whether she felt trapped, but she knew what Caterina would say: Of course not. Nobody made me have a baby. It was my choice. Everything always seemed so clear to Caterina. You did right even when it was unpleasant, and you shunned wrong even when you suspected it might be very pleasant indeed. The most infuriating thing was that so far it had all worked: here was Caterina sitting in her pristine blue-and-white living room, so milky, so serene, holding her baby aloft in the sunlight. Much as she loved Caterina, Maisie sometimes longed for the day when the moral system messed up, when Ed had an affair or the baby grew up and did cocaine. Then Caterina would come to her for advice for a change; and Maisie would listen sympathetically and then give the answer that, she was becoming convinced, was the only truly compassionate one possible: I don't know. It's not fair. Sometimes you do the best you know how, and things go wrong anyway.

"So how are things with Jack?" Caterina asked, rocking in the chair.

"Okay," Maisie said. She didn't want to talk about it, and she hoped Jack and Ed would get back soon with the Sunday papers. She was itching to light a cigarette, but Caterina didn't like people to smoke around the baby.

"Oh, well, it'll be easier when you go home for your vacation," said Caterina. "Then you'll have more time, and more privacy."

"The awful thing is I don't really feel like that's my home," Maisie said, and instantly regretted it. This was what always happened when she let herself be seduced into a conversation with Caterina: she would swear in advance to keep things light, to keep herself under control, and somehow the lid always came up off the box and all her troubles came swarming out. I am Caterina's screwed-up friend, she thought; she could imagine Caterina and Ed lying side by side in bed at night, sighing and whispering to each other that they hoped everything worked out all right for Maisie. But the truth was that she did feel at home here, where she had her own room with an unfolded old sleep sofa that had once stood on Caterina's parents' sunporch. Right now the baby was sleeping in a narrow dressing room off Caterina and Ed's room, but Maisie knew that the room she occupied was the apartment's real child room, and eventually she would have to get out so that Ellie could get in. "I could always get my own apartment, I guess," she said aloud.

"And have Jack move down here?" Caterina said, wiping the baby's face with the diaper she always had slung over her shoulder.

"I don't know," Maisie hedged. "I don't think I can really ask him to do that."

"Why not?" Caterina said briskly, the words coming out in a rush, as though she had wanted to say them for a long time. "Frankly, I've never understood why he and Maine have to be a package deal. Let him get someone else to run the place, and move down here."

"I can't," Maisie said again.

"Why not? If he cares about the marriage, he should put you first."

"Yes," said Maisie, pulling off another leaf. "But what if I ask him to move down here, and it doesn't work out?"

Caterina was silent, rocking with the baby, who had begun to whimper. If she starts nursing now, I'll scream, Maisie thought, but Caterina just kept rocking. After a moment Maisie went ahead and lit a cigarette anyway, because her hands were shaking and she knew that Caterina would not rebuke her now; and she thought again how much she hated Caterina when she was unfolding her problems before her this way, like describing the symptoms of some embarrassing infection to the doctor in detail because you know it is your only chance of proper diagnosis and cure. But Caterina couldn't cure anything; she could only anesthetize. Maisie remembered the day before her wedding, driving around with Caterina, saying, "I don't want to get married." And Caterina soothing, "It's all right, everybody feels like that right before, I felt like that, don't worry." And she had let those words coax her to the altar, like a cat coaxed down from a tree. Caterina knew something about love and safety that she, Maisie, didn't know; but she would let Caterina's words guide her there.

In the dark, in bed, something was waiting to happen. Come on, come on, it said to Maisie, and she knew she ought to ignore it, but there was this immense silence that needed to be filled with something immense, so childishly she put her small hand into its big one and let it pull her along. "You don't love me," she began in a soft voice, as though testing a microphone.

"What?" said Jack, not so much as if he hadn't heard right, but as if he wanted to give her a chance to change her mind: Are you sure you want to say this?

"You treat me like a chum."

"Oh, come on."

"Yes," she said, her voice shaking now and gaining volume. "I feel like we're hiking up the mountain single file, wearing lederhosen and *whistling*."

He had the sense not to laugh, or perhaps he was too alarmed to be amused. "That's not how you feel when we're in bed together."

"Oh, yes it is. That's how you make me feel."

The words lay in the darkness between them, out there with no way to get them back, like a letter dropped into the mail chute. Maisie wished them unsaid, but there was a strange exhilarating sense of having set something going. She had never thought before that making trouble could be a palpable physical sensation, like splashing in a still pond or bicycling downhill. I'm making trouble, she thought, and there was a reckless creative urge to make more. She pushed off the covers and got out of bed. Jack's discarded shirt was the first garment she came to, and she pulled it on and went to stand by the window. She felt that she should speak carefully, for posterity, but there was also an itch to get on with it already, like standing backstage before a play and watching the audience trickle in. She said: "You don't love me in a sexy way."

"Of course I do. All weekend I've wanted—"

"That's not what I mean. Your wants are so *healthy*. It's like wanting to exercise, or wanting to eat. It comes from the same part of you that likes to read, or see friends, or pet the cat."

"Maisie, what do you want?"

"I want it to be *dark,*" she said. "I want it to be involuntary, to come out of *need,* not affection. I feel like we're so damned *affectionate* all the time. Why can't you ever get angry at me?"

"Keep talking this way and I'll get there."

"You see? You see? You're so rational all the time. You're so good-humored. Don't you know I'm saying horrible things to you? Don't you know we're in trouble? Why don't you stop me?"

But Jack stayed propped on his elbow looking at her, as though she were a messenger riding wildly ahead of a cyclone, and he was torn between believing her warnings and looking at the blue sky and the safe, quiet countryside all around them.

Jack did not have to catch a train back until Monday afternoon, but Maisie had to work. She had a meeting at lunchtime, she said, so she could not see him then, and she felt terrible about it. She really did seem to feel terrible; she put her arms around his neck and cried and said she was sorry that things had not gone well. "It's just that we didn't have enough *time,*" she sobbed. Jack said it was all right, they couldn't expect things to be perfect every time they saw each other. "But don't let this one become indelible, okay?" said Maisie. "Because we won't see each other for a while, so please just don't think about this too much—" He promised that he wouldn't, and that he would call her the following night after work.

After she left, Jack went into the kitchen, where Caterina was ironing. She clearly had been taken into Maisie's confidence and was trying to pretend she didn't know anything was wrong; she blushed, and offered him tea, and questioned him gently about his work, and then, when he complained about the factory, said suddenly, sharply, "So why don't you sell it?"

He went into the bedroom and packed his suitcase, told Caterina he was going to spend the day in New York, and thanked her for having him. "Don't be silly," she said, kissing him on the cheek, "Maisie's part of the family."

The lockers in the station were full, so he left the bag in a checkroom and went out walking. As he walked, he had a conversation with Maisie in his head. I don't own you, he said. I want you to be happy. If it makes you happy to be in New York, then that's what I want.

And she said, If you don't love me enough to do something about it, then why should I give up everything to come live with you in that terrible lonely place?

All right then, I do miss you. Get back here now.

And she said, You don't own me.

When he was tired he went back to the station to get his suitcase, but, rummaging in his pockets, he couldn't come up with the claim check. "Sorry," said the clerk. "I can't let you have it without the token."

"But I can see it," said Jack, leaning over the counter and pointing. "It's that green leather one right over there."

"Sorry."

"Wait. What am I supposed to do?"

"After thirty days it goes over to lost and found. You can claim it there."

"That's stupid. Why should I wait thirty days when I'm here, now."

They wouldn't give it back to him. So he sat on a bench fingering his return ticket and waiting for them to call the next train. As he sat there, he began to get an idea. What if he got a taxi and went over to Brooklyn and knocked on the door just like that, and said I'm staying? But he could hear voices on the other side of the door, talking and laughing and interrupting one another, stopped suddenly by his knock; and there he was, standing in the doorway, gazing in on the startled faces of his wife and the people she lived with.

2

The Paper Anniversary

❧

"A lady on the plane said you had guts," Maisie murmured into his ear. It was a Thursday evening in May; they were in Boston, in a taxi, going from the airport to the hotel where they would spend the night.

"What made her say that?" he asked, surprised at how affectionate she sounded.

"I told her about you. She was sitting next to me. She was about sixty, but she was coming up here to see her boyfriend for the weekend. He teaches anthropology at BU."

"But what did you tell her?"

"Oh, just how you'd taken over the business when your father died, even though it wasn't doing very well. She said that took guts."

Jack looked sideways at Maisie. She'd cut her hair very short, like a boy's, and she wore long earrings he'd never seen before, silver with jade triangles that swung against her jaw when she spoke. The taxi was inching shakily ahead in the rush-hour traffic. She went on talking animatedly about the woman on the plane: her name was Anne, she'd gone to library school after her divorce thirty years ago because she'd needed to find a way to support herself and her son, and now she was the head of the research library at one of the New York investment houses. She'd been beautiful, Maisie said, nearly six feet tall and wearing the most wonderful stark clothes—bam, said Maisie, she just looked like bam! take me or leave me. That's what I want to be like when I'm sixty.

They hadn't seen each other for nearly two months, since that last New York weekend. Maisie had had the flu, and she'd said she didn't want him to come down and take care of her; she looked terrible and wanted only to sleep, and the apartment was too small to have him bustling around when there was really nothing he could do. Then she went out to lunch with the editor she worked for, an informal six-month review, and was told that while her typing and secretarial skills were perfectly fine, she couldn't expect to get ahead just by being, as her boss put it, "a good little girl": she had to show some initiative, start taking home manuscripts from the slush pile, start reading magazines and corresponding with writers who had possibilities.

"And the only time I can do those things," Maisie told Jack on the phone, "is weekends."

"Can't you bring the stuff up here and read? Or even if I came down I could give you some time alone. Go to museums, or something."

But no, she said, it would be too distracting, make too much of a break in her weeks.

"But if we lived together in New York I'd be there, wouldn't I? Underfoot?"

It was just temporary, she told him. Just until she established herself and got the boss off her back. She was already several years older than the other editorial assistants, she was under a lot of pressure to prove herself. *Underfoot,* he thought, why do I let myself sound like that?

He had finally convinced her to come this weekend for his company's annual picnic. He had business in western Massachusetts; he could meet her in Boston and they'd drive to Maine the next day. She'd agreed, out of shame or guilt, he thought. But just now she'd come bounding through the gate at the airport, red-cheeked, and kissed him with a brisk enthusiasm that had startled him. I'm glad you came, he'd said formally; and she'd answered, Oh, I'm looking forward to it, your picnic.

She was susceptible to other people's opinions, he knew, they rubbed off on her like chalk. But could the secondhand admiration of a stranger on a plane really have produced this sudden warmth? Maybe he'd been imagining her coldness. Maybe it was just that she was under pressure in New York, and she didn't realize how she sounded when she spoke to him. He reached for her hand and held it; it was small and very cool.

When they were in the Sumner Tunnel, the orange neon lights whizzing by, she said, "Oh. You know what's coming up?" A by-the-way tone.

"What?"

"Our anniversary." This said with ominous casualness: he'd missed giving the right answer.

"I know," he said. He squeezed her hand lightly.

"I wasn't going to say anything," she said. "I was going to wait for you to bring it up."

"You didn't give me much of a chance."

"But you did remember? You were going to say something?"

"Sure," he said. He'd thought of it once or twice, flipping through his calendar at work, but he'd assumed that any mention of it would annoy Maisie, make her feel that he was trying to corner her into something. "What should we do to celebrate?" he asked.

She drew her hand away and leaned to roll her window open a crack; the air in the tunnel made a muffled whistling sound. "Well, *I* don't know," she said. "I don't know that we need to do anything, actually. I just thought we should acknowledge it, that's all."

"Oh, no, we should *do* something," he said, his voice a little too hearty.

"It's not even a big one," she said. "It's paper."

"What do you mean?"

"There's this list of symbols for each one," she said. "Gifts. You know."

"No."

"Jack, everybody knows. The first one is paper, then there's—I don't know how it goes, but all these crappy little things like wood and tin and plastic. To hammer home to you that what you've gone through so far is nothing, you haven't earned anything yet. And then if you stay married long enough you're supposed to give the woman pearls and sapphires and diamonds." She looked at him. "You're just pretending you never heard of it."

He laughed, shortly. "No."

"Jesus," she said. "Forget it."

"Maisie, I'm sorry. I never did."

"All right. I don't want to talk about it anymore." She looked out the window, and he watched her face, her lipsticked mouth pushed out.

"Okay."

After a moment she said, "Everybody knows. Ed gave Caterina a framed drawing on their first anniversary. And this woman I work with, her husband gave her a subscription to *The New York Times*. Even though they already got it. So they wouldn't have to fight over it anymore." She looked at him, and he saw that her eyes were welling up. "And now you've made me sound petty for even caring about it."

"Oh, Maisie," he began, meaning to say, Why are we fighting about this? and unable to believe that all those other men had known, without prompting, of this codified system of anniversary gifts.

She cut him off. "And don't go out and buy some paper thing, because it won't mean anything now that I've had to ask for it."

The hotel bed was so big that Maisie didn't even know when Jack, lying at the opposite extreme of it, turned over or moved a limb. They watched the eleven o'clock news and then "Nightline," and then a movie came on: *The Benny Goodman Story.* Neither of them felt like laughing, but they couldn't help it, when Benny tagged along to his older brother's music lesson and wanted to play the horn but was handed something else instead.

What is this? he asked.

A clarinet, the teacher said.

What's a clarinet? asked Benny.

"And you didn't believe in fate," said Jack.

They laughed again watching Benny grow up: hands tootling around on a clarinet, bigger hands, bigger clarinet. His music stand shot up like a fairy-tale beanstalk.

Then he was rehearsing with his band for his first big concert, and someone said: I'm printing up the programs and I need to know—what do you guys call yourselves, anyway? What's that? The Benny Goodman Trio? Oh, come on. *Nobody*'ll listen to a group called the Benny Goodman Trio!

"This is a classic," Jack said.

Maisie was shaking with silent laughter, sweating with it. "It's not that funny," she kept saying. "It's really not." But her face was wet, and her cotton nightgown was sticking to her backside. Jack got up and broke into the minibar and handed Maisie a bottle of orange juice, which she drained at once. He took out a can of soda for himself and went back around to his half of the bed. Maisie didn't even feel the mattress move as he got back in. Maybe it was two mattresses under one big sheet; she slid her hand out to the side, still watching the movie, and sure enough she found a slight gap where her bed ended and his began.

Then Donna Reed, who'd been snobby about jazz, listened to Benny's concert with a dawning look of love and comprehension. Now I understand, she said to him afterward. It's like—like spontaneous Mozart!

Jack's face was bright red, and his eyes were squeezed up. "Hee—hee—hee—hee," he went. Maisie looked at him, startled. It was the most uncontrolled sound she'd ever heard him make. The look of him, shaking, losing it, practically weeping, made her laugh again, too, but she could feel that her eyes were nervously wide: who knew what might happen next?

The rest of the movie wasn't as funny, though she kept hoping for it to be. Just before the end she looked over and saw that Jack's head had slipped to one side and his eyes were closed. His big bony face was flushed with sleep, his skin pink and childish-looking beneath the black stubble of beard. He's so nice, she thought, I'm so lucky to be married to him; but it was an incantation made up of meaningless words; another part of her was saying: This is all falling apart.

After the movie came some commercials for financial magazines and dating services: money and love troubles, ads for insomniacs. Then another movie started, *The Glenn Miller Story*. Maisie lay quietly in the dark, waiting to laugh again, or to sleep.

The last time she'd been in a hotel was right after her wedding. The same sanitized stuffy smell in the room, the same weightless feel of the sheet and blanket, the slippery invincible pillow that refused to conform to the contours of her head and shoulders. A city outside, full of sights that should be seen; a plush locked room where lovemaking ought to happen; and the tired sense that she felt like doing neither of these things.

She was thinking now about her wedding, half-awake and half-dreaming. The long morning, getting ready. All she'd wanted was to see Jack, but they wouldn't let her. "It's bad luck," her mother said.

"I don't care, I need to see him," Maisie insisted.

While her mother was downstairs, talking to the caterers, Maisie went into her mother's bedroom and called the Sheraton where Jack was staying, along with his mother and the other out-of-town wedding guests. But there was no answer in his room. She asked Caterina to drive her over there; it was one of those rare times when she wished she had a license so she could drive herself. "It's bad luck," Caterina said. "Here, let me get you some brandy."

"I really want to see him," Maisie muttered, sitting on her bed in her lacy bridal underwear, one thin white-stockinged leg swinging out and back against the bed and out again. The bed wasn't made, a tumble of sheets and blankets. Maisie had begged Caterina to stay with her the night before, to talk her to sleep, but Caterina was the one who'd fallen asleep and Maisie had lain awake, drunk and tense from the rehearsal dinner.

The brandy felt like nothing until it hit her stomach, where it sat and burned, a hard hot knot. She knew that if she really put up a fuss she could make the Sheraton track him down, or make someone drive her over there; but she was afraid that if she got too insistent she would scare everyone else. Things were already in motion—the caterers downstairs, the musicians unpacking their instruments in the green-and-white-striped tent, the presents spread out on a white-clothed table in her mother's bedroom ("It's tacky to display them," Maisie said. "No, it's tacky not to," her mother shot back. "People who don't want to look at them won't even know they're here. I'll only direct them here if they ask. People like to know that their generosity has been appreciated"), flowers in baskets all through the house, roses, lilac, stock, filling the rooms with their dizzying mingled scents. It was too late to stop it all.

Caterina was looking at her seriously, her brown eyes suddenly wide and solemn. "Maisie, are you okay? Do you really need to see Jack?"

"No, I don't *need* to," Maisie retreated sullenly, sipping more brandy, leg still swinging. "I'd just like to, that's all." She just wanted to reassure herself that it really was Jack she was marrying, someone familiar, someone she'd chosen. He was smart, he was gentle, he adored her. She could tell him anything, and he made her feel safe. He could reassure her now, look at her and make all these frightening preparations fall away. She wondered if he was frightened, too, in his room at the Sheraton, but all she got was a picture of him methodically getting into his wedding clothes: one black sock and then another, two black shoes.

Caterina helped her into the dress, the same dress Maisie's mother had worn at her own wedding, twenty-eight years ago. It was long, fluffy, lacy, with three petticoats underneath and long sleeves that ended in points of lace on the backs of Maisie's hands. It was a fairy-tale dress, not the costume Maisie would have chosen for herself—she'd always imagined herself in something short, simple, a sort of flapper's wedding dress—but it seemed to mean so much to her mother that she'd given in and agreed to wear it. As Caterina fastened her into it (dozens of tiny, slippery, satin-covered buttons) she began to feel weepy at the thought of her mother choosing this dress, a princess dress, so optimistic, so innocent.

For weeks they'd been fighting about everything: the guest list, which Maisie had wanted to keep small but which her mother had kept expanding; the music—Maisie had wanted records on the stereo because it was simple and casual, her mother had insisted on a live band; and the menu, which Maisie had envisioned as champagne and cake, but her mother had said, "You can't make people come all this way and then not give them a sit-down meal!"

The worst fight of all was over the photographs. Maisie had just wanted snapshots, but her mother had secretly contacted a photographer who would do posed shots and candids and then bind them up in a big leather album with Maisie's and Jack's names on it and the date. "Absolutely not," Maisie said. The photographer called every night to find out if her mother had made any progress in persuading Maisie. She would hear her mother in the kitchen, whispering into the phone. Finally one night her mother held out the receiver to Maisie: "He says he wants to talk to you." Maisie glared at her mother: "I told you I don't *want* those kinds of pictures!" Her mother held out the receiver with a pleading look on her face. Maisie turned around and walked out of the room. She heard her mother speaking almost tearfully: "I'm sorry, she won't come to the phone," and then her mother hung up and came after her and spat out, "How dare you put me in the position of having to tell him you wouldn't talk to him?"

"How dare you put me on the spot like that?" Maisie shouted.

They stood there glaring at each other, and then Maisie started to laugh. After a moment her mother laughed, too, a bit uncertainly. "Oh, if you could have heard him, Maisie. The desperation. 'But I can preserve your daughter's wedding day, Mrs. Callahan. Who will preserve it, if I don't?' "

Flooded now with sudden love for her mother, and nostalgia, as though getting married were something that had already happened, Maisie thought that was another reason not to stop the proceedings: it would kill her mother. But wait—stopping the wedding? All she was feeling was nerves. All brides had nerves, everyone said so. Caterina had them on her wedding day, and look how happy she was, married to Ed.

"There!" said Caterina, straightening up from Maisie's buttons.

It was twelve-fifteen; the wedding was scheduled for one. It was like those nightmares of going in to take a big exam and realizing you don't know the first thing about the subject: why didn't I prepare better? why didn't I drop the course before it was too late? She couldn't stop thinking about the rehearsal dinner, nightmarish also. Brian, Jack's best man, a friend of his from college whom Maisie had never met before, sitting across the table from her, talking so intelligently about his business, which was manufacturing and selling skylights in Colorado. He was tall and sunburned and funny. He'd been a theology major in college, he said when Maisie asked him how he'd gotten into the skylight business, and when he was writing his senior thesis he worked his way into a philosophical corner and couldn't seem to work his way out. So he'd struggled with it for a year and finally gave up, left school, and started this business with three other guys from college. On weekends the four of them went camping and hiking together, skiing in the summer.

Next to Brian, Jack looked white, skinny, and academic. Brian told funny stories that made everybody laugh, Maisie most of all. She was aware of Caterina's eyes on her. She didn't care. She drank more wine and laughed louder. After dinner, when they milled around in the private room of the restaurant drinking coffee, she stood near Brian, asking him about flying (he and the three other guys had bought a plane together): how long did it take to get from here to there? letting her hair brush across his sleeve. But she hadn't been drunk enough not to notice when he started to edge away from her, looking down at her with a perplexed expression on his face, as though trying to ascertain whether she was really flirting with him; and just as she was beginning to feel ashamed of her own behavior, Jack showed up at her elbow and began to ask Brian questions about people they'd both known at college. Maisie stood there meekly, rescued.

But the fact that she had all but thrown herself at another man twelve hours before her wedding was hardly comforting.

She lit a cigarette and wandered over to the window, the train of the dress dragging heavily behind her. There were people in the garden already: her cousins from Kentucky, whom she hadn't seen in years; her cousin Charlie, who was going to take snapshots with his Nikon (Maisie had won that battle after all); and her friends Beth, Karen, and Nicky, who'd flown down from Boston. The sight of them all made her swear.

"What's the matter?" Caterina asked, coming to stand next to Maisie.

"Look at them!" Maisie said, inhaling and exhaling smoke. "They took me seriously. They really believe a wedding is going to happen."

"Oh, boy," Caterina said heartily, putting an arm around Maisie's shoulders. "We'd better find something to distract you."

Maisie shrugged her off; she was tired of being treated with jolly condescension. "I need to see Jack," she said again. "Will you go downstairs, please, and see if he's here yet?"

Something in her tone made Caterina nod this time, and she left the room. I could still get out of here, Maisie thought. I could still get away.

There was a knock at the door, a voice: "Maisie?" It was Jack.

"Don't come in!" Maisie exclaimed, rushing over to the door in a tangle of satin and lace. "It's bad luck to see each other."

A pause: she could see him smiling on the other side of the door.

"Are you okay?" she asked.

"Pretty much." His voice sounded hoarse. "You?"

"I don't know," she answered. She felt stupid now, talking to him through a closed door; yet if she were to open the door and let him in, a spell would be broken, the day flawed. She had already flawed it by flirting with Brian last night, by letting her doubts show to Caterina, by saying, "Shit," and smoking a cigarette while wearing her wedding dress.

"I'll be all right," she said, dismissing him.

"Well, then, I'll see you later," he said, and she heard a couple of footsteps, leaving.

"Jack!" she called, and when the footsteps came back, she said, "Are you sure you love me?" her voice tight with irritation: didn't he know how to be a groom?

"I'm sure," he said, and then in an even lower voice, "More than anything."

It was those last words, the coda he had added himself, without prompting from her, that got her through the next half hour and up to the altar, on her uncle Desmond's arm. The minister was a blur, and so was Jack, a blur she made vows to. Brian was a taller blur beside him, not even thought of as an object of flirtation now, but something she must resolutely turn her face away from. Her cheeks hurt from smiling.

"Will you love and cherish him and, forsaking all others, keep you only unto him?" the minister asked her.

It was like being crushed in a vise, no escape, the worst possible way of being put on the spot. Her life was narrowing down, doors were shutting. She tried to focus on Jack, aware of letting precious seconds go by, missing her cue. She saw a dark suit, a flushed face (he would come down with the flu later that night and would lie in bed shaking with fever for all of their two-day honeymoon). He looked solemn, hopeful, frightened. He loves me more than anything, she thought, and she said, "I will."

The company picnic was scheduled to begin at one o'clock Friday afternoon. Jack and Maisie got up at five and drove to the factory, which would be open just until noon that day. She'd awakened feeling penitent, determined to try hard today for Jack's sake; but the long drive north, the sparsening landscape and the enormous sky, filled her with apprehension. And at the sight of the factory, the bleak brick building leaning over a sluggish river in the middle of nowhere, the parking space stenciled RESERVED FOR J. ELDRIDGE, something inside her went still and grim.

When they got inside, Jack put on a paper hat. A long narrow one that reminded Maisie of Beetle Bailey, or the people behind the counter at McDonald's. He held out another one, for her to wear.

"Why?" she asked.

"Health regulations."

"You mean you wear this every day?"

"Sure." He had on an apron, too, white smeared with yellow grease. Jeans and a T-shirt. When they'd lived together in Maine, he'd left the house every day in a suit, and she'd assumed he wore it all day; but no, as soon as they'd arrived at the factory he'd gone into the men's room and come out in jeans, carrying the suit in a plastic bag.

"Why do you bother?" Maisie asked, jabbing the garment bag with the backs of her fingers.

He hung it up on the back of his office door. "I wear it for meetings, that sort of thing."

"But why not just leave the suit here and wear a fresh shirt and jeans from home every day?"

"What difference does it make?"

She shrugged. She couldn't explain why it disturbed her so much, that he set out each morning wearing one thing and ended up in something different. "Can I smoke?"

"Better not." He hunched his shoulders as he spoke.

"Not even in here?" She glanced around his office. It was messier than she remembered from the one other time she'd been here, right after his father's death.

"Well, no, you can in here."

She lit one and looked around for an ashtray to put the match in. He went out, and came back immediately with a green ceramic turtle whose shell was a hollowed-out depression, blackened by ash. She raised her eyebrows at him and dropped the match in.

"Mary's," he told her.

Mary was his secretary and had been his father's secretary for sixteen years before that. "How is Mary?" Maisie asked.

"Fine. She's taking the morning off, setting up for the picnic." He sounded relieved. Mary made him nervous, Maisie knew. She was an old-fashioned kind of secretary who expected Jack to be an old-fashioned boss. She wanted to get coffee, take dictation, and use her lunch hours to pick up Jack's dry cleaning. Once, fumbling through the closet looking for a pair of gloves, Maisie had plunged her hand into Jack's coat pocket and found a dirty coffee mug. "I smuggled it out of the office," he told her sheepishly. "Mary wanted to take it home and wash it for me, and I couldn't let her do that."

"Don't you get a temp when she's away?" Maisie asked now.

He shrugged. "What for?"

Maisie shrugged, too.

A man in a paper hat and smeary apron came into Jack's office and held something up. A french fry. Jack frowned and took it from him and held it up to the light, turning it this way and that. Then he reached into his back pocket and pulled out a little tape measure, and measured the french fry.

"What's the matter with it?" Maisie asked.

"There's something wrong with the crinkles," Jack said, measuring it again. "See, they don't quite match up. They're more widely spaced on one side."

"I see," Maisie said.

"Has it been this way all morning?" Jack said to the man.

He shook his head. "I opened a couple of bags at random. Most of them were okay, but the ones at the top of the stack definitely had some problems."

Jack sighed. "All right, you'd better work your way down through the stack until you stop finding the defect. Put them aside, and maybe we can repackage them as generics. I'll get on the machine."

Maisie followed Jack out onto the floor; he had to remind her again to put on her paper hat. Before she'd first visited the factory, she'd imagined a vast, dark place, volcanic open fires, vats of bubbling oil; and in the year since she'd been here, that imaginary factory had slowly grown up again in her memory, eclipsing the real one. She noticed with surprise now how small the manufacturing room really was, and how bright. Small windows, too high to see through, ran along one wall, letting in dreamy, greasy light. Cream paint peeled from the brick walls, and the gray cement floor was littered with squashed french fries.

She watched as Jack insinuated his fingers and tools into various parts of a machine that sat in a corner, innocently silent, as though it couldn't possibly be the cause of any anxiety. Other machines were roaring, spilling out great Niagaras of shoestrings and steak fries. Men and women in white smocks and clear shower caps, their faces glistening with oil, stacked trays of potatoes on tall open shelf carts and wheeled them away.

"How come you're doing this?" she asked Jack, watching him punch a panel of numbers.

"I'm reprogramming it now. It's all computer-controlled, you see."

"No, I mean how come *you're* doing it? Don't the guys who run the machines know how to fix them?"

"We can't afford to send all of them for training," Jack said, pushing a button and standing back. The machine hummed and clacked and began spitting out crinkled potatoes onto a conveyor belt. Jack picked one up and peered at it.

"Is it all right?" Maisie asked.

"Shit." He switched off the machine again.

"But *you* don't have any training."

"I do now." He pulled a small screwdriver from his pocket and stood on the base of the machine to reach up. "I went and took a course."

"You didn't tell me."

"Well. You know, I left the answering machine on, the whole time I was gone. I was out in Cincinnati for a week, at the machine factory."

She didn't answer.

Jack stepped down and punched in something on the numbers panel.

"So what are you now?" Maisie asked. "Certified in crinkle-cut technology?"

He turned on the machine and spoke loudly to be heard above it. "It makes sense to have one person who understands the machines. It used to be my father, and now it's me. There were a few bad months there when no one understood how to fix things, and we had to shut down and wait for a factory service guy every time the damn thing broke. Well, now we don't have to." He pulled a fry off the belt and looked at it, turned it over, measured it. "There, that's perfectly even."

"Well, thank God," Maisie said.

They were driving to a big empty field outside of town. It was surrounded by other fields, farmland, but for some reason this particular field had been fenced in for as long as Jack could remember and designated the Lewis B. Landry Memorial Recreation Area.

He was remembering a weekend soon after he'd met Maisie. It was his parents' thirtieth wedding anniversary; they had, uncharacteristically, been giving a party to celebrate. It had seemed too soon to bring Maisie with him, too much a family party. But he was drunk with her, unable to sleep away from her. The morning after the party he woke early and took his rental car to the state forest, to go bird-watching. He imagined that she was in the woods, seeing what he saw, listening, astonished by his ability to distinguish different species by their songs. When the morning warmed and the birdcalls died away, he'd driven into town and had coffee in the drugstore restaurant. And even there, he'd sat facing the doorway, envisioning again and again her sudden appearance in the store aisle, a look of hesitancy on her face as she came slowly toward him, and then, when she caught sight of him in the dark, smoke-filled restaurant, a speeding up, her familiar confident stride, her face full of happiness. He'd imagined walking down the main street with her, showing her the pizza parlor where he'd worked over school vacations, the old department store, now closed, where his mother used to take him for clothes, the farmer's co-op he'd joined when he and his sister kept a horse, where they'd shopped for oats and saddle soap and neat's-foot oil.

When he had finally brought her up, several months after that, she'd remarked that the town wasn't at all what she'd been picturing. "The buildings are too far apart," she'd said. "Like a mouth with not enough teeth in it."

"I like it," he'd told her fiercely.

The town was called Champs du Soleil, but only outsiders, or people who'd just moved there, pronounced it the French way. People who really lived there said "Shamdoosly," with the accent hard on the second syllable.

He drove through it now without thinking. The old red factories, mostly closed, that lined the river, the filthy-looking water that poured over the falls. The square-topped store buildings, the treeless streets, the gaping sky. The office of his eye doctor, whose phone number ended with "2020," the radio station with its continuous phone-in talk shows, where everyone thought everything was a communist plot, the Victorian building that had housed the Grosvenor Grammar School and was now condominiums, the Imperial Cinema, where movies played night after night to an audience of two or four or seven, the way people spoke of going "downstreet" rather than "downtown," the rich stink of the farms that surrounded the town in every direction. This was his landscape, the place he was from, inexplicable to an outsider, ugly but loved. Being here with Maisie, once something to be anticipated, instead had engendered a squirmy tension in him: quick, get her away before something bad happens. It was not purely for her sake that he'd suggested they live in the little beach community an hour south of here, although he'd rationalized it by saying they'd be closer to Portland, the bookstores, the concerts.

Now he said, "We should be able to get away by five or so. I've got some food at home, but I thought maybe you'd like to go out to dinner."

"That would be nice." She was smiling, looking out through the windshield.

"I thought we could go to the Stables," he said, naming Champs du Soleil's only fancy restaurant.

"Oh, Jack. I don't feel like baked stuffed shrimp," she said. "Besides, if we really get out by five, we'll have time to drive down to Portland for dinner."

"I hope we get out by five," he amended.

"Well, if we don't, that's okay."

She'd resumed the bright opacity he'd noticed the day before at the airport. She's trying, she's being a corporate wife, he thought, and he said gently, "Maisie, what are we going to do?"

"I don't know." The same tone, civil and impenetrable.

"How's your job going?"

"Shitty."

"Why?"

She said quickly, glancing at him sideways: "I don't know, it's not shitty, really. Not enough for me to quit."

"I didn't mean that."

They passed the turn for Jack's family's old house, and he forced himself not to look up the road, even though the house was two miles up and there was no chance of his seeing anything from here.

He had not driven by that house once since his mother had sold it a year ago, right after his father's death. It was a halfway house now, affiliated with the regional center for the mentally retarded. Jack's mother, who had moved full-time to Vinalhaven, where they'd always spent their summers, drove by it when she came back to Champs du Soleil to visit friends, and she kept Jack posted on its metamorphosis. They'd filled in the pool, she reported, and replaced it with a basketball court, surrounded by chain-link fence. There were two prefab houses in the back field, but the old forsythia bushes were still there, as big and tangled as ever. The house itself looked in pretty good shape, she told Jack, except that of course they'd had to run wheelchair ramps up to all the doors, and they'd put iron railings up along the front porch. It made her sad to see the changes, but, she said, sighing, she was glad the house was being used for such a worthy purpose. It was certainly a nicer place for those people to live than the concrete cell-like rooms in the regional center itself.

Jack, who had volunteered at the regional center during his summers home from Exeter, still had a clear memory of the center's low, dim rooms, the ubiquitous institutional smell of old mashed potatoes. He agreed that the house was being put to good use, but all the same he couldn't bear to look at it. He wanted to keep it clear in his head, the way it had looked and felt when he'd grown up in it: lying in bed as a child, with the comforting sounds of conversation and clinking dishes floating up from the dining room, where his parents were having a dinner party. The big old bathtub where the water came up to his chin, where he would lie after dinner listening to a Red Sox game on the radio, which he'd set up on the clothes hamper. The dusty second-floor hayloft of the barn, the old girly magazine some previous owner had stashed there, between the wallboards: *Cavalcade*, it was called, and its pages were puckered with the dampness of years of weather and excited fingers, and he, who at twelve had never seen anything like it before, would keep climbing up there expecting to find it gone each time, it seemed too incredible to be real, with its pictures of kneeling, pouting women in transparent nightgowns, or tight lacy brassieres that they pulled coyly down to reveal their breasts, bright pink nipples, thrusting forward, and the accompanying text in which they revealed their ambitions: to be a nurse, a forest ranger, to dance with Sadler's Wells Ballet. The square stained glass windows that swung out just above his bed, so that he could lie there propped on his elbows, watching the clouds move, or the lightning veining the pewter sky above the fields. The long, velvety shadows cast by the spruce trees on the lawn, late on summer afternoons. The field behind the pool, where he'd lain at night with Clarissa Moore the summer before college, fumbling with her buttons and zippers and expecting to be told any minute to stop, the wonder of not being told, easing his mouth down her body and wondering, just before he got there, What if I don't like it? and then, probing lightly with his tongue and hearing her breathing go jagged, her thighs on either side of his head tightening so that he could hear nothing but a roar, like the ocean; and then when they loosened, her shy whisper, "Now I'll do you," and she moved and he felt the cool night air on him for a moment before she took him in her mouth. The house floating like a ship on the rise above them, light spilling out of all its windows.

He still dreamed about that house at night. In the dreams he was never just living there, innocently, taking the house for granted. He was trying to buy the house and not being able to, coming up against shadowy but insurmountable obstacles; or he was walking through the rooms, but they were all different, because other people lived there now; or he was living there, but with the knowledge that he had already lost it.

Maisie blinked, climbing out of the car. The recreation field was flat and relentlessly sunlit. The high grass and clover grew in soft green clumps, flecked with occasional cigarette butts and metal tabs from beer and soda cans, Ring-Ding bags, and popsicle sticks, leftovers from other people's outings. The fence by the road was lined with cars and vans, many of them so old that their finish had gone dull. Jack had edged his Honda between a pickup truck and a big Chevrolet that had been severely rear-ended.

Two tables in stingingly yellow paper cloths stood over by the far fence, and people were massed there, as though too shy to take possession of the entire field. Maisie's first impression was of a crowd that had been bleached: the T-shirts and jeans and shorts, the dresses worn by some of the older women, were all in pastel pinks and blues and peaches. She was wearing a short black linen skirt and a sleeveless red top: too casually chic, too urban. Jack had forgotten to bring a clean T-shirt and jeans, so he'd had to change out of the greasy ones and into the navy trousers from his suit, and he had on a good white shirt with the sleeves rolled up and the first two buttons undone. He'd kept on his dirty white sneakers, so he'd be able to participate in the volleyball.

"Oh," Maisie said, picking out the one face that was familiar to her. "I didn't know your mother would be here."

"She's staying at Marion's for the weekend," Jack said vaguely, his eyes scanning the party. He put a hand on Maisie's elbow and steered her over to one of the tables.

"She must think we're so weird."

"What do you mean?" Jack asked.

"The way we live."

"She hasn't said anything."

Maisie took hold of his hand. "She doesn't like me."

"Sure she does."

"She never listens to anything I say."

"She doesn't listen to me, either."

Maisie delayed going over to talk to Jack's mother for as long as she could—getting a paper cup of lemonade, letting Jack introduce her to some of the people who were milling around the drinks table. Nearly all of them said to her, "So. You live in New York."

"Well, just during the week," she found herself answering, although she hadn't been here since Christmas, and Jack hadn't been to New York since the end of March.

"If you don't spend more *time* up here, you'll never start a *ba*-by," came a teasing, warning singsong. Maisie turned in annoyance to look into a shriveled, beaming face under a cap of dyed red hair.

"Mary!" she said after a second.

"Honey, so good to see you!" Mary said, enfolding Maisie in a warm, scrawny, Shower to Shower–scented embrace and rocking her back and forth.

"You too," Maisie mumbled, nearly weeping against Mary's craggy breastbone. She detached herself with difficulty and blinked, tucking a piece of hair behind her ear. She'd met Mary only twice before, once in the office and once at the wedding; so where was all this emotion coming from?

"Well, you *look* great," said Mary dubiously.

"So do you."

"Me?" She slapped the air. "I'm a tubba *lahd*."

"Oh, no, I was going to say you looked thinner than ever."

"Well. The drugs puffed me up," Mary said, resting a gnarled hand against each concave cheek.

Maisie nodded politely; she had no idea what Mary was talking about.

Mary leaned in closer and lowered her voice. Maisie smelled coffee on her breath. "He is so good, your husband. So good."

"I know," she said, smiling tightly.

"He told you about my cansah."

"Cancer! No, he didn't. Are you okay?"

"I hope so. I think so. I'm still doing the radiation now, and I had chemo for three months."

"Oh, Mary."

"And he was so sweet to me. Told me not to worry about the job, sent me the most beautiful flowers after the operation. Called me at the house every week, just to see how I was doing." She narrowed her eyes at Maisie: Don't you know what you've got?

"And how *are* you doing?" Maisie asked again. "You're fine? You're really fine?"

"Knock wood." Mary looked around, and then she leaned over to rap her knuckles against the paper tablecloth on the picnic table.

"Well, you look wonderful," Maisie said. They stood for a moment, smiling at each other, and then Maisie said, "I'd better go say hello to Jack's mother."

"Oh, sure," said Mary. "Where is she? I just saw her. Oh, there she is. Doesn't she look great?"

Janet was standing behind the other table, her head bent as she poured dressing on salad in a big flowered bowl, so she didn't see Maisie coming. Maisie bumped her way through a number of conversations—excuse me excuse me—wishing that someone else would waylay her.

She wondered, suddenly, how it worked with in-laws. You spent so much energy pretending they were your family: buying them Christmas and birthday presents, chatting easily with them when they called to talk to their child and got you by mistake. She supposed that after a few years these gestures would begin to feel less forced; the emotions would catch up with the actions. But what happened if a marriage broke up? Especially when there were no children. Would Janet still send her a birthday card, or expect a Christmas present? Would her own mother, who adored Jack, still keep in touch with him?

Janet looked up and saw her, put down the empty measuring cup she was holding. "Hi, dear." A big hug, light perfumed kiss on the cheek.

"How are you? Y'look wonderful," not looking, turning back to the salad—it was a potato salad, Maisie saw. "Some chives, do you think? Something to spice this up a little?"

"That's a good idea," Maisie said. "Where would we get chives, though?"

"Oh, Marion is bringing some from her garden," Janet said.

So you've already made the chive decision; why ask me? Maisie thought, watching Janet peel Saran Wrap from a platter of deviled eggs. And oh, shit, Marion. She'd forgotten about Jack's sister, who always greeted her coolly and received all of Maisie's attempts at conversation with an air of skeptical amusement, who wore dirty jeans and men's T-shirts or flannel work shirts that made Maisie feel trendy and frivolous. She felt she could count on Janet to be civil and cordial; but she dreaded seeing Marion, she could imagine Marion's half-closed eyes, her high toneless voice saying, "Why are you so crummy to my brother?"

The food on the table reminded her of one of those photo layouts in magazines where you were supposed to identify famous people by the things on their desktops or the contents of their handbags. Some of the dishes were pointedly anonymous, contributed by the company: the sandwiches and potato and macaroni salads in gargantuan plastic serving pieces made to look like cut glass, the bags of potato chips and Fritos and pretzels. But then there were the more personal offerings: the bowls of gently quivering Jell-O, with chunks of banana and pineapple suspended, amberlike, in translucent orange cubes; the Tupperware containers of macaroni salad looking cowed next to their tubbed company-provided counterparts. And scattered here and there, small jolts of chic—a heart-shaped yogurt cheese in a white ceramic mold, a terracotta bowl of gazpacho—which she recognized as coming from Janet's kitchen.

She was surprised not only at Janet's presence, but by the amount of effort she seemed to be putting into the picnic. Although Jack's father had left the company to Janet, Marion, and Jack in equal shares, both Janet and Marion had recoiled from any involvement in running the business. Maisie had assumed that Jack's mother was even more detached from the company (and from him) now that she'd moved away from Champs du Soleil, but apparently she'd gotten it wrong. She was always getting it wrong, with Jack and his family; it was always that feeling of lifting your foot to climb one more step when in fact you were at the top of the flight, putting your foot down, sickeningly, on air.

When Janet had sold the Champs du Soleil house, right after Jack's father's death, Maisie had thought: No, no, don't you know you'll never get it back? You won't feel the same in another house. You'll never have attics, basements, storage rooms full of things you've forgotten. Now you'll have to sort through, consider everything. Your life will never be a big slumbering mess again; you're going to wake it all up, stir it around. Don't you know how lucky you are, to have all those layers, to belong somewhere?

She had tried to say some of this to Jack, one night in their cold little Maine beach cottage; she'd thought she was probably articulating things he felt anyway but might not have words for; but he'd only looked at her and said, "Maybe my mother wants to shed some of that stuff, to feel free again. You should understand *that*."

She'd shut up. They both knew that she herself was already poised for flight; the mail was full of letters from New York publishers, saying they liked her résumé and would be happy to see her for an interview and typing test.

"Can I help you, Janet?" she asked now.

"Oh, no, no, no thanks, dear."

"But you will let me know if there's—"

"I will."

She ate a hot dog, a hamburger, salad, potato chips. She went back to the table twice for dessert, and then a tall thin man in a Disney World T-shirt pulled a watermelon from a picnic cooler and held it up above his head, and Maisie cheered with everyone else and pushed forward to get a piece. She admired babies, asked people what part of town they lived in and if they'd grown up here (nearly all of them had), and she explained over and over again that she lived in New York only during the week, that she came up here for as many weekends as she could manage. She met a man whose arms were spattered with white; he told her, without her asking, that he'd been splashed with hot oil once, twelve years ago, cooking up a batch of shoestrings. Workmen's comp had taken good care of him, he said, and he'd stayed home for a while, but then he'd figured what the hell, he was just staring at the walls, so he'd gone back. She met another man who bragged to her that his wife drove him to work every morning and then sat outside the factory all day long in their pickup truck, waiting until his shift was over, and then drove him home. Maisie said, Oh, come on, really? And he said, If you don't believe me, ask my wife, and dragged over a thin blond girl in a crinkled pink tube top. She smiled and nodded and said, Yup, that's right, swaying back and forth with a sleeping baby slung against her shoulder. What about the baby? Maisie asked, and they said that the baby sat in the truck all day, too.

Maisie was sweating in her dark clothes, even if they were bare; and when she put her hand up to touch her head, her hair lay in damp ridges along her scalp. Someone set up an urn of coffee on one of the tables, and Maisie drank a cup and then was sorry she had; it only made her feel hotter. There were no trees to stand under, but a wind came up, so at least the air was moving, blowing up bits of trash and loose dust from the grass. Jack and some other men were setting up a net for volleyball. Maisie went over to watch, digging her sunglasses out of her purse; the dust was getting in her eyes.

"So you're Maisie?" A man in a short-sleeved business shirt came strolling over to her, shading his eyes with one hand, holding out the other for Maisie to shake. "Dave LaPalme. Jack's sales manager. What are you, back from being a women's libber in New York?"

Maisie laughed, one elbow resting in the palm of the other hand while she smoked a cigarette.

He kept squinting at her. His face was big and shiny, with a dimpled chin, and his hair was layered nearly to his shoulders. He had a chunky gold ring on his little finger, with a tiny diamond that winked in the sun.

"You work for a publisher, or something?"

"That's right."

"Yeah, Jack said you were flying up last night, and he was going to meet you in Boston. He said he was taking you out someplace French —what was the name of it?"

"Maison Robert."

"Named after you, huh?"

"What?"

"Maise—Maise."

"Oh." She lowered her eyelids and let her breath out through her nose.

"You know what you can tell that husband of yours?"

"What?"

"Tell him to give us all raises, that's what."

"Oh, sure. Anything else?"

"No, just raises. So we can stay in fancy hotels, and go out to dinner at Maison whatchamacallit."

"Okay," she said.

He must have heard a change in her voice because he leaned in closer and said, "Don't get mad. I was kidding."

"Oh, I know," Maisie said.

"He's a good kid, Jack. It's not easy. Coming in on a sick company, trying to get things moving again."

"I know," she said again. She wondered if this guy, Dave, knew that Jack was thinking of selling the company. Was that the sort of thing you discussed with your employees, or did you spring it on them as a fait accompli?

"In the beginning we all thought he was a lightweight. I mean, you never even saw him. He was all dressed up, never came out on the floor, he never even came into the lunchroom, for God's sake. You'd go into his office at noon and he'd be eating bologna sandwiches from out of his desk drawer, like he was trying to hide something. I kidded him about it. I said, What are you, hiding out in your own company?"

She smiled faintly.

"But now he's really in there, getting his hands dirty." He looked around him and lowered his voice. "Much better than the old man."

Maisie frowned. "Jack's father?"

"Did you ever know him?"

She shook her head.

"Arrogant son of a bitch. I mean, he was in there too, he understood the business all right, but *he* knew best. Wouldn't take advice from anybody. I told him when things started slipping that he'd better keep a clean credit record with suppliers—I mean, wouldn't you think that's like a basic rule of business? But no, he lets that get all fucked up, excuse me, which means we can't ship on time, which means we start losing accounts right and left. He'd get this weird expression on his face when you tried to talk to him about it. Like he was a deer about to be hit by a truck, and he couldn't move to get out of the road. Like something in him just shut down."

Maisie nodded; she'd never met Jack's father, but she knew just the look Dave meant.

"You'd feel like, earth to Eldridge, earth to Eldridge." He paused for a moment. "I hope I'm not stepping on toes."

"No, no, it's interesting."

"It's funny, when I said 'arrogant,' I don't want you to get the wrong idea. He was a nice guy, Mike Eldridge. He sent presents when people got married or had babies, you know. He'd do stuff like change the health insurance around, when people were complaining about how we didn't get dental. He never laid anybody off, even when things got really bad. But he was like this really strange combination of dumb and stubborn. You know? He could quote *Hamlet* but he couldn't figure out how to smooth down some pissed supermarket manager."

"I think they're starting the volleyball," Maisie said. "We should probably go over."

She stood next to Jack, in the back row. His serves went where he wanted them, with tight efficient smacks and thuds. There was one big, bearded man on the other team whose shots were more powerful, roaring over the net like missiles; but Jack was faster, more agile and precise. She watched and registered his skill with some surprise but with no particular pride; it had nothing to do with her. She'd joined the game to prove she was a good sport, but now she was busy trying to survive, ducking the ball as it came whistling down at her, putting up her hands to defend herself.

"Fifteen–fourteen," the bearded man called out as someone on Jack and Maisie's team missed the ball.

"Oh, too bad," Maisie said, beginning to walk away.

Another man, older, the stubble on his concave face glinting silver, grabbed her elbow. "Hold it."

"What?" Maisie said.

"Hey, Jack," someone else yelled. "Better teach your wife the rules."

"I thought you only played to fifteen," Maisie said, rubbing her elbow, suddenly close to tears.

"You gotta win by two," the man whose wife sat in the truck all day told her kindly.

The other team missed a shot, and then it was Maisie's turn to serve. She balanced the ball uneasily on her fingertips and hit it as hard as she could with her knuckles, and it arced up and came down again, still on their side of the net. No one made a sound.

"Don't punch it, hit it with your palm," Jack said quietly beside her, pantomiming.

She turned her face away from him and closed her eyes, smacking the ball. When she opened her eyes, the ball was sailing away over the net, and she stood still and smiled at it. But there it was again, coming back at them, and Jack got under it with his fists, going down on one knee, sending it up into the air, and she thought how prissily he played, how much he cared about the right technique. Then she was sitting on the ground, holding the left side of her face.

"Didn't you see it?" Jack kept saying. "I called to you to get it, didn't you hear me?"

They got her some ice from one of the picnic coolers, wrapped in an extra cloth diaper someone came up with. Beneath the ice her face burned. Jack kept hold of her arm and led her over to a spot farther out in the field, where no one was, and crouched beside her while she sat. "Are you all right?"

"It hurts," Maisie said.

He ran his hand up and down her arm, lightly. She winced away from it.

"Will you be okay here? Would you rather go sit with my mother?"

"Aren't you going to stay with me?"

"I have to go back in the game."

She looked over his shoulder and saw that the game hadn't started up again. People milled around on both sides of the net, talking to each other and smoking, but clearly still divided into teams, waiting for Jack to come back.

"Can't you let someone else take your place?"

"Maisie," he pleaded.

"What."

In the car on the way home to the little beach cottage, an hour south of Champs du Soleil, they talked about Marion, who had never showed up.

"I didn't really expect her to," Jack said.

"But she said she would."

"Well."

"Why didn't she, you think?"

"Who knows."

"It doesn't bother you?"

"It doesn't surprise me." Marion, he thought, would call him a few days from now, more defensive than apologetic, as though Jack's having expected her had put an unreasonable burden on her. Most likely the explanation would have to do with Barry. She always hid behind Barry when she didn't want to do something. It was Barry's one day off, she would say, and he was really tired. Or: Barry just isn't comfortable with all that factory-owner stuff.

"But your mother's staying with Marion, isn't she?" Maisie persisted. "Won't it be embarrassing for Marion, when your mother comes home from this picnic and says 'Where were you?' "

"She won't say that."

"Your mother?"

"She won't say anything."

She raised her palms in a shrug and took a pack of cigarettes and some matches from her purse. He hated it when she smoked in the car, hated that she smoked at all—he'd read that the Indonesian cigarettes she liked were particularly dangerous, and he imagined her lungs perforated with black-edged holes. She lit a cigarette and put the pack back in her purse. Always, before this, she'd kept a couple of packs in the glove compartment, her stash for long car trips, but this time, it seemed, she planned to leave nothing behind. She rolled down her window and tossed out the match, and then she sat with her feet up on the dashboard, her city-white thighs and the gentle undercurve of her ass disappearing into the wrinkled black of her hiked-up skirt. There was a shiny red crescent shape on the side of her face, the beginnings of a bruise, where the volleyball had hit her.

"What are you *doing* there?" she asked suddenly.

"What do you mean?"

"I mean you can't like it."

"Why not?" He was answering without thinking, startled by her vehemence.

"Jack. I know you."

"So?"

"Jesus! What is the matter with you?" She held her cigarette out the window. A trail of sparks streamed out behind them. She brought the cigarette back inside and inhaled deeply. "Why are you pretending you like it?" Smoke came out of her mouth and nose.

"I'm not. I'm just saying I have a responsibility."

"To whom?"

"To my father. To all those people you met today."

"What about to me? Or to you?"

"I'm doing the best I can."

"No, you're not. You're—" She took one last furious drag on her cigarette and let it fly out the window. "You're making it so I'm this incredible bitch, I don't want to live here. Well, what about you? You don't want to live here, either."

"No."

"No *what?* No you agree with me? No you think I'm crazy?"

"No, I don't want to live here. Not forever."

"I feel like I'm just watching you drown," Maisie said. "And every time I try to save you, you tell me you're not really drowning."

"Look, I just don't see what screaming about all this, and fighting about it, will accomplish. I'm stuck here for now. I wish you'd come live here with me, but if you won't—I let you go to New York."

"You let me? Who are you to let me?"

He sagged down in his seat. "I didn't mean it like that."

"And why are you making me say these things?"

"Making you?" He didn't want to hear any of this, he didn't know why they couldn't just talk about the picnic, or her job, anything that would keep them in safe, calm territory.

"Why can't we talk? Why is it me yelling and you being calm?"

"I don't yell."

"Well, you're not *getting* it. I'm telling you something is wrong. For you, too, not just for me."

He pressed his lips together and drove for several miles in silence. Then he said, "Maisie, can I ask you a dumb question?"

"What?"

"Why did you marry me?"

"That's not a dumb question." Her voice was calmer, and he thought, So this is what she wants to talk about?

"You made me feel safe," she said.

"Oh," he said dismissively.

"No, I don't mean it like that. I mean I trusted you, I thought that even when I didn't know what to do, you would." Her tone regained some of its harshness. "But that's what I can't stand now. I don't know what the hell to do, and you're just sitting there like you don't even understand what I'm talking about."

"I do understand!" he burst out.

"You don't! Or you'd do something about it."

"I'm trying. I wasn't going to tell you this, but I met with a business broker in Boston a couple of months ago, to put the company on the market."

"Why weren't you going to tell me?"

"The point is, the right buyer hasn't come along."

"What do you mean, the right buyer?"

"Okay, no buyer."

She lit another cigarette and let the burning match fly out the window. "What did this broker guy tell you?"

"Well, the first thing he said was that the real estate the factory sits on might actually be quite valuable. Someone might want it for condos, or an office park."

"In Champs du Soleil?" she said scornfully.

"Listen, when the new highway gets finished—"

"Yeah, yeah, yeah. So what else did he say?"

"But I told him I'd prefer not to sell it as real estate. Because then all my employees would lose their jobs."

She sniffed, but he was sure she understood. She'd met the people today, she knew how much they depended on the business. With the exception of the one thread mill that was still going, and the old textile mill that made army uniforms, he was the biggest employer in the area.

"And I also said I didn't want to sell to anyone who'd do too much more automation, because that's another thing that would put people out of jobs."

"I see. So you're willing to sell your unprofitable business on the condition that whoever buys it wants to keep it unprofitable." She began to cough, and her skirt rode up higher. She leaned her chest on her knees, and her whole face got as red as the bruise. He kept the car at sixty-five. Finally she got her breath, and he saw, sneaking a glance, that her face had paled back to its usual color. "I'm sorry, I'm sorry. Well, then what about finding someone to run it? Some hot little MBA fresh out of school. Isn't this the kind of thing those guys love? A real challenge?"

He gazed sideways at her. "I'm trying that, too, Maisie. I've got listings with all the recruitment offices and headhunters I know of."

Maisie was quiet for a moment; then she said, "Did I ever tell you about the boys who die in the war?"

"What war?"

"It was a game Caterina and I would play, in the dorm. All about the boys who died in the war." She bumped her knees together lightly, as though they were hands she was clapping. The backs of her calves, so hard and taut when she was standing, trembled back and forth.

"What war?" he asked again.

"That was the point, there wasn't any war. We just pretended. We figured out who would die in it and how."

"Kind of cold-blooded."

"Oh, we knew that. There was one kid in our English class, Billy Carabillo."

"Uh-huh."

"Fat. Fat and pink. You were always looking away from him, in case his buttons were open and his belly was sticking out, or something. Anyway, he was the one who got captured by the enemy and tortured for years and years, and then he showed up again when the war was over, thin and brown and crazy."

He smiled uncertainly, relieved that she was addressing him so quietly all of a sudden.

"Then there was Denny Ford, he was the one who inspired everyone else and then got killed the day before he was scheduled to go home. And there was a guy named Schneider who we thought would get lost in the jungle with his outfit and survive by eating his dead comrades."

"Jesus, Maisie."

"So I've been thinking now, about you. And you know who you are?"

"Who?" he asked unwillingly.

"You're the one who dies because someone throws a grenade at him. That's all. Someone throws it, and you just reach out and catch it."

He glanced at her and turned the wheel hard, swerving into the emergency lane. He had his hands off the wheel and onto her leg before the car stopped, so that they went lurching, driverless, along the grass for a way. He pushed one hand up under her skirt, grabbing at the slippery silk and elastic, and pulled at the inside of her thigh with the other, trying to turn her toward him. He didn't know what he was trying to do, what he wanted. He was kneeling on his seat, with his face burrowing between her breast and her bare arm.

Maisie didn't move. Then she lifted her arm—he felt cooler air on his face—and said, "Oh, come on." She waited for him to raise his head as indifferently as she might have waited for him to pass through a door she was holding open. He sat up blinking, feeling his eyes and nose fill with liquid.

"That wasn't even real," Maisie said, looking at him with curiosity. "That was just what you thought ought to happen right then."

She sounded so calm, so certain, that he thought, nosing the car back onto the blacktop, she must be right.

3

Lost and Found

❧

The Sunday night after the company picnic, Maisie arrived at La Guardia at eleven and stood in line for a taxi. Rain was slanting down beyond the roof of the terminal, and she was shivering with fatigue. The dispatcher jerked his thumb at a cab: take that one. She opened the door, threw her bag on the seat, slid in, and gave Caterina and Ed's address. She leaned back and closed her eyes.

"Of course by that point what he was writing wasn't fiction," said the cabdriver.

"What?" she said, opening her eyes. She wasn't sure if the driver was talking to her or if she'd come in in the middle of some crazy monologue. It was too late to get out of the cab and find another; they were already sweeping out from under the terminal's protective canopy. Rain swarmed on the windows, making the lights of the airport and the cars in the next lane fragmented and blurry.

"Tolstoy," the driver said. "By that point he'd renounced fiction, he was only interested in didactic exposition."

"Oh, Jesus," she breathed, closing her eyes again. She'd forgotten that she was still clutching her copy of *Resurrection*, which she'd pulled out of the bookshelf in Maine last night. She'd been unable to read it then, lying rigid and sleepless, poking Jack to turn over whenever his breath began to buzz; and she'd been unable to read it on the plane because she'd been crying.

"I have the same edition," the driver went on. "I recognized the picture on the cover. So what do you think, you think it's a real novel, or not?"

She lifted her shoulders, hoping he'd see the shrug in the rearview mirror and take it to mean polite agreement, end of discussion.

"It's funny, because right through the scene where he rapes the girl—what's her name again?" A pause. "Anyway, until then it *is* a real story, don't you think? Like he couldn't help himself, he just had to make it dramatic. But then he gets all stern with himself—no, no, no, Leo, you're indulging yourself, this is vulgar, just expound those moral principles."

Maisie opened her eyes and looked at what she could see of the driver. Dark hair above a frayed white collar—a good oxford-cloth collar. Pale eyes in the mirror, deeply socketed; low straight brows. Not looking to get her reaction, just scanning the traffic, which was heavy. The wet road hissed beneath the cab.

The oxford-cloth shirt gave her courage. "I really don't feel like talking right now," she said softly.

"What?"

She opened her purse and looked inside. "Listen," she said. "I have a ten-dollar bill here, which I will give you over and beyond your regular tip, if you will just shut up."

He looked at her in the mirror. She fumbled for the door handle, ready to jump out onto the expressway if necessary.

"Nope," he said. "Sorry. Not worth it." His eyes left hers and went back to the road.

He did fall silent then. Maisie finally said, "Look, I'm sorry. But I've had a really awful weekend."

She saw his eyes move in the mirror. "Boyfriend?"

"Husband."

"Break up?"

"I'm not sure."

"Ah." Eyes back on the road.

Maisie looked out the window, rows of squat little bungalows hunkered down for the night. They blurred as she looked at them, cartwheeled and began to shimmer, starlike.

"Want some pot?" the driver asked.

"No, thanks."

"I'll tell you why I can't shut up, if you want. Have you ever driven a cab? Have you ever been stuck in a little box ten hours a day with nobody to talk to? Ah, you may say, but there are the passengers. You can talk to them. Ah, I say. Exactly. So what if they don't talk back. So what if they're wedged in the backseat bragging to each other about how much they just spent on room service at the Helmsley Palace. So what if it's two guys blowing each other back there. So what if it's a girl in a designer scarf who gives you an address down by the docks and then turns out to have a gun and wants all your money." He stopped for breath. "So when someone gets in carrying a book from my bookshelf, I go a little nuts. Sorry if I was a jerk."

He drove in silence for a minute or so, and she began to feel sorry for him. "At least you're not like the last cabdriver I had," she said. "He went on and on about how the Jews are trying to take over America."

"Let me ask you something. Why does everybody lump all cabdrivers together? I mean, there are all kinds of people who drive cabs. Why should I be anything like the last guy you had?"

He was watching her in the mirror. She shrugged.

"You think just because I drive a cab I'm stupid?"

She looked out the window again.

"I guess I'm lumping *you* with the last guy I had in here as a passenger. The one I took to the airport. I pick him up outside a brownstone on East Fifty-second—probably his mistress's house. He's spent the day at Sotheby's, I figure, trying to interest them in the boring safe collection of French landscape paintings his grandparents bought, when they could have been buying Monets. And now he's flying back to Boston, to his wife, who's spent the day with her lover, who teaches classics at Harvard. . . ." He glanced in the mirror to see if Maisie found this amusing. She didn't, especially. She decided that his offer of pot meant that it was okay to smoke a regular cigarette.

"Have you got a match?" she asked.

His right shoulder moved, and then his hand came back with a matchbook, which he put into the money cradle in the Plexiglas screen that separated them. She tilted the matches toward her.

"Thanks."

"Anyway, do you want to know what this turkey did, or not?"

"Sure," she said, exhaling smoke.

"He taps on the glass, with the handle of his *umbrella,* no less, and he says, 'Driver, oh, driver,' " here the cabdriver spoke in a haughty, faintly English-accented voice, "and I don't say anything, just keep on driving. And then he knocks again and says, 'Driver, please slow down.' Which I do, only I don't say anything about it to him, and I guess he doesn't notice. So then he starts tapping again. 'Driver, driver, oh driver,' and finally I turn around"—and now the cabdriver, who had fortunately stopped for a red light, wheeled around in his seat and glared at Maisie—"and I say, 'What's your problem, *asshole?*' "

She jumped a little when he roared and turned around. He held the glare for an instant, eyebrows raised, eyes bugging open, teeth bared, and then relaxed it into a grin. His features were almost exaggeratedly clean and sharp, as though a puppeteer had made him. In fact, he was so good-looking that the entire character of her nervousness suddenly changed: she stopped worrying about whether she could discourage his conversation and started to worry that she might say something stupid. She was beginning, uncertainly, to grin back at him when he closed his eyes, still smiling, and swiveled back to face the road again.

"So the poor guy goes 'Hrumph, hrumph, hrumph,' but he's scared shitless, I'm seeing the whites of his eyes all around in my mirror. I say, 'Don't call me *driver,* asshole. Driver is the name of a job, not the name of a person. Don't address me in that contemptuous way. I'm just as good as you. I went to Bowdoin and studied English literature'—all right, I dropped out after two years, but the guy doesn't have to know that—'and I would appreciate it if you would address me with a certain degree of respect.' "

"What did you expect him to call you—Tony? Mr. Bigelow?" Maisie asked, squinting to read the card posted on the dashboard.

"No," Tony said indignantly. "But he could just say, 'Excuse me.' Do you go to the library and yell, 'Hey, librarian'? Do you address the guy who cuts your hair as 'Hairdresser'?"

"People call waiters 'Waiter.' "

"I hate people who do that."

"Me too."

"Aha." He lifted his eyebrows at her in the mirror. She laughed.

"I knew I could make you laugh."

Maisie rolled her eyes and looked out the window. "Where are we?" she asked.

"Worried?"

Suddenly, she was. "About what?"

"That I'll kidnap you."

"Of course not. This just doesn't look—"

"Not that I wouldn't like to," he said. "But we're about ten blocks from your house."

"You're kidding." She'd never seen these streets before.

"Is it your house, or just a place you're visiting to get away from your husband?"

She hesitated.

"What I'm getting at is, do you live here or are you just visiting?"

She shook her head. "I live here."

"Work in the city?"

She nodded.

"Where?"

She told him.

"A publisher. That's interesting. Very interesting."

"Not really," Maisie said. "We don't publish very good books." There was the market she and Caterina shopped at, the newsstand, the dry cleaners. He was taking her home, after all.

"Tell me the names of some. Maybe I've read them."

"Well, let's see. *But You Look Like You've Had a Facelift. The Ultimate Dirty Joke Book. Dirty Jokes from Top to Bottom.*"

"Schlock."

"Oh, and Babette Stansfield."

"Who's Babette Stansfield?"

"One of the biggest romance writers in America. You've never heard of her? She gets her own cardboard display box in all the bookstores. Her latest novel goes at the top, and all the other ones go in compartments beneath. Only they print her name in such huge type, and the titles in such little type, that we're always getting angry letters from people who bought what they thought was her new book, only it turned out to be an old one that they'd already read." She stopped for breath.

"And you thought *I* was revved up," Tony said.

He pulled up in front of Ed and Caterina's building and switched the light on. "Fourteen sixty," he said, flipping off the meter. Then, "Don't you publish anything good?"

"Not that I'm aware of." She was distracted, fumbling in her purse, trying to calculate fifteen percent.

"Because I thought maybe I could send you some of my stuff."

She held out a twenty. "Uh, could you give me back three? What do you write, poetry?"

"No, I'm not a writer. I take pictures."

"Photographs?"

"That's right."

"Well," she hedged. "I don't think we do any art books."

"Don't you know?"

"We did a popular biography of Picasso last year. And a memoir by someone who knew Diane Arbus."

"Why do you sound so apologetic?" He was smiling at her, his voice was gentle, he knew why she sounded apologetic. He knows me, she thought, feeling weepy again.

She said briskly, "I mean, we don't do any books with just pictures in them."

"Okay."

She took her change. "But it was nice to talk to you."

"You too."

She sat looking through the rain-flecked window, at the yellow lights of Caterina's building. Tony got out of the cab and opened her door. She climbed out unsteadily.

"Well," she said. After a moment she opened her purse and fished out one of her boss's business cards. She crossed out her boss's name and wrote in her own. "Don't get the idea that I have any particular clout, even if I like your stuff. I'm just an editorial assistant."

He looked down at the card, dimpling with rain in his hand. "Maisie. Neat name. Irish?"

"English, I think. My father picked it out, and he was English."

"But Callahan's an Irish name."

"I think his parents came from Dublin."

"He's dead?"

"He died when I was seven."

He bent to reach behind her, into the cab. "Don't forget your bag."

"I won't."

He waited while she ran up the stairs to the front door. To her own surprise, she took them two at a time.

The apartment was dark when she let herself in. She went to the kitchen and poured herself a glass of wine from the open bottle in the refrigerator. The bottle was half-full, as she'd left it before flying up to Boston Thursday; Ed and Caterina hadn't drunk over the weekend, or they'd drunk their own.

She passed their closed bedroom door and went down the long hall to her own room, at the back of the apartment. There were clothes all over her bed and on the floor, bureau drawers gaping, manuscripts piled among the perfume bottles on the dresser. She lay on the mess on the bed, her head propped against the cool wall, holding her wineglass on her chest. She could smell her own smell, perfume and smoke and the faint scent of Jack, a familiar, peculiar burnt odor that clung to him from the factory. She lay there a long time. Waiting, she thought, and realized she was waiting for someone to come and stop things. She had the sensation of sliding: she was lying still and things were sliding all around her. This is the middle of the night, she thought, nothing is changing right now. Everyone is asleep. But she saw the dresser, the perfume bottles, the broken-slatted chair, the window shade with its looped cord flapping, all tumbling down a hill.

It occurred to her finally to take a bath. On her way down the hall to the bathroom she saw a dark shape by the front door: Jack's suitcase, which she had meant to return to him this weekend and had forgotten until just now. She'd picked it up at the Penn Station lost and found one night last week, using the birth certificate he'd sent her to show for ID.

The first time she'd gone, she'd told the attendant she was Jack's wife, and gotten a hard time.

"Your name's different," he'd pointed out.

"I kept my own name. Women do that nowadays," she'd said, smiling up at him.

"So you can't prove you're his wife."

"But I am."

"Honey, you've got to have proof."

So she'd asked Jack, over the phone, impatiently—why did he have to lose the damned claim check in the first place?—to send her some identification.

"Not my driver's license," he'd said slowly.

"No, not that, you need that." Trying to keep the irritation out of her voice.

"And I need my credit cards."

"Yes."

"Let's see, my passport is expired. Do you think they'd accept it anyway?"

Finally he'd sent the birth certificate, and she'd taken it down and gotten the same clerk.

"Still can't tell you're his wife," he'd said, bored amusement in his dark eyes. "You could've stolen this off somebody."

"Oh, come on. What if I describe what's in the suitcase?" But she couldn't remember one thing that Jack had worn or brought that weekend. "Here," she said, reaching into her purse. The old checkbook she'd used in Maine, Jack's name and hers printed together at the top of a check. She put it on the pitted wooden counter and spread out the birth certificate and her own passport and Bloomingdale's charge card.

The clerk scrutinized the documents, went back and looked at Jack's luggage tag, and then wordlessly heaved the suitcase at her over the counter.

"God damn it," she said aloud, looking at it now. She'd have to ship it back to him somehow.

There was a knock on the door while she was in the bath, lying beneath a carpet of softly hissing bubbles.

"Caterina?" she called, startled.

"Can I come in? How'd it go?" Caterina asked, yawning, sitting down on the rim of the tub.

"Not very well."

"The picnic wasn't fun?"

"No, it wasn't that." She wanted to say, I'm scared, don't you ever get scared?

He had never hurt her, or shouted at her, or done any of the crude or brutal things she had always supposed necessary to the death of a marriage. But—some idea was trying to get to the surface, and she shook her head, her face puckered in a grimace that made Caterina look at her oddly. Oh, get out of here, Caterina, don't look at me.

He doesn't *dance,* she thought suddenly.

That was it, the idea she'd been trying to think of. Every now and then she had dragged him to a club or a big noisy party, and he would sigh and roll his eyes and eventually agree to dance with her. That was the game: he was stuffy and blasé, and she was the spirited young breath of fresh air. So his demeanor on the dance floor—he pushed his fists back and forth in the air, he lifted each foot methodically as though checking for dog shit—seemed like a game, too. Or like something admirable: he was too modest and intelligent to cut loose.

But after a while she realized that he genuinely didn't hear the music the way she did, didn't have any instinct about what to do with his shoulders or his hips. In a slow dance he didn't lead her; he held her loosely and smiled apologetically into her face while he rocked her back and forth.

She'd tried to teach him once, in the living room. Now you go that way—now you spin me. No, you're too late—*now!*

He was willing to learn, anxious to please her. She snapped: Of course you can do it! Listen, it's one two three *four*. You're not *listening*.

But she glanced at his face just then and saw a look of such unhappiness that she stopped and laughed softly, consolingly, and told him he was doing fine, he was a perfectly good dancer, she was the jerky one to get so upset about it.

She never tried to teach him again, and she'd started to notice that same timidity in bed. He wanted her all the time, they could talk about anything, do anything; but when he touched her she began to feel that he was going through motions he'd read about, or seen in a movie. He kissed her here, circled there, began with his hands and followed with his mouth. There was no real hunger. He only thought he was hungry.

But she loved him. She thought everything he said was interesting. He was gentle and understanding with her, even when she was ashamed of her own behavior. You didn't stop seeing a man you loved just because he didn't drive you wild in bed. She had broached it once with Caterina, casually: Do you ever miss just plain fucking?

Fucking? repeated Caterina, smiling but looking a bit puzzled, as though the word were a foreign idiom.

As opposed to making love, Maisie said. I mean, making love is wonderful, it's great, but do you ever miss just—you know.

Yes, Caterina said frankly.

They laughed.

Not that I did very much of it, Caterina said.

Oh, me neither, Maisie lied hastily, and then she wondered why she had: Caterina knew she'd slept around, though probably not how much.

But I mean, is it really good, with you and Ed?

Sure it is. Sure, said Caterina. But anyway, even if it weren't, I still wouldn't miss casual sex enough to do anything about it.

Oh, casual sex, said Maisie, I'm not talking about that. I had casual sex one afternoon and it was the most boring thing I've ever done. I'm talking about the kind of sex you have in a really bad love affair.

Exactly, said Caterina. Is that what you want? A lifetime of bad love affairs?

Of course not, said Maisie, annoyed. This was what you got when you talked to Caterina: this terrific frankness that led you to confess emotions Caterina would then deny having felt herself.

"You forgot the suitcase," Caterina said now.

"I know."

"Did you get a chance to talk?"

"Sort of. He says he's trying to sell the company."

"Well, that's good." Caterina yawned again and drew the lapels of her seersucker bathrobe together over her chest. "You missed a steamy weekend here."

"It was hot there, too."

"This isn't the kind of rain that breaks the heat."

"No."

Caterina stood.

"What are you doing up at this hour?" Maisie asked.

"I heard you come in." She looked down at Maisie. "I wish there was something I could do."

"Oh, Caterina."

"Can I just say one thing? But you'll get mad at me."

"What is it?"

"I still think Jack's the right person for you."

Maisie pushed her hands through the dwindling bubbles, gathering them over her. She wanted Caterina out of the room; she was dimly aware, suddenly, of an interruption, a soft excited feeling she couldn't quite identify, as though she'd been wakened abruptly, and if only she could find her way back to sleep by the right path, she'd resume the same dream, whatever it had been, and see clearly what happened next.

"Well," said Caterina. "Go to bed soon." She shut the door softly behind her.

Maisie lay in the warm water and looked up at the gray, pockmarked ceiling. Once the paint must have come falling down in great flakes; but someone had painted over it, sternly—all right, that's quite enough of this nonsense—binding the shifting plaster into a permanent topography of craters and bulges, plausible and strange as a map from another civilization, or another point in history.

She reached for the soap and saw her body, white and blurred in the green water, and thought of Tony, how it would look to him.

4

A Prominent Local Businessman

❧

On a cool, late-spring evening, Jack drove from work to the Champs du Soleil Little League field, where he was to throw out the first ball of the season.

"We like to get a prominent local businessman," said the woman who telephoned him.

"Uh-huh."

He could remember his father doing it once, Jack sitting next to him on the splintery green bleachers, squirming with pride and embarrassment while his father stood, squinted down at the field for a long moment, rocked his shoulders from side to side, drew his right arm back and lifted his left foot, in its gleaming business shoe, and finally let go of the ball, a prosaic little toss that seemed to have nothing to do with all that preparation.

Jack's father had not been an athlete, but he had understood the stances, the gestures, of athletes. When he took Jack and Marion to play on the high school tennis courts Saturday mornings, he'd worn a white polo shirt and crisp white shorts, a sweater slung over his shoulders. Jack and Marion, fifteen and thirteen, wore cutoff blue jeans and stood across the net from him, yawning.

"Look at Daddy, in the Ready Position," Marion drawled.

Their father waited for her serve with bent knees, racquet lying across his palms.

Marion threw the ball up in the air and missed it, said, "Oh, shit," and hit it on the bounce.

Their father chased after it.

"Did it ever occur to you," Marion asked quietly, after Jack had returned the shot, "that maybe Daddy's stupid?"

"Why did you say that?" he asked her, while their father hunted for the ball in the bushes outside the fence.

She shrugged. "I was driving with him in the car the other night, and he ran over something. A cat, I think. And he didn't stop."

"Why does that make him stupid?" Jack asked. But he was disturbed by the story.

"It was like he wouldn't admit it happened."

"Maybe it was just a squirrel, or a rabbit."

"Even so, he should have stopped! But I'm almost sure it was a cat. I saw it for a second, in the headlights. We were passing a couple of houses, and I said I thought we should go ring the doorbells, and *tell* someone. But he said that would just cause trouble."

"He wasn't thinking," Jack said slowly.

He caught the ball when it came over the net; it was his turn to serve. He tried to do everything his father had told him: throwing the ball up straight, letting it fall four inches, and then snapping his wrist to put some speed on the ball.

Marion watched his serve soar over the net. "He looked scared," she said.

"Ace!" their father called. "See, that time your form was superb."

After they played, their father took them out for lunch, and then they all went to the factory. He did nothing there on Saturdays but leaf through the mail, which they picked up from the ground outside the locked front door. When they were younger, Jack and Marion had helped with the mail, claiming the rubber bands and junk leaflets for themselves, taking pencils and paper clips from their father's desk, weighing things on the postage scale. But now that they were older the visits were boring, endless. They ate M&M's from the glass jar on Mary's desk and read the books that were on their summer reading lists from school. They stood in the freezer until they began to shiver. They sneaked off to the empty manufacturing room and screamed, just for the way it sounded echoing off the bare concrete walls. Jack liked the feel of this room on Saturdays, the silent machines and still conveyor belts, the warm smell of oil from some permanent, invisible source.

Marion hated the smell of oil, she announced in the car on the way home.

"It's disgusting. It's not even healthy. You take perfectly good potatoes and fry them in enough fat to kill the entire population of—"

"It's not suet, Marion," their father observed mildly from the front seat. "It's vegetable oil."

"It's fat," Marion insisted. "Fat is fat."

"That fat is paying your tuition."

It was only after their father died that they discovered the fat had not been paying their tuition, or much else: not the summer house on Vinalhaven, not the semesters abroad, not the extravagant Christmases. The money had come from their father's inheritance, from his father and grandfather, who had run the company before him; and now it was gone. There was just enough left to pay off the personal loans their father had amassed to conceal from their mother the fact that the company had not been profitable for years.

The schools Jack had attended as a child were gone. Faced with a dwindling population and crumbling buildings, Champs du Soleil had added a new elementary wing onto the old high school in the mid-seventies, with orange stucco walls that had been etched with putty knives into rectangles meant to look like bricks. The Grosvenor Grammar School, grades K through four, had been turned into condominiums; and the middle school had been torn down to make way for an office building, which was never built. The Little League team played on the lot where the middle school had stood.

Jack parked in the old teachers' parking lot and walked across the shorn grass to the bleachers. The field was swarming with kids and their parents. He didn't see anyone he knew, and he wondered how he was going to find Laura Singerwold, the woman who had called him.

"Is that Jack?" someone said. "Jack Eldridge?"

He turned to see a plump black-haired woman in a navy blue windbreaker and pink stretch pants.

"Laura?" he said uncertainly. She looked much older than the crisp voice he'd heard over the phone.

"They told me you'd be here," the woman said. Her makeup was bright orange, with a precise red blush on each wrinkled cheek. "Don't you remember me? It's Cecily!"

"Cecily?"

"Cecily Beausoleil." Pronounced so that the first and last names rhymed. Suddenly he remembered: she had come twice a week to clean for his mother. A sharp delicious taste in his mouth: Cecily's sloppy Joes, made with peppers and onions and ketchup and mustard, simmered all afternoon for Jack and Marion's dinner on nights when their parents were going out. Once when he'd been sitting with his mother in the kitchen, home from Exeter for summer vacation, Cecily had come into the room holding out a box of Trojans, wistfully bought and still unopened, which she'd found in Jack's bureau. "From now on, stay out of the drawers," his mother had told her coolly.

"Cecily!" he said now. "How are you?"

"They told me you were going to be here," she said again, "but I'd never have recognized you. You're so grown up!"

For some reason, this made him like her. He wished she would hug him.

"Do you have a son playing Little League?" he asked.

"Jack! A grandson." She pointed into the knot of children. "Right over there. Dominic's little boy. He's such a good boy. He lives with me, he and his mother."

Good boy, he thought, that's what she always said about her sons. They stole cars and got into bar fights, but they were good boys.

"You know her," Cecily went on. "My daughter-in-law. Brenda Beausoleil. She works for you."

"But I had no idea she was your daughter-in-law!" he said, trying to summon an image. A sullen-looking heavy girl in the packing room. "And what about Dominic? What's he up to?"

"I can't tell you," she said wistfully. "We haven't heard from him." Then, "Hey, did I hear you got married?"

"That's right."

He had a sudden cold sick feeling, which was followed by a rush of gratitude for the woman who came up to them then, holding out her hand.

"Jack Eldridge? I'm Laura Singerwold."

She apologized for interrupting the conversation, and he introduced her to Cecily.

"Oh, we know each other," said Cecily.

"That's right," said Laura. She had a long, pink-and-brown face, with dark eyes that narrowed to dashes when she smiled. She was tall and strong-looking, wearing blue jeans and a striped man's shirt. "Cecily's going to sing the national anthem."

"The national anthem!" Jack repeated. It seemed a little grandiose for the Champs du Soleil Little League.

"Well, we figured why not," Laura said. "It'll make things more exciting for the kids. And I'm told you have a wonderful voice," she said to Cecily.

"Well. Jack remembers. You remember my singing, don't you?"

"Of course," he lied.

"I better go sit, if I want to keep my seat." Cecily hugged Jack and kissed him on the cheek, though by then he didn't want her to, and scurried off toward the bleachers. Jack and Laura followed, more slowly.

"Thanks for doing this," she said after a moment.

"Oh, that's all right."

They found seats in the third row. They watched pairs of kids play catch on the field while other kids practiced batting.

"This is amazing," Jack murmured finally, the silence beginning to weigh on him. "There was nothing this elaborate when I was growing up. They just showed up and played."

"Oh, did you grow up here, then?" Laura sat with her long legs propped on the bench in front of her, her arms wrapped around her knees. She sounded surprised.

"Yes. In fact," he said, peering over her shoulder, "I think that's my sister over there."

She turned her head to look at Marion and Barry coming across the grass, Barry limping a little on the foot he'd broken over the winter.

"Will she see you up here?" Laura asked.

"I don't know." He excused himself, made his way down the row, and jumped off the bleachers. He loped over to them. "Marion."

His sister looked startled and perhaps annoyed, but she gave him a light, cool kiss on the cheek. Barry, who was either very shy or contemptuous, Jack hadn't ever figured it out, raised a hand and strode off in the direction of the quilted steel hot-dog wagon.

"Hey," Jack said to his sister. "Where were you, at the picnic?" He had not intended to ask her this, but it just came out.

"One of the dogs was sick." Marion and Barry crossbred German shepherds and beagles to produce ugly dogs that they claimed were smart, gentle, and had a sense of humor.

"Maisie was here."

"What an occasion!" said Marion, stuffing her hands into the pockets of her Indian-print skirt. Her voice was as high and rapid as a child's. "Yeah, Mom said. She didn't look too happy."

"Mom?"

"No, Maisie. Mom said she sulked the whole time."

"That's not true. She was trying, I think she really was." He was surprised and disturbed that his mother had said anything overtly critical of Maisie, but maybe Marion was just trying to make trouble. He changed the subject. "You know who's here? Remember Cecily?"

"Oh, her," said Marion. "She used to tell me I was going to go to hell."

"She did?"

"Because I didn't clean my room. She said if I was her kid, she'd whip me."

"She never said anything like that to me."

"She liked you. Also, she always made me scared I'd grow up to have bad taste. Remember we used to drive over to her house every Christmas to look at the decorations? And Mom and Dad would go on and on about how it was bad taste."

"I remember the decorations. I don't remember the bad taste."

"Well, I used to like the way her house looked. I thought all those Santas and elves and flashing lights were really beautiful, and I used to sit in the back of the car not saying a word because I was so scared I'd grow up to have bad taste."

He laughed. "You always remember everything awful."

She narrowed her eyes at him. "Sometimes I think we must have grown up in different families. Where were you?"

"I don't know. Away at school, I guess, some of the time."

"Well, you always act like they were so benign."

"They were benign. Anyway, they must have had some hold on you, too, or you wouldn't still be living here."

She shrugged. "Barry's here."

"What are you guys doing at a Little League game?" he asked.

"We like 'em," she said. "We come to all the games. I've never seen you at one before."

"I'm throwing out the first ball," he confessed.

"Ooooh, corporate guy."

"Be quiet," he said to her back, and he thought that in some peculiar way this had been the most affectionate conversation he'd had with her in years.

When he got back to his seat, Laura said, "They ought to be starting soon."

He nodded.

"So, did you play in the Champs du Soleil Little League?" She gave it a French pronunciation.

"I wasn't big on team sports."

"See that girl with the red ponytail? The one behind the plate? She's the catcher. You throw to her."

"Yes, that much I figured out." He knew he sounded cool, snotty, but he couldn't help it; he was thinking of Maisie, prompted by Marion's remarks, adding to a running list in his head of all the reasons he believed she really loved him, in spite of the way she was acting.

The day his father died, she had come and waited outside the room where his afternoon class had met. Marion had telephoned her at the apartment, and Maisie could have called the registrar to track him down and give him the message, but instead she'd taken a cab to Harvard because she'd wanted to tell him in person.

In the car that night, on the long drive to Maine, she'd been quiet. She had come with him the next day to the church to make the arrangements for the funeral, and to the funeral home to deliver a suit for his father to be buried in. She'd cooked and washed dishes and answered the phone when it rang, and she'd gone up to bed early so that he and his mother and Marion could be alone to talk, even though they hadn't talked, they'd sat around the dining room table reading murder mysteries. She'd come down the hall from the guest room to his bedroom each night, after everyone else was in bed; once, the one time he'd lost it and cried uncontrollably, she'd sat beside him and waited for him to stop and then held him until he slept, and another night she had taken off her nightgown and his pajamas and gone over his whole body with her mouth—his face, his ears, his ankles and thighs—with a patience and attention that at first had made him self-conscious and then sad and then, finally, when she'd lain on top of him and he'd exploded inside her without having realized he was going to, astonished at what he was still capable of feeling. At the end of that week, he'd asked her to marry him.

He hadn't thought much, before then, about marriage. Maisie had been the one to bring it up, over and over again, at first teasingly, then more insistently as time went on. Her old friends were getting married —not all of them, but it seemed as though every couple of months she was getting an invitation, shopping for a present, convincing Jack to spend a Saturday driving seven hours to New Jersey or Vermont for a wedding. Some of the brides she didn't seem to know that well: they had lived across the hall from her at boarding school, or waitressed with her one summer; and they were surprised that she had actually come so far in response to a casually mailed invitation. Of course I came, Maisie cried, squeezing their white taffeta shoulders, I had to see you get *married!* In the car on the way home she would complain that she hadn't known anyone else at the reception, and the ceremony had been too long and sappy, or that the groom seemed boring, or vain. "He's going to be trouble," she was fond of saying. Jack, listening to these critiques, kept thinking, So then why the hell did we have to go? but he didn't say anything. Maisie seemed, in the midst of all her fretting, to have a dauntless awe for the moment of transition. "Four hours ago at this time," she would say, looking at her watch, "they weren't married, and now they are." "Yup," said Jack, deliberately taciturn, and she would look at him and then laugh.

Caterina's wedding was the hardest on her. She couldn't distance herself from it with criticism: she liked the groom and loved the bride. Maisie was the maid of honor, and there was a whole weekend of festivities, hectically bright, culminating in the moment when Caterina climbed the stairs to throw her bouquet and the guests in the hall below moved back to make a space in which all the unmarried young women would gather, waiting to catch it. Maisie moved forward into the space, no one else. After a moment Caterina's seventeen-year-old sister joined her, giggling, along with two of her giggling friends.

On the car ride home that day, Maisie said, "I was the only one." Caterina's bouquet lay on the backseat, weeping petals.

"Well, but that was just a fluke," Jack said. "Every other time we've been to a wedding, there have been a million women waiting to catch that silly thing."

"They're all married," Maisie said.

"Maisie, you're only twenty-six."

"Will we get married, do you think?" she asked after a silence.

"Sure, probably," wanting to reassure her, but still uncomfortable with the question.

"What are the odds, do you think? Seventy–thirty? Eighty–twenty?"

"Ninety-five–five," he'd retorted, hating the idea of quantifying but wanting to shut her up with his extravagance. You see, Maisie, there's nothing to worry about.

"What's that five percent for?" she wanted to know.

"Maisie!" He laughed at her and kissed her, and hoped she would forget about that five percent, whatever it was.

But then, the week after his father's death, when his life suddenly seemed bare and clean and numb and he saw things with a sweet and painful clarity that would soon vanish and never return, he did ask Maisie to marry him; and she said she wasn't sure.

After all her pushing, he was startled by her hesitancy, but at that point he thought he understood everything, the entire sad strangeness of life. He told her that he loved her and wanted her to be his family, but it was all right, they had time; and he thought now that his gentleness had tricked her into marriage, lured her in by seeming not to want to lure her, the way he could get Egg, the cat, to come back into the apartment after a desperate break for freedom simply by cracking open the door and looking at the ceiling, humming a little.

Laura was talking. "The season's starting a little later than usual, as you probably noticed. They thought it made sense to wait until summer vacation to get started."

"I wondered about that," he said automatically. Then he made himself sit straighter and asked, nodding out at the field, "Is one of these yours?"

"God, do I look that old?"

"Actually, no," he mumbled, embarrassed.

Laura went on easily. "No, I'm just volunteering to help out this year. I figured it'd be good for business."

"What kind of business?"

"Advertising."

"Oh, really? What exactly do you do?"

She told him she worked free-lance, designing ads, brochures, and packaging. She'd worked in a big agency in Chicago for several years, and then moved here a year ago when her grandmother died and left her a camp on a lake an hour away. It was her favorite place in the world, she said; she was sick of living in the city and she wanted to be near enough to be able to use the camp on weekends.

"Did you grow up in Chicago?" he asked. The teams were lining up along the dirt paths that ran from home to first, from third to home. He was beginning to feel nervous.

"No. I was born in London, and then we lived in Brussels, and then Washington for a while. Then Beirut. I went to school in Chicago, though."

"Why all those places?"

"My father was in the Foreign Service."

"And where do you live when you're in town?"

"Grosvenor Court."

"Oh, my old grammar school. I don't know why they've given it such a pompous name."

"Watch it," said Laura, "that's my pompous name."

"You made that up? But why 'Court'?"

"You always call condominiums 'Court.' Unless they're for old people, then you call them 'Manor.' Or if they're on a golf course, you call them 'Blah Blah Greens,' and if they're on the water you call them 'Blah Blah Landing.' "

"Or 'Cove.' "

"Or 'Cove.' Right."

She smiled at him, and he liked her; she reminded him of the women he'd had as friends in college.

"Have you ever done french fries?" he asked.

"No. But I bet I could. I've done baked beans. And pickles."

Everyone around them was standing up, and on the field the teams were taking off their caps. From somewhere he heard a faint, mournful alto begin: "Uh-oh, say can you see . . ."

The moment the singing started, he remembered the sound of her voice, Cecily kneeling on his mother's kitchen floor, scrubbing, sweating so that the dye from her hair ran blue down the back of her plump neck. She would sing:

Mama's little baby loves shortnin', shortnin',
Mama's little baby loves shortnin' bread.

And:

Love my mama and my papa too,
Love my mama and my papa too,
But I'd leave them both to go with you.

When she finished the anthem, everyone sat down, except Jack. Laura handed him a baseball, clean and white. He took it and, making his movements as casual and quick as he could, let it fly into the air toward the catcher's mitt.

5

A Real Separation

❧

Maisie and Caterina were in the kitchen, baking cookies for a Fourth of July potluck supper. The heat from the oven throbbed in the little room, so that the air shimmered and the shiny dingy walls were sweating. "This was so stupid," they kept telling each other. "Why didn't we just buy ice cream or a watermelon?" But they had mixed up the dough, filled it with expensive butter and brown sugar and bags of soft, melting chocolate chips; they couldn't stop now.

"Watch out," Maisie said, turning from the oven with a hot sheet of cookies.

Caterina straightened at the table, where she was spooning dough in little mounds onto another cookie sheet. "Oh, no, are they done?"

"Where am I going to put this?" The heat of the pan was beginning to seep through the frayed oven mitt Maisie was wearing; she felt a burning in the soft place between her thumb and index finger. Caterina's face was red, and there were white circles beneath her dark eyes. Wisps of black curly hair stuck to her forehead. She looked plump and moist, and Maisie, wheeling away from her with the cookie sheet, felt suddenly that Caterina was to blame for much of this heat; she was exuding it. If she would only get out of here, I could finish the baking so easily. She closed her eyes and saw a coolness, lavender, while she let the pan rest on top of the stove.

"Maisie?" Caterina said in a funny voice. Slow, and as though the word had to fight its way up from under something else.

Maisie turned again and saw Caterina reaching out, a look of great concentration on her face. Then Caterina's legs bent and she began to fall forward. Maisie left the cookie sheet on the stove and put out her hands, the right one still encased in the blue-and-white-striped pot holder, and caught Caterina by the shoulders, staggering for a moment under the weight. Then Caterina seemed to come back into herself. "Let me sit down," she mumbled.

Maisie stretched out her bare foot to pull a folding chair away from the table. Caterina sank heavily onto it and brought her palms up to meet her face.

"Put your head down between your legs," Maisie said, gently pushing at the back of Caterina's thick damp hair. Caterina bent, and Maisie saw the wide outline of her bra—four rows of hooks—through the wrinkled white cotton stretched tightly across her back. The room smelled of sugar and warm chocolate, and of sweat, a dank sweetness that reminded Maisie of canned peaches. She slipped her hand out of the oven mitt and leaned over the table to tug at the closed window, and Caterina, without raising her head, said, "Don't."

Maisie nodded and went to the sink, where she turned on the water and waited for it to run cold. The kitchen faced onto a broad alley that ran down the center of the block. Thick, limp ailanthus trees grew with their leaves plastered right up against the window, a greenness that Maisie had thought cool and enchanting at the beginning of the summer. Now, like Caterina and Ed, she found it claustrophobic. They were all uneasy about the things that went on beyond that smothering green, things they could hear but couldn't see. Cats lived in the alley, tough wild ones who sang and screamed at night in such anguish that Maisie, whose room also faced onto the alley, sometimes got up from her bed and went to the window, peering out vainly, knowing it was the cats but wanting to see, to be sure. She heard traffic honking, and sirens, and the distant drums and bass notes of radios, and the constant, urgent howling floating up from the weeds and cracked cement below.

When the water was cool she took the dish towel that was threaded through the refrigerator door handle and held it under the faucet, wrung it out, and put it into one of Caterina's limp hands. "Here. For your forehead."

Caterina kept her head down. "I'm so embarrassed."

"Don't be silly."

Caterina made no move to lift the dish towel to her face, so Maisie knelt by her chair and took the towel, pushing aside Caterina's hair to press the wet cloth against her cheeks and forehead. "We were crazy to bake today," she said again. She dabbed at Caterina's face, enjoying her own brisk competence in meeting this little crisis. She would get Caterina to lie down in the bedroom, run to the corner to buy her a fashion magazine and some sherbet, finish the baking herself, and then clean up the kitchen so that when Caterina got up in a few hours, refreshed and feeling better, she would find that Maisie had taken care of everything.

"Maybe you're getting the flu," she said. "Or maybe it's because you're dehydrated. Let me get you some water, or juice."

"No," said Caterina, "it's because I'm pregnant."

She sounded so dejected that Maisie's first reaction, before she could even take in the news, was to say, "You're not glad?"

"Oh, no, I am." And Caterina rose quickly to her feet and picked up the spatula, to take the cooled cookies off the baking sheet.

Automatically Maisie reached out to take the spatula from her. "No. You sit." She slid the blade under the cookies, three at a time, with a light hand on top of them to make sure they didn't fall off on the way to the metal cookie tin. "Well, listen, that's wonderful. When is the baby due?"

"November," Caterina said, holding the damp cloth to her throat. Maisie took it out of Caterina's unresisting hand and went to hold it under the faucet again.

"November," she said. "But that seems so soon!"

"Not really," Caterina said. She was holding on to the cookie tin, where it rested on the table, and rolling it back and forth between her hands. It was supposed to look like needlepoint, with bumpy little flowers on it and a rhyme picked out in cross-stitch: *Monday's child is fair of face, Tuesday's child is full of grace . . .*

"Did you just find out?" Maisie asked carefully, handing back the wet cloth. But she knew even as she asked that of course Caterina hadn't just found out; she must have known for months.

"Well, we've known for a little while. But we haven't told anybody. We didn't want to, until we were sure. You know a lot of people have miscarriages in the early months."

Maisie nodded, sliding the last of the cookies into the tin. She was so upset she didn't trust herself to speak. Had Caterina put off the announcement because she'd so dreaded Maisie's reaction? Caterina certainly had seemed tired the last few months and hadn't wanted to cook much—Maisie had cooked, happily, because it made her feel as though she had a role in this household and wasn't just a fifth wheel, or they got take-out food, which Caterina barely touched. Maisie thought of what an effort it must have been for Caterina to conceal the pregnancy in her own home.

She sent Caterina off to lie on the bed under cool sweeps of the fan, and she put the cookie sheets into the sink and ran water onto them. They warped suddenly, with a loud metallic moan; she hoped she hadn't ruined them.

The kitchen seemed stiflingly hot, and she went to open the window, cats or no cats. She had to lean over the table to do it, and the front of her T-shirt, hanging loosely, knocked over Ed's jar of vitamins and Ellie's bottle, which lay on its side and began dribbling milk onto the wooden tabletop. "Damn it," she said aloud, tugging at the window. She needed more leverage, which she couldn't get without moving the table; the window was swollen shut with heat.

After giving the window one last shove, she abandoned it and the messy kitchen and went to sit in the living room, which was strewn with toys and books and magazines. It was incredible to her how much chaos a one-year-old child could make. Nothing, it seemed, was out of her reach. Last week Maisie had come into her own room to find Ellie sitting on the floor, surrounded by perfume bottles and tubes and jars of makeup, which she'd somehow managed to pull down from Maisie's dresser top. "No," said Maisie, grabbing things out of her small, strong hands. "No! No!" She tried to imitate Caterina's way of saying no, which was stern but not angry, but she was afraid that her own panic came across in her voice. Ellie hadn't actually managed to open anything, Maisie saw once she had gathered everything up and replaced it on the dresser top, and she smiled apologetically down at the baby. Ellie was still sitting in the same spot on the floor, looking up at Maisie with a curious expression on her face, as though asking: What kind of person would get so upset over a few silly bottles? This feeling that the baby could see through her, knew exactly how flimsy and shallow and frightened Maisie really was, made her view Ellie with fear and a kind of propitiatory awe. She simply couldn't imagine how anyone dared to have children, little witnesses who would be there all the time, watching you.

She sat in the blue armchair until Ed and Ellie came back from the playground where they'd spent the morning. They were damp and pink, and Ellie's fat arms and legs, protruding from her sunsuit, were speckled with heat rash. "Caterina's lying down," Maisie said.

"Is she okay?" Ed asked, putting Ellie on the floor. She immediately held up her arms to him and began to whimper. "She wants lunch," he said, scooping her up again.

"I'll fix it," Maisie said, taking the baby. "You go see Caterina."

She strapped Ellie into the high chair and sliced half a banana onto the tray, to hold her until Maisie could make her a grilled cheese or something. The sink gave off a humid odor of food, and the milk from Ellie's breakfast bottle that had spilled onto the table was sticky and beginning to smell. Maisie, scrubbing at it with a sponge, thought that just the addition of two more bodies, Ed's and Ellie's, seemed to raise the temperature in the apartment even higher. It wasn't a big apartment, really, for all of them to live in, and it would seem even smaller when the new baby came. She scrubbed harder, a crease between her brows. Caterina would want the baby to sleep in the small dressing room off her and Ed's bedroom, which would mean moving Ellie out of the dressing room. They would want Maisie's room for Ellie.

Maisie rinsed out the sponge and began washing the dishes in the sink. In the high chair, Ellie sang to herself, pounding a piece of banana against the tray with her palms. That was why Caterina had been afraid to tell her about the new baby—she knew it meant that Maisie would have to move. And while this was worrisome—how would she find a place she could afford? What would Jack think when he saw her signing a lease on her own apartment and realized she was never coming back to Maine?—it was better than the notion that Caterina had kept silent because she was afraid that Maisie was too fragile, too messed up, to handle such happy news.

A few nights later she and Tony were in a midtown McDonald's, having dinner. They'd met several times now, always last minute, casual suppers. She would come out of her office to find the cab parked at the curb, Tony sitting on the hood. His coloring was completely different from what she thought she'd seen that first night in the cab, with its tricks of mirrors and shadows. His hair, eyes, and skin were all the color of sand. He was not as tall as she'd thought. He was growing a beard. He had long, flat forearms, full of tendons that moved when he moved his hands.

They went to coffee shops, or bought hot dogs on the street and ate them on the front seat of the cab. She liked to look inside the glove compartment, where he kept novels, two cameras, and food, a jar of pickles or a wrapped-up sandwich; once she found carrot sticks in a Tupperware container of water, which for some reason struck her as moving and sad. She found out he'd been the middle of seven children; his mother was a psychiatrist in Georgetown, his father was a lawyer, and his brothers and sisters were all doctors, lawyers, research chemists. The two youngest, both sisters, were still in college; he spoke of them affectionately, and Maisie pictured them as beautiful and solemn, innocent, on the verge of interesting, dangerous lives. His mother did a lot of charity work and every few years would impulsively donate all the furniture in the house to a shelter for the homeless; Tony would come home for Thanksgiving to find his father standing against the wall of the living room, watching football on TV.

Maisie told him about her own childhood in Los Angeles, her father who had taught dance and had danced in the movies, who had left her mother but still taken Maisie out to lunch on Saturdays until he'd died of pneumonia.

She kept her account factual and general, not wanting Tony to think her hysterical. She didn't tell him that for her the overall lesson of childhood was simple: anything could happen, good or bad. When she'd heard her parents fighting, she had thought: But they can't get divorced. And after her father moved out, and she barely saw him except for their occasional Saturday lunches, she thought, But at least he's still *there.* When her mother told her that he was in the hospital with pneumonia, Maisie thought she'd said "ammonia." She figured out that by climbing on a kitchen chair she could reach the cleaning supplies, and she would take down the bottle of floor cleaner and stare at the label. "Mr. Clean, with the Power of Ammonia," it read, and Mr. Clean's expression, his little smile with one eyebrow raised, reminded her of her father's face, the grin he would give her sometimes when he dropped her off outside the apartment door. Mr. Clean looked frightening (he was bald and fierce), but funny: she gazed at him and got the idea that everything would work out.

Her father's death had astonished her. She didn't cry until her mother told her they were moving to Virginia; then Maisie had a tantrum. She was afraid that if they moved, her father wouldn't know where to find them when he came back. But she couldn't tell this to her mother; she let her mother think she was hysterical because she didn't want to change schools.

For a long time after he died, she'd waited for her father to come back. Narrow dark men getting out of cars, sitting in restaurant booths that adjoined hers, striding jauntily down the street, jingling the change in their pockets. A Cockney voice overheard through the dense stacks at the town library—her heart jumped. She couldn't believe he would go without slipping her some sort of message. At school she daydreamed, expecting to be called out of class at any moment to meet her father in the hall. He would find her, even in Virginia. He would apologize for having been out of touch, and he would give her a note telling her where to reach him in case of emergency—not to be used for any ordinary daily problem, but something she could count on as a last resort, in case the world turned upside down. His death had turned the world upside down; that was the thing she really needed to talk to him about. She knew he was dead, unreachable, but she thought that God might make an exception and let her call on her father again in the case of a real disaster, if only her father could slip her that little note. The fact that he couldn't, or didn't, somehow came to seem like a greater enormity than the fact of his being dead, as though he were being kept away from her now by some foolish technicality.

In the first few years after his death, it had come to her occasionally, doing the most mundane things—walking down the aisles of the supermarket with her mother, or rinsing her hair in the tub at night—that she was very young, there were many years in front of her. Things would happen during those years, and she would not have her father to talk to or to protect her. Her mother was useless as protection; sometimes, lying awake in bed at night, Maisie would hear her mother crying, across the hall in her own bedroom.

At some point, she wasn't sure when, in junior high school, maybe, she had stopped waiting. She'd grown reckless, she'd stopped wearing her cousin Elsa's hand-me-downs and begun dressing in clothes she found at the thrift shop: cashmere cardigans worn with the buttons down the back, cowboy boots and transparent Indian skirts. She bought a peach-colored 1940s silk slip and wore it as a dress to a school dance; her mother said she looked trashy, but it attracted the attention of the senior she was interested in at the time. She began sneaking out to meet him secretly at night, making love to him under bushes and in ravines and once standing up in a gas station men's room. He broke up with her and she went out with someone else. She drank, she smoked dope and cigarettes, she had pregnancy scares.

But all the time she was being reckless, another part of her was coolly protective of what she saw as her own distinction: she was smart. She knew it in those days, though she would forget it later. She read every English and Russian novel she could get her hands on. She learned history through reading biographies of the opinionated sort that were no longer in print or in fashion; she got them from the library, musty, their pages limp from dozens of long-ago readers and stained with the readers' long-ago jam and coffee spills: a study of Mozart that began with Mozart's mother's labor pains, Stefan Zweig's Freudian analyses of Marie Antoinette and Mary Queen of Scots. She read her way through the Modern Library and Everyman Classics series, solemnly accepting their editors' judgment of what constituted a well-read person. She forged her mother's signature on an application to Concord Academy; when she went to her mother with the news that not only had she been admitted, but they'd given her a full scholarship, her mother had looked baffled and then fought with her about how she was too young to go away. Finally, though, she'd said: Oh, well, it'll be a chance for you to make connections. At Concord Maisie met Caterina, with whom she'd gone on to Harvard.

In college she'd run out of gas. The first day of her freshman philosophy seminar, she was the only person who had heard of Hobbes and John Locke, who could rattle off "I think, therefore I am" when the subject of Descartes was introduced. She lapsed into a semester-long daydream of herself as an intellectual. When she finally woke up, in January, with five papers due and five exams, she recognized with a panicky start that the rest of the class had learned something, they had moved into philosophical discourse that she no longer had a hope of following, while she was still proudly toting her old Penguin edition of Plato's *Symposium* to every meal in the dining hall. She'd floundered through to graduation, and finally she had met Jack. She'd felt relieved: if she couldn't be incredibly learned herself, at least she could get an incredibly learned person to love her.

But meeting Jack, marrying Jack, being married at all—these were things she didn't talk about to Tony.

She did give Tony an account of her time at Harvard, mocking her intellectual pretensions the way he mocked his own artistic ones. She suspected that he, like her, could mock them and simultaneously, secretly, still cherish them. She talked about the town in Virginia where she and her mother had moved after they'd left L.A., how her mother still worked as the secretary to the owner of a local restaurant chain. She told him about the Tuckers, a family she'd become attached to as a teenager, who lived on a farm outside of town and kept horses, and how Mr. and Mrs. Tucker each had a male lover, and the two lovers had come out to the farm for a family dinner every Thursday night. She'd gotten a postcard a few years ago from Bernadette Tucker, who had been her friend; Bernadette was living on an ashram and had changed her name to "Gita."

Maisie had the feeling, talking to Tony, that he sometimes listened and sometimes didn't; his attention opened like the doors of a subway car, and she had to speak quickly to get in before the doors closed. Sometimes she was aware of abbreviating so much that what she said didn't make sense. She went home after these dinners feeling as though she had talked herself hoarse, listened so hard her head hurt. She couldn't sleep after she saw him.

Tonight they had his portfolio open on the small table, the oily wrappings of their Big Macs pushed to one side. He had not shown her his pictures before, and she'd never asked to see them, afraid she might not like them. Photography, like music, made her uneasy; she couldn't tell the difference between good and bad and charlatanism; she might admire something trite or disparage something accomplished and original. She let him turn the pages.

"It's mainly portraits," she said uncertainly.

"That's what I'm most interested in. I've been doing them for a few years, and lately I've actually made a little money off commissions."

"What's the difference between a commissioned and an uncommissioned portrait?"

He showed her two pictures, side by side. The first was a head-and-shoulders view of a middle-aged man in shirtsleeves and a knitted vest, smiling, his head drawn back proudly on his neck so that his chin and nostrils seemed especially large. "He's a security guard at my father's office building, in Washington," Tony told her. "I took this one for him to give his mother as a birthday present. In exchange he posed for the other one."

The photo on the facing page showed the same man, in his uniform, at the end of a long dark hall, with a light coming from an unseen source above and behind him. The badges on his hat and lapel gleamed. He was sitting on a chair, and he was asleep, holding his revolver on his lap. Beside him a German shepherd lay sleeping with his muzzle resting on the man's shoe. Maisie admired the picture; then she asked, "Was the guard really asleep when you took this?"

"No, I just told him to close his eyes and drop his head. I didn't tell him why."

"You don't think it's manipulative, to do something with your subject that he's not aware you're doing? It's almost like you're making fun of him."

"Maisie, Maisie," said Tony, smiling. She looked at him: What? "Relax," he said.

She was self-conscious, saying "Uh-huh" when she was ready for him to turn the page. The pictures were all in black and white. Some of the compositions seemed to her too beautiful for the subjects. A man curled on the sidewalk, his pale raincoat rippling over the subway grating. An old lady running down a New York street, her mouth and eyes wide open in a laugh or a scream, and people turning to look after her, some smiling, some looking alarmed. A pretty girl in a white dress, with sober, frightened eyes.

"I like that," Maisie said.

"That's my sister Helen."

"Was she going to a party?"

"Her debut."

"I didn't know people still had debuts."

He shrugged.

There was another picture of three girls, young women, really, naked, outdoors, crouching in a children's rubber wading pool. She recognized one of them as the sister from the debut picture. She skipped over the picture quickly, not wanting to ask about it. More female nudes, different women, lying on beds, standing in front of windows. One of a middle-aged woman sitting on a chair, her legs crossed widely, so that one ankle rested on the opposite knee, naked except for a pair of thin, high-heeled sandals.

"I'm going to get some coffee," Tony said. "You want some?"

She nodded. When he left she turned back to the picture of the women in the wading pool. The sunlight bleached their bodies, so their pale backs looked like eggshells, and they were shot from above, so that their eyes looked closed. The one closest to the foreground was gripping the edge of the pool with one hand, but all their other hands were invisible behind the inflated rubber walls, supporting them in their crouches and squats. The middle one was kneeling, slightly higher than the others; one small pointed breast was visible in profile, so smooth it appeared to have no nipple. Maisie thought that Tony must have staged this shot; it seemed to her vaguely exploitative, and she wondered what he had said to his sisters, if they were his sisters (but he only had two younger sisters—who was the third woman?), to get them to pose.

When he came back to the table she had closed the book and was holding it on her lap. He stood behind her, resting his hand on her shoulder. "Well," he said, "you like 'em?"

"I do," Maisie said stiffly. "I think you're very good." He's going to ask if he can photograph me, she thought.

He put the coffees on the table and sat down. "I need to get off my ass and start showing them around," he said. "I know I could get some more commissions. What I'd really like is to get a show somewhere."

"I bet you could." The coffee burned her tongue.

"Or magazine work. But that seems to be a closed little mafia. They use the same few guys for every shoot."

She started to think about who she knew, the magazine art directors she'd been introduced to at publishing parties. But there was no one who would recognize her name if she called on Tony's behalf.

"What about an agent?" she asked. "Do photographers have agents?"

"They have reps. But it's a catch-22. They'll look at you if you're hot, but you can't get hot without one. Oh, well. What the hell. But I'm glad you like them."

"You're so lucky to have something you like, that you're so good at," she said.

He smiled at her, leeringly, she thought. Poor Maisie, always stating the obvious, Jack had said, but he'd said it affectionately. She held on to her coffee cup, letting its warmth seep into her hands. Tony took a french fry from the nearly empty bag on the table and tried to feed it to her; she kept her lips closed, but then opened them and bit the fry so far down that she tasted his fingers. His elbow knocked the bag to the floor, and the remaining fries fell out. The woman at the next table stared at Maisie and Tony. "You're making a mess," she told them. She was reading a paperback, underlining in yellow highlighter. Maisie saw that she was highlighting every word.

"What about book jackets?" Tony asked. "Those pictures of writers on the back. Who takes those?"

Maisie chewed and swallowed. "I don't know."

"You don't know?"

"I think the writers are on their own, pretty much. Their husbands take the pictures, or friends."

"But some of them must use photographers."

"I don't know," she said again. "But I'll try to find out for you."

The woman at the next table was still staring at them disapprovingly. She had very short hair, and a little gold cross on a chain around her neck. Tony stared back at her, and then he grabbed Maisie's hand and pulled her to her feet. The portfolio slipped under the table, and Maisie bent to pick it up. Tony leaned in at the woman sitting next to them and pointed at a red U-shaped scar on his forehead, which he'd gotten, Maisie knew, as a child, when a swing had hit him. "See that?" he said ominously. "They don't call me Yasha for nothing."

Maisie laughed, and she was still laughing when he pulled her out the door and into the cab, which was parked at the curb, ticketed. He reached across her and locked her door and began to kiss her. He'd never kissed her before. His mouth tasted of coffee. Her tongue was in his mouth, but she put both thumbs on his collarbones and pushed him away.

After a moment he slid back behind the wheel and started the motor. "Don't worry about it," he said. He looked at her. "Maisie. It's all right."

She didn't know if he meant It's all right, give in, or Don't worry about not giving in. He squeezed her shoulder, and she leaned against him. They sat like that with the motor running until she looked up at him and agreed that everything was all right.

He drove her home to Brooklyn, walked her to the front door, and kissed her quickly on the mouth. A sophisticated friends' kiss, she thought. She was letting herself into the apartment when she realized he hadn't asked her to pose for him.

Caterina was in the kitchen, folding laundry. "Jack called," she said.

"Oh."

"He said he'd be up till around midnight." She held one of Ellie's shirts against her chest, tucking in the sleeves. "You will call him back, won't you?"

"Sure," Maisie said. He'd been calling and calling. Whenever she heard Caterina or Ed talking to him on the phone, she froze for a moment and then scribbled a note, which she slipped in front of them. *Tell him I'm in the bath*, the notes read. *Say I've gone to sleep.* They would read the notes and nod, continuing to ask Jack how he was doing. Maisie would go into her room and shut the door so she couldn't hear them lying. Neither of them had said anything to her about the phone calls, but now, with Caterina, she heard the faint note of reproach she'd been dreading.

"I'll call him now," she promised.

"You can use the phone in our bedroom," Caterina said, laying the small white shirt on a stack of folded clothes.

Ed was sitting on the bed, legal journals and papers spread around him.

"Oh," said Maisie, backing out.

"No, what?"

"Nothing. Caterina just said I could use the phone."

"Oh, sure." He stood up, gathered things off the bed.

"But I didn't want to—"

"No, no, it's okay," said Ed. His movements were awkward, hasty. Maisie wondered again if he and Caterina talked about her and Jack, what they said. He liked Jack, Caterina had said so ("Isn't it wonderful that our husbands get along so well?"), but she'd never been sure what Ed thought of her.

When he left the room, shutting the door behind him, Maisie sat down on the floor beside the bed, leaning her back against the quilt and dust ruffle. Ed and Caterina had a real bed, with a brass headboard. They had matching white dressers, one horizontal, one vertical. There were white shutters and lace curtains at the windows and a little blue-and-white upholstered armchair with a basket of magazines beside it. Her own married bedroom had never looked like this, settled, married. She and Jack had never gone out shopping for furniture together; they'd pooled what they already had, Salvation Army chairs and hand-me-downs from Jack's mother's house. She'd always viewed their scraggly possessions as a sign of independence; there was something banal and middle-aged about "decorating." But when she looked at Caterina's bedroom, she thought it wasn't so bad to have nice-looking things. In fact, she loved nice things. She took the phone down from the nightstand, which Caterina had painted dark green, and dialed Jack's number.

His voice sounded dull, and she thought, He knows what I'm going to say, which made it seem even more necessary that she say it; any choice she might have had was somehow removed. She looked at the pale blue wall, the framed Bonnard poster over the bed, and said, "I think we should have a separation." She kept her voice low so she wouldn't wake Ellie, sleeping in the dressing room.

"We do," he said.

"I mean a real one."

"You mean a legal separation?"

"No, not that." The idea of going to a lawyer scared her. "I mean I don't want to have to worry, every time the phone rings, that it's you." There was a long silence, and she said, "Okay?"

"If you think so," he said slowly.

"That's it? You're not going to say anything?"

"What would be the point?"

"So you want this, too?" Aware of sticking the pins in, trying to figure out where it hurt.

"No, I don't want it," he said. "I want you, you know that."

But it sounded stagy to her, forced. And she thought of Tony and felt she was in a jet streaking down a runway, gathering speed; a quiet voice saying "Stop" could not stop her.

"We should set it for a definite time limit, I think."

"And then what?"

She didn't know. "Why don't we say three months. At the end of three months we'll talk."

"All right."

But this was too simple. She'd imagined fending him off, pushing her feet against his chest. "And you won't call me that whole time."

"No."

She wasn't going to get anything out of him. "So," she said.

He didn't answer.

6
Focus Group

❧

Jack sat on a plush folding seat next to Laura Singerwold, on the second floor of an office building in Portland. The room was dark and narrow, like a single row of a movie theater. In front of them was a ledge spread with the gratuitous refreshments that always seemed to accompany anything having to do with advertising: baskets of muffins, grapes, popcorn, and a bowl of M&M's into which Jack kept dipping his hand compulsively, even though he wasn't hungry and was convinced that the tiny sliding clicks of the M&M's in the bowl would somehow be audible to the people in the focus-group room, tipping them off that the innocent-looking mirror on the wall was actually a sheet of one-way glass. How they could imagine that it *wasn't* one-way glass, and that the room wasn't bugged, was beyond Jack, but they seemed to have very little curiosity about why they'd been brought here.

"What I heard," one of them was saying, "is that Catherine gets pregnant and then dies, and then they're going to just have Vincent go around looking for the baby."

"Well, Shop 'n Save has them two for eighty-nine," a woman in a bright yellow sweater said to someone else. "But I think you have to buy six to get it."

"What I'm going to do," said Jim Lyman to Jack and Laura, "is to offer them three individual opportunities to try the fries." His voice sounded shockingly loud and close compared with the overheard voices from the focus-group room. "The first, which we'll call Batch A, will be your new microwave fries, actually fried in a deep-fryer. That'll be kind of a control batch; we *know* they'll like *them.* The second, Batch B, will be the microwave fries actually microwaved, using a browning tray. And the third, which we'll call Batch C, will be the microwave fries microwaved on a piece of paper towel. I gather Batch C is the crucial batch?" He said it with the air of a clothing salesman who has just shown you three suits and suspects you are about to opt for the least expensive. He actually looked something like a clothing salesman: he wore a dotted bow tie and a gray suit and a bewildered air of not quite liking his profession, as though it were a beach he'd washed up on by accident.

"Now that's Batch A, Batch B, and Batch C," Laura said as soon as the door shut behind Jim, counting them off on her fingers. "Think you can remember that, Jack, or should I repeat it for you?"

"No, I think I've got it," Jack said, grinning faintly and reaching for more M&M's. He was paying Jim Lyman a lot of money to do this research, and he had a gloomy premonition that he was not going to like the results.

"He's an ass in some ways," Laura said, as though reading his thoughts. "But he's good. He'll get us the data we need, you'll see."

"That's what I'm afraid of."

Jim reappeared on the other side of the one-way mirror, armed with a clipboard for taking notes. "Now, ladies, we're here to talk about french fries. The first thing I want to ask you is: Which brand do you usually buy?"

Everybody bought Ore-Ida.

"And what else?" Jim asked encouragingly. He had a special jaunty buoyancy for talking to the ladies.

With prompting, they admitted to buying Heinz and McCain.

"Anything else?" Jim asked.

Finally, a young-looking woman with red hair said that she sometimes bought Eldridge, but her kids didn't like them.

"Why not?"

She wasn't sure; they just didn't.

"Anybody else ever buy Eldridge?" Jim asked.

A vague, lukewarm murmuring.

"All right," Jim said with renewed energy. "Now I'm going to ask you to try some french fries. Be right back."

"Jesus," Jack muttered, leaning back in his chair.

"Ssh," Laura said. "Let's hear what they say now that he's out of the room."

The woman in the yellow sweater leaned forward and addressed the group at large. "Are we getting paid for this, does anybody know?"

"Twenty bucks, they told me."

"I couldn't believe it, I hung up the phone and I didn't ask. My husband says, 'Are they paying you or what?' and I says, 'Gee, I don't know, I forgot to ask.' "

"We'll probably get more if they use us in a TV commercial."

"This is for a TV commercial?"

"Well, he didn't say. But it might be, right? I mean, you never know."

"Do you think that's his real hair or a toupee?"

"O*kay,* ladies," Jim said, sailing back in with a plate of fries.

("Batch A," Laura whispered to Jack.)

Batch A was a big success, except with one woman wearing a Florida sweatshirt who spoke up suddenly in a raspy baritone voice. "I have a FryDaddy," she said.

Jim looked startled. "Yes?"

"Well, the point is, I always make my fries in the FryDaddy, so it's just what I'm used to. That's all."

"Oh. Well, what would you say if I told you these were microwave fries?"

"Microwave?"

"They can't be, they're too good."

Their disbelief was a bit forced, Jack thought, as though they had decided that there was a hidden camera, after all, and they were auditioning for a commercial. "What's he talking about?" he said to Laura. "This is the fried batch, not the microwaved."

"No, no, no," Jim said. "I didn't say they *were* microwaved, I said what *if* they were microwaved. These, as it happens, were not microwaved, but fried."

"I think he was just trying to establish that nobody expects good french fries to be microwaved," Laura said.

"Well, he's confusing the hell out of them," Jack said, eager to blame Jim if the results of the focus group were negative.

"I think it is a toupee," the young-looking woman said as soon as Jim left the room to go get Batch B.

The fat woman said: "You know what I don't understand? Is guys that wear them sometimes, and then don't wear them. Like Willard Scott—some days he's got hair, and other days he's bald."

The FryDaddy woman lit a cigarette and waved away the smoke.

The fat one went on, "I mean, what's the point? We already know he's bald, so it's like, who's he fooling?"

They all liked Batch B, and expressed amazement that it had been microwaved. Then Jim told them he'd used a browning tray and asked how many of them owned browning trays. No one did. "They're awfully expensive," the woman in yellow said.

"Only around twenty-five dollars," Jim said. "And when you think of how much you've already spent on your microwave, and how much time you could save doing fries in it—"

"Nice try, Jim," Laura said.

"I have a FryDaddy," rasped the woman in the Florida sweatshirt. "Why should I make fries in the microwave?"

Jack stood up. There was no room to pace, but he jammed his hands down in his pockets and rocked from foot to foot. "We're in trouble," he said. "If they won't invest in browning trays, they'll never buy this product."

"Why not?" Laura asked.

"Wait," said Jack.

"Eeeew," said the woman in yellow, when she tasted Batch C.

"These are disgusting," said the fat woman.

"In what way?" Jim looked surprised.

"Well, they're soggy. They taste—I don't know. Stale, or something."

The young-looking woman wrinkled up her nose and put her french fry down on her napkin, unfinished. And the woman in the Florida sweatshirt shook her head and muttered, "Like I said, I have a FryDaddy."

"You know, maybe you should look into packaging the product in its own browning tray," Laura said. "Disposable ones. They can do that now, I know."

Jack shook his head. "Too expensive. I have to keep my price points lower than Ore-Ida and those guys, or I don't have a prayer."

In the focus-group room, Jim was handing out twenty-dollar bills and shaking hands with the women. Batch C had left them with a dazed, anticlimactic air about them, like passengers coming off a transatlantic flight. "Is this for a commercial?" the woman in yellow asked, bending to retrieve her handbag from under the table.

"No, just research," Jim said, apologetically cheerful.

"For what brand?"

Jim gave a glance at the one-way mirror, as if asking permission. "Uh, Eldridge," he said finally, shrugging a little, and the women nodded at each other, as if to say: That explains it.

After the focus group, Jack and Laura walked through the Old Port section of town to have lunch in the kind of brass-and-wood restaurant Maisie had always referred to as "J. T. Terwilligers," because, she said, there was a whole genre of restaurants with names like that.

It had been six weeks since she'd called him to say that she considered them officially separated. He'd done as she'd asked and not tried to reach her since then. He'd gotten drunk the night of that phone call, really drunk for the first time in years; but now, knowing that he couldn't call, he was actually relieved. Something terrible was going to happen, but it couldn't happen for another six weeks at least.

"I never know what to have in these places," he said to Laura, flipping the pages of the menu. "Look at this. 'Chicken Sate.' 'Buffalo Wings.' 'Our Own Special Mini-Burgers, Hand-Pressed and Caressed.' How are you supposed to put together a meal out of this?"

"You're not," Laura said, closing her menu and putting it aside. "You're supposed to 'graze.' Order several small dishes and thus spend more money."

"You didn't write this menu, did you?" Jack asked suspiciously.

She smiled. When the waitress came she ordered a salad, and then she folded her hands and said, "So."

"So," said Jack. "The microwave fries are going to be a disaster."

"Not necessarily," Laura said. "Although I'm glad you're so honest about that possibility. Most of my clients are so convinced that their product is the greatest thing since sliced bread that they won't even listen to me when I play devil's advocate. Then when the ad appears and it doesn't work, they blame me." She picked up her water glass, and he thought how different her long tanned hands were from Maisie's small freckled ones.

He sighed. "What I'll have to do is go back to the office and take a look at how much we've invested already in the microwave fries. It might make more sense just to stop the whole thing right now."

She rested her chin on her closed fist. "You really would consider stopping? Not introducing them at all?"

"Doesn't it make sense? Rather than going out there and getting killed?" He picked up a packet of sugar from the ceramic dispenser on the table and rubbed it between his fingers.

"There's such a thing as being too cautious."

"Yes, but do you honestly think I am being too cautious now? If it were your business, would you introduce these—these loser fries?"

"See, that might be a great marketing strategy. 'Loser Fries.' Like—what is it? What's that cola they sell that's deliberately full of sugar and caffeine?"

"But would you? If it were your business?"

"I don't know," she said. She must have seen his disappointment then; she added, "I'm sorry. But frankly, that's why I do what I do. I don't understand how business works. And I don't want to take risks myself. I just want to come in, do something clever and hopefully effective, and then leave."

"I don't understand how business works, either," Jack said.

The waitress brought Laura's salad and his hamburger, surrounded by thick steak-cut fries. He looked at them in dismay. "Oh."

"They're not Eldridge?" Laura asked, squeezing lemon juice on her lettuce.

"I just don't want to look at another french fry today, that's all."

"Send them back," she said, glancing around for the waitress.

"No, no, it's okay." He picked one up and put it down again; it had the weight and heft of a real potato, rather than the light mealiness of a fry made from reconstituted potato granules. It depressed him that he knew this.

Laura's fork probed lightly through her salad. "So then why are you in the business?"

"What?" he said through a mouthful of hamburger.

"If you don't understand business, why are you in it?"

He had trouble swallowing, watching her, but her expression was simply one of curiosity, not of accusation or challenge. He drank some of his beer. "Oh, family loyalty, mainly," he said. "It's been in my family four generations. It wouldn't seem right to just let it go down the drain now." He paused, preparing further explanations, but she nodded and ate a piece of tomato.

He found himself telling her, as they ate, about his latest business pressure: Sam Lowry, who was one of their largest distributors, had just canceled his agreement to sell Eldridge. "We missed a couple of shipping deadlines. It was stupid of me to agree to those dates in the first place, I knew we'd never make it, but I was trying to turn cartwheels for Sam because I knew we were in a precarious position with him."

"Why did you miss the deadlines?" Laura asked.

"Oh, the damned suppliers. They're still sending us stuff, but never when they say they will. Our credit ratings aren't what they used to be."

She nodded, wiping her mouth. Let her think he'd messed up the credit; he wasn't going to tell her that it had been his father.

"But the awful thing," he said, "was that Sam Lowry was a friend of my father's. They were playing golf together when my father—that was when he had his heart attack. He died while Sam was off trying to get help."

"So that makes this a lot messier?"

"Exactly," he said. "I kind of—well, not kind of, I mean, I really did go crawling to Sam, threw myself on his mercy, in a way. And he listened, he let me do it, and then he started crying, and talking about how much he'd respected my father. He didn't understand that my father thought he was a jerk, and only pretended to—you know, because it was good for business. So here's this guy crying with emotion for this friendship that never existed, and at the same time he's cutting me off at the knees, do you know what I mean?" He was running out of breath, his eyes flickering from Laura's narrow, concerned face to the things around and behind her: two girls sharing a fondue, an oil painting of an intersection with a traffic light hanging above it, a tanned couple in business suits holding hands across a table. And he was seeing his father and Sam out on the golf course that last day, his father maybe groveling the way he, Jack, would have to grovel a year later. (A decent interval, Sam said. Frankly, Jack, this trouble's been brewing quite some time now, but I wanted to wait a while after your father passed on.) Groveling, feeling the snaking pain in his chest and arms and ignoring it, wanting to make Sam see his point. Come on, Sam. . . .

"Sure," Laura said.

Jack shook his head and ate one of the steak fries, appalled at how close he was to losing it in front of her. He ate another fry. "They're not bad," he said aloud, surprised.

Laura said, "Do you sell much to restaurants?"

"Some."

"What about schools? Airlines? From what I gather, the institutional side of the business can really be quite profitable."

"I should look into it more."

"Don't you have someone in the company who's checking this kind of stuff out for you?"

"I'm not too good at delegating."

"Well, that," she said, putting her fork down on her plate, "is pretty silly."

He looked at her, startled.

"I mean, I'm sorry, I don't know you very well, but it seems to me you can do a lot more with this business than you have so far."

He made an effort, then, to tell her some of the ideas he'd had for the company, back in the beginning. Bigger allocations for new product development, a small-scale employee incentive program to cut down on quality glitches, tuition reimbursement. They talked about advertising in a general way, though Laura said that they shouldn't spend money saying anything until they'd figured out what they wanted to say. Check out Sunday circulars, she advised; and he was pleased to be able to tell her he'd already done that, he had a coupon program up and running now.

When the check came, Laura reached for it.

"I'll get it," said Jack.

"No, that's all right."

"Really. Let me. It's on the company, anyhow."

"I know," she said, and she put the check down, keeping her hand on top of it, and said, "I pay the check to make you feel pampered, because God forbid the client should ever have to feel unpampered. And then when I send you my bill, I stick this lunch on it under 'travel and entertainment.' "

"That's ridiculous," Jack said.

"Isn't it?" She picked up the check and frowned at it. "You can't imagine how nice it is, how refreshing, to have someone like you for a client. Most of the people I deal with . . . well, you know how all the hotels now have telephones in the bathroom? So you won't miss that crucial phone call? Well, most of my clients are the kind of people those hotels are thinking of when they install those phones. The guys who look at the phone hanging next to the toilet and think, Gee, I must be somebody pretty important."

She bent to pick up her purse, and Jack studied the top of her head, the sharp white part that divided her dark hair. He was wondering why she stayed in advertising, since she seemed to dislike it so much and to dislike herself for doing it; but that was a dumb thing to wonder about, he supposed. Look at him, obsessed with slotting fees and quotas and profits per linear foot of freezer space. He spent his days inventorying the contents of the light and heavy storage areas, meeting with brokers and distributors, pacing the slippery floors in the manufacturing area, correcting mistakes on the production line, keeping his temper, never yelling, making sure that all his employees felt they had a voice in the operation. Taking home *Frozen Food World* and *Grocer's Spotlight* to read in bed. He almost never thought about his dissertation anymore, and he tried not to think of Maisie. The thoughts he did have came as shocks: opening the linen closet and seeing the little stack of perfumed bath soaps, shutting his eyes and inhaling the faint scent of her, naked, freshly bathed. Forgetting why he'd opened the closet in the first place, gazing stupidly at the piles of towels and sheets.

After Laura paid the bill, they walked slowly, almost aimlessly, back to the office building where the focus group had been and where they'd left their cars. The summer afternoon had turned cool, and the light was clear and lemon-colored against the storefronts. The air smelled of salt and, faintly, of the beginning of someone's cookout.

"Portland," Laura said, glancing into the window of a clothing store as they passed, "really is one of my favorite cities."

"I know," Jack agreed, although all he saw was a city that had not been good enough for Maisie: the bookstore that hadn't had the feminist novel she'd wanted, the posters for the chamber group she didn't want to hear, so that the concert tickets he'd brought home as a surprise had lain on the desk in the living room until a month after the concert date, when he'd finally thrown them away.

"I wish I got down here more often," Laura said. "It's only an hour from Champs du Soleil. But it seems like another world." They had reached the parking lot and were standing beside Laura's Jeep.

"I've actually been living down here," Jack said.

"In Portland?"

"Just outside. A place called Higgins Beach."

"And you commute every day? That's a lot of commuting."

"I know," Jack said. "Actually, I have just about decided to move back up to Champs du Soleil. I found an old farmhouse I might rent, off

LaRue Street." (Maisie had loved the name, when he'd driven her down it once. "Kind of redundant, don't you think?")

He'd already signed a lease on the new house, in fact, but he still couldn't make himself think of it as something definite. He had given notice to the landlord of the little beach cottage, and he'd reserved a U-Haul for the coming weekend. Yet all this week, beginning to throw his own stuff into boxes and Maisie's stuff into separate boxes, he'd been telling himself that it was hypothetical, something he was doing just in case he did move.

"Well," said Laura. "So are you driving back up again now?"

He looked, unnecessarily, at his watch. "It's not worth it. I think I'll just go home and pack."

She held out her hand. "Call me when you figure out what you want to do about the microwave fries. Or if you just want to talk. I'll think about it, too, and see if I come up with any ideas."

She pulled herself into the Jeep with one swift motion, waved, and drove away. He stood looking at his own car but didn't get in. He walked instead to the post office, where he took from his pocket the postcard to Maisie he'd been carrying around for the past week. He'd debated sending it at all, knowing she might view it as a break in their separation. He'd gone through several drafts, trying to get the tone right; he didn't want it to sound angry, or as though he were trying to make her feel guilty. He had ended up with very few words, though he knew that Maisie might read anger into the very brevity of it.

He read the card once more before he sent it.

Dear Maisie:

As of the first of next month, I'll be moving. The new address is:

RD 3

CHAMPS DU SOLEIL, ME

Will send you the new phone number when I have it, but for now, just wanted you to know where I am.

7
Fortification

❧

Now, all of a sudden, Caterina looked pregnant, her belly lifting her blouses away from her hips. It was as though making the announcement had given her body permission to go public. The bigger she got, the smaller Maisie felt. "How are you doing?" she kept asking, and Caterina would look surprised and say, "Fine."

No one had said anything about Maisie moving out. She'd begun to look at apartments, but she couldn't afford any of the places she would have liked, and the ones she could afford scared her. She thought she would put off the decision for a while; maybe Caterina would need her help after the baby was born. Caterina and Ed went out and bought a second crib, and it stayed in its box, leaning against the living room wall.

At the beginning of September, she got Tony an interview with the publicity director at her publishing house. She waited in her cubicle for him to come and tell her how it had gone. She was trying to type a letter to an author, but she was having trouble deciphering her boss's handwriting, and she finally gave up and began on a manuscript she'd been meaning to read. It was a saga about the Navaho, several generations of the same family. She didn't care about any of the people and couldn't keep them straight, but she kept reading dutifully because her boss had said that the subject sounded promising and the book might make a good first project for Maisie to handle on her own. Maisie had better get cracking, her boss had said, smiling, if she wanted to get anywhere in this business.

At five-thirty she put down the manuscript and left her desk.

She ran into her friend Dennis in the hall. They hadn't gone out for drinks in a long time, and he was rumored to be having an affair with a woman in the art department. He reached out and grabbed the collar of Maisie's bright pink blouse. "Where'd you get the shirt from, Pepto-Bismol?"

She smiled tightly at him and walked down the hall to publicity. The door of the director's office was open; there was no one inside.

"Where is she?" Maisie asked the assistant, who was shrugging on his jacket.

"Gone," the assistant said, bored.

Maisie went back down the brightly lit hall to her cubicle and put the dust cover on her computer. She was thinking of the publicity director, a beautiful Irish woman named Jill whom she saw sometimes in the ladies' room, outlining her eyes in olive pencil. Maybe Jill had swept Tony off for a drink, or maybe he'd swept her. She could see them leaning toward each other over a small table. She picked up the Navaho manuscript and put it down again; it was too heavy to lug home tonight on the subway. I could have managed it in the cab, she thought. She would have to take it home in sections, but some other time: she was suddenly too tired to think anymore.

"Leaving?" her boss said in that ominously cheery tone that let Maisie know that everything she did was being noted.

Outside the building she glanced involuntarily at the space where the cab usually was, but it wasn't there. She was almost at the subway stop when she heard an insistent honking behind her, and she turned to see Tony pulling up at the curb.

"Hey, sweet," he said when she got in, kissing her.

"I almost missed you," she told him.

"I know. I was parked outside, but there was a cop on the street, so I've been circling around. I figured you'd know to wait."

"Why didn't you come find me inside?"

"That place gave me the creeps. Besides, what's-her-name shepherded me in and out. She walked me to the elevators."

"Yes, but she would have understood if you'd told her you wanted to say hello to me."

He shrugged. "Next time I will."

"So did she give you some work?"

"Sort of. She told me to go take this guy's picture, and if she likes it, she'll pay me."

"What guy?"

"I wrote down his name."

He pulled away from the curb, into the stream of traffic. She leaned her elbow on the window and put her forehead in her hand. They drove down to the Village and had dinner in a little health-food restaurant, barely speaking. When they were in the cab again, she noticed he was heading west, away from Brooklyn.

"Where are we going?" she asked.

"Home."

She looked at him.

"My home," he said. "This time I am kidnapping you."

The dazed sadness she'd been feeling was still there, but in her center something warm was beginning. She looked at people walking on the streets, the lighted awnings of restaurants. Grocery stores, with piles of fruit and flowers outside. The glowing windows above the stores, where people lived. None of those people knew that she and Tony were in this cab, driving to his apartment.

"Don't you have to return it?" she asked once, clearing her throat. "The cab, I mean?"

"Not till one," he told her. He patted the dashboard. "Like a pumpkin."

He led her up a flight of stairs to a cold, large living room with brick walls. The high ceiling was painted black, studded with black lights. He turned them on, and she saw that the walls were covered with photographs she recognized from his portfolio; she wondered, while he poured some wine, how he'd gotten the nails into the brick. She sat down on a big leather couch. He put on some music, Duke Ellington, she thought, and handed her a glass of wine.

"Hey," he said. "When I was sitting in the reception area, I started thinking about a book I could do for your company to publish."

"Really?" She saw bookshelves full of books, a cage on the floor with a hamster running around and around inside a metal wheel; she'd seen those wheels before but never seen a hamster actually using one.

"I was looking at your fall catalog, and you were right, it does seem to be mostly trash. So how's this? A book of dumb proverbs."

"What do you mean?" She looked at his eyes, his beard shimmering above a black-and-white plaid flannel collar. Behind him she saw two bicycles leaning against the wall and, on a chair, a plastic bag that said "The Needle Nook," with a red knitted sleeve trailing out of it.

"Like here's one," he said, putting his glass down on the coffee table. He made his voice deep and theatrical. " 'Sleep not, wake not.' "

"I like it," she said. Her eyes followed his wineglass to the table, where, in a jumble of books and papers and crumb-covered plates, she picked out an Anne Tyler novel, a copy of *Vogue*. An open can of Tab.

"A real checkout-counter book," Tony said. "The kind of thing that people put in Christmas stockings."

"Right," she said.

"Of course, that's only one. We'd need to come up with some more."

"Maybe we could think of more now."

"Not now."

"No," she said, not quite fast enough, so that she mumbled it against his mouth.

Think of nothing, think of nothing, she sang in her head to the music; and yet for some reason when Tony was unbuttoning her blouse (maybe it was the nimbleness that did it, the air of practice that momentarily repelled her), she said, "Whose knitting?" gesturing with her head over toward the corner.

"Oh, God," said Tony, reaching back for the hook on her bra.

"It's in the front," Maisie explained, guiding his hands. "It's okay, I won't get mad. Are you married?" She was proud of herself for maintaining such a light tone, when really she didn't want to hear about the woman—partly because she didn't want to think about whom she might be betraying. The Tab, the Anne Tyler: these scattered possessions made their owner seem real, vulnerable.

But she'd asked, and Tony told her, his hands cupping her breasts: "It's my fiancée. Louisa. But don't worry, she's in Atlanta on business."

"Oh," said Maisie, and she lay back on the couch and tried to clear her mind by watching his hands moving over her body. Tony's hands. That was exciting. Think of that.

"You know, you never talk about your husband," Tony said, brushing her with his mouth. "You never even mention him. Well, Louisa's the person I never mention."

It was when he took her hand and pulled her toward the bedroom that she said, "I don't have my diaphragm."

He kept pulling her. "I'll be careful."

"No, that's not safe. Don't you have a condom?" It was ridiculous to be talking about this, when she should have been desperate to get into bed with him; but she was, suddenly, adamant, one little part of her brain still thinking coldly and clearly: she would not take a chance on getting pregnant. AIDS she couldn't even begin to contemplate; she thought about it and decided not to think about it.

"Just come lie down, then," Tony said in her ear. "We'll just mess around. Come lie down."

The bed was made. Maisie wondered whether the sheets were fresh or left over from Louisa. She lay down with Tony next to her, and then on top of her. Then she said, "No!"

He rolled off her and didn't say anything for a moment. In the light that spilled in from the living room, she could see his eyes blinking impatiently at the ceiling, and then he said, "Maybe Louisa left hers here."

It took Maisie a moment to figure out what he meant. Then she said, "Would it be in the bathroom? I'll go check." She sprang out of bed. When she got into the bathroom and locked the door behind her, she realized she had reacted automatically, saying the thing that would get her away from him most easily.

She looked at herself in the bathroom mirror, a vast one surrounded by movie-star bulbs. Her face and body were flushed, her eyes big and dark, with the light making white pools of the pupils. There's a man out there who is waiting for me to put in his fiancée's diaphragm, she thought, as clearly and slowly as though she had spoken the words aloud.

Finally she made herself look for it, just out of curiosity, half hoping she wouldn't find it, that Louisa had taken it to Atlanta and was cheating on Tony. But there it was, a little blue case in the second drawer. It was so exactly like her own, in her flowered cosmetics bag in Ed and Caterina's bathroom, and it had been left there so trustingly, amid a jumble of tweezers and Q-Tips and miniature free-sample bottles of moisturizer, that she had a momentary impulse to put a note in it for Louisa, expressing camaraderie, warning her not to marry Tony.

When she came out of the bathroom she had begun to cry. Tony followed her into the living room and asked her once, sharply, what the hell was going on, and when she didn't answer he threw up his hands and turned away. She put on her skirt and blouse and shoes and stuffed her underwear into her purse and left.

She took a taxi home to Brooklyn, welcoming the high fare as penance for what she had almost done. When she unlocked the door she saw that Caterina was awake, sitting up cross-legged on the living room couch. She looked so safe sitting there, so welcoming, that Maisie was drawn irresistibly into the room. She sank down into the rocking chair and sat in silence, too tired to rock, her feet turned in so the toes touched. Even in this room, at the front of the building, the cats' yowls came through, a muted rumbling that Maisie noticed more when it stopped for a moment than when it was going. Someone had put Ellie's toys away into two red plastic milk crates, closed up the sheet music on the piano, and fluffed up the pillows on the chairs, so that the whole room seemed to be resting, preparing for morning. Only around Caterina were things in disarray: on the couch beside her was a basket of fabric, spilling scraps onto the cushions and the floor. She was piecing together squares of a quilt for the new baby—purple and gray and white, with surprising small triangles of red and black. Maisie wondered what it would be like to have an eye that was so sure, an unfailing and original sense of what was right. She found herself saying, "Caterina, there's this man . . ."

Caterina looked up quickly, and across her face there flashed a look of such alarm that Maisie stopped. She felt that Caterina was barring her from confessing. But who was Caterina, to sit there sewing quilt pieces and fending off the intrusion of anything that was sordid or messy? Maisie began to rock, sullenly, letting the chair thud back and forth on the polished floor. She looked up at Caterina and saw in her face that she was ready to listen, if Maisie wanted to talk; and it occurred to her that Caterina had been trying to protect Maisie, to warn her against telling things she might later regret having revealed. She felt suddenly that Caterina loved her and would always love her, but that the love was laced with a full understanding of Maisie's weaknesses, as though she were a pet, not too well trained. "Caterina," she said, nearly whimpering with need, "why didn't you tell me you were pregnant?"

"I don't know," said Caterina, looking surprised. "I told you, we didn't want anyone to know."

"But you could have let *me* know."

"Oh, Maisie, let's not talk about it, okay? I'm sorry." Her hands were still moving, the needle flashing white, impatient, in the lamplight.

"It was because you thought I couldn't handle it, right? You thought I'd be really upset."

"Maisie, it's not like I purposely excluded you from knowing. I just wanted to keep it to myself."

"You see? That's what I mean," Maisie said. "You don't really care if I'm upset or not. You just live your life the way you want to live it, and you don't really include me."

Caterina bit off a thread. "You're being totally irrational."

"So what! If you really cared about me, it wouldn't matter that I was irrational. What would matter is that I'm hurt."

"I said I was sorry. I don't see what else I can do."

"You can act like you care about what I'm feeling."

Caterina said, "All that matters is what you're feeling? You never ask me how I feel about anything. Here I am having a second baby right on top of the first one and we don't have any money and I can't get any work done now, let alone when the new baby comes—"

"And all we do is talk about me and my little problems," Maisie finished bitterly.

"Oh, God, Maisie, that's not what I meant."

"Well, what did you mean? You burst out with this big list of things that are bothering you, like I should have known about them"—she thought guiltily, saying this, that she *should* have known—"but you never tell me anything important. It's always me telling you *my* stuff. You don't trust me."

"That's not true."

"It is! When you ask my advice, it's always something like does this blouse look good on you, or should you paint or wallpaper the bedroom."

"Well, I just don't happen to like sitting around having heavy discussions about—Oh, skip it."

"No," said Maisie, breathing fast. "Tell me."

Caterina put the quilt square down beside her on the couch. "Whatever I say now will be wrong, so I just think it's better not to say anything."

Maisie began to cry, helplessly; and Caterina, tight-lipped, gathered the scraps of fabric into little piles, sorting by color. She put them all into the sewing basket, then clenched her hands in her lap. "You think that's why you're my friend, so I can ask you about painting the bedroom?"

"Then why?"

"Jesus! I'm not going to sit here and give you a *list.*" Caterina looked away. "And, I don't understand why you have to turn everything into a *scene.* You push and you push—" She stopped.

"Caterina," choked Maisie, "don't be this way."

"What's going on in here?" Ed said from the doorway. He was wearing green-and-white-striped pajamas, and Maisie looked away; the sight of him was at once intimate and formidable. She wondered how long he'd been listening. She wiped her face with her hand.

"We're arguing," she said disingenuously. "We're tired. It's stupid. I'm being a jerk."

"Well," said Ed, frowning, "it's late. Why don't we all go to bed." He held out a hand to help Caterina up, then put his arm around her. "Good night, Maisie," he said.

He wants to show me there are no hard feelings, that this is between me and Caterina, thought Maisie. "Good night, Ed," she said, almost gratefully. But she couldn't let Caterina go without making some gesture, whether for his sake or Caterina's she really wasn't sure. "Caterina, I'm sorry," she said. "I didn't mean it. This is just a crazy night, I guess . . ." trailing off.

"Forget it," said Caterina, but her voice was so tired Maisie couldn't tell if she was still angry. Her own anger now seemed irrational and impossible—had she really said all that?—and all that was left was fear that she had done damage.

She watched as Ed and Caterina receded slowly down the hall. His arm was still around her, and they looked solid, like a wall, a fortification. Maisie couldn't say whatever she felt like to Caterina anymore, because Ed would always be there, holding her accountable.

She sank onto the rocking chair again and tried not to think about anything that had happened that night. But she saw herself half-naked on Tony's couch, trying to manufacture ecstasy, she heard the irritation in his voice when he sent her to look for the diaphragm. Still, nobody knew. Not Caterina, and not, thank God, Jack. She heard Caterina asking why she always had to make everything into a scene: her voice had been cold, impatient, but Maisie thought now that there had been something else there, a kind of fear for Maisie's safety. Like a mother shaking a child: Why did you run out into the street? And then Ed had come to shepherd Caterina off to bed. Caterina was lucky to have him. He took such good care of her. Like Jack took care of me, she thought, and she remembered the time she'd had stomach flu and thrown up in front of him, on her way to the bathroom, how he'd gotten her back to bed and cleaned up and made her feel it didn't matter, though she'd been so ashamed when it had happened.

The rockers made a steady thunk-thunk on the bare wood floor. The room blurred. She wanted someone to come and help her up, put her to bed. It was silly that Jack wasn't there. Nothing had really happened tonight. She had not slept with Tony, and Caterina had said of the fight: Forget it. The slate was still clean; Maisie was pure.

She sat there rocking, making up her mind, and finally she realized that if she thought about it too long she'd never do it. She went to her room and found her address book. She hadn't called since his move north, and she had to look up the number. Flipping through the pages, she felt ashamed, and then frightened: what would he think if he could see himself listed in her small clear handwriting—*Eldridge, Jack*—as if he were a mere acquaintance to be cataloged coolly among all the other people she knew whose names began with E? She would throw this address book away, she thought, going to the kitchen to make the call, and she would buy herself a new one.

When he answered, his voice blurred with sleep, she said, "Jack? I'm coming home," and then she said it again, just for the pleasure of deferring the moment when he would tell her how happy he was to have her back.

8

Greetings from Lake Chaugoggagogman-chauggagogchabuna-gungamog

❧

Already he was conscious of sleep as an excuse. Look, I'm sorry, it was the middle of the night. You put me on the spot. I didn't really have a chance to weigh what I was saying.

But all the while he was rehearsing this future conversation, he was continuing with the real one, standing beside the bed with the cold telephone receiver tucked beneath his jaw. "Oh. Great. When?"

She laughed and said, "Whoa. Whoa."

I know I didn't sound that impetuous, he thought. She's hearing what she wants to hear.

He yawned, audibly. "Excuse me."

"Well," she said, subdued, "there are some things I'll have to wrap up here first. Quitting my job, telling Ed and Caterina I'm leaving—"

Oh, no, he thought, don't do all those things. Don't do them and then blame me for leading you to do them. And he began to feel that rather than planning how he would undo this whole conversation later (Maisie, I was half-asleep), he ought to begin undoing it now. "Maisie . . ."

"But you're pleased? You're really happy I want to come back?"

"Of course." It was like waves off a beach: every time he tried to get to his feet, another one came and knocked him over.

"And you believe me, that I want to try again?"

"Uh-huh."

A small laugh. "Was that a skeptical 'uh-huh,' or are you just tired?"

"I'm tired."

"I just feel so awful, Jack. I mean, I feel I've been awful to you. And I've been trying to analyze it, and I don't know why I've been so hard on you. And—"

"Maisie," he said.

"What."

He sighed. "I really am tired. Let's talk about it in the morning, okay?"

He heard her exhale, and got a clear picture of her hunched over a cigarette and the telephone, her small legs drawn up to her chest. "Is Egg there?" she asked.

"What do you mean?" he asked, with the confused idea that she was asking to speak to the cat. Egg had been Maisie's cat originally, a kitten, which she'd gotten a week before Jack had met her.

"How is he? I haven't really seen him for months," she said.

"He's fine." He's a cat, how do you expect him to be?

"So. We'll talk tomorrow?" And her voice was suddenly smaller.

"Right." He hung up.

The floor was cold beneath his bare feet, and he was aware, for the first time, that as soon as he'd realized who was calling and what she wanted, he'd gotten out of bed and stood, as if to meet some emergency. The numbers on the digital clock beside the bed glowed orange: 2:12. She had called at 2:08; he had noted and memorized the time. Four minutes, he thought. How much damage could be done in four minutes?

He was cold. He was sleeping naked still, in the second week of September, trying to eke out the illusion of summer; but the air in the room made him shiver, and the sky outside the window was filled with luminous, fast-moving autumn clouds. He went to the closet and found his plaid flannel robe and a pair of ragg wool socks and felt his way down the creaky staircase to the kitchen.

He flipped the wall switch, and the neon ceiling circle clinked and shuddered full of light. This kitchen, in the farmhouse he'd rented, was old but pleasantly anonymous, like a laboratory in some remote country hospital. The floor was tiled with gray linoleum, and the high white wooden cupboard doors sagged on paint-encrusted hinges. The brightness of this room, at night, always made him feel as though a storm were slashing around outside; it had an alert, battened-down feeling.

He took the kettle from the bulbous old gas stove and went to fill it at the kitchen sink. The thermometer outside the window read thirty-seven degrees, and the sound of the wind made him picture trees rocking, corn stalks withering. When he lit a burner, the blue flame jumped out suddenly, as though startled to be awakened in the middle of the night.

He could not make himself take it in: Maisie wanted to come back. It was like standing too close to an abstract painting; he couldn't seem to get back far enough to see what was in front of him. Last time he'd thought of it at all, the idea of her coming back had seemed desirable but unattainable. Lately he hadn't thought about it, and now he simply couldn't.

Instead he thought about the vegetable garden. It had been here when he'd moved in, planted by the people who'd had the farmhouse before him. He knew nothing about them, since he'd rented through an agent. He thought it was peculiar that they'd put in all these late-summer plants and then left before they could harvest anything. At first, when the tomatoes had flushed red, he'd looked around furtively, carrying them back to the house, expecting someone to appear and accuse him of plundering. But now he took tomato sandwiches to work every day, and stood by the trellis in the evenings, cracking the swollen pea pods and raking off the coarse, uneven peas with his tongue.

The herbs, though, made him feel stupid. Laura, the one time she'd come for dinner, had told him what was what: oregano, she'd said, pointing, and rosemary, and that's thyme, and that stuff is mint—you'd better watch it, that can really take over. And that's basil—boy, you've got tons of it. You can make batches of pesto. After she'd left he'd gone out and stood knee deep in a tangle of fragrant green and found himself unable to remember a thing she'd told him.

So he'd let the herbs go all summer, watching them flower and grow wilder, thinking that Laura knew all about them. He imagined himself bringing bunches of herbs to the office, casually handing them to her at the ends of meetings, having her smile and thank him. Having her go home to cook up wonderful food which she would invite him to come and share with her. But he kept seeing in his head some real or apocryphal Norman Rockwell painting of a cowlicked little boy, with a gosh-aw-shucks foot-scuffing stance and a freckled, blushing face, proffering a bunch of scraggly weeds to a gallant lady patron.

He made a cup of instant coffee and checked the thermometer again several times as he drank it. He opened the kitchen door to the outside, which seemed to roar with an exhilarating coldness. A wild, mischievous chill that might freeze vegetables even though the thermometer wasn't quite down to freezing. Did wind chill affect plants?

He took a steak knife from a drawer and went out to the garden, a rectangular patch that ran nearly the length of the old gray barn, which was slowly, inexorably, collapsing in on itself. There was a low summery chorus of crickets, but the trees hissed as the wind rifled through them. He leaned down, grasped a handful of some herb, and hacked away at the base of the plant until it came free in his hand. The leaves felt clammy and gave off a rich, bitter smell. The moon was high and bright, and he could see the plants clearly, although he still couldn't identify them. He worked his way down the row, tossing the cuttings on the shaggy grass behind him. He was aware when he finished one herb and moved on to the next; the smells changed, became sweeter or sharper. After one vigorous slice he felt something soft and floppy in his hand; he looked down, alarmed, and discovered that he was holding, amid a bunch of greens, the severed flannel belt of his bathrobe.

Egg came and snaked around his legs, and he stopped cutting for a moment to scratch the cat between the ears. "What is it, Egg Man?" He felt unusually protective of Egg—what did Maisie mean by suddenly asking about the cat in that wistful way when she'd abandoned them both months before? Egg rolled over to let Jack scratch his belly, and then he leapt to his feet, as though summoned by some silent alarm, and streaked off. There were all sorts of things Egg could see and smell at night, Jack thought, and he had a moment of bereft disorientation, like a blind man whose arm had just been let go of in a crowded street. Well, he thought, it's a good thing I know someone out here who really understands how darkness works, and who can lead me back inside if things get too bad. No, no; he shook his head and got his bearings from the lighted kitchen windows: this was just a backyard, and he was harvesting vegetables.

He went inside and slept for a few hours before the alarm went off. Then he dressed and went out again, with burning eyes, to gather up the limp piles of herbs into brown paper grocery bags.

He pulled them out from under his desk after his ten o'clock meeting with Laura, in which they'd discussed her ideas for completely repositioning the Eldridge brand as The Low-Fat French Fry. He had imagined all sorts of offhand remarks he might make, giving her the bags, but all he came up with was, "Here."

"Oh," Laura said. "Thanks." She put her face down, inhaling. "Listen," she said, "I was wondering. I've told you about this camp I have, on the lake? Well, I'm going out there this weekend, and I was wondering if you might want to come."

He felt himself frowning at her.

"It's very restful there. Silent, really. Nobody bothers you. You wouldn't see another person the whole time you're there. Not even me."

"That would be great," he said finally, smiling, and then, when she left, he realized he'd said that it would be great not to see her.

Late that afternoon he was actually staring at his phone, trying to figure out what he'd say to Maisie if he did call her, when the phone buzzed, and Mary's voice said: "Jack, it's your wife."

He pressed down the button. "Maisie?"

"Jack?" Her voice sounded high, possibly upset. "I have to talk to you."

"Oh, well, I'm kind of in a meeting," he hedged. "Listen—" but Maisie cut him off.

"Jack, I've been thinking, and I don't want to be less than totally honest with you."

"Uh-huh."

"The thing is, I'm *pretty* sure I want to come back to you, but I'd be lying if I didn't say I had some doubts."

"Doubts?" He found a paper clip on his desk and began bending and unbending it with one hand.

"I mean it's possible that I'll get up there, and we'll try, and things won't work out."

He didn't say anything.

"Jack, the truth is things have been really awful for me lately. I haven't told you because I always had to make it sound like everything was great in New York, to justify myself to you for being here, but I really hate it."

It was like the middle-of-the-night phone call; he couldn't think of answers to anything she said. He felt as though he ought to be allowed to go away between her sentences, to a separate little room where he could collect his thoughts and then come back and say what he really meant.

"Yes," said Maisie, as though answering something he'd said, "the job is boring and degrading, and it gets lonely living with Ed and Caterina. I mean, they're so happy, and so focused on each other, and now they're having this baby—"

"Another baby!" Jack said. "You didn't tell me that!"

"Well, we haven't really been talking—"

"A new baby. Boy, that's great."

"So that's another reason why I might be coming back to you, because I'm feeling sort of pushed out of their lives *anyway*—"

"Maisie, please don't—don't—" The paper clip snapped into two pieces that went flying off in different directions.

"Don't what?"

"I don't know," he said.

"I'm just trying to be honest with you about how I'm feeling."

"What you're doing," he said slowly, "is bending over backward to tell me every reservation you have so that you can reassure yourself later about how scrupulously honest you were. You're already setting it up so that when things don't work, you won't have anything to reproach yourself with."

She didn't say anything.

"So what do you think I am? Some kind of laboratory animal, that you can just keep experimenting with?"

"Of course not!"

"You decide it's time to try again. Then you say you still have doubts. You'll decide whether it's working or not. What am I supposed to be doing while you're doing all this deciding?"

"You'll be going through the process with me."

Jack let out his breath. "I don't want to go through any 'process,' Maisie. I'm not interested in having a marriage that's an ongoing case study. I just want to relax and have a nice life with someone I care about and who cares about me."

There was a silence, and then Maisie said, "You met somebody, didn't you?"

He hesitated. "That's not the point."

"That means you did meet somebody. You did, didn't you?" Maisie insisted.

"I'm not sure. Maybe."

There was a silence, which stretched itself out for what must have been minutes. The longer it went on, the harder it would have been to break it. Jack had no intention of breaking it; he was just waiting to see what Maisie would say. He sat with his elbow propped on his desk, his fingers pressed against his temple, feeling the silence lengthen with a kind of fascinated horror. It became a presence, rather than an absence, like a third person on the line with them. He couldn't even hear Maisie breathing. Finally there was a soft click, and then a more utter, but somehow lighter silence, and he realized that she'd hung up.

"Of course it was different when my grandmother was alive," Laura said, pocketing the key of the Jeep and leading Jack down a trail slippery with pine needles. She was wearing khaki shorts and ancient white Keds, with a long stretch of bare brown leg between. Through the tree trunks, the lake shimmered white and silver. "We used to laugh, to hear her talk about 'roughing it.' She would have all these strong young men working for her—guides, she called them, but really they were Ivy League college boys, doing this as a summer job. So one of them would drive her here, to the boathouse, and then paddle her across the lake to the camp. If there were guests, more college boys would appear, as if by magic, enough to paddle everyone across." She stopped outside the boathouse, whose door was hanging by a single hinge.

"Shouldn't you get that fixed?" Jack asked, and Laura shrugged.

"My attitude about the camp, and everything connected with it, is laissez-faire. Which is lucky, since I wouldn't have the money to fix it up even if I wanted to."

Inside, the boathouse was dark and dusty smelling. Jack stood just inside the doorway, blinking, while Laura plunged ahead, going either by superior eyesight or on pure memory. "There's a door here that leads to the dock," she said. "But the planks are really starting to rot, so we're better off going out the way we came in, and just carrying it around ourselves."

His eyes adjusted enough to make out two wooden canoes, on racks against the side walls. He wondered, helping her to lift one down and grunting a little at the weight of it, how she'd managed to get it up there the last time, who had helped her.

"This is the less leaky of the two," she said, swinging her end around smoothly to precede him out through the doorway. "But we'll still have to bail."

They carried the canoe over their heads to the lakeside, and made another trip back for the paddles and their backpacks. They sat on the beach for a moment and undid their shoes. Bending to slide the canoe into the water, Jack paused, listening. "A hermit thrush," he said.

"We get them here all the time." Laura gave the canoe a shove. "That's right, I forgot you're a bird-watcher. Remind me to show you the bird log when we get to the camp."

"The bird log?"

"Gram loved birds, too. She had this special leather book made, where she'd write down everything she saw, and guests wrote down what they saw, too." She smiled. "The effect is a bit tyrannical, or at least it is if you knew my grandmother. I always imagine her standing grimly over the guests, forcing them to write in the book before she'll let them eat breakfast."

Jack smiled back at her. "Do their comments sound so desperate, then?"

"Not desperate. But a kind of determined enthusiasm, do you know what I mean? 'Two yellow warblers in maple tree by big rock' exclamation point."

"Bird-watchers always sound like that. Sometime I'll show you the bird notebook I kept as a child. I made up my own set of symbols to describe weather conditions, wind directions. And whether the sightings were lifers, or new for the year, or new for the locale, or new for the year *and* the locale. I think I imagined it would be discovered someday, and published, and everyone would marvel at how a little boy could do such accurate, detailed research."

Laura smiled, tucking her sneakers up under the bow.

Holding the canoe steady in the water while Laura loaded it, he remembered telling Maisie once, long ago—maybe in the course of their first, all-night, talk? Was this becoming a seduction line, a poignant bit of his past he tried out on potential lovers?—about the birding notebooks, his desire to be recognized as a scientific prodigy. He felt sick, thinking of her, and he was relieved, looking up, to see Laura's long smooth arms reaching into the canoe to lay the paddles neatly across the gunwales. "Why don't you get in," she said. "I'll push us off."

It took them nearly three hours to paddle to the camp. The pace Laura set from the bow was fairly easy, but still Jack found it tiring, his arms and shoulders aching from the unfamiliar, repetitive motion. Laura wielded her paddle with expert strength and grace, slicing silently into the water, feathering after each stroke. Her back, with her black braid dividing her cotton shirt into two neat navy wedges, took on a kind of hallucinatory quality for him: there it was, always four feet ahead of him; he could strive and strive and never catch up. Tactfully (he thought), she stopped sometimes—to catch her breath, she said, although her voice sounded not at all winded when she said it.

"How do you manage this when you're alone?" he asked her during one of these breaks.

She shrugged. "It takes longer to get across, that's all." She rested her dripping paddle across the gunwales. "I'm used to it. I almost always do come alone, you know. You're the first person I've asked here in a long time."

"I don't mean to keep talking about my grandmother's day," Laura said, "*but,* in my grandmother's day, there would have been a college boy here as a cook, and he would have had a big hot lunch waiting for us, and a homemade blueberry pie." They were sitting on the stone-slab steps in front of the house, eating the fruit and chocolate Laura had brought along.

"I don't care about the hot lunch," Jack said, putting a section of orange into his mouth, "but I am sorry about the pie. That would have been nice."

"We can make one later, if we feel like it. There should still be plenty of berries left on the bushes up the hill."

So after they finished their oranges they went to pick blueberries, with an old tin bucket Laura got from the shed behind the kitchen. Jack had never picked berries before, and he was surprised at what hot, slow work it was; but he didn't mind, after his initial sense of impatience wore off. What difference did it make if it went slowly; they were in no hurry; there was nothing they had to do after they finished doing this. In fact, he found that his movements were getting slower and slower, as though some tight spring inside him were winding down. His forearms were faintly pink with sunburn. He would have liked to take off his shirt, but he was embarrassed to do it in front of Laura.

Laura picked the way she did everything else: quickly and unfussily. She didn't talk. Glancing at her surreptitiously as she filled her hands with berries, it occurred to him that she was probably the most self-sufficient person he had ever seen. "That should be enough," she said finally, straightening up and giving the pail a shake.

"Do you ever get bears here?" Jack asked.

"Not in the daytime. But you see them at night once in a while, if you get up to go to the privy. If we decide to sleep outside, we'll probably want to bring along some pot lids to bang, just in case."

"Sleep outside?"

"In the lean-to. It'll be pretty cold—"

"That wouldn't bother me," he said instantly, and knew then, clearly, that he was close to falling in love with her: why else would he be leaping to subject himself to discomfort? He honestly wouldn't feel the cold, sleeping outside with her; and he thought of the steward on the *Titanic* who'd gotten himself so drunk while the ship was going down that he'd been able to paddle happily around for hours in the cold water waiting to be rescued, while everyone else drowned.

Inside, the house was dim and wooden and smelled of woodsmoke and pine and mildew. The scale of the rooms was tremendous. Downstairs there was a kitchen and a large living room with a gigantic black stove right in the middle, a bathroom with a tapless tub and a marble basin set in a heavy oak dresser, and a bedroom with a swaybacked double bed, where Laura left her knapsack. Glancing in, Jack saw a bathing suit and a nightgown hanging from pegs on the wall, curling photographs stuck in the frame of a mold-spotted mirror, a pile of paperback books on a table next to the bed: evidence that Laura belonged here, that this weekend was only a little piece of her ongoing life.

"You can have your pick of the rooms up here," she said, leading the way up a narrow, enclosed stair. Four identical bedrooms opened off the landing—he knew, with a sudden nostalgic certainty, that to someone who lived here the rooms would all have names distinguishing one from another: this one would be the Red Room, perhaps, because of the color of the blanket folded at the foot of the bed; or that one would have been referred to as Uncle William's Room for so long now that no one could remember why, or even remember anyone called Uncle William.

He stowed his knapsack in one of the rooms overlooking the lake, hurriedly, not wanting to linger over the choice of a bedroom. The slight melancholy that had begun to grip him when he looked into Laura's room now sat like a weight on his neck and shoulders. Of course she had given him his own room. He was grateful for that, and for her matter-of-factness, the way she had led him up the stairs as though there were simply no question about where he would sleep. And grateful for her tact: in all the time she had known him, she had never once mentioned his wife, although he still wore his wedding ring and she could not have failed to notice it. Or maybe she *had* failed to notice it: maybe he was an incredible egotist, to imagine that she would look at his left hand. She had asked him here because she was a nice person who liked him; maybe she'd seen that he was troubled and she wanted to help.

He looked down at the gold band on his finger. It had looked wrong to him ever since the day Maisie had slipped it on: not because he'd had any bad premonition about the marriage, but simply because he was unused to jewelry of any kind, and felt flashy and conspicuous wearing it. It was still so bright, so new-looking. He supposed that after years of marriage it would have developed a patina, myriad tiny scratches, a look of legitimacy.

He itched, suddenly, to take it off. But it seemed so sleazy: to reappear in front of Laura newly ringless. So he left it on and went back down to the kitchen. At the foot of the stairs there was a bookcase, full of old books. Poetry, murder mysteries, Peterson's field guides: birds, stars, wildflowers. Tacked above the bookcase, a number of postcards. "The Brooklyn Bridge," one of them read, over a picture of a wooden foot-bridge suspended a couple of feet above a stream. "Brooklyn, Connect-icut," read the small print at the bottom.

Another card said, "Greetings from Lake Chaugoggagogmanchaug-gagogchabunagungamog."

The name was so long that the postcard people had had to set the type as an arc, like a great rainbow stretching over the picture of the lake. Jack, haltingly, tried it aloud.

Laura, coming up behind him from the living room, laughed and rattled it off; she sounded like a car trying to start in the dead of winter.

"That's quite a name," Jack said.

"It's an old Indian saying," Laura said. "It means, 'I'll fish my side, you fish your side, and no one will fish in the middle.' "

"Is there really such a place?"

"Oh, yes, it's in Webster, Massachusetts. I went there once, with a friend of mine."

He pulled a book from the shelf and opened it. John Donne.

"Good," Laura said. "Are you going to read?"

She sounded so eager that he said, startled, "Not out loud."

"No," she agreed, with mock seriousness.

"Oh, you meant—well, yes, I thought I would, if that's okay," he said, thinking then that she'd sounded eager because she wanted to read for a while herself.

But she said, "Great. That'll give me a chance to go for a swim," and she went into her bedroom and shut the door, leaving him feeling guilty and burdensome. And morose, and somewhat annoyed with her—why had she invited him, if she wanted to be alone? And annoyed at himself, for showing his hand too soon. Maybe she would have been perfectly happy to have him come swimming, if she hadn't thought he was dying to read John Donne. He stuffed the book back onto the shelf and took instead a John Dickson Carr he'd already read, and went to sit on the couch, which had wooden arms and damp green upholstery full of holes, as though mice lived in it when no one was there. After several minutes Laura came out of the bedroom in a black bathing suit with a faded blue towel slung over her shoulder. She raised her hand and waved at him, brisk and sleek as a racer on a high school swim team. The screen door banged behind her.

He stretched out and looked unseeingly at his book and sometimes up at the windows, blinding oblongs of light that reduced the rest of the room to darkness, and wondered about Laura's friend, the one who had taken her to Webster, Massachusetts. I'll fish my side, you fish your side, and no one will fish in the middle.

Maisie was swimming in the lake, fancily, like Esther Williams in a late-night movie: a few strokes of the crawl and then a sleek rollover, like a seal, for a quick backstroke. Her white arms paused halfway through each stroke, perpendicular to the surface, wrist bent and hand rotating slightly, like an inquisitive animal nosing the air. He could see her wedding ring as it caught the sun, an occasional flash of light. Then he was watching from above, and she sank away from him, spiraling down through the green water. A doctor came and looked down at her. "It's too late," the doctor said. "We'll have to flush her." On the lake, an Indian with a long black braid paddled a canoe. "Wait," Jack tried to say. "Wait." But he couldn't say anything, and in the effort of trying his face came up against something rough and damp: the cushion of the couch at Laura's camp.

He opened his eyes and saw that the light had changed, and the shadows thrown by the clumsy summer-house furniture had moved on the floor, like the hands of a clock. He sat up and rested his forehead in his hands, then stood up stiffly and walked to the kitchen, where he could hear Laura moving around. "What time is it?" he asked her thickly.

"Quarter of five. You really slept." She had put her shirt on over her bathing suit and was making the pie, rolling out the crust on a rough wooden table beneath the windows. Her black hair was still wet, combed back from her forehead.

"Sorry."

"Oh, don't apologize. You must have needed it."

But he was apologizing for his dream, which seemed so obvious that it must have been visible, like a filmstrip running above his head as he slept.

"Do you want tea?" Laura asked, laying the pie pan upside down on the dough and cutting a wider circle around it with a knife. "Or some wine?"

"Wine, I guess." With clumsy, trembling fingers and the corkscrew on his Swiss Army knife, he opened one of the bottles he'd brought. "Damn it."

"What?"

"The cork broke."

"So we'll drink cork." She had the pie assembled now, and she was pinching the edges into a neat, up-and-down rippling pattern with her fingers, rotating the plate after every few pinches.

He stared. "How do you do that?"

"Crimping the edges?"

Crimping. That was what it was called. She had a whole vocabulary he didn't know about, a whole catalog of unfamiliar skills. The idea was at once fascinating and intimidating, as if he were out walking and had come across a road sign that pointed toward his destination and told him how many miles away it was.

Still, he thought, might as well start walking. He leaned against the door frame, holding his glass of wine. "My wife—Maisie," he amended (*My wife* sounded so dramatic), "wants to come back to me."

Laura nodded slightly and made slashes in the top of the pie. He couldn't tell from her face what she was thinking.

He went on, carefully, watching her. "But I don't think I want her to."

"Uh-huh," Laura said. Was she embarrassed that he was talking about something so personal? Or neutrally friendly? Or dreading the pass that she sensed might be coming? "Um, how long have you been separated?"

"About a year. Only it hasn't been an actual separation. I mean, we haven't called it that, until just recently."

"I didn't know, I mean, I wasn't sure—" she stammered. Her awkwardness filled him with elation: if she were neutral, wouldn't she sound more smooth? "I thought maybe she just lived apart from you for logistical reasons." When Jack didn't answer, she said, "I don't mean to pry, I mean, it's really none of my business—"

"No, it is your business," Jack said quickly, and then she looked up at him, swiftly, a look of such unguarded happiness that for a moment he could barely breathe.

Finally she turned and picked up the pie. "Do you mind opening the oven for me?"

He leaped to do it for her, as though he'd been asked to throw his coat over a puddle in her path. She put the pie into the oven and then moved away, going to pour herself a glass of wine.

"It was for logistical reasons, in the beginning," Jack continued. "At least, I thought it was. But then after a while I began to see that she'd been unhappy all along."

"And you?"

"Me? No, I was happy. I was fine," he said hastily, not wanting to make it sound as though he'd been *too* happy. "I mean, I would have been fine, if she'd never left."

She looked at him for a moment. "It's so hard to imagine you married." She added quickly, "Not that you don't seem like you could be married, but I just keep forgetting you are."

"Well, frankly, I'd been forgetting it a lot lately, too. That's why I was so shocked when she said she wanted to come back."

Laura said, "I hate this conversation."

"I know."

"I really do," she said, "So why don't we just shut up about it."

They had vegetables from the garden for dinner—beans and gnomish, stunted-looking ears of corn that were the sweetest Jack had ever tasted. They washed the dishes with water Jack carried up from the lake. The sun went down and the house got very cold, as though the cold had been locked up somewhere all day and only just released. Laura lit a fire in the big stove in the living room, and they ate their pie and drank coffee. "This stove is hideously ugly, I know," Laura said, "but I put it in because it makes the house usable all the way through October." They pulled their chairs very close to it, so that the sides of their faces grew hot, and they sat facing each other, leaning forward and talking. Jack held one of her hands in both of his, but other than that he didn't touch her.

He was yearning to know what would happen with Laura. But mixed with the almost unbearable curiosity was a hot, languid confidence: he already knew what was going to happen, and knew that he didn't have to worry about anything. They slept inside that night (Laura said, "Why freeze? What are we trying to prove?"), apart. They spent the next day chastely: swimming, weeding the garden, walking in the woods. In the late afternoon they packed up the canoe, paddled back over the lake, and drove to Jack's house, where they fell into bed. It was as though a declared moment of silence had come to an end. They had acknowledged Maisie, bowed their heads briefly in remembrance of her, and now they were free to talk and laugh again, like normal people.

He woke that night to the sound of the bedroom door opening (he had shut it earlier, to keep Egg out), a footfall, then silence. He felt, but could not see through the impenetrable rainy-night darkness, that someone was standing in the doorway. He stayed where he was, lying on his side with his arm beneath the pillow, watching futilely through half-closed eyes, trying to figure out what to do. But as he was debating, the footsteps began to move, hesitatingly, toward the bed. He could hear breathing: soft, fast, a closer version of the sound of the rain in the grass outside. Just as he was about to jump out of bed, shouting, he felt a light hand on his face. "Jack?"

It was Maisie.

"What are you doing here?" he whispered. Laura, so close that he could feel her warmth mingled with his own beneath the covers, was still sleeping, and all he could think of was that he wanted to get Maisie out of there before Laura woke up.

"Oh, God, Jack," Maisie said. She was crying. He thought it was because of finding Laura, but as she went on he began to realize she hadn't noticed, yet, that Laura was there. "I hurt my hand. I tried to get in through a window, but they were all locked. I had to break the glass in your kitchen door."

"How did you get here?" he whispered.

"I took a bus, then a cab. I've been traveling all day. Oh, Jack," and then she got down on her knees beside the bed, and words came pouring out of her: she knew it was probably too late, but she couldn't let him go without a fight, because the things you really wanted were worth fighting for, weren't they? and she understood why he was acting the way he was, she couldn't blame him, but wouldn't he please give her another chance? not even another chance, a first chance, because really they'd never given their marriage a real chance, at least she hadn't, she saw that now, she'd set it all up to fail right from the beginning, which wasn't fair to him, and she understood now how he'd felt all this past year, desperate, she'd never understood that before, but he couldn't have felt that way about her if he didn't love her, right? and now she knew she loved him, too, and so they had all the ingredients to make it work this time, if they both really tried. And she'd thought that what she wanted was to be independent, she'd been afraid that it would swallow her up to be someone's wife, but she'd finally realized that independence had nothing to do with being married or not being married, that it had to do with choosing the life you wanted, and she knew now that she wanted Jack. And she thought maybe the real problem all along had been that she had no work of her own, nothing she really cared about, and she'd blamed that on Jack because it was easier than realizing it was up to her to solve it, and she still didn't know what she wanted but she knew what she didn't want, and that was to be alone. . . .

Could Laura really be sleeping through all this? But she didn't stir, barely seemed to breathe. Several times Jack tried to break through the torrent of words, but it would have taken more than his discreet whisper to stop Maisie. Even with her low sobbing right in his ear, he barely listened to what she was saying, wanting her out of this bedroom, out of this house. These were the kinds of things no one should say and no one should have to listen to. But he heard her when she said she didn't want to be alone, and his mouth tightened. Panic, that's what was driving her. It always has been panic, he thought. First it drove her away from me, now it's driving her toward me.

"Well, come downstairs," he said suddenly, pushing back the covers as gently as he could, willing Laura to keep on sleeping, willing Maisie not to see her. "We'll get some tea and fix up your hand."

Maisie held tightly to his arm all the way down the stairs, and he let her, because the house was dark and, to her, unfamiliar; but once they reached the bottom he shook her off and said, "What the hell are you doing here?"

She began to cry again, great hiccuping sounds. He took her arm again and shepherded her into the kitchen. In the harsh light of the neon ceiling circle, she looked terrible: her thin hair plastered in wet snakes to her cheeks and neck, her pale face blotchy with crying, blood on her hand and on her wet shirt and jeans. He narrowed his eyes at her, even while tending to her hand with wet paper towels and looking for a clean dust rag to use as a bandage, feeling that he was being subjected to some insidious waifish manipulation. When he got her hand cleaned he saw that the bleeding had stopped, and there wasn't any one big cut, just a series of small nicks. She might even have given them to herself on purpose. She'd broken the glass with a rock, she said, and cut herself fumbling for the doorknob. The jagged hole in the glass let the wind in, and the rain was gathering in a shiny puddle on the linoleum. He kept his eyes averted from her and slowly went about the business of making tea: filling the kettle, getting out the pot, the mugs, the spoon, measuring tea into the pot, one spoonful, two, three. She watched him with reddened, brimming eyes.

When he put the steaming mug in front of her, she caught him by the wrist and said, "So will you? Will you at least try?"

"No." He went back and took up his own mug and stood leaning against the counter.

"So that's it? You won't let me stay?"

"You can't stay, Maisie."

"But I quit my job. I told Caterina I was moving out."

"Well, you shouldn't have done that. Not after our last phone call."

"You mean you're just going to throw me out? In the middle of the night?"

"All right, just for tonight. But on the living room couch."

"What, are you afraid you'll be tempted?" she sneered.

"There's someone here."

It took her a minute. "You mean here? Now? She's *here?*"

He nodded.

"You mean in bed? You mean she was there in bed the whole time I was—" She got swiftly up and over to him, and drove her fist, the unhurt one, hard against his stomach.

"Christ, Maisie," holding himself, but with the other arm he managed to catch hold of her wrist.

"Let go," she cried out. "Let go! Let me get to the sink."

Startled, he let her go and stood by helplessly while she hung over the sink, retching. Finally she turned on the faucet and straightened up, keeping her back to him.

"Here," he said, handing her a piece of paper towel. She held it under the water and used it to wipe her face. "You look thin," he said, in spite of himself. Maisie was always thin, but this was different: she looked as though flesh had literally deserted her, leaving nothing but bones, ready to snap.

"I haven't been eating," she said dully.

"You want something now? A sandwich?"

She looked at him, incredibly, with hope. "You always take such good care of me, Jack."

He got out bread, peanut butter, strawberry jam. Then, on his way to the cupboard for a plate, he turned to her and said, "Listen, Maisie, I want to get something straight. I don't want you reading meanings into everything I do. Just because I make you a sandwich doesn't mean we're getting back together."

"I know that," she snapped. Then, when he turned his back on her again, she whimpered, "I know this sounds pathetic, I know it, but I have to ask, what do you get from her that you don't from me?"

He was silent for a moment, incredulous. Comfort, he wanted to shout at her, comfort. He finished spreading the peanut butter and wiped the knife clean with a paper towel before putting it in the jam. "The freedom to be dull," he said.

He slid back into bed and pulled the covers up around his shoulders.

"Where is she?" Laura asked in a low voice.

So she had heard. Well, of course she'd heard. No one could have slept through all that. He would have had to tell her anyway, in the morning, so that she could stay out of the way until he drove Maisie into town to the bus station. He didn't think Laura should have to go through the mess of running into Maisie.

"I let her sleep on the living room couch."

"Is she all right?"

Something fell on his feet: for a moment he thought it was Maisie, back in the room again, reaching for him. Then he realized it was Egg, stepping delicately over the mound he and Laura made, purring and purring, and settling down finally between them, so that the three of them nestled together, their backs touching.

Part II

9

Objects in the Mirror

❧

Loveless, jobless, Maisie went home to Virginia, to stay with her mother. Her room seemed to have grown smaller; at night, lying in bed, she could feel the ceiling pressing down on her. The bed was the one she had clamored for at the age of eleven: not the white canopy bed that all her friends had wanted at that age, but a massive old mahogany four-poster from her grandparents' house. "Not that bed, Maisie," her mother had said, horrified, when the house was being sold and the possessions divided.

"Why not?"

"It's too big for you. It'll depress you."

"I like it," Maisie said. Her grandfather had died in this bed, which was why Maisie's mother didn't want her to have it. But that was one of the reasons Maisie liked the bed: things had happened in it. At night she lay there making up stories. The bed was a raft, and she was out in the middle of the ocean with someone who loved her. He'd been allowed to choose one person to save from the sinking ship; he'd gone down the line of passengers, and when he came to her he'd stopped. On the raft he held her fiercely, pinning her down with his body so she wouldn't be swept off. The bed was a big ceremonial court bed, with red velvet curtains all around it. She was a princess from a foreign country, who had been brought to this country to make a state marriage. She and the prince were being put to bed with a great deal of ceremony, and they lay there stiffly, surrounded by courtiers and burning candles, afraid to look at each other. Then the candles were extinguished and they were alone, and slowly they began to look at each other and then to smile.

The pillow was the lover in these stories. Maisie moved it around the bed to suit her: propped it up against the headboard when she wanted to have a conversation with it, put it at the foot of the bed when the lover was feeling shy and deferential, lay beneath it when he was being protective. Sometimes she addressed the pillow by the name of a boy in her class, whichever boy she happened to be interested in at the moment; but attaching the identity of a real person to the pillow seemed to spoil the game. She would suddenly imagine how Jim Wile really would act if they were on a raft together: scared to death, no doubt, and scared of being shipwrecked with her, a girl. Or Michael Hewitt: concerned with the science of survival. He would be all wrapped up in the mechanics of making a sail or distilling drinking water. It had worked better to keep the lover anonymous, shadowy: someone she hadn't met yet, someone who was coming, in her future, mysterious, adult life.

Now, out of habit, lying in the dark in this bed at night, Maisie found herself hauling out the same old stories, trying to get herself to sleep. It felt literally like hauling; it was heavy work to get herself back into bed with the virginal young prince. It was funny, thinking back to her younger self, to realize that sex, at least overtly, had had no part in these stories. It was not that she had been unaware of it, although at that age she had put no name to it. She had discovered it around the age of nine, she thought: dating it by the fact that when she'd been sent to camp the summer after third grade, she was afraid the people in her tent would catch her sucking her thumb; but by the next year she was afraid they'd catch her doing that. When she gave it a name at all, she thought of it as blowing a gasket: a phrase she had read somewhere that seemed to describe the feeling. She had continued to think of it as that until the age of fourteen, when her mother had given her a book on sex and she'd read, in the chapter on masturbation: "Oddly enough, many young people masturbate for years without realizing that this is what they are doing." Oh, Maisie thought, I wonder if that's what I'm doing. None of the techniques described in the book seemed to have anything to do with what she did; none of them, when Maisie tried them, tentatively, seemed remotely capable of bringing her to the point of blowing a gasket. What she did was to lie on her stomach with a pillow between her legs, thinking about the Greek gods. Hera taunted Zeus, laughed at him. But he grabbed her, forced her down. "Take off your cortege," he ordered. (And again, when she learned the true definition of cortege, and realized that the word she had confused it with was "negligee," Maisie felt vaguely disappointed.)

Gaskets, corteges—these were solitary things, so private that she had to make up her own words for them. What she wanted to do with the lover was different: embraces, kisses, words of love, valorous acts. The bed was big and empty, but invitingly so. One day a man would come and lie in it next to her.

Now, in bed alone, she cried, thinking of Jack in bed with someone else. When she was through crying she sometimes gave herself an orgasm to help her sleep, as she might have given herself a sedative. She thought of nothing as she touched herself, not Jack, not other men. Afterward she felt her body sink down toward sleep, as reliably as it had in the days when she'd lain here telling herself stories.

"What I think," said Maisie's mother, "is that you should learn to drive." She was standing at the sink rinsing the coffee cup that Maisie had just put down.

Maisie went to the cupboard for a clean cup. Her mother picked up the ashtray from which Maisie's cigarette butt was still sending up a dying plume of smoke, and emptied it over the garbage disposal in the sink. "You have got to do something productive," she said. She was small and neat, carefully groomed even in the morning, when she bustled around in a short flowered garment she referred to as a "model's coat." Whenever she called it that, Maisie felt a brief, irrational flash of irritation: "model's coat" was so much a manufacturer's euphemism; surely there was some slangier, less fancy word that could describe this particular garment.

"Some people aren't meant to drive," Maisie said, pouring coffee. "Grace Kelly always said she was uncomfortable behind the wheel, and look what happened to her."

"That is nonsense," her mother said. "You are perfectly capable of operating a car."

Maisie sighed. She had a bad history with cars. At sixteen she'd taken driving lessons and felt fairly confident behind the wheel. The morning of her road test, she'd gone out with the instructor for one last hour of driving, and he'd said to her, "You're doing fine, except for one thing. You just need to get a little more aggressive."

She got 100 on the written test and got through all the tough parts of the road test: parallel parking, the three-point turn on the access road behind Kmart. Then she came to an intersection and put on her signal to make a right turn. A car was approaching from the left, and she hesitated, staring it down, trying to decide if she had enough time to turn before it reached her. Aggressive, aggressive, she thought; and, still watching the approaching car, she stamped on the gas and swung the wheel hard to the right. The car surged up onto the sidewalk and headed toward the plate-glass window of a savings bank. The inspector, who had sat silently through everything she'd done right, yelled, "Young lady! Young lady!" and grabbed the wheel and straightened out the car. "Go straight back to the Motor Vehicles Department," he said.

Two weeks later, on the first day she was eligible to take the test again, Maisie showed up at the Motor Vehicles Department, where she was promptly sent out on the road with the same inspector. The sight of his grim, dubious face (how would she endanger his life this time?), and the heavy, rapid, frightened sound of his breathing, rattled her so much that she started to pass a truck that was backing up. "Young lady!" he shouted. "Young lady!"

Since then she had never driven a car. She had come to believe that a car, like a horse, could sense fear at the reins and would take advantage of her because she didn't know what she was doing. Not driving had never been a problem for her: first she'd been at boarding school, then at college, then in Boston, where the public transportation was so good that she and Jack hadn't owned a car, and finally up in Maine, where there was no place she would have wanted to drive to. Jack took her everywhere she needed to go: to the supermarket, to the dentist, to the outlet stores in Freeport. (How good he had been, to drive her around, and she had never thought of it as good at the time. To her, it was just the way things were. And he'd never tried to pressure her to learn to drive, just said, "What time should I pick you up?") She sat listlessly watching the roadside whip by: pine trees, huddled carcasses of skunks and raccoons, sudden small houses where people lived unimaginable lives, with front yards full of rusted cars and running children.

On one of these rides she'd noticed that there was something printed on the mirror outside the window, white stenciled words as faint as a whisper: OBJECTS IN MIRROR ARE CLOSER THAN THEY APPEAR. Slumped in the passenger seat, Maisie read them over and over. They seemed ominous to her, a cryptic warning. Things are not what they appear to be. Make the appropriate adjustments. The problem was that she couldn't figure out what the appropriate adjustments would be. If the objects were closer than they appeared to be, did that mean you had to react more quickly? More cautiously? The words paralyzed her. She could imagine herself behind the wheel, seeing these mysterious objects in the mirror, coming inexorably closer and closer, and being unable to do a thing to stop them. So she let Jack drive; and then she took the job in New York; then, when she quit her job and went back to Jack in Maine and found he'd fallen in love with someone else, she took a Trailways bus down to Virginia, where her mother met her at the station.

The driving school was called Ace Auto Instruction. Maisie signed up for six weeks of lessons, her mother's treat. As far as she could tell, she was the only student; at least, she never saw anyone else around, and there was nothing that resembled the formal group lectures with slides she'd sat through the first time she'd learned to drive.

The teacher was a chunky young man—she realized, startled, that he was younger than she was; at twenty-eight she was just beginning to have the odd sense of being overtaken by younger people, an implicit message that by this point she was supposed to know what she was doing. The first time Maisie met him, he stuck out his hand and said something that sounded like "De name's de name."

"Excuse me?" said Maisie, confused but at the same time intrigued by what she took to be a philosophical statement of profound simplicity, something along the lines of "A rose is a rose is a rose."

"The name's Dunnane," he said, enunciating carefully, with a slight grimace that made her think that he often had to repeat things to make himself understood.

"First name or last?"

"Last. But everybody calls me that."

Now she felt that there was something familiar about his accent, something definitely not Virginian. "Where are you from?"

"You mean originally? Boston."

"Oh, really? Where in Boston?"

"Charlestown, actually. You know Boston?"

"Oh, sure," she said warmly. "I used to live there."

"Oh, yeah? Were you in school, or what?"

"My husband was," she said, and as soon as she said it she knew that she'd been steering the conversation that way. She had the same bereft feeling that had come upon her the other day in the supermarket, when she'd gone to the freezer aisle for ice cream and overheard a mother and children arguing over french fries. The market carried Jack's brand; Maisie's mother had badgered the store manager for months until, she told Maisie proudly, he broke down and ordered Eldridge. Maisie had carefully avoided the french fry section since she and Jack had separated. But she couldn't help overhearing this mother and her two little kids.

"But, Ma," the older girl whined, "what kind should we get?"

"I don't care," the mother said. "Anything that says Ore-Ida."

"But there's shoestrings, and hash browns, and Tater Tots, and—"

"I said I don't care," snarled the mother. "Just so it's Ore-Ida."

And Maisie felt a surge of indignation on behalf of Jack's poor, slighted brand, and then that feeling of utter loneliness, knowing it didn't matter anymore whether she was indignant or not.

Dunnane simply nodded when she mentioned her husband and motioned her to get into the car, so Maisie didn't get a chance to tell him then that she and Jack were separated. Not that it would have mattered: she'd had no interest even in flirting with anyone in the past four months, since the night she'd broken into Jack's house and hit him, and anyway, this man was regarding her with a look of pure boredom. He wasn't her type: his black hair was cut very short except at the nape, where there was one long ratty tail of hair that made her itch to take a scissors to it.

"We'll start real basic," he said. "That's the gas, that's the brake."

"I know, I know," Maisie said. "I've driven before. My problem isn't ignorance, it's fear."

He looked at her with more interest then. "You're afraid of driving? What's there to be afraid of?"

"Crashing," said Maisie. "The fact that all it takes is for one stupid person to do one stupid thing."

"Well, but you don't. You just don't. You get to the point where you see something out of the corner of your eye, and you just instinctively react. Like last week, I'm on the highway, in the left-hand lane, and this car jumps right in front of me going about fifty." He said the word *fifty* contemptuously, as though it were a turtle's speed. "And there's a truck to the right of me, one of those big ones about a mile long. So what I did was, I just swerved up on the median strip and went around them," he made illustrative zigzags with his hand. "And it wasn't till later, when it was all over, that I realized I came this close to having an accident."

"Thanks."

"No, but the point is, I did the right thing. Without even thinking. I mean, I was around that other car before I even knew what I was doing."

"What if there hadn't been a median strip? Sometimes it's just a fence, you know. Or what if you'd lost control of your car on the grass? You must have been going awfully fast, if you couldn't slow down enough to keep from hitting a car going fifty."

Dunnane whirred his window down and tossed out his cigarette. "No offense, but I think you're thinking too much. What I would say is, just shut up and drive."

So she did. His attitude annoyed her, but the annoyance seemed to help. If this jerk can drive, then I can drive, she thought. They were coming up to an intersection, where the road divided into three lanes. "What do I do? What do I do?" she asked frantically.

"We're going to turn left," Dunnane said. "So put on your blinker and get into the left lane."

"Can I do that? Am I in the clear?"

"Use your mirrors."

She glanced, blindly, into the rearview mirror, swung the wheel to the left, and, miraculously, found herself in the left-turn lane.

"Now just wait for the arrow," Dunnane said.

She waited, felt herself beginning to relax. The cars to the right of her got the green light and began to whip through the intersection. Then, behind her, a car started honking. "He wants me to go," Maisie said, looking nervously in her rearview mirror.

"Tough," said Dunnane. "Wait for the arrow."

The car kept honking. "What should I do?"

"Give him the finguh," Dunnane advised.

Maisie laughed. He'd said it in exactly the same calm tone he'd used when he told her which was the gas and which was the brake. She felt that nothing she could do would faze him—unlike the driving inspector, who'd acted as though her driving were beyond the pale. The green arrow came on, and she swept the car easily through the intersection.

One afternoon Maisie and her mother went to a shopping mall and stayed out for dinner and a movie. The movie they saw was *She's Gotta Have It,* which Maisie's mother vaguely remembered reading a review of. "It's supposed to be a charming comedy," she said. Maisie sat in the dark theater watching the heroine being licked, kissed, sucked, and brutalized by three different lovers, trying to choose among them, and finally deciding not to choose because she liked her life the way it was. Sure, thought Maisie, she's going to end up alone. Tears were running down her face at the sight of so much lovemaking, and she tried not to sniff audibly, conscious of her mother's tiny movements in the seat next to her. She wondered what her mother made of all this merry promiscuity: it occurred to her, not for the first time, that in all her twenty years of widowhood, her mother hadn't had so much as a date. Of course it was possible that she was incredibly discreet, but Maisie didn't think so. Her little body was so taut and trim, her movements so brisk, that she gave the impression of being a completely self-sufficient organism.

"Well," said her mother when they came out. "Not quite what I expected, but it was fun."

When they got home there was a letter from Jack, which Maisie took into the bathroom to read. He was writing to say it was time for them to start thinking about a divorce. "I don't want to rush you, though," he wrote. "Clearly this is a painful time for both of us, and I don't want to add unnecessarily to it. On the other hand, I don't want to keep wallowing in something that's over."

When she finished reading the letter, Maisie pulled the phone from the hallway into her bedroom, all the way into the closet. She punched in Jack's number with a shaking hand. The phone rang and rang. The machine always picked up after five rings, but this time it just kept ringing. She didn't hang up for several minutes, and by then she was thankful that Jack wasn't home; she didn't know what she would have said to him if he'd been there.

She wandered into the kitchen, where she lit a cigarette and left it resting on the edge of the counter, its lit end hanging, while she went to the freezer and got out a container of butter-pecan ice cream. "Don't do that," her mother said, walking in and plucking up the cigarette. "You could burn the Formica." She got down an ashtray, balanced the cigarette on its lip, and put it down beside Maisie. "And I wish you would quit smoking. Or at least cut down. You're going to have to quit one day anyway, if you plan to get pregnant." Then she said, "Oh, dear."

Maisie spooned up ice cream, said nothing. This was the kind of hapless thing her mother always said, and then felt terrible for saying. There was nothing malicious about her remarks; but they were reliable barometers of what was going on beneath the surface, indicators of the subjects her mother had told herself not to mention. She never meant to wound, but she could wound nevertheless; and Maisie, who at other times reacted by getting angry, now just felt worse about herself. She knew her mother thought she hadn't worked hard enough at being married. She had never understood, for instance, why Maisie would leave Jack to go live and work in New York. "I'm not leaving Jack," Maisie had explained patiently. "I'm leaving Maine. There's nothing for me in Maine."

"Your husband is in Maine," her mother said. "I don't understand how you can expect to have a marriage when you don't put each other first."

"Mom, Jack understands, and he doesn't mind."

"If you believe that, you're sadly deluded."

And when Maisie had finally called her from New York in tears to say that, yes, the marriage had fallen apart, her mother had said, "It can't fall apart if you don't let it. Why are you giving up so easily? Go up to Maine and see Jack, tell him you want to work it out."

Now her mother said, "Maisie, I'm sorry. I truly am."

She let her hand rest on Maisie's head, and Maisie started to cry, with her face against her mother's stomach. She had not meant to tell her mother the contents of Jack's letter, but she found herself sobbing out, "Jack wants a divorce." Her mother made soothing sounds. After a few minutes Maisie became aware of the buttons of her mother's blouse mashed against her cheek, and she sat up and looked at her mother.

"Well," said her mother. "Maybe it is time for both of you to think about moving on, even if it is painful. You can't go on being this miserable."

Maisie was shocked. She had expected her mother to talk some more about making the marriage work, to give her suggestions that maybe weren't useful but at least implied there was hope. "So you think this means he'll never take me back?" she said, and was instantly appalled at how pathetic she sounded.

"Not if he's with another woman," her mother said.

Maisie stiffened. That had been a mistake, to tell her mother that Jack had fallen in love with someone else. She had let it out during that long tearful phone call she'd made to tell her mother she was coming home, and she'd known as soon as she said it that it gave her mother ammunition of a particularly deadly kind.

"I'm not trying to hurt you," her mother said. "But I think you need to look at what's really happened."

"So you think one woman is as good as another, that if he has this new girlfriend what does he need me for?"

"Oh, Maisie, that's not what I mean at all. And why are you jumping all over me? It's Jack who's hurt you."

"I thought you liked Jack."

"I do. I like him very much. But I'm trying to get you to see that what's over is over. He's living with someone else."

"And you think I pushed him into it." She was having trouble with such frankness, coming from her mother of all people.

"I didn't say that. But what I do think is that you should let yourself get good and mad at him, and then maybe you can get over him."

"Well, I'm not good and mad at him," said Maisie, beginning to cry again. "I'm mad at myself."

"Well, don't be," her mother said helplessly. "You'll meet someone else."

"Oh, God, Mom," sobbed Maisie, thinking suddenly of Dunnane. "You don't know who's out there." As she said it, she wondered if perhaps her mother knew perfectly well who was out there, and that was why she'd been alone so long.

"Sssh," her mother said, turning into a mother again. "Sssh. Eat some more ice cream. I'm so glad to see you eating. You can't not eat. You'll make yourself sick."

Dunnane had two cars: an old green Pontiac, which had ACE AUTO INSTRUCTION painted on its doors, and a Chrysler LeBaron, which he referred to as being "for my own personal use." Whenever Maisie showed up for her lesson he was doing something to that car: washing it, or putting on new windshield wiper blades, or simply caressing it slowly with a piece of chamois cloth. The thing he was proudest of was that the car talked. "Listen to this," he said, reaching in to turn on the engine. "A door is ajar," the car said promptly. "Fasten your seat belt. A door is ajar." It had a peevish, wounded sort of voice, as though it expected all its good advice to be disregarded.

"That's a riot," Maisie said uncertainly. She couldn't tell if Dunnane regarded the talking as something campy and funny or as a sign of class.

But he turned to her with a perfectly serious look on his face. "This is going to be a collector's item," he said. "They don't make 'em anymore, cars that can talk."

"I can see why," Maisie said. "It would get on my nerves."

"Yeah, they bombed pretty bad," Dunnane said. "It's funny how when stuff bombs and they have to stop making it, that's when it gets really valuable."

"So, you going to paint Ace Auto Instruction right about here?" Maisie teased, touching the gleaming maroon paint lightly.

"Not in a million years," Dunnane said, putting a hand on her arm and steering her in the direction of the Pontiac.

"The key is in the ignition!" the Chrysler called after them.

Dunnane had gone into the navy after high school and had spent three years stationed in Hawaii. He'd moved to Virginia to live with his older brother, who was dying of cancer. When the brother died, he'd stayed on, working as a car mechanic and then opening the driving school. "Named it Ace because there already was an Acme Driving School, and I wanted to come first in the phone book. Pretty smart, huh?"

He had all sorts of theories which he would tell Maisie about as they were driving. Once he told her that carbon dating was all wrong, that scientists were now deciding that a piece of quartz they'd always thought took millions of years to form instead had taken 2.3 seconds. The world, by this reckoning, was only eleven thousand years old. "And there's this fish," he said, "I forget the name of it. But they thought it was extinct, and you know what? They caught one."

Another time he told her that there was a secret third party in this country that was quietly engineering a socialist revolution. "They have a four-stage plan," he said. "The first stage was the oil embargo. The second stage was the breakup of the utility companies. Then they broke the independent farmer. Now they're breaking up the nonprofits."

"That's ridiculous," Maisie said. "Even if there were something like that going on, which is crazy, what would it have to do with socialism?"

"The destruction of private enterprise," Dunnane said. "That's how they pave the way for their coup."

❧

Long before the six weeks of lessons were over, Dunnane told Maisie she was a fine driver. But she couldn't believe him. She still felt that every time she made it from point A to point B, it was by special dispensation. Dunnane tried comparing her with other drivers on the road. "Look at this woman—look at her! Her brake light's coming on every two seconds. You would never do that," and "See how this guy's slowing down on the entrance ramp? That's something I've never seen you do. Your instincts are better than that." Finally, on the morning of her road test, he showed up at her house to take her out driving for an hour, in the Chrysler. "But, Dunnane, I thought you said you would never let a student near your car."

"Shut up," he said, handing her the keys.

It was a bigger car than she was used to, and its constant stream of admonitions disconcerted her ("Your oil level is low. Proper maintenance is essential"), but she drove it all around the town and out on the highway. It was a clear February morning, and the willows spinning by were beginning to soften and yellow. She found herself passing trucks, just to prove she could do it. "See, you're fine," Dunnane said, and she took her eyes from the road for a second to grin at him. Then, aware of her lapse, she swiveled her eyes back, dreading to find some unseen car about to sideswipe her. But the road all around them was empty.

"What does 'Objects in the mirror are closer than they appear' mean?" she asked him.

"What?"

"That's what it says in those outside mirrors."

"It does? I never noticed that." He leaned sideways, looking at his mirror. "No, it doesn't."

"The letters are very faint," Maisie said, frowning.

"No, there's nothing. Maybe in your mirror," and he leaned over her, so that his head was practically in her lap and she could smell tobacco and shampoo. "Nope."

"Maybe it was just the car we used to have, up in Maine," she said. Although she wasn't superstitious, it gave her an absurd sense of freedom, to know she was driving around without those ominous words.

"You are exceeding the speed limit," the car said sternly. "Please slow down."

"Nag, nag, nag," Maisie said to it. She was feeling a new sense of being in control, which, perversely, seemed to engender a kind of recklessness. Right ahead of her an exit ramp went spinning off the highway, and she flipped on her turn signal and jumped across three lanes to get there in time.

"What's up?" said Dunnane.

"Just driving," she said airily. She had the feeling she could drive forever. The exit brought them out on a road lined with fields, an occasional farm. She drove along it, enjoying the fact that she could keep a constant speed, accelerating a little in the valleys to carry her up the hills. "Oh, I know where we are," she said. "Just coming up to the Scenic View."

And sure enough, there was the turnoff at the top of an especially high hill, with a sign that said in big black letters SCENIC VIEW. "In case you can't tell," Maisie said, putting the car into park and turning off the motor. Dunnane was smoking a cigarette. She lit one, too, and thought about kissing him; it seemed a decision that was entirely hers to make.

"Come over tonight, and I'll cook you a celebration dinner," Dunnane said. "I'm a killuh cook."

"That's assuming I pass," said Maisie.

That night, while Dunnane was making dinner, Maisie suddenly said, "I have to make a phone call."

She went into the bedroom, locked the door, and dialed Jack's number, charging the call on her credit card. The phone rang eight times before he picked it up. Laura, the woman he lived with now, never answered; she probably dreaded finding Maisie on the other end as much as Maisie dreaded getting her. For the same reason, Maisie had finally stopped leaving long tearful messages on Jack's answering machine; she couldn't bear the thought of Laura standing next to Jack with a sympathetic hand on his arm, while they both listened to Maisie's recorded voice spilling out of the machine with all the reasons why Jack should agree to see her. "Hello," said Jack, and even that one word sounded faintly wary to her, and she wondered: Did I do that? The idea that he was afraid to talk to her depressed her but was also vaguely reassuring: perhaps she hadn't lost all her power after all.

"Hi," she said lightly. "It's me." She meant to move crisply and immediately to the subject of divorce, to tell him with her newfound sense of control that she didn't think they should do anything right away, that they both needed some time to think calmly. But instead she found herself saying, "Guess what? I passed my driver's test." Next she would tell him how she'd gotten the same inspector, still there after eleven years, and how the inspector had looked at her with horror and said, "You!" Her not driving had been such a big part of their life together that Jack would know how much getting her license would mean to her; even if their marriage was over, this seemed to Maisie to be a legitimate occasion for truce and celebration.

"Great," he said.

Subdued by his tone, she tried once more for some of their old intimacy. "Now I won't have to pull out my passport for ID every time I want to write a check."

"That must be a relief." His voice was polite, and she wondered whether it was an effort for him to muster up this cool politeness, or if this was really all he felt.

"So what do you want to do about the divorce?" she asked, suddenly businesslike herself.

"I'd like to have my lawyer start drawing up the papers," Jack said with no hesitation.

"Oh, no, Jack. Please, let's wait." It came out as a wail, a child clinging to its father's trouser leg as he tried to leave for work.

She could hear his sigh through the telephone, but his voice when he spoke sounded as though nothing she said could upset him anymore. "Fine. There's really no hurry."

"You know," Maisie said suddenly, "I really should give you this other phone number, in case you have to reach me."

"Aren't you living with your mother?"

"Some of the time. But most of the time I'm over at this other place. This guy I've been seeing."

"Oh, really?"

Perceiving a tinge of hurt in his voice, Maisie thought: What if he was thinking of getting back together, and now he'll never say anything because he thinks I'm with someone else? "It's no big deal, really," she said. "Nobody important."

"Well, it's none of my business anyway."

"I mean, he's not even my type. He's kind of dumb. I don't even really like him much."

"Then what are you doing with him?"

She stood mute for a moment, and then hung up the phone.

"Who was that you were talking to?" Dunnane said when she finally unlocked the door of the bedroom and came out. The living room was filled with sharp-smelling smoke, and she could see more smoke curling out in the light from the kitchen doorway.

"My husband," she said.

"The dinner burned," said Dunnane. "I was cooking us a special dinner, and it all burned up."

"Why didn't you just turn it off?"

"If your husband's so smart and I'm so dumb, why don't you just go back to him?"

"You were listening."

"What are you doing calling your husband from my phone, anyway? What kind of jerk do you think I am?"

The look on his face as he came toward her frightened her, and she thought swiftly, He's going to hit me, and then, with sudden alarming clarity: He's going to be tough to get rid of. But she pushed both thoughts away, and when his arms went around her, hard, she shoved her hands roughly down into the back pockets of his jeans.

And when they were in bed, and the headboard was slamming against the wall, she was childishly, savagely glad, as though someone were in the next room to hear. You want to know what I'm doing with Dunnane? This is what. This and this and this and this.

10

The Dream Stealer

❧

Dunnane always overdid it. He was the kind of man who went through life saying "Keep the change." He overate, overtipped, overslept. He was not big or fat, but he was fleshy. He had long Buddha earlobes that swung like bell clappers when Maisie flicked them with her tongue. A round white ass that she would cup her hands around when they kissed, kneading. He had a soft belly, and although his calves were taut and hairy, his inner thighs were a surprise: smooth and luminous as the moon. He was always talking about how he needed to stop eating or drinking, slapping himself as he stood naked before the mirror. But Maisie found his fleshiness erotic, a thick layer of butter spread on her bread, and she grabbed his body in handfuls and hung on.

She stayed with him three or four nights a week. He picked her up at the bank where she was working, and they kissed for several minutes before he put the car in gear. She didn't care if people from the bank saw; she hoped they would see. On the way home Dunnane's hand would slide up her leg, and she'd rest her hand against his groin, moving her fingers sometimes and watching how his eyes slipped closed and then jumped open again, gauging the traffic. He would cook some huge, fancy dinner ("You're too fucking skinny," he said, wrapping his thumb and forefinger around her upper arm and squeezing) while she cleaned his apartment: he was an unbelievable slob, dirty clothes and dishes everywhere. Sometimes he went out to a meeting after dinner (he was starting on some new business scheme, selling household paper goods). If he stayed home, Dunnane turned on the TV, and Maisie, who during her months in Maine with Jack had watched sitcoms and game shows and police dramas with fierce attention, now sat in Dunnane's brick-colored armchair obstinately reading Turgenev and Flaubert, and flinching with annoyance whenever the laugh track or gunshots rang out especially loudly. She went "Ttttk" with her tongue, and Dunnane, stretched out on the couch, went "Ttttk," because she was breaking his concentration. But at ten fifty-eight, when the closing theme for the last prime-time show of the evening started to play, they began to smile, almost sheepishly, at each other; and by the time the eleven o'clock news came on, they were gone.

The nights when she wasn't with him, she was home with her mother. They would concoct a low-calorie dinner together out of frozen ingredients and talk about what had happened during the day. Her mother had worked for years as secretary to the president of a local chain of pancake houses. "Nothing much," her mother would say cheerfully, and Maisie, trying to match her tone, would answer, "Me neither." After the dishes were washed they watched TV and did needlepoint. Maisie had never done it before, and the "project" her mother had bought for her to learn on—a checkbook cover with pansies printed on it—was coming out all balled and lumpy. Every time she pulled it out, it made her feel sad, and she would thank her mother again for buying it for her. Her mother was stitching neat, perfect spouting whales on the panels of a tote bag. "You get into a rhythm," she told Maisie. "That's the trick for keeping the stitches even."

Her mother knew Maisie was "seeing someone," but she never asked questions. Maisie and Dunnane had run into her one Saturday at the mall; Maisie had said, "This is my mother, Alice Callahan," but Dunnane's name had gotten lost in her throat and she wasn't sure if her mother heard it. After a moment her mother had said, "How do you do," and extended little white fingers; it was strange for Maisie to see them clasped for a moment in Dunnane's big hand, with her knowledge of all that hand could do. They'd been in the linen department at Bullocks, where Alice was buying towels and Maisie had dragged Dunnane for new sheets; he only had one set, and they had tiny brown old bloodstains halfway down.

"Well," said Alice. "I'm glad someone has finally taught my daughter to drive."

"Yeah," said Dunnane, grinning at Maisie, "she's a natural."

That was the whole conversation, but Maisie kept rerunning it in her head, even while they were standing there with nothing else to say—her mother's politely contemptuous use of the word *someone,* the dazed look on her face, as though someone had slapped her. "She's a natural," and all three of them knew what he meant she was a natural at. She clutched the packages of queen-size sheets to her chest until her mother walked away, but when Alice did walk away she looked so little and lonely that Maisie wanted to drop the sheets and run after her; and she was in a bad mood with Dunnane all the rest of that day.

"Excuse me, sir," Dunnane said. "I was wondering if I could ask you a question."

"Sure," said the gas man, with his head in the oven. "Do you have to light this thing, or is there a pilot?"

"No, there's a pilot," Maisie said. It was eight o'clock on a Tuesday morning, and she was still in her bathrobe.

"This may sound like kind of a crazy question," Dunnane warned.

"Hey," said the gas man.

"What I want to know is, are you making as much money as you'd really like to?"

The gas man laughed rudely inside the stove. His kneeling legs jutted darkly out into the room, dusty gray canvas trousers baggy and wrinkled as elephant skin.

"I'm serious, man. Are you?"

"Who is?"

"I am," Dunnane said. "Or at least, I will be."

The gas man hauled his big torso out of the oven and, still kneeling, turned his head to look up at Dunnane. "What is this?"

Dunnane leaned against the chrome edge of the counter and took a cigarette from the pack lying there. "What would you say," he began, and then there was a long pause while he lit up and screwed up his face to take the first drag, snapping out the match. He blew a stream of smoke. ". . . if I told you I know of this really exciting business opportunity?"

"I'd say"—the gas man imitated Dunnane's dramatic pause—"that you were probably full of shit."

"Dunnane," Maisie said. He made lists of friends and relatives, friends of friends, and spent evenings on the phone, calling people all over the country. A few days ago, driving Maisie home from work, he'd stopped the car at a red light, whirred down the window, and shouted to a woman who was crossing the street: "Excuse me, m'am, but are you making as much money as you want?"

"Sssh." Dunnane looked at her and pushed his hand down on the air. He turned to the gas man again. "You know, that's exactly what I said to the guy who first told me about this opportunity. The guy's one of my best friends, I mean I really trust this guy, but he tells me this and I say, 'You're full of shit, man.' "

The gas man stood up, slowly, and reached into his chest pocket for his own cigarettes. It was a new pack, and he busied himself with peeling off the narrow gold plastic strip that bound it shut, crumpling the cellophane top in his hand, turning the pack upside down, and tapping out a cigarette. He was in his late thirties, with pale eyes blinking in a battered, sun-browned face. He didn't look at Dunnane, but he was paying attention now. "How much money are we talking about?"

"Well, let's see." Dunnane flicked ashes into the sink. "Of course, I'm pretty new to all this, so it hasn't started to really pay off for me yet. But this month I'll be getting my first check, for two fifty, and next month I expect to get more like six hundred."

"This is full-time work?"

"No, part-time."

"That's not bad," the gas man conceded.

"Man, that's nothing. You know what the average earnings are in this? We're talking ten *thousand* a month. And that's average. That means there's a bunch of people making even more."

"No shit."

"The guy that brought me in? The one I told you about? Well, the guy that brought *him* in, he was a lawyer. You know how much money those guys make, right? Well, this guy, this lawyer, is now planning to give up his law practice. And his wife, she's, I don't know, something in some corporation, and she's quitting her job, too. You know why? Because they're making so much money with this thing."

The gas man nodded, smoking. He was leaning against the stove, with his tools on the floor around his feet.

"The guy who brought me in, he asked me what my goals and objectives were. So I said, 'I don't know, I'd kind of like another car.' And he said to me, 'Dunnane, go down to the dealer today. And don't just look at new cars. Pick one out and order it.' "

"Uh-huh. Uh-huh."

"So did you mention yet what it is, exactly, this business opportunity?" Maisie prompted, on the gas man's behalf. She always felt guilty when Dunnane didn't tell people right off what the business was. The product is secondary, he told Maisie, although of course it's a great product. It's the opportunity that counts. I'm not going to make my money selling paper towels and tissues and toilet paper, I'm going to make my money recruiting new distributors to work for me. If I can get five distributors working steadily for a period of three months, I become an Executive.

Dunnane kept his eyes on the gas man. "Have you ever heard of multilevel marketing?"

The gas man shook his head.

"The name's Dunnane, by the way," Dunnane said, putting out his hand.

"Charlie Benavy," said the gas man.

"Hey, Charlie. Want some coffee or something, while we talk?"

"That'd be great."

They'd both adopted new, smooth, doing-business tones, speaking softly with their eyes fixed on each other's face. Dunnane gestured the gas man into the living room. Maisie understood then that she was supposed to make the coffee, and she banged drawers and cupboard doors, getting what she needed. Dunnane was very picky about everything he ate and drank, so she ground the beans carefully, then ground them again and waited until the kettle sent up a really good shriek before she poured the water into the filter.

While she was waiting for the coffee to drip, she opened Dunnane's freezer and stood looking in at the two bags of Eldridge steak fries she'd thrown into the cart the last time she and Dunnane had shopped for groceries together. Dunnane didn't know her husband's last name, and he'd paid for all the groceries as usual. *Jack,* she said silently, looking in at the bags, *oh, Jack.* The cold mist from the freezer enveloped her face.

She poured the coffee into three of Dunnane's bright white melamine cups and put them on a metal tray that had the Boston Celtics logo on it. When she carried it out to the living room, Dunnane was saying ". . . so that's four guys I've got now in my front line, and since one of 'em's in L.A., it means I have an L.A. office. All my trips to L.A. from now on are deductible."

She put down the tray on the floor at Dunnane's feet and picked up her own cup and saucer. Both men glanced at her, and then the gas man asked, "So what do I do? I mean, how do I get into this?"

"There's a meeting tomorrow night. Just come to the meeting."

"Did you ask what the product was?" Maisie said to the gas man.

He looked startled and then frowned.

"We'll go over that at the meeting, Charlie," Dunnane said. "The important thing is, it's a terrific opportunity."

Maisie took her coffee and went to get dressed for work. As she shut the bedroom door the gas man was asking, "So can I bring my wife to the meeting? And her parents?"

When she came out of the bedroom fifteen minutes later, Dunnane was alone in the living room.

"Is the stove fixed?" Maisie asked, trying to join the post of a pearl earring Jack had given her to the slippery earring back.

"I guess," said Dunnane. "Or it will be. I don't know. He's back in there"—he shot his thumb in the direction of the kitchen—"working." He had dropped his mellow business voice. He tossed the *Penthouse* he'd been reading onto the floor and stood up, worming his keys out of the pocket of his fatigue pants. "Come on."

In the car, he said, "You see?"

"See what?" She knew what he meant.

"That guy signed up. *He* saw that it was an opportunity."

She laughed. "Oh, not again."

He shook his head, smiling, his eyes on the road. "Maze, I'm not giving up on you. Come on. You're hardly making any money at the bank."

"I just don't want to."

"Why? You haven't given me a good reason."

"Dunnane, stop it." She pushed in the lighter and opened the glove compartment, where Dunnane kept a carton of cigarettes. She could never tell, with this PaperWorth business, whether he was serious or not.

One morning a week ago, the phone had rung early, when they were still in bed. Maisie, groggily, had picked it up. "Hello?"

A man's voice. "May I speak to Kevin Dunnane, please?"

"What?" She wasn't used to hearing Dunnane's first name; it seemed weirdly brand new, like the unfaded upholstery she saw when she pulled the sofa out to clean behind it.

"Kevin Dunnane?" the voice repeated patiently.

She handed the telephone to Dunnane, who took it, still lying down.

He cleared his throat and mumbled monosyllables into the receiver. When he hung up, he threw off the covers and said, "Shit."

"What."

"He asked me what my goals and objectives were, and I couldn't tell him."

She sat up. "What?"

"Shit, how am I supposed to remember my goals and objectives at six in the morning?"

"Who was that?"

"Jerry. My Executive. He said I should always have my goals and objectives right at the forefront of my consciousness. Shit. Why did I have to sound like such a dope?"

He got out of bed and headed for the door.

"Where are you going?" Maisie asked.

"He told me to write down all my goals and objectives."

"Right now?"

"Yup."

"And you're going to do it?"

Dunnane looked back at her, and after a moment he grinned. "Nah."

But when he was lying above her, grinding his hips against hers, she had looked up into his clenched face and saw that he was staring at a spot somewhere over her head, and his lips were moving.

Now she said, "If you really want to know why I won't do it, it's because it's a pyramid scheme. A few people on the top will get rich, and the people on the bottom get screwed."

"Yeah, well, this time I'm one of the people on the top. You would be, too, if you got in now. If you'd just come to a meeting." He motioned her to light a cigarette for him. "Think of it like a pie," he said. "Every time one of my distributors sells something, I get a certain percentage of the pie. And every time one of my distributors recruits another distributor for my organization, I get a piece of that pie."

"But if you keep cutting the same pie in more and more pieces, won't the pieces keep getting smaller?"

He inhaled, and said after a moment, "No, because we keep adding more pies."

She looked out her window, at the white shopping centers gliding by.

"You should talk to Jerry," Dunnane said. "He can explain it better than me."

"I don't want to talk to Jerry." They were passing the street where

Maisie's mother lived, and she glanced down it involuntarily, as though her mother might be standing in the middle of the pavement, watching for her, like a crossing guard.

They drove the rest of the way to the bank in silence and pulled up in front of the LOAD AND UNLOAD ONLY sign. They usually sat here and kissed for several minutes before she went inside, but today she reached immediately for the door handle.

"All right," said Dunnane. "At least do one thing for me." He jabbed an index finger at the bank. "Find out who in there I talk to about selling PaperWorth."

Maisie's title at the bank was "Secretary 2." If she stayed for six months, she would be eligible for a promotion, but there were Secretary 1s and Secretary 3s, and she hadn't figured out which direction she was supposed to aspire in.

When she'd taken the job, she hadn't realized it was secretarial. The ad in the newspaper had said "Editorial exp. required," and when she'd gone in for the interview they'd told her the job involved editing the bank's employee newsletter. Great, she'd said, that's right up my alley. Job hunting, she had adopted the persona of a fifties college girl: clean, eager, deferential. She wore a Black Watch plaid skirt and swept her hair back from her face with a tortoise-shell band. She didn't think at all about whether she wanted the job, only about whether or not she could get it.

When she did get it, she found that most of the work on the newsletter was done by an outside consultant. The front-page headlines in the current issue were NEW IBM PCS FOR TRUST DEPARTMENT and THEFT PREVENTION SEMINAR ENLIGHTENS DRIVE-UP-WINDOW TELLERS. These stories, Maisie's boss had told her, were considered "hard news" and were handled by the consultant. Maisie would be responsible for writing the "Let's Talk People" column, which contained the monthly branch news—branch managers who had bought new cars, tellers who had just become grandmothers. She would also report on staff appointments and promotions. The first promotion had occurred when she'd been at the bank a week, and she'd called the Mortgage Department to interview the new vice-president. He turned out to be a man who'd played minor league baseball with the Louisville Cardinals for two seasons, then smashed up his hand in a car door and decided it was a sign that God wanted him to go back to school for a degree in accounting. "So I figured, let it lie where Jesus flung it," he said. Maisie liked him—he told her all this with a sheepish, goofy light in his eyes—and she wrote up a funny little promotion story, peppered with his quotes. Her boss read it and said with gentle dismay, "Oh, no, no, no," and she showed Maisie a promotion form in the files, a model that all the stories were supposed to follow.

> The ____ department is proud to announce the promotion/appointment of ____ to the position of ____. Before joining us, ____ worked for ____ years at ____ in the capacity of ____. He/She graduated from ____ in ____, with a degree in ____.

After that Maisie had tried to make her mark by showing extraordinary efficiency. The job had been described to her as being sixty percent newsletter and forty percent other. Yet within the next two days she was able to finish all she had to do for the upcoming issue. "Boy," said her boss, "this is terrific. Keep this up and in a year or two we'll be able to let our consultant go and turn over the whole newsletter to you." Then, seeing the look of disappointment that crossed Maisie's face, she added, "You have to be patient, Maisie, we can't make these changes overnight. But don't worry, we'll find plenty to keep you busy in the meantime."

The "plenty" had turned out to be more secretarial work.

Today she sat down at her desk and opened a big envelope of monthly workmen's compensation amendment sheets that had come in the mail the day before. They all had headings like "Page B-2476 c (replaces Page B-2476 b)," and Maisie began slowly going through the enormous black workmen's compensation binder, taking out the old pages and putting in the new ones. After several minutes she realized she hadn't gotten her coffee yet, and she picked up her mug, which had PEOPLE HELPING PEOPLE and the bank's black-and-mustard logo printed on it.

Her desk was in the elevator hall of the Claims and Benefits Department, which was a subdepartment of Personnel. Behind her was a burlap-covered wall with HUMAN RESOURCES spelled out in foot-high steel letters. The letters seemed to hang there of their own volition, with no visible source of support. They made shadows on her lap, and she pushed her chair back carefully, as always a little afraid that any sudden movement would cause them to fall on her.

The coffee machine was set up on a small refrigerator near the elevator.

When she reached in for the cream, she looked at the expiration date printed on the cardboard container. May 3, it said. Today was April 24. She allowed herself to check the cream date several times each week. It gave her the sense that time was passing and would continue to pass. She saw the year as a series of connected cream dates, firm and visible as telephone poles, with the other, unmarked days strung slackly between them.

When she sat down again the phone on her desk buzzed. It was Dunnane.

"You still mad?" he asked without greeting.

"No."

"It drives me crazy that you won't let me help."

"You do help, Dunnane."

"I do?"

"Sure."

"Well. What do you want for dinner tonight?"

"I don't care."

"Beef Stroganoff?"

"Oh. You know, let me call you later. I might want to go to my mother's tonight."

She heard the click of his lighter, a pause while he lit up. "You've already had dinner with her twice this week."

"She's my *mother,* Dunnane."

"Yeah, and what am I?"

She swallowed some coffee. "Here's an idea. What if I cook for us tonight?"

"Cook what?"

"I don't know. Scrambled eggs, maybe. Or a hamburger."

"Why have hamburger when you can have beef Stroganoff?"

She couldn't think of an answer. Her phone buzzed, one of the other lights at the base was flashing, but she was afraid to put Dunnane on hold.

"You've never *had* my Stroganoff," he said. "I *make* it with hamburger."

Her phone buzzed again. "All right, then."

"I'll pick you up?"

Her boss came out of her office and frowned at the blinking phone. "Maisie?"

At eleven the mail came, tossed onto her desktop in two stacks bound by rubber bands. Maisie pawed through it feverishly, looking for a letter from Jack. How he would get the address of the bank, or why he would write to her here, rather than at her mother's house, she didn't know; but any pile of mail these days was a temptation, a garbage heap that might contain hidden treasure.

And when the bell went off above the elevator door opposite her desk she held still and watched, on the chance that it might be Jack. Sometimes he was coming simply to get her, looking around angrily at the bare little anteroom in which she sat and then grabbing her by the hand and pulling her out of there. Sometimes he walked in without knowing he was going to find her: he'd had a tremendous success in the french fry business, he'd made a fortune, and he was looking for a bank to deposit it in. Maisie greeted him calmly and laughed and said, Not this department, silly; she took him to the right department and introduced him to the trust people, and everyone at the bank was amazed—to think that Maisie Callahan could be the source of our biggest depositor ever!—and *then* he took her out of there.

Dunnane was waiting outside the bank at five, parked in the Chrysler beneath the LOAD AND UNLOAD ONLY sign.

"Load," he said, pulling her across the seat and placing her hand on his lap.

Maisie gave him a squeeze and took her hand away. "We need to go by my mother's." She got a pack of cigarettes from the glove compartment and lit one for herself. Sideways, she saw Dunnane's face darken as he pulled the car away from the curb.

"You *said* you weren't going there."

"Not for dinner," she said hastily. "I just need to pick up some things. No, I'm looking forward to your Stroganoff."

"I didn't make the fucking Stroganoff."

"Oh."

"I made something better."

"What?"

"You'll see."

"No, tell me, what?" But she pulled at the cigarette, not looking at him. What's so mysterious about a goddamned dinner?

"I said, you'll *see*."

Her hands were shaking. "Well," she said brightly, "I hope it's not tuna fish. I had that for lunch."

"Tuna fish," spat out Dunnane. "I don't cook with tuna fish."

"I know you don't."

"What, you think I made you tuna casserole? *Tuna wiggle?*"

"What's tuna wiggle?"

"Noodle crap. My mother used to make it."

"Oh." She had no curiosity about Dunnane's parents, who still lived near Boston; Dunnane barely mentioned them.

"No, I made you something much, much better."

Maisie looked out the window. They were driving past an office park, nowhere near her mother's house. Nowhere near Dunnane's apartment, either.

"Dunnane," she said.

"Sssh." He reached over and took her half-smoked cigarette, putting it into his own mouth for a long drag and then throwing it out through the open window. The soft warm evening hissed by. It was strange, she thought, that she'd grown up in this town, yet so little of it looked familiar to her.

Dunnane had stopped the car by the side of the road that ran behind the office park. The radio was on, a female disc jockey purring between songs. Two free tickets to see some band Maisie had never heard of. Dunnane's hand was between her legs. You do love me, you do. See? You love it. Say it. Say what I'm doing to you.

Maisie whispered it in his ear, what he was doing.

A song started, a deep thudding drum. A car drove by, slowly, and she froze against Dunnane's hand. It's okay, he whispered. They can't see us. They don't know what I'm doing to you. And what if they did know? What if they were watching? Aaah, you see, Maze? What if they were standing outside, looking in the car window?

Oh, shut up, she thought, flooded with shame, stop talking. But she pressed herself forward, on top of him, confined by his hands and the steering wheel.

What would they see? Dunnane said, easing her nylons down, touching her from behind. His fingers were cool and light. No, come on, Maze. Tell me.

Despite herself, she told him.

Maisie's mother was standing by the stove, wearing a nightgown—she had always, as long as Maisie could remember, changed into a nightgown as soon as she came home from work—poking with a wooden spoon at a plastic bag tumbling in a pot of boiling water. A Lean Cuisine Swedish Meatballs box lay on the counter by the stove.

Maisie kissed her on the cheek.

"Oh, dear," said her mother. "I don't know what else is in the freezer."

"That's okay. I'm not here for dinner."

"Is—" Alice jerked her head toward the window.

"He's in the car. I'm just going to run upstairs and grab some stuff."

"Doesn't he want to come in?" Alice asked, holding her spoon in front of her stiffly as though it were a weapon.

Maisie shook her head and ducked out of the kitchen. She stopped at the table by the staircase to check her mail—a Harvard alumni magazine, a catalog of fancy cookware, no letters—and went slowly up to her room.

The bed was spread with neat little stacks of clothing: underpants and bras, nightgowns, socks paired and balled, and two odd ones, a purple and a green, lying on the edge, waiting for their mates. Oh, God. She'd forgotten that she'd started her laundry when she'd been here for dinner the other night. She took three blouses and a skirt from the closet, hurriedly stuffed the clean laundry into the empty plastic basket at the foot of the bed, and carried the clothes downstairs, stopping at the foot of the stairs to put the cookware catalog into her basket; she would pass it on to Dunnane. She carried the alumni magazine into the kitchen and stuffed it deep into the trash can under the sink.

Her mother was still standing over the stove.

"You didn't have to finish my laundry," Maisie said reproachfully.

"It was beginning to smell mildewy. I ran the stuff in the washer again, with fabric softener."

"I would have done it."

"Well, I didn't know when you were coming by again."

"You must have known I'd run out of underpants," Maisie said, humorously, she thought.

"I don't know anything," Alice said, poking at her dinner.

Maisie leaned on the counter, looking out the window at Dunnane's car, idling by the curb. "What are you so upset about?" she asked softly.

"I don't know where you are half the time, who you're with, when you're coming home—"

"I'm almost thirty years old."

"You act like you're sixteen."

"*You* act like I'm sixteen."

The bell on the timer dinged, and Alice reached out and flipped off the burner. She carried the pot over to the sink and stood, holding it, as if uncertain what to do next. Maisie reached into the jar of utensils by the stove, pulled out a pair of tongs, and handed them to her mother.

"I'll come for dinner tomorrow," she said reasonably. "Okay?"

Alice pulled the plastic bag from the pot with the tongs and held it, dripping, over the sink. "Look, it's not like I'm saying come have dinner with your poor lonely mother."

"I know."

"I'm saying, what are you *doing?* You have this foolish job—"

"It's no more foolish than yours."

"I don't have your education," Alice snapped, dropping the bag onto the counter. "You're seeing this—*kid,* this redneck—"

"Don't be a snob," Maisie said.

"Well, don't pretend that you're not."

"A snob? No, I am one. I know that. But I'm trying not to be."

"Oh, Maisie. If I weren't your mother, I'd laugh," said Alice, beginning to laugh anyway. She cut a hole in the bag and recoiled from the escaping steam. Maisie watched her pour the brown mess out onto a plate. Then Alice turned to look at her. "You know, with all the boys you brought home in high school, there was never one I really worried about. And when you married Jack, I thought, Good, now I'll *never* have to worry."

Maisie bit her lip. "Well, I'm sorry, Mom, that you don't have that luxury anymore."

Alice tightened her mouth, but she didn't answer. She put her plate on the table, set down silverware and a napkin, and poured a glass of diet soda.

Maisie picked up her laundry basket and went to the door.

"Jack didn't call, did he?" she asked suddenly. She knew he hadn't, but she had to ask, superstitiously: she believed if she didn't ask, it would mean that he *had* called, and the message would be lost and he'd think she didn't care.

"Maisie," her mother said sadly, impatiently.

"I'll see you," Maisie said, rushing out.

Dunnane had made lobster Newburg. "No, no, it's good," Maisie assured him.

"Then why aren't you eating?"

"I did."

He pointed to her plate, where several large chunks of lobster swam in coral-colored sauce.

"It was just a little rich for me, that's all." Then she said, "You know, I always thought food was supposed to be relaxing."

"Yeah, well, do you know what it's like to watch you eat? It's like you're doing it with *tweezers*."

Her eyes filled with tears. "I'm not hungry. Why does it have to be such a big deal?"

"You're not hungry for the things I cook, you mean."

"Dunnane."

"You're getting skinnier and skinnier on purpose."

"All right," she said, putting a big forkful into her mouth.

"You're starting to look like an old lady. The one in that ad where they talk about women not getting enough calcium."

Maisie ate some more.

"The one on the *train,*" Dunnane said. "Don't pretend you don't know what I'm talking about."

She put down her fork.

"Oh, that's right, I forgot. You're too smart to watch television. Just like you're too smart to sell PaperWorth."

"What does PaperWorth have to do with it?" Her voice was shaking.

"Oh, nothing. It's just something dumb Dunnane does, when he's not doing his dumb cooking. Did you ask, did you even *ask* who I should talk to at the bank?"

"No."

"You act like it's this *poison* I'm trying to bring into your office. All I'm trying to do is give the people there an opportunity to do a little better. That's all. If they don't want to, they don't have to."

"Then why won't you listen to me when I say I don't want to?"

Dunnane reached across the table, picked up her plate, and threw it, Frisbee-style, into the sink. It broke with a clatter. Then he ladled some more food onto his own plate and began to shovel it into his mouth. "Nothing I do is good enough," he said, his tongue and lips coated with orange cream.

"That's not true."

He stared at her, then scraped some sauce and fish from his plate and held the dripping fork out to her. Hesitantly, she put her mouth around it.

"It's delicious, really." She struggled to swallow. He had the fork filled again, waiting. "Really. What did you put in the sauce?"

"Oh, fuck you."

She waited.

"Don't talk down to me."

"No, I'm curious. What was it, onions?"

"Shallots." He pushed the fork against her mouth. "And sherry. I put in a little Tabasco, for flavoring. Can you taste it?"

She nodded, fighting nausea.

"And the rice," he prompted.

"Ummmm."

"I boiled it in fish broth, instead of water."

She nodded again, her eyes brimming. He swore and pushed back his chair so hard that it fell over. She heard the bedroom door slam. She sat with one hand holding her stomach and smoked a cigarette, dropping the ashes into Dunnane's smeary plate. The exhaust fan in the kitchen picked up the smoke and drew it, swirling, upward and in.

She stood up and did the dishes, wrapping the broken plate in newspaper and throwing it into the garbage. There was no sound from the bedroom.

She went and knocked softly on the door. When he didn't answer she opened the door and walked in. He was lying on the bed, wearing only his jeans. His work shirt was on the floor, and the shiny pinstripe suit he would wear to his PaperWorth meeting lay on a chair.

"I'm sorry," she began.

He watched her. "Come here," he said. She hesitated for a moment and then started to unbutton her blouse.

When she was naked, he reached up and turned off the light. She went to him and lay on the bed, and felt the mattress give as he got up. The shades were down, outlined by a thin crack of evening light. His chunky silhouette crouched on the floor, rustled his clothes. The sound of his jeans falling, his belt buckle thudding against the carpet. He came back to the bed, and she heard a click and saw a flame leap up: his lighter. He held it over her and she could see his face, expressionless. She breathed faster, looking at the flame, not knowing what he was going to do. Then he flipped its lid shut; the room was dark again, and he lay at her feet with his elbows gripping her knee; he ran the warm steel body of the lighter inside her legs, going higher, sitting up to kindle it again when it grew cold. He pushed her arms above her head and kept one hand there, holding her. She pushed her fingertips into the soft underside of his forearm. She sighed, her legs wide, and he whispered, "Am I hurting you?"

"No."

She was pressing down through the mattress. An insistent little point of heat, climbing and climbing.

After Dunnane left for his meeting, Maisie put on her robe, leaving the front undone so that the belt trailed behind her like a tail as she wandered around the apartment. The air was soft on her belly and thighs. She felt languid and strange, a record being played at the wrong speed. She made herself a cup of tea and then sat on the couch with a book, but she didn't open it.

She had a picture in her head of her whole life, past, present, and future, something she could see from a distance though she couldn't fill in the details: a heedless downhill slide and then redemption. She'd messed up, messed up, and messed up; now she was at the bottom of the abyss, atoning; and soon it would be time to begin climbing uphill again. What she did while she was at the bottom was unimportant—Dunnane and the job at the bank could just as well be some other man and some other job, or no man and no job. Her real job now was waiting. This was the Bad Time; it would be followed by Jack's return and the Second Chance.

Her mother and Caterina kept trying, gently, to warn her. Jack was not coming back, they said. Her marriage was over. And even if, by some wild chance, he *did* come back, her marriage would still be over, because all the things that had been wrong between them in the past would still be wrong. Maisie answered by saying, with a confidence she sometimes actually felt, that she was different now, she thought she could change.

But what about Jack? they said. He won't have changed. He'll still be stuck in the company, he'll still be someone who doesn't talk. You always said there weren't sparks between you, he wasn't passionate enough—

And Maisie would shut out the sound of their voices and wish she hadn't told them so much, all the things that had been problems with Jack before. They wouldn't be problems now, she was convinced: they would either have disappeared, miraculously, or they would still be there and she would make her peace with them. Her life now was a dream, the ghosts that visited in the night to show her that she'd been caring about all the wrong things. When she woke up in the morning the ghosts would be gone, and she'd have a chance to put everything right.

She swallowed, and the taste of Dunnane's dinner was still in her mouth. I'm using him, she thought, I should get out. He's *real.* This is my real life—but oh, God, it can't be.

And she felt a sudden tenderness for him, the way he tried so hard with his dinners, the way he went after her in bed. Hey, Maze, he said, and her eyes would fill with surprised tears: he meant *her.*

Just *get up,* she told herself. Go into the bathroom and brush your teeth, and then you won't have this taste in your mouth anymore. But she couldn't move.

After a long time, she reached for the phone. She hadn't spoken much to Caterina during the last few months. Caterina had called Maisie from the hospital Thanksgiving weekend to announce that she'd had a boy, and Maisie kept meaning to call her after that, to see how things were going; but she never seemed to think of it until late at night. And after the fight they'd had last fall, the night she'd almost slept with Tony, she had been afraid of appearing too selfish or needy.

Caterina sounded tired. "Are you okay?" Maisie asked.

"Yes, just—I guess I fell asleep."

"I'm sorry!" Maisie said. "What time is it?" She looked at her watch; it was a few minutes past eight.

"No, it's all right. I have to do the dishes anyway."

"Where's Ed?"

"In the other room," Caterina said. "Working. So, how are you?" Maisie knew this opaque tone that Caterina got sometimes, a tone that hinted at unhappiness but wouldn't admit it. Tell me! Maisie always felt like saying, but she was afraid that pumping Caterina would be slightly malicious: Come on, your life cannot possibly be as rosy as you think.

"I'm fine," Maisie said carefully. "How about you?"

"Fine." The same brittle tone, and now Maisie wondered if it had to do with her, if Caterina was upset that she hadn't called lately, or if she was still angry about the fight.

Caterina went on, "So, who is this man you're seeing?"

"Oh. No one."

"Your mother says he's a greaser."

"My mother? You talked to her?" Her mother rarely had occasion to speak to Caterina on the phone, but when she did she always told Caterina the things she couldn't tell Maisie. After Maisie met Jack, it was "I wish they would get married," and then, after they were married, "Do you think they're thinking about children yet?"

"A couple of nights I called to get you, and you weren't there."

Maisie lit a cigarette. "Where did she get a word like 'greaser'?"

"I don't know, Maisie. I'm sorry. Don't be mad at her. She's worried about you."

"She's probably told all the waitresses, then, at that place where she works."

"The pancake place? Is she still there?"

"Yes."

"I used to love that place. Remember how I'd always make you take me there, when I was visiting?"

"I was always afraid someone would see us."

"I liked their Belgian waffles." Caterina sighed. "So, anyway, what's this guy really like?"

"Dunnane?"

"That's his name?"

"His last name. That's what he likes to be called." She paused, defiantly, but Caterina didn't say anything. Maisie sighed. "I don't know what everyone's making such a big deal about. I'm not serious about him." She realized she sounded like a sulky adolescent and thought, Oh, I'm tired, I'm so tired.

"So you're not—serious?"

"Only in bed," Maisie said.

"Oh."

"I don't know why, but I seem to let go with him in a way I never have before."

"Well, that's good," Caterina said dubiously.

There was a silence. "How are the kids?" Maisie asked.

Caterina's voice warmed. "Oh, they're fine. Ellie's really talking, you know."

"Is she? What does she say?"

"We have this whole game now where she sits on my bed and pretends to make a birthday cake. She says, 'Now butter, now chocolate, now eggs, now sugar—' And then she pretends to bake it, and then we have to sing and blow out the candles. She's been doing it since her birthday last month. Oh, Maisie, thanks for the books."

"She liked them?"

"She loves them. Especially *Blueberries for Sal.* I've been meaning to write to you, or call. . . ."

"That's okay. How's the baby?" In the background Maisie could hear him crying.

"A wild man. Ellie still naps, but he hardly does, and he's awake five times a night."

"Do you have to go now and get him?"

"Ed can get him," Caterina said shortly.

"But everything's okay?"

"Sure."

A silence, while they both listened to the baby's cries.

"Caterina, do you ever hear from Jack?"

"Sometimes," Caterina said, and Maisie heard a new caution in her voice. "He and Ed talk occasionally. His sister's getting married."

"Marion."

"And I guess the company's doing better. He seems excited about it, anyway. They're introducing a new low-fat french fry."

"Uh-huh." Maisie waited. She couldn't hear the baby anymore.

"We saw him, you know."

"Jack?"

"We had dinner with him, the last time he was in the city."

"When?"

"About a month ago."

"Where?" Maisie asked.

"Here."

"At your house, you mean?" Now she could put them in a specific setting, could see Jack leaning against the pitted door frame of the kitchen, while Caterina made dinner. His shirt would be untucked in the back. He'd be holding a beer, which he'd drink—but she didn't remember how he drank a beer, whether he sipped or swallowed it down all at once, whether he liked it in a glass or right out of the bottle. How could she have lived with him all that time and never noticed how he drank a beer?

In Ed and Caterina's apartment, her absence that evening must have been something they'd all considered. She could feel herself haunting that dinner; she must have hovered over it, shaping the words they said to one another and the thoughts that went through their heads. "Did you talk about me?"

"No," Caterina said. Then, "Listen, Maisie, I'd better tell you, because you might find out some other way and I don't want you to be hurt."

"What," said Maisie, beginning to tremble already, sensing the shadow of the thing about to fall on her.

"Laura was here, too."

"Laura?"

"The woman who Jack—"

"I know." She kept silent for a moment, reminding herself to be careful with Caterina. But she couldn't help herself. "How could you have her in your house?"

"Maisie"—Caterina spoke rapidly—"I didn't invite her. I didn't even know she was coming. He just brought her along, without telling us."

"Well, what do you mean? He just showed up on your doorstep out of nowhere?"

"Of course not. We invited him."

Maisie didn't say anything. The fact that Ed and Caterina still saw Jack, which a few minutes ago had seemed like a precious thread still connecting her to her husband, now seemed suspicious in itself, threatening, with or without Laura.

"He was in on business, and he wanted to meet Ed for a drink, and so I said why not just come over for dinner. I didn't want him to feel like an outcast, just because—"

"Okay, okay." She lit another cigarette. "But I don't know why he'd just bring her, without asking. That is so inconsiderate. Don't you think so?" She was proud of herself for sounding so detached, analytical.

"It surprised me, yes."

"Really out of character for Jack. To put you in that position."

"Well."

"He must have known it'd get back to me."

"Exactly."

"Well," Maisie said. "What was she like?"

Again that hesitation in Caterina's voice. "Well, it was hard for me to see her clearly. On principle, I hated her guts. And she didn't talk much."

So Caterina had liked her, Maisie thought. "But I do understand how it happened. Really, Caterina."

They talked for several more minutes and then said good-bye. Maisie held the receiver in her hand and heard a faraway recorded voice telling her to hang up and try her call again.

A few nights later Dunnane picked her up at the office and told her curtly that they were going bowling. He was sulking because she still hadn't approached anyone at the bank about becoming a PaperWorth distributor. He wanted to get someone high up, he said, like even the president, because the president could put pressure on his employees to become distributors and they wouldn't dare say no to him, and all of them would be in Dunnane's network. Maisie had started hanging up on him when he called her at work.

His friends were already bowling: Donna and Fred, Priscilla and Jimmy, and a short ominous woman named Marsha who had been Dunnane's girlfriend the year before, and who'd once got drunk and whispered to Maisie, in the ladies' room at Kentucky Fried Chicken, "I'm gonna get you." Since then Marsha had met a new guy, Pat, who was there with her tonight. He had bushy blond hair and an earring and a vague, bombed-out-building look about him.

"You're on my team," Marsha told Dunnane, and he finished tying his shoes and followed her over to lane six.

"What about me?" Maisie asked after a moment.

"She's in lane seven," Marsha said without turning around.

"It figures," Maisie said under her breath. She was with Donna and Jimmy and Pat, the worst bowlers in the group. She was worse than any of them. She did all right in practice, but by the time they started scoring, her arms and legs were tired, and she'd had a couple of beers, and her balls went wild, drawn as if by magnetic attraction into the gutters and sometimes even jumping into adjoining lanes. ("Jesus Christ!" yelled Marsha. "Who the hell did that?" "Me," Jimmy said quickly, and Maisie shot him a grateful look.)

Jimmy bowled badly because he tried to get fancy, imitating the stances he'd seen on "Candlepins for Cash." Pat was completely spacy; when told it was his turn again, he invariably said, "Huh?" And Donna was eight months pregnant. The only way their team managed to knock over any pins at all was by cheating. They let Maisie bowl six balls, seven balls, eight. She'd made the mistake of wearing a bra that hooked in front; every time she let go of the ball, the clasp came springing open, and she could hardly wait for her turn to be over so she could go into the ladies' room and fix it. "Go, go, keep going," her team hissed at her as she straightened wearily after eight unsuccessful balls.

"Is she cheating?" Marsha shouted from lane six.

"Of course not," Donna said loyally.

"Huh?" said Pat.

After three games they sat on the benches behind the lanes and drank. The bowling had made Maisie thirsty, and she had another beer. She felt unpleasantly full and pleasantly dizzy, floating somewhere up above the conversation.

"When they traded Klimo two years ago," Dunnane said, waving his hand so his drink sloshed, gleaming, over the lip of his plastic glass. "That was what *really* fucked things up."

Maisie looked at him, startled. His face was a dark, angry red. She put her glass down underneath the bench. "We should probably think about getting home."

"Home?" Dunnane said. "We can't go home. There's someplace we have to take you first."

Dunnane insisted on driving, which made Maisie nervous. How many drinks had he had time for? Three? Four? When you read in the paper about people who went ninety miles an hour on the wrong side of the interstate and smashed into other people, they always seemed to have seven beers in their system. How did seven beers compare with four stingers? He was driving the way he usually did, fast, but not weaving between lanes once they got out on the highway. She was wedged between Dunnane and Priscilla in the front seat; Jimmy and Marsha and Pat were in back. Donna and Fred had gone home, but the others had abandoned their cars at the bowling alley and come along for the ride. There was a lot of random hooting in the car, laughter: all the sounds she heard when a car full of drunk people passed her on the road, only this time she was in the car.

They swung off the highway onto a dark exit ramp and then into the parking lot of the Holiday Inn. What were they planning to do to her in a motel room? Would anyone hear her if she screamed? "What is this?" she squeaked.

"Shut up," Dunnane told her. He threw open his door and got out of the car, then turned around and took hold of her arms. "Get out."

"Dunnane!" Her arms began to hurt where he was squeezing them, ten little points of pain.

"Get out of the car!"

His friends had all climbed out and were standing around in the parking lot, tactfully looking away. Maisie began to feel hopeless, like a toddler throwing a tantrum in a store. She pushed Dunnane back with her foot and slowly emerged from the car, holding longingly for an extra second to the steering wheel. Dunnane took her by the hand.

Crossing the parking lot, she saw other people: a man in a khaki jacket walking a dog in the bushes, a pair of plump ladies getting out of a small Toyota and heading for the motel, just ahead of Maisie and her group, their high heels making light click-clicks on the asphalt. She began to feel as though all these people had been sent to get her out; they were all agents on her side, who'd infiltrated the situation and had it all under control, blending in so well that Dunnane wasn't aware of them. If she got close enough, one of them might try to reassure her with a quick wink, or just a glance. It was only a matter of time before they made their move.

The lobby was brightly lit, momentarily comforting although nobody paid any attention to them. Maisie gazed at the desk clerks. They were people in uniform, they would help her. They had taken Holiday Inn training courses, where they'd learned to be courteous and alert and to call security if there was a problem; they wouldn't let anything bad happen to her.

But Dunnane swept her past the desk clerks, down a long, maroon-carpeted hallway lined with vast fake panel paintings of Henry VIII and his wives—in backward order, she had time to notice; she recognized Catherine Howard, dumpy Anne of Cleves, Anne Boleyn with her dark gaze and her hands playing with a little flower, and she remembered how, as a little girl, she'd been able to list all the different wives and their fates. A carved wooden sign over an open door said TUDOR ROOME, and beneath it hung a paper sign that said WEIGHT WATCHERS. Maisie thought of the plump ladies from the parking lot; she wanted to run in and hide herself between them, burrowing into their comforting flesh.

"Here it is," Jimmy said, stopping in front of another doorway: YORK ROOME. Dunnane steered her inside, behind Jimmy and Priscilla. Marsha and Pat came in after them.

Maisie saw rows of folding chairs, men in business suits or jeans and sweaters, young women and middle-aged women. Her darting eyes could discover no immediate common denominator except cleanliness; the room smelled faintly of shampoo. At the front of the room was an enormous chalkboard on legs. Someone had written, in glowing orange chalk: PAPERWORTH = SELF-WORTH.

She smiled, in spite of herself. The relief made her legs shake. She couldn't stop smiling, and she bobbed up and down jauntily, unnecessarily, sliding down a row of folding chairs between Priscilla and Dunnane. Now she remembered that Jimmy and Priscilla had been the ones who'd introduced Dunnane to PaperWorth. She didn't know if Marsha and Pat were distributors, or if Dunnane was trying to recruit them tonight. Priscilla glanced at Maisie and smiled, and Maisie smiled back. She felt suddenly fond of Priscilla, though they'd never had much in common.

A man in a dark blue suit got up at the front of the room, introduced himself as an Executive, and began to talk about the combined monthly earnings for the Central Virginia PaperWorth organization. He was around forty, with glasses and soft brown hair that ringed the sides of his balding head like a monk's tonsure. Maisie felt affectionate toward him, too, even though she had no intention of listening to a word he said. All she had to do was sit here for an hour or so, surrounded by these benign people. She was aware of Dunnane breathing beside her, and every rise and fall of his pinstriped chest repelled her. His big black-haired hands, with their bitten-down nails, folded and unfolded in his lap, and she wondered how their touch could have excited her so. But the moment she thought that, she began to imagine what would happen tonight when they got home and into bed, when the hands would reach for her, roughly she was sure after this evening, and she felt, horrified, a small thud of excitement.

She turned her attention to the front of the room. The man had given way to a succession of people talking about their goals and objectives, and how much they were making. A woman in a cream-colored turtleneck was standing next to the chalkboard, saying, "Well, I woke up one morning and I had the realization, This is it. This is all I'm ever going to have." She stopped for a moment, and looked around the room. "Do you understand what a terrible feeling that is? I don't mean just in terms of money—well, I mean, sure, that's important, who wouldn't want to be makin' tons of money?"—here the audience laughed, but softly, automatically, showing they were still with her, they understood that this wasn't the main point of the story. "But just, I mean, I just had to put my mother in a nursing home. She goes along with it. I move her in and it breaks my heart to see her in there, with her little plaid suitcases. But she's great. Kisses me and tells me not to worry, I did the right thing. But then the next time I go visit, she grabs hold of my hand and she says, 'Why couldn't I stay in my own house?' " The woman cleared her throat, nostrils flaring. "So that's when I decided, screw this. Excuse me. There was this neighbor of mine, Prudence, well, I thought she was a flake." Her eyes sought someone in the audience and bestowed a quick, apologetic smile. "She's been tryin' to get me to come to a meeting, no high pressure or anything, just come and see what it's all about. So I came with her, and, well, I've been doing it five months now, and I expect to make almost a thousand next month. We'd already sold my mother's house, but I'm hoping soon I'll be able to buy her a little place near mine, and hire someone to live there with her." She smiled as everyone started clapping, and then looked as though she might cry. Maisie watched her sit down and lean her head briefly, lightly, against the shoulder of a big woman in a striped blouse.

The Executive stood up and waited for the applause to die down. "Any problems, questions?"

Dunnane raised his hand and stood up.

"Yes?" the Executive asked.

"This woman I live with," Dunnane said, not looking at Maisie, "she keeps trying to talk me out of doing this. She acts like there's something shady about this whole setup."

The Executive was nodding before Dunnane finished speaking. "We see this all the time." He lifted his hand to the chalkboard and wrote out, BEWARE OF THE DREAM STEALERS. Then he turned back to the audience. "Do you all know what I mean by the dream stealers? The people in your life who tell you you can't make it, you can't succeed, you can't meet your goals and objectives. Not bad people, often it's people who love you. But the only way to handle them is just to barrel right past them. They can't stop you from achieving your goals and objectives, only *you* can stop you. You have the dream, don't let anyone steal it from you."

He put down his chalk and gave an emphatic, end-of-the-meeting nod. Everyone applauded.

After the meeting Dunnane dropped his friends off at the bowling alley.

"So," he said, when he and Maisie were alone in the car. "What did you think?" He sounded cautious and polite. He was driving slowly now, stopping for yellow lights.

"You know I said I didn't want to go to a meeting."

"Well, but so I knew if I told you where we were going, you wouldn't come."

"I'm not a little doll that you can just pick up and carry from one place to another."

"You're not? You're not my little doll?"

She slapped his hand away. "It's not funny."

"So, yeah, but what'd you think?"

"It was about what I expected."

"So were the people criminals?" He waited.

She said, "No."

"Were they weirdos? Were they crazy?"

"No."

"And what about what I said?"

"You mean about me?"

"Did you understand why I had to do that?"

"Do what?" The beer had worn off, and she was feeling sad and tired.

"*Tell* them. They want you to be honest about people in your life who are trying to trash your dreams."

"Sure." She yawned, desperate to get into a bed and sleep, too exhausted to decide whether it should be Dunnane's bed or her old one at her mother's.

"So now will you become a distributor?"

She couldn't help it, she smiled.

"Will you?"

"Dunnane, you got me to the meeting, all right? Now let's drop it."

"It's not like I'm asking for your life savings. All you have to do is invest three hundred fifty dollars."

"That is my life savings."

"Oh, come on."

"Pretty near."

He was shaking his head. "I knew you'd pull this. Your poor act."

"It's not an act."

"You don't pay rent, to me or your mother," Dunnane pointed out. "You hardly ever pay for food. And *anyway*"—he cut her off—"I knew you'd say this. So here." He handed her a piece of paper, which she couldn't read in the dark. "I signed you up. And I put out the three fifty.

You don't even have to pay me back, until you start really raking it in."

Maisie looked at the white oblong of paper. "This is ridiculous," she said, trying to hand it back to him.

He wouldn't take it.

"Dunnane, you can't make me do something I don't want to do just by giving me a piece of paper."

He kept driving. "You can say whatever you want, but that piece of paper makes you an official PaperWorth distributor."

She whirred down her window and let go of the paper. Dunnane slammed on the brakes. "You asshole," he said.

She shrugged.

"That was a *document*."

She looked down at her hands.

"So you better find it. Go on. Get out and find it."

"Dunnane, why can't this just be something you do, and I don't want to do, and that's all?"

He put his arm along the top of the seat and backed the car up a hundred feet. Then he said, "It's not 'something I do.' It's my life." On the word *life*, he hit her, hard across the face. Her nose made a cracking sound. Then he threw open his door and got out. Maisie sat, her face numb. She watched him walking, bent-backed, in the grass at the side of the road. The white stripes on his suit glinted silver in the headlights. After a moment she lifted her hand and jiggled her nose from side to side. It seemed to be all right, not broken, not bleeding, but it hurt. Then she got out and began wordlessly to help him look. She found the paper flapping in a bush and took it over to him. "Here, Dunnane." Then she said, "Take me to my mother's."

"I'm really sorry, Maze. I never did that before to anyone."

He opened her door for her and reached around to cup her face in his hand. "Did I hurt you?"

"No," she lied. He drove, hunched over the steering wheel.

Her mother's car was not in the driveway. She and Dunnane sat in his car with the motor running. "So," he said, "should I pick you up after work tomorrow?"

"No," Maisie said.

"You think I go around slugging women?"

She shook her head.

"Then why? Because I made you go to the meeting?"

"Dunnane," she said gently, "I guess I'm just not over my husband."

His face hardened in the dashboard light. "Are you getting back with him?"

"No." She opened her door. When he realized she was going, he leaned over to shove her out of the car; but it was too late, she was already out, and she felt only a light press of his fingers on her leg. Her hand in her pocket was already clutching the key, and she hurried up the path to the front door. The key rattled in the lock, she heard a car door slamming. Her fingers turned the key—hurry, hurry, let it be the passenger-side door, which she'd left hanging open. Just as the front door of the house fell open, the car's motor gave a great roar and Dunnane's headlights swept over her, backing out into the street. She sighed and went inside.

The empty house seemed small and hot and cloying, the rooms scented with small bowls of cinnamon potpourri. The china dogs on the mantelpiece looked down at her; actresses smiled from the covers of the women's magazines on the coffee table. The clock from her grandparents' house ticked loudly, like a tongue clicking against teeth. It was past midnight. Her mother was never out this late. She never had dinner with friends, dates with men, never went alone to the movies; she just sat here, on the nights when Maisie was home, drinking cocoa and watching TV and working on her needlepoint whales. Maisie went back into the kitchen and then into her mother's room to check for a note. In her mother's wastebasket there was a pair of panty hose trailing out onto the floor, and she pulled them out and ran her hands along the cool, empty legs. The room otherwise was perfectly neat, with that overpowering smell of cinnamon.

She didn't leave a note because she thought I was spending the night at Dunnane's, thought Maisie, and felt better, although still faintly worried. She sat down on the bed and dialed her mother's work number; a recorded voice told her the office was closed and invited her to leave a message. "Our restaurants are open daily from seven A.M. to eleven-thirty P.M.," the voice told her, so there was no way to find out if any of the waitresses with whom her mother was friendly knew where she might be.

She had trouble sleeping, worrying about her mother. She tried to pacify herself with what had become her latest falling-asleep story. She was walking into a hotel bar. Jack had called, to ask her for a drink. It was the bar at the Ritz in Boston: richly dim, with tables looking out over the Public Garden. He was already there, and he watched her come in. That was as far as she got. He was already sitting at a table, and he half rose when he saw her. It was not a gesture of courtesy, but of longing. The Maisie in the Ritz never even noticed it, she was checking her coat, laughing a little with the man who hung it up. But the other Maisie, the one picturing the scene, saw over and over the expression on his face.

Tonight the charm failed. She told herself: I come into the bar. . . . But she couldn't get any further. She saw her mother bleeding in the tangled wreck of a car; her mother mugged and beaten, lying unidentified in a hospital bed wondering why Maisie didn't come; her mother locked overnight in the refrigerator at one of the restaurants, shivering among the frozen cartons of pancake batter and orange juice concentrate; her mother saying, The hell with my life, and driving west or north all night.

She was sitting at the kitchen table the next morning when she heard a car in the driveway. She stood up, stiffening her shoulders, and then let her breath out when she heard her mother's key in the lock.

"Oh," said Alice. "I thought you were out." She was wearing what she always referred to as a "dress-up dress": rose-colored silk.

"I was, but I came home."

"Well," her mother said shakily. "Let me go freshen up."

Maisie heard the shower running. All the pictures that had run through her head last night vanished, to be replaced by an image even more difficult for Maisie to visualize: My mother is seeing someone.

"Did you have breakfast?" Alice asked, coming back into the kitchen. She was wearing a red linen suit, a white blouse with red dots on it.

"I'm never hungry in the mornings."

"That's funny, I couldn't manage without breakfast," Alice said. She smiled at Maisie, her shadowed eyes wide. "Oh, good. You made coffee." She poured some for herself and then sat down at the table. "Maisie," she said. "I'm sorry I wasn't here last night."

"No, no, don't worry about it."

"I just feel bad that I wasn't here when you came in."

"Mom, you can do whatever you want. It's your house."

"I don't want you to think that—well, I feel I should have been here." She turned her coffee cup in the saucer. "You know, it's not as though this was just some sort of casual date."

"Oh, I didn't think that."

"This is a man I've been seeing for some years."

"And you haven't ever told me about him? Or gone out with him on the nights when I'm here? You didn't have to do that."

"No, it's just that we don't see each other as often as I'd like."

"Well, I'd love to meet him, sometime."

"No, that wouldn't work," Alice said.

Maisie understood then: the man was married. They drank their coffee, looking out at the bird feeder in the backyard, draped with squirrels. The man's name was Ralph, Alice said. He'd been her boyfriend in high school, and they'd lost touch until Alice moved back to Virginia, after Maisie's father died. That was twenty years ago, Maisie thought, but did not say. There was an alcoholic wife, Alice said, three grown sons, but another still in high school, so Ralph can't leave. And he wouldn't leave anyway, Maisie, he's the kind of man who honors his commitments. And I admire him for that.

"So do I," Maisie said. She wanted to ask, How could you stand this for twenty years? And: How could I not have known? "What does he do?" she said.

"He's a doctor. A urologist." Alice ran a hand through her hair. "Two years ago we went to Quebec together, for a week. He had a conference. We had a room that looked over the river. I got to use my French."

"That must have been so nice," Maisie murmured.

"It was. And once he took me to Chicago. Wait." She left the kitchen and came back in a minute carrying a small blue leather album, like the red one she kept Maisie's baby pictures in.

She showed Maisie a photograph. A tall, somewhat heavy, balding man, smiling across a table, a half-eaten plate of spaghetti in front of him. Maisie recognized, behind him, the Impressionist reproductions that hung on the wall of her mother's dining room. "That was a few years ago," Alice said, peering at it. "He doesn't really look like that."

That night Maisie had a dream. She was climbing down a cliff, a movement that, once begun, could not be stopped. The surface was crumbling away. Every step pushed down boulders and soft chalky earth. She had to get to the bottom. Suddenly there were steps, a steep wooden flight like a ladder. She flung herself down them to the beach. A woman was lying there, in a red two-piece bathing suit. Maisie went and lay down next to her, and the woman rolled on top of her. She had to get away, but she couldn't; she was pinned, with the other woman's knees locked around hers. Then the woman held her head and began to kiss her, slowly, and Maisie moaned in her sleep and woke up sweating, knowing instantly that the woman in her dream had been Laura.

She was still trying to fall back to sleep, the first morning light seeping in under the window shade, when her door opened and her mother's voice whispered hoarsely, "Maisie?" Then, louder, "Get up. Come on. The strangest thing."

She sat up in bed, and her mother padded quickly across the room in her furry slippers and sent the shade cracking to the top of the window. Maisie blinked out at the front yard. It had snowed in the night, and at first she thought that was what her mother was trying to tell her; and she struggled foggily to come up with some reason why that might be a big deal. Oh, yes, she thought, I'm in Virginia, and the cream date yesterday was May 11.

"What the hell," Alice said slowly, almost gently, "what the *hell*?"

That got Maisie out of bed; she'd never heard her mother say "hell" before. And when she got to the window she saw that it had not snowed. The whiteness was paper. The wet black trees were festooned with toilet paper, loopy garlands that swooped up, up, and twisted themselves around higher branches and then sagged nearly to the ground and then swooped up again. The green lawn was gone, completely carpeted in long slanting lines of wet paper towels. Here and there the empty cardboard rolls were dark shapes against the grayish white, like stones and tree branches poking up through melting slush. Even the station wagon was shrouded in a translucent veil of paper that softened its lines and made it look like a ghost car.

"What in the *world*," Alice murmured, already beginning to recover her decorum.

It did not occur to Maisie to answer. She was staring and thinking that before she allowed herself to get upset—to imagine him out there all night doing it, to anticipate the cleanup and the curiosity of the neighbors and the trouble she would certainly be having with him in the next few weeks—she would memorize how lovely it looked, how still, how white.

11
Lists

❧

"Tell me why you're here," Nona Reese said.

Jack looked away from her, and then remembered that of course, he'd expected her to ask that. He said: "I feel like I'm stuck, and I want some help to get moving again." He told her that he was separated from his wife, leaning toward divorce but unwilling to push it. His wife, as far as he knew, still hoped for a reconciliation; she'd put quite a lot of pressure on him about it, but that was a while ago. He hadn't spoken to her in over six months. He was seeing someone else, anyway. A very nice, bright, calm woman. He didn't know how serious it was, whether or not he would eventually want to marry her. That was part of the problem. He ought to want to marry her. She wasn't pushing him, but she was a few years older than he was, thirty-six, and he knew she wanted children. And the other thing that was making him feel paralyzed was his work. The factory had been doing very badly, but lately things had begun to turn around, thanks in large part to ideas he'd come up with together with this woman he'd mentioned, the one he was living with. So now it would be easier for him to find a buyer for the business or to find someone else who'd be willing to run it, yet he couldn't seem to walk away and pick up German literature once again. His life wasn't turning out at all the way he'd expected, in any way. And his wife used to always yell at him, when they were fighting, that she thought he was incredibly passive, he really ought to go talk to someone. "And so," he finished, frowning vaguely at the complicated abridgment of his life, "I got your name from the Yellow Pages."

Nona moved her head slightly, a nod, but with more gravity. Almost a bow, he thought nervously. "Well, that's certainly a lot to contend with." She smiled.

He was simultaneously comforted—he'd handed over the story to an expert, it wasn't all his anymore—and disappointed: was that the wisest thing she could think of to say?

"So in a way," she said slowly, "it was your wife who suggested you see a therapist."

He flinched when she said "therapist." In her gentle voice the word sounded floppy, falsely soft. Still, he didn't know what else she could call herself.

"Well, not really. I haven't even talked to her in months. It was something she used to say to me sometimes, when we fought."

He didn't want to be held to what he had just said. That was the problem with going on the record: you said things that you didn't think were important, and someone else insisted that they were.

"I just said that because you asked me why, and that was the only reason I could think of. The whole idea of—of therapy wouldn't have occurred to me, except for Maisie. I don't come from a family where, you know, people—" He couldn't bring himself to say "therapy" again, and "get help" was even worse. "Go talk to other people," he ended lamely.

Despite his wish not to be held accountable for what he said, he could feel himself, almost against his will, handing Nona the bits and pieces she would need to construct the collage that would represent him.

"I guess that also I wanted to talk to someone who wouldn't be judgmental. Somebody who wasn't involved, who could just listen to what's going on and give me a neutral assessment of it." He listened to himself, then smiled. "In other words, a judge." He felt slightly dizzy, trying to be precise and contradicting himself, trying to be honest about the contradictions and wondering what Nona was making of them.

Nona smiled, too.

"Look, I don't know what to expect," Jack said, after a moment. "It's not easy for me to be here, I don't like to talk—"

"That's one reason I'm pressing you a little about why you *are* here," Nona said.

He stared at her face, exaggeratedly wide at the cheekbones and narrow at the jaw. Her eyes were lined with black beneath her black bangs, but aside from that she wore no makeup. Her long hair was all swept forward over one shoulder, pooled shinily in the crook of her arm. She wasn't writing down anything he said, only listening. In one hand she had a Kleenex, and she dabbed at her nose occasionally. Her sweater was purple. When he went home and thought about this hour, he would remember exactly what Nona had looked like, the silhouette of her head and body on the couch, but nothing else about the room.

He began to talk about the company, telling Nona about the new brand they were introducing, SunLights. "Laura, this woman I live with, really was the one who came up with the idea. I was about to introduce a new microwave fry, which would have been a complete disaster, and she was the one who came in and said, Whoa, hold on here, let's do some research. And when we found out that there wasn't a demand for a new microwave brand, but there was for low-fat products, she was the one who found us a culinary engineer—"

"A culinary engineer?" Nona interrupted.

"Yes, there really are people who call themselves that," said Jack, smiling back at her, liking her for the first time. "Anyway, this guy completely reformulated the cooking process and figured out how to eliminate thirty percent of the fat. So now we're about to introduce this new product, and Laura's working on the packaging—"

"She sounds incredibly supportive."

"She is," he said firmly. "But—but I think she just assumes I'll do this forever. Make french fries. I mean, she has a sense of irony about it, and about what she does, but she doesn't see any reason for us to get out of it."

"And you do?"

"I think I do, but I can't tell if I'm really dissatisfied, or if it's just left over from Maisie. My wife. She couldn't believe it when I took over the business, she kept saying, My God, is this what you want to do with your life?"

Nona shifted her position, tucking her foot beneath her. "Tell me about your marriage."

He was silent, and Nona let the silence go on for several moments. Then she said, "I'm just curious about why you and she broke up."

He stared at her, at her pleasant, inquiring face, and then turned his eyes to look out the window. "She said I wasn't passionate enough, or romantic enough. I didn't talk enough. She was always asking, What are you thinking? What are you feeling? and when I said, Nothing, she didn't believe me."

"So she was the one to break it up."

Oh, come on, can't we drop this? But Nona's scrutiny was also weirdly fascinating: maybe she was working her way up to some amazing diagnosis.

"Well, at first. Then she wanted to come back, but by that time I'd already met Laura."

"Why did you marry her?"

"Maisie?" he asked stupidly. Nona waited. "Well, I don't know. We used to just—talk about things. I don't know why she said we never talked. Even if we were really tired at night, we'd sit up till one in the morning. I don't even know what we talked about. And I just felt—she was just the most—I know this sounds stupid, but when she was out of the house, I would just go open the closet and stand there looking at her clothes."

Nona said, "I don't think it sounds stupid."

He sat twisting his hands together. He said, "And I think she found me reassuring. She had a strange combination of confidence and, I don't know, terror—"

"Uh-huh," Nona said encouragingly.

He looked out her window again, into a tangle of bare tree limbs. He didn't know why he was babbling about Maisie, when he'd come here to talk about Laura and the factory and his life now, but on the other hand, maybe it was better to get Maisie out of the way in this first session. Assuming there was a second session. All he had to do was get through this one, and then he could call Nona and tell her he'd decided not to come back.

"Go on," Nona prodded.

"Well, nothing. I was just thinking about the first time I met her, it was at a party, and she was talking to this other man and taking cigarettes out of his shirt pocket, just kind of plucking them out, talking and laughing, like we can take this all for granted, we're so cozy and intimate. I just thought, What a phony. But then we got into a conversation—she asked me to open a bottle of beer for her, and I couldn't get it open, either, and then it finally exploded all over me. . . ." He was smiling.

Tone it down, he told himself. "We were silly together, that was another thing. One night we put her cat in a roasting pan and floated him around the bathtub—" He stopped.

Nona smiled. I sound pathetic, Jack thought.

He said coolly, "She just wasn't the sort of person who was usually attracted to me. So when things started getting bad, in a way I wasn't surprised. Somewhere inside I guess I always thought she'd leave. Anyway"—he took a deep breath, got hold of himself—"it took me a long time to realize she was really treating me like shit. But finally I did see it."

"Why did you say 'terror'?"

"What?"

"You said she had a combination of something—sureness—and terror."

"Oh." He didn't want to talk about Maisie anymore, but he didn't know how to say this to Nona without sounding rude, or as though he were trying to hide something. "Terror"? He thought suddenly of the first time he'd gone home with Maisie to Virginia, how she'd apologized for everything. The hot southern summer, the suburban shopping strips of her town, the smallness of her mother's house, the braided oval rugs from Ethan Allen, the strings of plastic onions hanging in the kitchen. "It was supposed to be a 'starter house,' " she said, "only we never got out of it." Someone rang the doorbell one afternoon, and Maisie's face went gray: the chimes played the first bars of "Oranges and Lemons." Jack went out and rang it again, just for the fun of hearing it; but Maisie dragged his arm away with a fury that startled him and filled him with bewildered tenderness.

"Not terror, exactly, it was more a kind of—I don't know. She used to tell me she felt she came from noplace. I think her whole life was a kind of construction that she was always working on—the way she dressed, even the kind of cigarettes she smoked. She worked really hard not to be boring. She—" He stopped. There was a long, terrible silence. "Anyway," he added finally, "Laura's not like that."

"What is she like?"

Why had he thought this would help? Nona was asking perfectly reasonable questions, he knew, but he didn't want to have to answer them. Not now. Maybe if he had a few weeks to go away and think about the questions, prepare some coherent responses.

"She's very independent," he said coldly.

"In what way?"

He counted the ways off on his fingers, impatiently, as though he'd already told them to Nona a hundred times and she'd forgotten. "She has her own *business,* her own apartment, she's lived all over the *world,* she's older, she knows when to talk and when to shut up."

"So she's completely different from your wife."

"Yes." The fierceness of his own voice startled him. Were they just going to sit here harping on the obvious? But that wasn't fair—when Nona said something obvious he was irritated, but when she'd pushed him about Maisie, which he hadn't expected, he'd been annoyed at that, too. She just doesn't get it, he thought, she doesn't know me.

But Nona, as though thinking the same things, said after a moment, "You know what might help us get started?"

"What?"

"Well, first of all, of course, you'll have to decide whether you want to keep seeing me."

"I do want to," said Jack, to his own surprise.

"Good. So for next time, what I'd like you to do is to make me a list."

"A list?"

"Write down what you want."

It sounded gimmicky and facile to him. "What do you mean, about"—he swallowed—"relationships?"

"Relationships, work, whatever. Your life in general. It may be helpful or it may not be. But sometimes it's hard to think in a therapist's office, and it's easier to give yourself a sort of jump-start at home. Just write it all down."

He sat that evening at Laura's kitchen table, with a pad of legal paper and a mug of herb tea. LAURA, he wrote, and then looked at the word. They had finished dinner, and Laura had cleaned up the kitchen and gone into the bedroom so that he could be alone to make his list.

Her apartment was settled, in a way that made him feel simultaneously at home and uncomfortable. There was a white sofa and two white chairs, a big old Persian rug, framed pictures on the walls. There was a small bamboo bookcase full of books and large built-in bookcases filled with everything but books—tapes and records and a tremendous collection of fish: wooden ones, china ones, glass ones, neatly arranged on the white wooden shelves. As he spent more time in the apartment, he saw that the fish were a running subtext: Laura's salt and pepper shakers were shaped like dolphins, the butter dish was a white china whale, there were blue damask fish borders on the white dish towels. The hallway was lined with framed collections of old cigarette cards, beautifully colored, each with a picture of a fish and the proper bait to catch it with. In the living room was a big green tank, humming, filled with gleaming, flickering guppies and platies. He couldn't decide if it was endearing or annoying, to keep finding the motif in unexpected places, to write something on the telephone notepad and notice that it was silk-screened faintly with goldfish, or to grab an oven mitt and find himself stuffing his hand into a crudely colored flounder.

Her kitchen was full of things put away in places designed especially for them. Mugs hanging from hooks in diagonal symmetry. A ledge behind the stove lined with white-capped spice jars, labeled in Laura's strong black capitals. Behind closed cupboard doors her dishes were piled in matching stacks: eight of everything, in a plain thick white china that could be easily replaced if anything broke. She had a separate silverware basket for each kind of utensil—teaspoons, tablespoons, forks, knives, steak knives—each piece lying on its side, nestled neatly with the next. The sight of such order, in such secret places (who ever looked at anyone else's silverware? You arranged these things carefully only for yourself), had at first disconcerted him: how could he live up to it? He tried to dissuade her, unsuccessfully, from washing the kitchen floor every night before she went to bed. Did it mean she was compulsive, anal? Would she think he was a slob?

But she'd accepted the mess of his presence (which by any other standards couldn't have been considered a mess) easily, almost, he thought, gratefully. One night, letting himself in late with the key she'd given him, he'd skidded on one of the small rag rugs that lined her hallway. The next morning, following her out of the bedroom, he saw her smiling at the rug that was awry. You can't imagine how sad it made me, she told him, having those rugs in perfect alignment day after day after day.

And she had taken in Egg, who leaped every morning to the top of her bedroom door and lay there watching Jack and Laura dress, one paw trailing down, tail flicking. She'd said it was fine for Jack to put the cat box under the bathroom sink, and she'd found a place for Egg's dishes next to the refrigerator.

So she'd welcomed the mess, and Jack had relaxed into the neatness and begun to find it soothing. In the lamplit kitchen, the clock ticked softly on the maroon wall, the black-and-white floor tiles shone, the refrigerator was papered with exuberantly sloppy drawings, done by the children of Laura's friends. The plants were bright green against the tall, cold, black rectangles of the windows—the same schoolroom windows on which Jack, as a fourth-grader in Mrs. Kalishes's classroom, had once pasted cutout jack-o'-lanterns and snowflakes.

He looked down again, at the glowing yellow paper. The word LAURA looked so stark and lonely that he drew a square around it, going over each line hard, with a pencil, again and again. The square swelled and darkened, making shiny black cradles in the paper. But now it looked overly emphatic, almost defensive. He could imagine Nona's calm voice: Why did you have to reinforce Laura's name so many times? Did you think I wouldn't believe you? He tore off the sheet of paper and balled it up, intending to write the name again on the sheet beneath. But there on the paper the rectangular indentation repeated itself; he imagined Nona scrutinizing it: What had you written on the sheet above that you felt so strongly about and then rejected?

After his father's death, they'd found lists everywhere, in his careful beautiful handwriting. Christmas shopping lists in his jacket pocket, lists of phone calls to make, To-Do lists in the pages of the datebook on his desk at work. The desk itself, like the business, had been a mess, and the lists had seemed to Jack to indicate a wistful devotion to method and order, his father's stubborn hope that by writing down numbered items in order of their importance, the chaos could be minimized and conquered.

He pushed back his chair and went down the hallway to the bedroom, pushing open the half-shut door. "This is hard."

Laura was sitting on the bed, folding laundry and watching a documentary. A bobcat ran across the screen. "It must be," she said.

"I keep feeling like it's a trick question, as though she's going to read all sorts of meanings into what I write down."

"So you're trying to figure out what she's going to say and kind of head it off?" She smiled at him and then, when he said nothing else, turned her attention back to the screen. He sat on the bed with her and watched, folding dish towels, pairing socks. The bobcat was chasing something, a rabbit. Close-up of the rabbit in a brief, panicky halt, eyes darting, nose twitching: what next? Then a blur of movement: flight. The announcer droned on calmly, giving nothing away, making simultaneous implications of slaughter and reprieve. "The bobcat has formidable advantages—speed, strength, teeth, and claws. Yet the rabbit is not without defensive mechanisms. It too has speed, a network of holes in the ground. And a quite remarkable talent for camouflage."

"And so?" Jack prompted.

"Four different seasons, four different protective colorations," the announcer said, off on a detour. Jack sighed. He got up and went over to Laura's bureau and began putting his clothes away in the bottom drawer. He had a restless wish that she would ask him more about what had happened with Nona. But of course she wouldn't question him; she would consider it wholly private, unless he initiated the discussion. And he couldn't figure out what to say. I feel like I've put my foot into the bog, and now it has me by the ankle and it's pulling me down. I want to sort of talk to Nona, not really talk to her. I want some things to be off limits.

"This time the outcome is not so happy," the announcer concluded mournfully. Jack glanced up in time to catch a last glimpse of the cornered, skittering rabbit, a whirl of brown fur. Then a quick cut forward, a discreet lapse of vision. The bobcat, sated, picked lazily at a tangle of unrecognizable blood and bone.

All the rest of that week he thought about the list. He didn't repeat the humiliation of sitting down with the blank sheet in front of him, but in his head he could see the paper, glowing yellow. TO GO BACK TO SCHOOL, he wrote on it, and immediately crossed it out; he didn't know if it was true. It had been true once, but now he wasn't sure. TO GO AHEAD WITH MY DIVORCE: but that one, also, was questionable, a rash statement made only to shut a door in Nona's face.

He thought maybe the trouble was that he was trying to be too specific, in making the list. Maybe he should write down in the broadest sense what he wanted, and then Nona could help him figure out how to get there. TO BE HAPPY, he wrote on the imaginary sheet of paper. That seemed unimpeachable; it had a stark, dumb simplicity that pleased him. He actually did write that one down, on a blue Post-It at work, and he stuck it inside the top drawer of his desk, to see whether he could live with it. He saw it when he opened the drawer to lend Dave LaPalme a pencil, and again when he reached in for a paper clip. Laura came in at eleven for a meeting and found him looking into his gaping drawer; he shut it irritably, as guilty and ashamed as if she'd caught him gazing at himself in a mirror. By the end of the day the words embarrassed him; they seemed smart-alecky, trite, and he tore off the piece of paper and threw it away.

Foiled by Nona's list, he began his own: the kind he liked best. He set the alarm for five-thirty the next morning, got dressed without waking Laura, and went out. He stopped by his own house to pick up the leather pouch his grandmother had given him, long ago. His worn green hardcover Peterson's was inside, as well as a pack of checklist cards, with a piece of fragile, yellowed cellophane folded around them. He took a fresh card and filled in the spaces at the top for his name and the year. The cards had come with the pouch; there had been twenty-five of them originally, but now he was down to three. He wondered where he'd get more cards when these were gone. The Audubon Society probably had them, but he didn't know if they'd be the right kind, these austere slippery vertical ones with barely any room to write, and with their familiar, comically clipped abbreviations (Hum'gbrd; Wrblr; Frigbrd, Magnif.). The pencil that had come with the pouch, in its own special outside compartment, had been used up a long time ago, but the one he'd been using for the past few years was still inside, worn down to a comfortable stub. He sharpened it carefully before putting it back in the pouch; he wouldn't sharpen it again until next spring, even though his recordings would grow noticeably duller and heavier as the year went on.

As a child, the excitement of beginning a new list had been so great that he'd awakened early on New Year's Day, gone out before breakfast into the fields below the barn, and noted a few juncos, chickadees, finches. These birds in winter were as common as clouds, so this first observation was purely ceremonial, done for the intense pleasure of writing on the clean white card, embarking on his work for the year.

Now he was more patient, or perhaps less passionate: it was the third week of March, and he was just beginning his list. The winter birds were still around—he noted down a few juncos and finches hopping around in the dead, flattened grass next to his driveway. Over the next few weeks their numbers would begin to dwindle: a sign that spring was coming.

He drove to the reservoir twenty miles away. He sat in the car and drank coffee from a thermos until it was light enough to see, and then headed out across the field to the water. His boots crunched over a lace of ice. He saw some redpolls, grosbeaks, and a crossbill. In the lake itself he saw the first sign that the spring migrations had begun: a pair of

American mergansers, paddling slowly around in an ice-ringed patch of black open water. He watched the male, who looked like a mallard only more rakish—the sports-car model, he thought—and female as they sailed along with their heads into the wind and then dove, together, disappearing for almost a full minute before bobbing up again in the same spot. The wind scraped across his face.

While he was setting up his telescope to get a closer look at the birds on the ice in the middle of the lake, another group of bird-watchers passed him, heading back to their car. Two old ladies, and a young man with wire-rimmed glasses and a beard. "Scaup, buffleheads, goldeneyes," they said to him, and he nodded, trying not to listen. He wanted to see for himself, not knowing what he was looking for. Sometimes other bird-watchers told him things that he knew were dead wrong. Did you see the gannet out there? And Jack would look through the telescope and see, instead of the nearly impossible gannet, a much more common gull. That is amazing, he agreed.

On the way back to the car, edging the woods again in case something had changed in the past half hour, he heard a male cardinal singing.

How do you know it's the male? he remembered Maisie asking when he'd taken her bird-watching after his father died.

Because the females don't sing.

Are you kidding? So it's always the male you hear? Just cardinals, or all birds?

All birds. All songbirds, anyway.

What about ducks and geese?

No, they're different. You know that honk-honk, honk-honk you hear when a pair of geese flies overhead? Well, that's actually both of them, honking back and forth to each other. It's how they keep track of each other as they fly.

She'd taken his arm, smiled at him. That sort of thing had momentarily interested her, the anthropomorphizing part of bird-watching. Other than that the whole thing had bored her. She didn't understand what he loved about it: being silent in a beautiful place, watching something that had no awareness of him. Writing down what he saw, trying to fill up all the blanks on his card. Competing with himself, with last year's list, hoping to see more, identify more. Knowing what was normal for the place and the time of the year, enjoying the certainty that the same birds would come back in roughly the same order; but also knowing that it was always possible to see something rare and startling, blown off course by a storm.

That, more than politeness, was the reason he looked through the telescopes of novice birders who were trumpeting improbable sightings: they might be right. A gannet in an inland reservoir—it was almost certainly a mistake, but it might be a miracle.

"I didn't do the list," he said, sitting down in the rocking chair in Nona's office. This time, determinedly, he looked at the room, damned if he was going to be too awed to see it. A long, dark velour couch, on which Nona sat, in a green sweater this time and gray wool trousers. She held in one hand the leash of a small terrier, for whom she'd apologized when Jack came in. We have to go to the vet, she'd said, wrapping the leash more tightly around her hand as the dog strained and moaned to get to Jack, and the only time he could see us is right after your session, so I had to bring Flaky to the office today. The dog sat quietly now at Nona's feet, and Jack didn't mind it at all; in fact, it seemed to humanize Nona. He liked the idea of her on the phone, flustered, pleading with the vet to squeeze her in.

The light in the office this morning seemed at once cooler and more general; it took him a moment to realize that the last time he'd been here it had been snowing, and the lamp beside the couch had been turned on. Today, there was just daylight. On the wall above the couch was a poster from the Metropolitan Museum, TREASURES FROM THE KREMLIN: an icon of a sad, olive-skinned Christ riding a donkey. He was surprised that she'd have such an overtly religious, sorrowful picture in her office; but on the side wall there was another museum poster, this one showing a Matisse goldfish bowl. The second poster took away some of the power of the first: see, this is just decoration. The theme here is museum posters, that's all. There were two chairs for patients to sit in, facing the couch: a soft leather armchair and the rocker.

"The list," Nona repeated, as though she had to fish in her memory to understand which list he meant.

"The list you told me to make, of things I wanted."

"Okay." The way she said it was practically a shrug, so he found himself explaining to her (irritably: he'd anticipated a battle) why he hadn't done it: everything he wrote down seemed either too specific or too vague, and also frankly, he'd felt it was a gimmick, an oversimplification.

"Okay," Nona repeated. "I only suggested it because I thought you might find it helpful."

He ground his hands together.

"You know, you should feel free to disagree with me whenever I say something that seems off-base."

He sighed and slumped back in his chair. He'd forgotten it was a rocker, and the sudden motion disconcerted him. His feet groped for the floor. Already he was exhausted.

Nona looked to one side, in the direction of the Matisse but not at it. She's trying to figure out what to do with me, Jack thought. He was proud and ashamed of how difficult he apparently was, and reminded himself again: She only knows what I tell her, and I don't have to tell her anything unless I want to.

But he felt sorry for her, and when she turned back to him and said, "Tell me more about the relationship you're in now," he drew his eyebrows together and made an honest effort to tell her about Laura. This was private, but not excruciating; and after all, he was going to have to talk to Nona about *something*.

Laura, he said, had basically saved his life. At a time when he was very depressed, when he'd been convinced that the dissolution of his marriage was all his fault and that he was probably incapable of having a good relationship with any woman, Laura had come along and made everything seem easy.

"In what way?" Nona murmured.

He thought. "She just accepts me. She's *like* me. With Maisie, I always had to explain everything. It was so easy to hurt her feelings!"

"Can you give me an example?"

He thought, So, she's got me talking about Maisie again, and then he shrugged: So what. "Oh, for instance, she was always very insecure about how intellectual she was. She was really smart, but she was convinced that she was dumb, or that everybody thought she was dumb, anyway. Like, she never let herself read any junk. It always had to be *Daniel Deronda*, or *Buddenbrooks*." He stopped. This seemed underhanded to him, pure disloyalty. Stop talking about Maisie's private fears, and get to the point of the story. "Anyway, one night we had some people over to dinner, some friends of mine from grad school and some others, all these high achievers, and I could just see Maisie getting more tense and more insecure as the evening went along. She was smoking a lot, talking in this intellectually pretentious way. Anyway, when the people left, she just wilted. Told me she hated her job—"

"Which was?"

"She was working as a secretary. Until she figured out what she really wanted to do with her life. Anyway, she was holding this tray of dirty wineglasses when she said it, and I was seeing her through the glasses, and she looked so beautiful, she had on a dark green shirt and she just sort of shimmered, and I said—I don't know why I said this—but I said, 'Don't worry, you could always be a cocktail waitress.' " He stopped, looked at Nona's face, thought he saw acute distaste. "It was an unbelievably stupid thing to say, I could have shot myself right after. I was trying to say the most absurd, far-from-the-truth thing I could think of, you know, that no matter what happened she'd never end up as a cocktail waitress."

He frowned and blinked, waiting for absolution. But Nona simply watched him. He had time to remember how he'd led into the story: Maisie's feelings were too easily hurt. But this wasn't a good example—so far, at least, the story seemed to be about him being tactless, if not downright cruel. "Well, the point was that I apologized right away, only it was as though she couldn't hear me. For days she was asking, Why did you say that? Is that what you really think of me? Are you sure it's not what you really think?"

He stopped again, thinking how vindictive and petty he sounded. "The point is, if I were to say something like that to Laura now, something tactless, and then I apologized, she would understand and forget it."

"Because she's more secure?" Nona asked. "Or because she's less invested in what you think?"

"Not less invested. Less dependent."

"But your wife was the one who left you, right? Why do you say she was dependent?"

"Well, I told you: she left me, but then she wanted to come back. I was the one who didn't want her back."

"Because you'd been hurt so badly?"

"No, because I'd met Laura."

"Do you love Laura?"

There was a low table next to the chair where he sat, and on the table was a box of tissues. Oh, so I'm supposed to cry, he thought.

"I don't know," he said.

"But you do know you loved Maisie?"

"Yes."

From time to time from then on he glanced at the tissues and thought, Well, at least I won't need *that.* Then he began to worry that he was sounding too dispassionate, telling random anecdotes that weighed Laura against Maisie: Nona would think that he was unemotional, cold. He was talking about Maisie's habitual flirtatiousness, how she couldn't go into a convenience store to buy milk without getting into a snappy little conversation with the clerk.

"So did that bother you?" Nona asked.

"No."

"Did you admire it?"

"Well, I thought it was kind of endearing, actually. And it was so different from how I am. I know I can come across as rude or snobbish, when I'm really just awkward. Or worried about disturbing someone's privacy. But Maisie really did have this interest in other people. She'd pick up on little details of their lives, their clothes or their accents. Or if they had some interesting profession or hobby, she'd find out all about it."

"She sounds charming."

Jack ignored her. "But for her all these conversations were little successes. The flirtations—and they weren't just with men, they were with everybody, only I guess they were mostly with men—were her way of making people like her." He waited. "She was very amusing, but I don't think that's what she wanted. She wanted to be taken seriously."

"By whom?"

"I don't know." He looked at his watch. "I feel like I'm not doing a very good job of describing her."

"Well, what I'm hearing is that she's very charming and seductive. Nothing wrong with that. It's not as though she was out having affairs." Nona paused. "Was she?"

"No. I don't think so. I don't know. Maybe she was." He straightened up in his chair. "I feel like I'm still not giving you any coherent reason why our marriage broke up. I can't make you understand. There weren't affairs, there wasn't any big blowout."

"It sounds to me like *you* don't understand."

"I don't." He felt tremendous relief in saying it.

"You said last time that Maisie thought you were too detached, or not passionate enough, I think you said."

"But I wasn't detached. I was incredibly upset when she took the job in New York."

"What about before that?"

"It depends on what you mean by detached. I wasn't throwing myself down in front of her every night telling her I loved her."

"Did she expect you to?" Nona asked.

"No. But when I inherited the business, there were a lot of things on my mind. I just wasn't all there, the way I had been before."

"And you'd just lost your father."

"Yes. He died, I took over the business, we got married, and we moved."

"Those things all happened at once? I can understand why you might not be 'all there,' as you say."

He frowned, at what seemed to him to be facile sympathy. Now she was going to ask him about his father, and he didn't think he could bear to talk about that. Instead he began telling Nona about the trip to Europe he and Maisie had been planning, for their honeymoon. They'd made lists of places they both wanted to see: Madrid, Cornwall, Scandinavia, Vienna, Italy, the south of France. Too many destinations for one trip: they would have to narrow it down. She'd brought home guidebooks, and they'd spent evenings mapping out different possibilities: three days here, four days there. He'd promised to call a travel agent, but never had.

"Why not?" asked Nona.

"Oh, money, partly. We were pretty broke then, it was before I really got going at the factory and I thought we ought to be careful. And partly because—I don't know, we hadn't figured out any definite itinerary, and I just kept waiting for her to tell me where she most wanted to go."

"But you never talked to her about money, or said: Okay, so let's pick the places and make the reservations?"

"I thought talking about the money would upset her. And—"

"But would it have, do you think?"

"Not as much as my doing nothing." He felt better, admitting this, and thought: What is there about self-abasement that's so refreshing? "And I think I was preoccupied with the company. It was hard for me to plan anything."

"So did you have a honeymoon?"

"We went to Washington for a couple of nights."

"Was Maisie happy about that?"

"No. In fact, we had a big fight on our wedding night. She blamed me for not pursuing the Europe trip, and I said, Well, if it was so important to you, why didn't you say anything before this? And she said she'd been waiting for *me* to say something."

He'd been going on and on about Maisie, and he looked at his watch again, trying to gauge how much time was left in which to come up with some new revelation about Laura.

"Yes," said Nona, following his glance. "We need to stop now."

"So I'll see you next week?"

"Right." She seemed surprised that he'd needed to ask.

Laura had grown up all over the world. Her father was in the Foreign Service, a couple of ranks below an ambassador. She'd lived behind walls and fences, in houses that could have been anywhere, except for the language being spoken by the servants when she walked into the kitchen to ask for something.

She'd been raised to be considerate. Once, she told Jack, she had started to choke on a piece of empanada at an embassy dinner party, and rather than interrupt the table conversation to tell them she couldn't breathe, she'd gotten up and floundered down the corridors looking for a bathroom, where she'd been able, finally, to cough it out. He took her hand when she told him this, and she looked a little startled: she didn't see anything moving about the story, she simply found it ridiculous.

She'd told him, at first, that she'd moved to Champs du Soleil solely to be near her grandmother's camp. Now more of the story came out: there'd been a man in Chicago, another art director at the ad agency where she'd worked. If you think *I'm* fastidious, she said, grinning, you should have seen Craig. He was the kind who wore tweed sport coats with flecks in them and socks that picked up the colors of the flecks. He was always vacuuming—I knew the woman who lived downstairs from him, and she told me she'd hear his vacuum rolling over the floors at two in the morning. And he was always taking self-improvement courses—wine tasting, public speaking. I thought all these things were charming quirks. I guess I loved him, she said coolly, but it was more that I'd decided it was time to get married. I was thirty, and I just thought, All right, it's time. (Here she looked away from Jack, acknowledging that the subject of getting married for the wrong reasons was a touchy one.) But, she said, right around the time we started having serious discussions about marriage—in fact, I'd actually begun telling people we were engaged—he fell madly in love with his speed-reading teacher. She was forty-five and she rode a motorcycle. He told me when we were having dinner. I had a mouthful of mashed potatoes, and I remember thinking: I have to swallow these somehow. He said: I just feel like she has her finger on the button of life, and I want to be around when she pushes it.

She told Jack this story wryly, ruefully. She said, Now, of course, I bless that speed-reading teacher. She never asked Jack for the story of his marriage, and he never brought it up, because he knew he couldn't tell it the way she'd told hers, as though it were an embarrassing lapse that had happened to someone else. But after she told him, he had, for the first time, a small, silent sense of pressure: someone had led her on and then dumped her; it mustn't happen again.

Sometimes, when Laura embraced him, he would think, Her arms are too long. He lay in bed beside her in the morning while she slept and looked at her with combined love and dismay. He made himself see that her arm was beautiful, the curving sheen of her shoulder, the slight smooth indentation of the triceps, like whorls of water following the sinking of an oar, the sudden darkening below her elbow and down the strong flat forearm, where the sun lay when she impatiently pushed up her sleeve, the fine, barely perceptible shadow of hair.

He put his hand on her face and saw the flicker of a dark eye beneath the eyelid; she woke and turned, reaching for him. The sheets crackled. This was new to him, making love in the morning: something slow and heavy and wordless, as though they were underwater. She breathed but made no other sound; he was free to be alone in this, as she freed him to be alone in every other way. With Maisie he had wondered, always, how she was feeling: his excitement had come largely from watching hers. With Laura he closed his eyes and felt.

But afterward, he thought. He saw the long arm falling away from him, and he thought of what Maisie had said once, about Egg: Don't you think he makes all other cats look wrong? And he wondered, after all his years of staring at Maisie: How long would it take him to get to the point where all other women, even Laura, didn't look wrong?

The spring migration built up very slowly, as March blurred into April. He could see it happening, not only out at the reservoir, but also by looking at his list. On March 18 he'd seen twenty-four pine siskins, while now he could go days without seeing a single one. In their place he was noting down fox sparrows, brown creepers, grackles, red-winged blackbirds. Thrushes and warblers were singing in the softening branches of the trees that ringed the reservoir; and one morning, he heard a chorus of high, barking laughter overhead, and he looked up to see a long, white, wavering line of snow geese.

He loved the sense that he was observing a great, inexorable pattern, keeping track as the birds came back from the hot places where they wintered, settling here to breed or sweeping past him on their way to Canada.

Most mornings he went straight from the woods to the factory, stopping at Vernet's bakery on the way to pick up muffins for breakfast. But on Thursdays he skipped the bird-watching, drove down to Portland, and went to Nona's instead. He talked to her about graduate school, about the factory, about Laura choking on the empanada. He told her about his family. One morning he talked about his father in a cool monotone, staring out the window. He'd assumed Nona would shove him around more, manhandle him into dramatic revelations. But mostly she let him lead the conversation, only introducing a new subject when he fell silent. When he left her office he was often unable to remember what they'd talked about, and he began to try to write it down in a pocket datebook, as he sat in his parked car outside her office. But that didn't help; he felt better after talking to her, and seeing the topics they'd discussed reduced to four or five bulleted points on lined paper seemed to diminish, rather than preserve, the feeling. They went over the same ground again and again; written down it looked as though he were only going in circles.

"I think that's why I married Maisie," he told her. "Because I couldn't believe my own good luck. I knew if I didn't find some way of holding on to her, I'd never get a chance like that again. I found her—romantically fascinating, in a way I've never found any other woman."

Nona nodded and crossed her legs.

"She—I don't know if she ever really understood how I felt. When we moved to Maine, to take over the factory when my father died, she thought I was somehow neglecting her, because it wasn't what she wanted at all."

"Well, here's my theory of marriage. You want to hear it?"

He nodded.

"I think that there are times in every marriage when one person starts sounding the alarm bell. And if the other person doesn't hear it, or hears it and doesn't respond, that's when things start to become dangerous. Did you not hear it?"

"No, I heard it. I just didn't—"

"Understand that it was an alarm?"

"Believe that she had the right to get so upset over something I couldn't change. I thought she was testing me."

"Which you resented."

"Yes, because I guess *my* idea of marriage is that it can't be perfect and equal every minute. Sometimes one person has to bow to the other. Over the years, it equals out. She used to say I was taking her for granted, and I thought, So? People always think taking each other for granted is a terrible thing. But to me it seems like a part of love. It means counting on their loyalty. I thought that if she really loved me, she should just accept the fact that our life was going to veer off course for a few years."

"You accused her of testing you, but then you said, 'If she'd really loved me, she would have . . .' "

"You mean I was testing her? It didn't start out that way. But maybe you're right, maybe that's what it turned into."

"So you were sounding an alarm, too."

He cleared his throat. "I guess." He looked at the tree branches outside her window, then down at the box of tissues. It took him a few moments to feel certain of controlling his voice; then he said, "So what if the things she was accusing me of were all true?"

"Well, let me ask you a question," Nona said, pressing her palms together. "Did it ever occur to you that she was treating you pretty badly?"

He stared at her. "Yeah, when she left me the thought crossed my mind."

"But before that."

"When she was moping around the house, you mean?" He coughed. "No, at that point I was so worried about her, and so afraid she'd leave, that I wasn't really angry at her."

"You were missing your father and taking over this failing business, and it never once occurred to you that maybe she ought to be taking care of *you* for a change?"

This was it, the revelation he'd been coming for. He sat there waiting for the big "Ah-hah!" He tried to picture Maisie in her nightgown on the couch in the dark cold living room watching "Wheel of Fortune" night after night, he remembered her saying, You don't love me; and,

You're the one who would catch the grenade, just because they threw it at you. He tried to conjure up the flatness of her voice when she'd proposed the three-month separation. He knew these things had happened, but there was no sudden avalanche of emotion now. Oh, so *she* was neglecting *me,* he told himself dutifully. He looked at Nona. Her eyebrows were raised, and he thought she must be feeling calmly triumphant. He was sorry to let her down, but there was another part of him that was proud of how honest he was about to be.

"No," he said.

Disappointingly, she didn't seem surprised. "You still can't admit you're angry at her."

"Sure, I can. I told you. She left me, she treated me like shit."

"But you can't admit that the anger goes back farther than that."

Nona! he wanted to say. But maybe he was supposed to call her Dr. Reese; he never called her anything. He couldn't just say Hey!, could he?

But while he was quibbling with himself, she moved on.

"Why didn't you try to stop her from leaving?"

Because I was already angry at her. That was what Nona wanted him to say. That was why he'd never wanted to go "talk to someone." That was the big cliché of therapy: You're angry. Let it out. Come on. Admit you hate your wife. And here was Nona, sensible, unpretentious Nona, pulling it on him. Nona, this is Bad Taste, he thought, and he got a sudden picture of Cecily Beausoleil's house decked out in Christmas lights; and he began to laugh.

He laughed and laughed, harsh, solitary, barking laughter, and every time he came close to stopping, the sight of Nona's earnest face set him off again. Tears were running down his face. He pulled a tissue out of the box to wipe them away and then held it to his mouth, trying to smother the sounds he was making.

Nona watched him patiently, as though she knew exactly why he was laughing. Well, screw her. She couldn't know about the sleigh on Cecily's roof, the lit-from-within Santa Claus and the red flashing lightbulb on Rudolph's nose, the Mr. and Mrs. Snowman standing next to the Virgin Mary on the lawn, the speakers under the eaves blaring out "O Holy Night". . . . But itemizing Cecily's Christmas decorations in his head suddenly made the whole thing less funny. He felt bad for Cecily, and for Nona—it couldn't be very comforting to have your big insight greeted with laughter. He coughed into his tissue and said, soberly, "I'm sorry."

"That's all right," Nona said, nodding almost jauntily, so that he began to be annoyed with her again. "But I want you to think about something, for next time."

"What's that?" he asked. A few belated snorts escaped him, and he covered his mouth again with the shredded tissue.

"Think about what I said about your maybe being angry with Maisie from a long time ago. I may be way off base, and if I am, you can tell me. But think about how it might be affecting your behavior now."

"What behavior?" Oh, no, are we going to have to dissect exactly why I laughed?

"Your affair."

"Laura?" Now he was, quite straightforwardly, angry. "That's not an affair. An affair implies a betrayal, and I'm not betraying anyone. My marriage was over before I met Laura."

He told Laura he thought he'd stop going to Nona; he couldn't see that it was doing any good. "It's just self-indulgence. I sit on her chair and whine, and she tells me I'm not whining loud enough."

"I think you should at least give her a chance," Laura said. It was late Thursday afternoon, and she was here for a meeting with Dave LaPalme on the new low-calorie, cholesterol-free french fries.

"It's repetitive, it's boring, I'm getting sick of myself."

Laura shrugged. "If it's really not helping at all, maybe you should stop."

He went to the window and looked out at the pines and spruces drooping over the ravine. Nona, he thought. It was a primally comforting name, the sort of name little children make up for their grandmothers or their stuffed animals. He was still standing there when Dave tapped on the open door and walked in.

Laura stood up and shook his hand. "Dave."

"Laura." He spoke with exaggerated politeness. (The first time he'd met her, Dave had gazed into Laura's eyes and said, "Laura. That's my daughter's name. But you know what I call her? Numb Nuts." "What a lovely nickname," Laura had replied, shaking his hand. Since then Dave had treated her with a kind of baffled, sweaty courtesy.) He held up a piece of paper, crumpling it slightly, shaking his fist. "I gotta tell you," he singsonged, looking back and forth between Jack and Laura. "I gotta tell you."

"What," Jack said, sitting down at the round table he'd installed in his office, in place of his father's old couch.

"Ten thousand units, first of next month."

"Who?"

"Rose Foods."

Jack put his hands on the table and let out a long breath. Rose Foods was one of the biggest distributors in the Midwest, supplying supermarkets and schools, and Dave had been courting them for months. This business, finally, would begin to make up for the loss of Sam Lowry's.

" 'Course, we won't *send* them ten thousand," Dave continued, dropping into a chair.

Jack frowned. "Can't we do it?"

"Sure, we could. But if we send them ten, they'll have product left over, and we won't look so great to them. I say send them eight, and let them beg for more."

"Isn't that how you got into trouble last time?" Laura asked. "Not coming through on your promises?"

Dave leaned toward her, grinning. She recoiled almost imperceptibly. "Ah, my dear lady, but I didn't promise. I told him demand is so hot right now that I could only promise him sixty-five hundred. He'll be happy to get eight." He blew on his finger and pretended to replace it in an imaginary holster, then sat back, his shiny face flushed and smiling.

"Well," Jack said slowly. "Sounds great." Thank God for Dave, he was thinking. I can't stand him, but he's smarter about this stuff than I am.

Now Laura was showing them sketches for the new logo and how it would work on new packaging. She'd been working on the designs at home, hunched over her drafting board in the study, but she hadn't shown them to Jack.

"What's that?" he asked now, pointing to a corner of the package.

"A potato plant."

"It's ugly. Get rid of it."

"I thought it helped to reinforce the message of 'all-natural.' "

"Then let's say 'all-natural' somewhere on the package. But that plant is weird-looking, and no one will know what it is anyhow."

"No problem," Laura said smoothly, moving on to the next layout.

He was being unusually brusque with her, but it had nothing to do with her, he thought. He couldn't keep his mind on her sketches, couldn't stop thinking about Rose Foods. That was a real achievement on Dave's part, and he had barely acknowledged it. So what am I supposed to do, pat him on the head? No, but like it or not, you're the boss.

"Excuse me a moment," he said to Laura, and pushed down the intercom button on his phone. "Mary? Can you come in here?"

When Mary appeared, her ubiquitous dingy cardigan slipping down from her thin shoulders, he handed her fifty dollars and his car keys. "Do me a favor," he said. "Do you mind going into town to the liquor store? And buy two bottles of good champagne." He looked at Dave. "One we'll drink now, and one you can take home to Nancy."

"Oh, boy," Mary said, adjusting her cardigan and scurrying out.

They watched her go. Laura drawled, "Don't you kind of feel like Perry White, and you've just given Jimmy Olson the chance to get his first big scoop?"

"She's been desperate for an assignment like this from the day I got here," Jack said. "I have to fight her off when it comes time to pick up my dry cleaning and I tell her I'd rather do it myself."

"Let her make you coffee tomorrow morning," Laura said. "Go on. Make her day."

"Then she can die happy," said Dave.

Jack shot him a look. Everyone knew about Mary's cancer. Was this a hapless slip of the tongue or a doltish attempt at wit? He could see a flash of distaste on Laura's face, too. Well, it didn't matter. He was going to drink champagne with Dave and think about a bonus. He couldn't afford to lose him now.

Laura stood up. "I'm just going to run to the ladies' room."

Dave watched her leave and then ran a hand over his hair and turned to Jack. "Boy," he said. "Wouldn't you like to have those legs wrapped around you?"

His birthday came: May 5. On his dinner plate was a package wrapped in corporate-looking gray paper. A fountain pen, with a gold point and a green swirled marble pattern down the barrel. "It's great," he told Laura, kissing her.

"My birthday was Monday," he told Nona. "And Maisie didn't send me presents!"

"You say it like it's a triumph of some sort."

"It is."

She'd sent a box at Christmas. Laura was with him when the UPS man came to the door; she'd looked over his shoulder to see who the package was from, and then she'd disappeared into the kitchen so that he could open it in private. He'd slit open the mailing box reluctantly but dutifully: it was probably something of his that Maisie still happened to have, books with his name on the flyleaf, or his silver christening mug, which she'd used for her makeup brushes. He'd pulled back the flaps and saw, nestled in shredded packing material, gift-wrapped packages, tasteful medieval-looking motifs balanced with funky, shiny, silk-screened artist gift-wrap, each package neatly labeled in Maisie's small handwriting "For Jack," as though he might not be certain for whom these presents were intended. He'd actually lifted the presents out of the box. A light oblong—clothing of some sort? A small cube, surprisingly heavy. Could be anything. And two that were clearly books. He ran his finger along the gentle indentation between cover and spine, before replacing them exactly as they'd been in the packing box. He slapped the flaps shut again and pushed the box away, with a muttered exclamation. Laura came to see what was wrong. "Christmas presents!" he said, and she looked thoughtful and then slowly shook her head, smiling a little. The memory of her expression helped to fortify him the next day, as he drove the box to the post office and sent it back to Virginia.

"It was so manipulative!" he said to Nona now. "She just wanted me to have to acknowledge her. And anyway, it was completely out of character."

"How do you mean?"

"We never gave each other presents."

"Never?"

"Well, not for Christmases and birthdays, anyway. We agreed that when we found something great for the other person, we'd buy it, but that we didn't have to tie the presents in to specific occasions."

Nona said gently, "You didn't expect much of each other, did you?"

He looked sideways, at the Matisse. "I don't know. I guess we felt that there were enough empty obligations in life—Christmas shopping, thank-you letters. We thought that if we loved each other, the least we could do was let each other off the hook."

"The way you and Laura do?"

"I suppose," he said dully.

On the drive back to Champs du Soleil, there were no rest stops, and he could feel all the coffee he'd drunk pressing inside him. He pulled the car off the road and walked down the grassy slope, flecked with buttercups, into the woods. He went in about a hundred feet; a friend of his, back in college, had once been arrested for indecent exposure, pissing innocently by the side of a road, and had had to cut his hair and shave his beard and go to court to convince a judge that this had been an isolated instance of deviant behavior.

The woods were cool and quiet; the canopy of fresh rustling leaves muffled the noise of the passing cars. As he was zipping up his pants, he heard another sound: a fuzzy, insectlike chirp. The moving trees made a confusing veil of light and shadow, and it took him several minutes, with his hand shading his eyes, before he saw it: a splash of red on the white branch of a birch. A scarlet tanager. That was one for the year's list. He wished he could see it more clearly, but his binoculars were in the office. He squinted at the bird again. Was its wing black, or not? If not, it could be a summer tanager, which would be something really extraordinary, almost a lifer. They never got this far up north; in fact, he'd only seen one once, in Virginia, the week before his wedding. "That?" Alice had said, surprised by his excitement as he'd pointed from her kitchen window. "We get those at the feeder all the time. I always thought they were cardinals."

And Maisie had pushed herself back from the breakfast table and come back in with a package. "Not a wedding present," she'd said, thrusting it toward him—telling him she didn't expect a wedding present from him.

It was a pair of binoculars, good ones. "I noticed your old ones seemed to have some sort of permanent condensation in one lens," she said.

He'd kissed her and looked at the summer tanager. The bird had seemed overly large and vivid, and he'd realized it would take him a while to get used to such powerful vision.

This bird in the birch was so far away that he'd never identify it definitively with his naked eye. And he couldn't record it on his list, either as a scarlet or summer tanager, unless he was sure. But he continued to stand in the woods, looking up, unable to relinquish the possibility of such a rare sighting. The yellow sun came sifting down through the trees, and he had to close his eyes. And he saw in his head, suddenly, the glowing yellow paper of the other list, the one he hadn't been able to do. Written on it in handwriting so faint that he could barely read it, let alone recognize it as his own, were the words: *I miss her.*

12

A Sensible Longing

She left Virginia like a refugee, secretly, at night. Dunnane had begun calling her in the middle of the night, making threats if he got her, hanging up if he got her mother. "Who is this? Who *is* this?" she heard her mother demanding weakly from across the hall at three o'clock one morning, and just as her mother's face looked faded and worn without her customary layers of makeup, so her voice sounded alarmingly old in the middle of the night. Maisie broke her rule of not speaking to Dunnane and called him back. "How dare you wake my mother?"

"Hey, I'm not getting any sleep. Why should she?"

"The point is, this is between you and me. You cannot harass my mother."

"Who's going to stop me?"

And it went on this way until Maisie hung up, and then there was a silence, and then the phone rang again.

"Maisie, what is going on with this man?" her mother demanded, quite reasonably, in the morning. She was neatly turned out now in a matching dotted blouse and skirt, her cheeks determinedly blushing pink, as though the weary old lady Maisie overheard in the night had been just a mirage.

"I don't know, Mom," Maisie said earnestly, shaking her head. Since casting Dunnane off, she'd been feeling wistful toward her mother, wanting to be the sort of daughter who shared things. "I just can't seem to make him understand that I don't want to see him anymore."

"Were you serious, with him?" her mother asked, frowning.

"Of course not."

Her mother half closed her eyes. "Well, you played with him, then. That's even worse."

Maisie opened the refrigerator door, looked in, and shut it again. "So what do I do?"

"Do you think he's dangerous?"

"I don't know," Maisie admitted. So far Dunnane's violence was all implied—the night phone calls, waiting in the Chrysler outside the bank when she came out and got into her mother's car, tailgating them as they drove home, and then speeding off when they turned into the driveway. But already he had her too scared to sleep—she was so afraid that she wouldn't be able to grab the phone before her mother did.

"I've got to get out of here anyway," she said to her mother; and Alice nodded.

"Will you go back to New York?"

Maisie shook her head. "Boston." She had a clear memory of herself in Cambridge, reading *Middlemarch* on a stone bench in a Radcliffe garden lined with blue iris. That was the clean point from which the mess of her life diverged. If she could get back to that, she could erase everything else. Nothing irrevocable would have happened to her. "It's more manageable, and besides, I can't descend on Caterina and Ed again."

"I wish there was something I could do."

"Well, thanks. But there isn't."

"And, you know, if there was, I'm not sure I would do it." She held her cup of coffee and stirred Sweet 'n Low into it, and watched Maisie. "You're twenty-eight, and you'd better start straightening out your life."

Maisie took the nine hundred dollars she had in the bank and went to a car dealer. He sold her a twelve-year-old Toyota that had a hole in the floor just to the left of the brake pedal; when she glanced down she saw the pavement rolling by beneath her. She left the night she bought the car and drove up through the mountains, around Washington and into Maryland. She didn't want to spend the money for a motel, but it didn't matter; she kept waiting to get tired, but she was so frightened and excited that she never did. Big trucks came and sandwiched her in, and she just kept looking straight ahead, at the white lines swarming toward her and the tangle of white headlights and red taillights stretching ahead of her to the horizon. In the morning, just outside New Haven, she pulled off the highway and into the parking lot outside a Greek diner, and she slept for two hours. When she woke up it was raining, opaque sheets of water slanting down from the sky. She got out of the car and ran to the diner, where she ate scrambled eggs and peppery orange home fries, waiting for the rain to stop. After four cups of coffee she paid her bill and dashed for the car again.

I am driving alone through a night and a day, she thought, and she remembered how in Maine she'd been afraid to get behind the wheel, even though Jack had offered to teach her and pointed out that there was hardly any traffic in their neighborhood. Now she was driving into blinding arcs of water thrown off by the car just in front of her, and more water was gushing up through the hole in the floor, soaking her feet. Her fingers were white, gripping the steering wheel; soon I'll have to bail, she thought. But when the rain let up, suddenly, around Hartford, she let out her breath and patted the dashboard. "Good car. *Good* little car."

Her old friend Nicky had a small apartment, which she never used, on the wrong side of Beacon Hill. She'd been living with her boyfriend for the past four years, but she hung on to the apartment just in case. Maisie, jumping up and down on the dusty doormat trying to knock down the key Nicky had left for her on top of the door frame, wondered how many apartments and houses there were, unlived in, maintained so that people wouldn't feel they were closing off options. She let herself in and traced the source of the stench that filled the rooms to an old carton of milk in the refrigerator. She poured it out, and while she was at it threw out a lemon and a pineapple, green and furred with mold.

"Educational background?" asked the woman who interviewed her, her pen poised over the answer space on the printed form. "Any special skills?"

Maisie answered the questions, looking at a print of Monet water lilies on the wall behind the interviewer. She didn't want to know a thing about the woman, didn't want to be curious about her. She wanted to go to work and get paid, that was all.

"How fast do you type?"

"Seventy words a minute," she said, hoping it was still true.

"Word processing?"

"I've used a Macintosh."

"But not an IBM?"

"No."

"And why are you seeking temporary employment?"

"Because I won't have to work more than once for people I don't like, and if they don't like me, I'll never know," Maisie said without thinking. The woman looked up at her. "Oh," Maisie added hastily. "And because I'm interested in a wide variety of work experiences."

The interviewer stared at Maisie, then shook her head and laughed and wrote something down on the form. She was wearing a charm bracelet that clanked softly as her wrist rose and fell.

"What do most people say when you ask them that question?" Maisie asked.

"Most people talk about how they're writing a dissertation and need extra money, or they're putting their husband through med school, or their kids just went off to school and they're at loose ends."

"Oh."

The woman tapped her pen on her desk, which was very neat but crowded with things: pencils with birthday cakes and hearts mounted on them instead of erasers, a large scallop shell with rolling plastic eyes, outstretched arms, and a sign that said: I LOVE YOU THIS MUCH, a plastic snow dome with a flamingo and a palm tree inside, a coffee mug with an intricate pattern of rabbits copulating, and a picture of a dimpled toddler laughing in a red-bordered frame made to look like a *Time* magazine cover, with BABY OF THE YEAR printed on it. There was also a black-and-white nameplate, which Maisie, against her will, found herself looking at: KRISTINE PINEDA. "I don't know what to put you down for. We have these specialties—word processing, front desk—" She had a very slight Spanish accent, a furry edge to all her words.

"Don't you have one that's just called 'miscellaneous'?"

"Not really. We like to make our temps feel like specialists. We like them all to have a sensible longing."

A sensible longing for what? Maisie wondered. A longing to get ahead? To have some expertise in something, even if it was something as nebulous and dreary as "front desk"? She hoped Kristine Pineda wasn't going to ask about her longings, with the aim of crisply determining whether they were sensible or not.

"Is that your baby?" she asked, pointing to the *Time* magazine frame. Kristine Pineda nodded and smiled, her strong, haughty face dimpling. "That's Jared. He's two." Maisie suddenly felt that she looked familiar.

"But your hair is different," Maisie said slowly. "You used to wear it pulled back, in a bun."

"How do you know?"

"And you have a daughter named Felicia." Then she noticed that Kristine Pineda was looking alarmed, so she said, "I used to see you on the train in the mornings."

"But how do you know my daughter's name?" This was a demand.

"Because once she wore a beaded belt that spelled out FELICIA," Maisie said, thinking that she had now certainly blown her chances for ever getting called by this temp agency. Oh, well, there must be others. She'd check the Yellow Pages as soon as she left here, start making a list. And order herself to be bland and discreet during all her interviews.

"I remember that belt," Kristine Pineda said. "But that was a long time ago. We got that at a roadside stand in Arizona, when Felicia was like seven."

"How old is she now?"

"She's twelve." Kristine was speaking automatically, still with that frightened look in her eyes. She looked the way Maisie had felt once when she'd been getting dressed in her room at Caterina and Ed's and she'd seen a man watching her from the apartment across the back alley, and she'd realized, groping for a towel, the light switch, that he might have been watching her for months, that she'd been visible all that time.

"I used to have a whole group of regulars I would watch for on the train," Maisie said, trying to sound harmless, sociological. "You, and this really gorgeous old lady who always had on pearl earrings and white gloves. And a baby who wore glasses, who always came with his father. They would share slices of apple out of a plastic bag. And there was a nervous little man in a trench coat who I always thought of as the Dostoyevskian civil servant."

Kristine Pineda smiled a little.

"You and your daughter looked so nice. She was always asking you questions and you would answer them. I don't know." I'm sorry, she felt like adding.

Kristine Pineda stood up and held out her hand. "Well, I'll call you if anything miscellaneous comes up," she said.

Her voice sounded warm, but Maisie left feeling dubious. On the other hand, she thought, she'll definitely remember me. To her surprise, Kristine called her at eight the next morning, to send her to work in a dentist's office; the regular receptionist had called in sick and ended up in bed for a week, so Maisie went back several times and pruned the plants and the grubby collection of magazines and got down on the floor and colored with small children who were waiting for their appointments and turning pale at the sound of the drill.

"Dr. Badookian really liked you," Kristine said at the end of a week. "Any interest in a permanent job there?"

"No thanks," Maisie said.

She worked in an auto showroom, taking people's names when they walked in the door and asking them to sit on the blue plastic chairs to wait for the first available sales representative. She offered them coffee and gave them brochures on the cars they were interested in, and bent to murmur the dealer cost into their ears, so that they'd know what to bargain for. During the month she was there, the dealership sold more cars than they ever had before, and though the owner shook his head at the profit margins, he had to admit that they were making up for it in sheer volume. He was a genial old man with a heavy Boston accent, and he said, "We can offah you a puuhmanent job, if you like."

"Oh, thank you so much," Maisie said. "But no."

She went from one temp job to another, and soon she felt confident enough of her ability to earn a basic living that she began to look for an apartment. The place she found was just outside Harvard Yard, in a building with turrets and an enormous swooping stairway modeled after the one in the Paris Opera. Maisie's apartment was in the basement, one room and a bathroom. There were bars on the window and feet walking by all day, and a noisy freshman dormitory across the street; but it was rent-controlled. And it was the first place she'd ever lived in by herself. She liked the fact that she had so few possessions, and was free to decide where each of them should go. She put her table in the curve of the bow window and covered it with a cloth one of her college boyfriends had brought back from West Africa. She found a secondhand futon through an ad on the Harvard Book Store bulletin board, and used it as a couch during the day and a bed at night. She stacked orange crates next to the two-burner stove: one for dishes, one for pots, one for books. Her clothes all fit into the tiny closet: the blouses and skirts she wore to work, and the jeans and T-shirts she wore the rest of the time. She still had a lot of stuff stored in Jack's house, and someday she would have to go up there to claim it; but for now she was enjoying living like a student again: unencumbered.

Two weeks after she moved, she got a phone call from Caterina. "I thought I'd come up and see you for a few days, if that's okay."

"Sure," said Maisie, looking around the apartment and wondering where Caterina would sleep. "Are you all right?"

"Not really," Caterina said. "I'll tell you when I see you."

She came the next evening. Maisie was setting the table for the two of them to have supper when she saw the cab pull up outside her window. The driver came around to open the door, and then there was a flailing of arms and legs: Caterina struggling to emerge, holding the baby, prodding Ellie to get out before her.

"Kayo me! Kayo!" Ellie was pleading, her arms reaching up to Caterina, when Maisie got there.

"I'll carry you," she suggested to Ellie, who started to wail and clung still more tightly to Caterina's legs.

The taxi driver, who had unloaded an alarming number of canvas suitcases, stood patiently at the curb while Caterina fumbled with her handbag.

"Give me the baby, then," Maisie said, reaching for him. He was bald, with a dark silent gaze, dressed in denim overalls and a red-and-white-striped shirt. He came to her willingly, but he kept his eyes on Caterina. "Hey, Evan," Maisie said to him, stroking his arm lightly with her finger. "Ellie, do you remember me?" But Ellie frowned and tucked her head between Caterina's legs.

"Oh, well," Maisie said.

Caterina, holding her hand out for change from the driver, said, "Come on, Ellie, you remember Maisie."

"It doesn't matter."

"No, no, she remembers. All the way up here on the train she kept saying, 'Maisie? We see *Maisie?*' As if she couldn't believe her luck. Thanks," she said to the driver, who got quickly into his cab and drove off. "Ellie, this is *Maisie.*" She tried to turn Ellie's head.

"That's okay," Maisie said again. The baby was getting heavy. "Why don't you go in with the kids, and I'll bring the bags," handing Evan over to Caterina. "The door's open. It's the third one on the left, on the street side."

Caterina hobbled off, Evan slung against one shoulder, Ellie clinging to the other hand. Maisie surveyed the baggage strewn over the brick sidewalk. If she took the Port-a-Crib in one hand and the two big canvas bags in the other, she could wear the diaper bag over her shoulder and get it all in one trip.

"Oh, God," Caterina said when Maisie came staggering into the apartment.

"What." Maisie dumped the bags on the floor.

"You didn't tell me it was this small."

You didn't tell me you were bringing your children, Maisie thought, but she shrugged.

Ellie was running in and out of the bathroom, laughing each time she emerged and each time she disappeared. "I see you, I see you," Caterina said automatically, watching Evan, who was crawling purposefully toward the windows. She swooped over and caught him just as he grabbed for the tablecloth. "Well, I would never have descended on you with these guys if I'd known," she said, her voice sounding close to tears.

"Listen, it's okay," Maisie said with an emphatic calm she didn't even recognize. She stood for a moment with her hands on her hips. "I don't think we should even try to have dinner here. Would Ellie like a hamburger?"

"Hooray!" Ellie shouted.

Caterina grinned shakily. "You can tell this is a child who's been read to. How else does a two-year-old know to shout 'hooray'?"

"So we'll go into the Square and get a hamburger," Maisie continued, "and then we'll come home, put these guys to b-e-d, and figure out how to childproof the apartment."

"Okay, but we're only staying a day or two," Caterina said, pulling a changing pad and a big box of wipes out of the diaper bag.

"Don't you feel like we're going to get caught at any minute, and put on probation?" Maisie asked. She was sitting cross-legged on the chipped tile floor of the bathroom holding a glass of wine, and Caterina was on the toilet lid. The bottle, which they'd just opened, was on the floor between them.

"Probation, nothing," Caterina said. "We'd have been kicked out."

"What did you think, that first time you walked into our room and saw me with my bottle of Drambuie?" Maisie continued. In this bright light, with the children out of the way and sleeping in the next room, she was getting her first good look at Caterina. She hadn't lost the weight she'd put on with Evan. The flesh that hung from her upper arm shook heavily when she reached for the glass she'd balanced on the rim of the sink. Even her hair seemed puffy. But the worst thing was her face, doughy and jowly and grayish. It reminded Maisie of something.

"I thought you were bad," Caterina said darkly, and then Maisie knew: Caterina looked like Nixon, right before he resigned. "I thought you were weak and flaky and self-indulgent, and I couldn't believe I was going to have to live in the same room with you for a whole year."

Maisie smiled. Why was it so comforting to have this conversation with Caterina about how much they'd hated each other at first? They had it every time they saw each other, a warm-up ritual to other, more important talk. "Well, I thought you were a snob."

"A snob!" Caterina hooted. "With all those rich kids in that school? What did I have to be a snob about?"

"A moral snob. You were a snob about your own goodness."

"That's true," Caterina admitted.

"But then you sat down and drank with me. Why did you?"

"Oh, I don't know. I'd just tried out for that play, and I got up on stage and realized everyone else was a better actress, and you were nice to me about it." She put her glass back on the sink and sat with her big legs apart, her hands hanging between them, twisting.

"You look kind of tired," Maisie said gently.

"I know."

"Maybe it would be good for you and Ed to get away for a weekend. You know. Without kids."

"A weekend wouldn't be long enough."

Maisie didn't say anything.

Caterina said, "You must think I'm a spoiled bitch. Here I am with this nice husband and these nice kids, complaining."

"You're not complaining. You haven't said anything."

"No, but you know why I'm here. You know this isn't just a fun visit."

"You and Ed haven't broken up," Maisie asked, keeping her eyes down, but her heart was beginning to beat faster. Shut up, shut up, she said to it. If Caterina's marriage split up, then she'd be in the same boat as Maisie, and then she'd see. Shut up.

"Of course not," Caterina said, sounding genuinely horrified.

"Good," Maisie said.

"He's my *family.*" Her tone was offended, but she opened her eyes wide and looked at Maisie pleadingly, as if for confirmation. Then she started to talk. "He's gotten on this fast track at work, trying to make partner. He gets home after I've gone to bed, and he leaves for work before I'm awake in the morning. I mean, he is never home. Even when he says he's going to be home, he's not home. So finally I said, 'It wouldn't hurt you to call, would it?' So then he has his *secretary* call, to tell me he's not going to be home." She tightened her mouth. "It's like this fifties marriage. I'm home all day cleaning, and watching 'Sesame Street,' and making homemade Play-Doh. I mean, how did this happen? One of the reasons I married Ed is that he wasn't like that, he believed everything should be equal."

"Have you talked to him about it?"

"Of course I have! He agrees it stinks, he thinks it's disgusting that he should have to work so hard, that he'd be penalized if he didn't work so hard, and then he goes right back the next morning and I don't see him again for a week."

Maisie poured some more wine into Caterina's glass. "Maybe you should think about getting a job. At least a part-time one."

Caterina smiled evilly. "Oh, no, we agreed that it's very important to have a parent home with the kids."

"He was home a lot with Ellie, that year I was living with you."

"Well, that was before he took this new job. He even sat down with me before he took it, and we had this whole talk. About how it was going to be tough on me to be home all the time with no help, but wasn't it lucky that we'd spaced our kids so close together, they'd both be in school before we knew it. And anyway, I said, this is such a fun age. I wouldn't want to miss one minute of it." She swallowed some wine. "Well, here's what it's like. I realize there isn't any apple juice in the house, and Ellie's screaming for it. How about some orange juice? I ask. Apple apple apple! she screams. So I scream back at her to stop being such a rotten little brat, and she gets this look on her face so I say, All right, let's go to the store. I get one kid dressed and the other kid poops, and by the time I get that changed the other one's done it. Then I look out the window and I realize it's snowing, and I have to stuff them both into their snowsuits. And their boots and gloves and hats. Which it turns out I've left in the stroller, in the basement. By the time I get them both into the stroller, they've started screaming for lunch, but there's no way I'm turning back now. So we go to the supermarket and Ellie screams for lunch the whole time, and she screams when we pass the bagels so I give her one and she takes one bite and throws it away, and then we get to the juice aisle and I get the bottle of apple juice and she screams, No, the box! So I stand there telling her I'm getting the bottle, not the box, and she's screaming bloody murder and all these old ladies are walking by shaking their heads at me, so finally I give in and get the damned box, and all the ladies shake their heads at me for saying no and then giving in. So then she drinks some and pulls out the straw and throws it on the floor, and then ten seconds later she says she wants more and I say No, because you threw your straw on the floor and now it's dirty, and she screams she wants more! She wants more! And finally I get through the checkout line and she's still screaming and everyone's looking at me like I'm a terrible mother and then I see that Evan's fallen asleep right there in the cart, which means he won't nap in the afternoon, and I pull him out and his booties fall off on the floor of the supermarket." She took a deep breath. "And then I call to arrange a baby-sitter for the following morning, so I can have a few hours to myself, and when I tell Ed that night he says, 'You're leaving the children with a stranger?' "

"Boy," Maisie said, and then, "Well, but Caterina, you're wonderful with them. You really are."

"I know I am," Caterina said grimly. "They're not the problem. They're babies, they're acting the way babies act. Ed's the problem."

"Why doesn't he understand that you need some relief?"

" 'You're leaving the children with a stranger?' I couldn't believe that. I said, 'Would you rather have them with a stranger or a crazy person?' and he said, 'Who's the crazy person?' and I said, 'I am.' "

"Well, you just get yourself a sitter. The hell with how he feels." But be careful, she told herself, Caterina never said anything really nasty about Jack the whole time our marriage was breaking up. Don't criticize Ed.

"I can't just say the hell with how he feels. I get this disapproval from him."

"That's ridiculous. It's not like you want to dump the kids in some twenty-four-hour day care center and leave them there till they're eighteen. You just want some breathing room."

"We used to talk about moving to Vermont," Caterina said, leaning down for the wine bottle. "We were going to buy an old farmhouse, grow vegetables, have a bunch of horses. Our kids were going to see the seasons change, know about nature—all that crap. Everybody talks that way when they first fall in love, I guess. Only we really believed it." She set the bottle back down. "And Ed still believes it."

"Ed does? Then what's he doing in a Wall Street law firm?"

"Because, as he puts it, we came smack up against the brick wall of reality." She drank. "I'd like to smack *him*."

For some reason this, out of Caterina's mouth, struck Maisie as unbearably funny. She started to laugh and couldn't stop, glancing guiltily at Caterina through teary eyes. Caterina was laughing, too.

When they stopped laughing Caterina swirled the wine in her glass and said, "But you don't think I'm a bitch?"

"What, because you and Ed are fighting?"

"No, because just being home with the kids is driving me nuts."

Maisie shrugged. "It sounds honest."

Caterina poured more wine into Maisie's glass. "To me it's like natural childbirth. I was really militant about going through it with no drugs, and then in the middle of it, I thought, What is this? Would I have an appendectomy without anesthesia? And come to think of it, I had a fight with Ed. In the middle of labor. I'm saying, Give me the epidural, and Ed is saying he wants it to be all natural."

"Oh, Caterina."

"What?"

"I never knew you got so angry about things." Maisie said it sadly, and she was sorry for Caterina; but she drank more wine and the little bathroom reeled. She thought: For once it's not me complaining and Caterina being wise.

"It must seem like a pretty dinky set of things to get angry about." Caterina reached for the wine bottle.

"No, it doesn't."

"I mean, I sound like I've been *hoarding* all these things, just stewing about them for months. But it hasn't been that way, really. I love Ed, I'm happy with my kids. I think if I could just find some time to get some painting done, or there's this silk screen I've been wanting to work on. . . ." She trailed off.

"So, but was there a particular *thing* that made you want to get away for a few days?" Maisie asked. Suddenly she wanted reassurance that that was all it was: Caterina fleeing for a few days, nothing more.

"You mean one big moment?" Caterina thought. "No," she said finally, and this made them both smile.

Caterina poured more wine into Maisie's glass and emptied the bottle into her own.

"Hey," said Caterina. "You're not smoking."

Maisie shook her head. "I quit. I hope."

"What made you stop, finally?"

Maisie shrugged. She didn't feel like talking about Dunnane, but he was the reason she'd stopped. The two of them had smoked all the time, at breakfast, at dinner, in bed, passing cigarettes back and forth, lighting new ones off the dying old ones. There were overflowing ashtrays all over Dunnane's apartment; wherever she went she kicked one over, or knocked one accidentally from a table. When she thought back to those months now, she saw them enveloped in smoke, flapping at it ineffectually with their hands while they lit up and made more. The smoke was what she'd walked out of when she left Virginia.

"So what's going on with you and Jack? Anything?"

"Not much." Maisie got to her feet to go after another bottle of wine. "We talk from time to time, but it's always about something practical. The taxes, or something like that." In fact, Jack hadn't called her in months, even about a practical thing, but Caterina didn't have to know that.

The next morning the temp agency sent her out to Somerville, to work for a woman named Liliana Vardaro. "*Doctor* Vardaro," she said, opening the downstairs door of a triple-decker and motioning Maisie into the first-floor apartment. She was at least seventy, with dyed red hair pulled back into an excruciatingly tight bun, and she wore a black leotard, tights, and brand-new-looking white sneakers. Behind her, on a big television screen, Jane Fonda in a leotard said, "Okay, everybody, let's wash the windows. Around and around like this. Great exercise, washing windows."

"Sure, Jane," Dr. Vardaro said to the screen. "You wash windows all the time. That's a good one." Then she turned to Maisie and said, "You work out?"

"Not enough," Maisie said.

"You should. You think you have the figure, and then one day you don't. I used to be tiny like you. You believe me?"

She still had sticklike arms and legs, but the middle part of her body looked like Humpty-Dumpty. "I go to the video store every day and rent one of these tapes." She turned to the screen and began a halfhearted imitation of Jane Fonda's movements. "I've done 'em all—Callanetics, Kathy Smith, Raquel Welch, even . . . what do you call them? those

Playboy videos. Only those weren't about exercise, as you might guess." She turned to grin at Maisie. "Let's be honest, I knew they weren't about exercise when I rented 'em. I was curious, like anyone else."

"Hula!" commanded Jane Fonda.

"Sit, sit," said Dr. Vardaro, hulaing and waving her hands at a soiled cream-colored brocade sofa piled with books and newspapers. "You can watch me while I finish." She hulaed off in the other direction while Maisie gingerly shifted things to make room for herself on the couch.

"This tape I like," Dr. Vardaro said, panting a little now, "because it has a subversive on it."

"A subversive?"

"A guy in the back row who tries to make trouble for Jane. Makes funny noises, does the steps wrong. Probably on drugs or something. Jane tries to act like she thinks it's funny, only she's really uptight, it really bothers her. You'll see."

Maisie saw, sitting there for the next twenty minutes, aware of her own meter ticking as though she were a taxicab. Did Dr. Vardaro really want to pay her to sit here and watch Jane Fonda? She also saw that the apartment was truly filthy. The venetian blinds, shut tight against the sun, were black with grime. Books and papers and clothes were everywhere, mixed in with other, odder objects: an upturned colander, a miniature garden rake, the thick pieces of a broken seventy-eight record, a Chock Full o'Nuts can lying on its side and spilling out fabric loops that looked like the ones Maisie had used to make pot holders at camp. The table in the corner was piled with dirty dishes, an open ketchup bottle, an open jar of grape jelly; on the floor beneath it were three half-eaten TV dinners, the meat gone, a few peas and carrots congealed in white gravy and clinging to the foil sides. There was a sharp pissy smell that Maisie recognized from Jack's mother's house, only this was ten times worse: the smell of cat. The cats themselves were right there in the room, but it took her a few minutes to see them, like objects in an Escher print. There were three of them, four—no, five—hunched here and there on the floor, unbudgeable and randomly scattered like houses in a suburb that hadn't yet been landscaped. The beige carpet (it was ridgy, like a topographical map, and it made her nervous to look at it, and then she remembered: it was the same kind of carpet Dunnane had had, only his was green) was stained and encrusted with something reddish brown that Maisie realized was cat food, and with hairballs that looked like miniature tumbleweeds.

"You want some coffee?" Dr. Vardaro called out, lifting her knees.

"No thanks," Maisie said; she was afraid to go into the kitchen.

Finally Dr. Vardaro said, "There!" and switched off the TV. "Now I can feel virtuous all the rest of the day." She smiled at Maisie, and Maisie smiled back, suddenly liking her.

"The agency said you needed secretarial help?" she hinted, not wanting Dr. Vardaro to waste any more money while she sat around.

"Well, yes, that's part of it," Dr. Vardaro said, squatting down creakily to stroke one of the cats between the ears. The cat didn't move, just blinked wearily. "I'm working on a book, you know? Did they tell you that?"

"Yes, they did mention it," Maisie said. What Kris had actually said to her was: This woman may be a bit of a nut. I don't know. She talked my ear off for half an hour about sex and some kind of all-grains diet and the postmenopausal woman. I'm sure she's harmless, but if she's at all weird, just *leave,* okay?

"Well, maybe we'll do some work on it later, but first, I thought if you didn't mind, you might do some tidying up in here." She kept her head down, saying this, kneading the loose skin of the cat's neck, and then she looked up at Maisie. "I know you weren't hired to clean, but if I'd told them what I really wanted, you wouldn't have come."

"There are cleaning services," Maisie said, as gently as she could.

"Yeah, rip-offs," Dr. Vardaro said scornfully. "They charge twenty-five bucks an hour, and your agency will send me a college graduate for ten. Besides, that's what I want, a college graduate. Anybody can vacuum. I want someone who can vacuum and *talk.*"

"I don't know if I can vacuum and talk at the same time," Maisie said. "I can vacuum and scream, if you want." Somehow, it seemed, she was agreeing to clean this woman's house.

Dr. Vardaro laughed and punched Maisie in the arm. "And you're funny! Ten bucks an hour—a bargain!"

When she left Dr. Vardaro's at six (she had stayed an extra hour, and when Dr. Vardaro had worried aloud about whether overtime was extra, Maisie waved her arm grandly and said, "No charge"), it was still light out and there was a soft evening wind blowing, fluttering the new leaves in the spindly sidewalk trees. Without consciously deciding to, she started walking home. The wind was behind her, blowing her hair around her face and giving her little pushes as she walked. Blowing the dirt of the day away from her. She had done the best she could, but she hadn't managed to make much of a dent in the apartment. Dr. Vardaro hadn't minded. She'd followed Maisie from room to room, watched her scrubbing the bathtub and swirling tubful after tubful of gray, cleanser-laced water down the drain, and when the tub was still black after forty-five minutes Dr. Vardaro had said, "Enough! Move on to the sink!" as though Maisie were a game show contestant stumped by one category, needing to cut her losses and go on to the next.

While she worked, Dr. Vardaro talked. She had taught high school biology in Italy before the war, had fled to America with her husband, who was Jewish, and gotten a master's degree in nutrition. "So I call myself a doctor," she said. "So what." She told Maisie that knowing so much about nutrition was a burden. "You think I follow my own advice? You're crazy. When I was in practice I spend all day telling the fat ladies how to eat and then I come home and have doughnuts for supper. So now I write this book. Grains and old ladies and the libido. And me with a freezer full of Sara Lee." By the end of the day she'd gotten curious about Maisie, peering at her. "So you married?"

"Separated," Maisie said, stuffing the gray sheets she'd pulled off Dr. Vardaro's bed into a pillowcase. She could say it easily now, it didn't make her teary the way it once had.

"But not divorced?"

"No."

"Well, as long as you're not divorced, there's hope. Me, I've been a widow since 1968."

"That must have been hard."

"Terrible. I still miss him. Which is not to say there haven't been guys in the meantime," holding up an emphatic index finger puffed and warped with arthritis, "but no one who counts."

"I miss my husband, too," Maisie said.

"Of course," said the doctor.

The last thing Maisie did, and the worst, was to vacuum the living room. Dr. Vardaro's ancient Electrolux coughed and retched as Maisie dragged it back and forth over the carpet, and she looked at the machine with sympathy: she knew just how it felt. The cats didn't move, even when the vacuum cleaner came perilously close to them. "Just go around them," Dr. Vardaro shouted. The carpet, when she finished, was still stained, and there were still some spots that were hopelessly encrusted, but the beige had lightened by several shades, and she realized, putting away the Electrolux and glancing involuntarily into its black furry mouth, that she'd vacuumed up a veil of cat hair dating back God knew how long. When she backed out of the broom closet Dr. Vardaro was scooping cat food from cans into bowls. "Here," she said, handing two of the bowls to Maisie and taking three herself. "They're so fat and lazy they won't even come into the kitchen to eat," and she took the bowls into the living room and put one in front of each cat. The cats slowly opened their eyes and mouths and began to eat, dribbling food onto the newly cleaned carpet.

"I'd better go," Maisie said.

"Next time bring your leotard," Dr. Vardaro said, walking her to the door.

She was halfway home before she remembered Caterina and the children, waiting in her apartment. She sprinted to Porter Square, caught a bus to Harvard, and ran home from there, feeling as though she were running from one kind of chaos to another. But when she got there, the apartment was surprisingly tranquil. Caterina was in the bathroom, and both children were in the tub, playing with Maisie's plastic measuring cups. "Jack called," Caterina said.

"What?"

"Jack."

"Jack Eldridge?" Maisie stood there, still short of breath from running, her face in the mirror flushed, her hair wild, and she thought, I knew it, I knew he'd come back. "How about that," she said, letting her raincoat slide from her shoulders and tossing it across the room to the futon. "Did he say what he wanted?"

"To me? Of course not."

"Am I supposed to call him back?"

"Yes, but not till tomorrow. At first he said he'd call you, but then when I explained you were temping, he said you should call him at the office. After ten, or before ten, or something. I wrote it down." She began to get to her feet.

"That's all right," Maisie said, motioning her down again. "No rush."

She went into the other room, which was strewn with the children's things but which looked to her wonderfully, miraculously clean, and she knelt before the tiny refrigerator and found the second bottle of wine, the one they hadn't gone all the way through last night. Caterina had been shopping, she saw; the refrigerator was stocked with more healthy food than she bought in a year: oranges and miniature rice cakes, muesli and broccoli and goat cheese. She poured herself a glass of wine and saw, on the table next to the telephone, the slip of paper on which Caterina had written the message: "Jack. After ten." And then Jack's office number. He doesn't want Laura to know he called me, she thought triumphantly.

"Maisie," Caterina said, coming heavily into the room. "Don't get your hopes up."

Maisie shrugged, annoyed. "Did Ed call?" she asked, quietly, so the children wouldn't hear.

"No," Caterina said.

The next morning, when Kris called to send her out on another job, Maisie said she was sick.

"Gee, I'm sorry," Kris said. "And what did you do to that Vardaro woman?"

"Do to her?"

"She loved you. She called me already. The phone was ringing when I came into the office. She said it was like having Groucho Marx for a secretary."

"I think she's overstating things a little," Maisie said.

"Well, whatever, she said she wanted you to come back next week. I said I didn't know if you'd be available." Then she added sheepishly, "She was a nut, I guess, huh."

"Kind of, but a nice nut."

"Well, listen, Maisie, take care of yourself. Is there anything I can do?"

"No thanks," Maisie said, surprised. "I'm sure it's just one of those twenty-four-hour things."

"Okay, well, call me as soon as you're ready to work again."

"Sure," Maisie promised.

She hung up and looked at her watch. It was a quarter to nine. She'd worn the watch all night, jolting awake every half hour or so to check its crawling luminous dial, trying to match her breathing to Caterina's, lying next to her in bed. Still over an hour until she could call him. She wanted a cigarette. Think of Dunnane, what he looked like with a butt hanging out of his mouth, flipping up and down when he talked. Wet, nicotine-tasting kisses. She went to the refrigerator instead, got out a carton of pineapple yogurt, stuck a spoon in it, and left it there. Not hungry.

"We're going to the playground now," Caterina said, straightening up from changing Evan's diaper on the folded futon.

"There's a playground near here?" Maisie asked in surprise.

"Right in front of the library."

"Oh, yeah," Maisie said slowly. She'd never noticed it, though she'd been to the library several times. And Caterina had found it in a day and a half. Children must make you develop a kind of radar.

She helped Caterina finish dressing the children and put shoes on Ellie, who said, "Playground."

"That's right, you're going to the playground!" said Maisie, amazed and flattered that Ellie had addressed a remark to her. But her enthusiasm was too much: Ellie recoiled suspiciously. Maisie carefully ignored her then and began washing the breakfast dishes in the sink. Caterina opened the door to leave, and Ellie darted back to tell Maisie one more thing.

"We going to sing."

"Sing?"

"No, *sing*."

"Swing," said Caterina.

"Oh, great. Have fun," Maisie said casually, smiling over her head at Caterina, who seemed to be carrying nearly as much baggage to the park as she'd come with. She looked so laden down, with Evan in the stroller and Ellie clinging to her hand, and the diaper bag over her shoulder. And it was so tactful of her to get out of the apartment now.

"I'll miss you," Maisie said as they left.

"Maisie," Jack said.

She didn't say anything. He wanted to talk to her, let him talk.

"How are you?"

"Pretty good. I moved," she said, "but you know that. How did you get this number?"

"From your mother."

"Oh." She wondered what kind of conversation they'd had.

"Caterina's there with you."

"Just for a visit." Maisie hesitated, and then said, "I guess she and Ed have been having some trouble."

"Serious trouble?"

"They're not splitting up, if that's what you mean."

"Oh. Good."

"So," she said, "how are you?"

"Fine."

"And"—in a slightly higher voice—"Laura? How's she?"

"She's fine."

Silence. Now, she thought, is when I would light up. The telephone cord was long enough to get her across the small room, all the way to the closet. Maybe there was a half-smoked pack somewhere, forgotten, in a compartment of her handbag or a jacket pocket. She rummaged, and sure enough, there in her winter coat was a pack with three cigarettes left, crumpled, leaking tobacco crumbs, but still smokable. No matches, though. No matches in the whole damn apartment. She backed over to the stove, turned on one of the burners, and held the tip of the cigarette over the flame, tapping her thumb on the filter end to create a draft. She got so engrossed that she jumped and nearly burned her hand when Jack spoke.

"Listen, I want to see you."

"What?" She flipped off the burner and put the cigarette between her lips, taking a deep drag. But it was awful, nauseating, like the first cigarette she'd ever smoked, in the woods behind the junior high school.

"I said, I want to see you." It was an angry, between-gritted-teeth voice that she'd never heard from him before.

She blew out a dizzying cloud of smoke and leaned her elbows on the table, trying to breathe. "Why?" she said.

"Do you want to see me or don't you?" he asked in the same voice.

"Yes," she said.

"All right."

"When?"

"This weekend."

"Oh," she said.

"What?"

"I don't know if I can."

"Why not?" he said, even more sharply.

"It's just that I don't know how long Caterina is planning to stay, and I can't kick her out."

The cigarette was still burning in her hand, and she looked down at it. The thought of another drag made her sick, but it was a precious thing, one of only three she had left. She held on to it and tapped the hanging ash off into the sink.

He said after a moment, "Then maybe we should talk again in a few days."

"Okay," Maisie said. Without thinking she drew on the cigarette again, and then she did smash it out, hard, on the floor of the sink, coughing out smoke. When she stopped coughing she said, "Can you tell me what this is about? Please? If you want to talk about getting divorced, will you just tell me and not leave me hanging until we see each other?"

"I don't want to get divorced. Not yet, anyhow."

"Oh."

"But I'm not making any promises, either," he said, and she agreed: "No."

"So I'll call you back sometime soon."

"Fine," she said, and she hung up the phone, exhausted. She wanted to smoke but she still felt sick from smoking. She went and lay on the futon (in its couch mode it was too short, she had to curl up with her knees and neck bent), and looked out at the sky, but the sight of the big clouds rolling by made her queasy. After a few minutes she went to the phone and called Kris, and said she was feeling better and was willing to work today, if Kris had anything for her.

Kris said, "Oh, boy, am I glad you called. Have you ever taught aerobics?"

At the end of the day she went by the temp office to pick up her check for the week. Kris, putting a plastic cover over her computer, said, "So how was it?"

"Not bad." She'd taken aerobics classes with another editorial assistant in New York, but she'd never taught before, and she was proud of herself for still being on her feet. "When I went, 'Wooooooo!' halfway through my classes, they went 'Wooooo!' back. What a relief."

"So you passed the Woooo test," Kris said, handing her the check. She poured what was left in her coffee mug into the philodendron on the windowsill and hurried back to her desk. Maisie, admiring the long line of her head and neck, her brown glowing skin, watched her rummage in her purse for a fistful of coins, pluck out a subway token, and put it into the pocket of her flowered skirt.

"Are you doing anything special this weekend?" Maisie asked.

Kris smiled. "Arturo's birthday. I've got him taking the baby out for pizza tonight, so Felicia and I can make a cake. Of course he doesn't suspect a thing."

"Of course," Maisie said. She picked up a troll doll from the corner of the desk and ran her fingers absently through its fluffy purple hair. "Can I ask you something?"

"Sure," Kris said, opening a compact and swiveling up her lipstick.

"When you interviewed me you said you wanted all your temps to have a sensible longing."

"Uh-huh." She outlined her mouth in coral.

"A sensible longing for what?"

"What do you mean, for what?"

"I mean, what do you want them to long for? And why sensible?"

Kris closed the compact and stared at her. *"What?"*

"How can a longing be sensible? Do you think people can learn to long only for what's good for them?"

"Maisie," Kris said. "I said, a sense . . . of . . . belonging." She bared her teeth, stretching out the words, and kept them bared, grinning expectantly and lifting her eyebrows twice, quickly.

"Oh," said Maisie.

On the way home she passed a new clothing store that had enormous helium balloons flying out front, anchored to a sandwich board that said GRAND OPENING TODAY. She went inside and asked if they were about to close, and the saleswoman, who had red hair and freckles and wore a white sari, said they were.

"Then could I take home two of those balloons for my kids?"

"Oh, I don't know."

"Come on," said Maisie. "The helium's going to die overnight. You wouldn't be able to use them tomorrow anyhow."

"Okay," said the saleswoman.

Maisie watched as she rummaged in the drawer for scissors. "How was the grand opening? Did you have much business?"

"Not much."

"Oh, well, that's because the students have mostly gone home. Wait till summer school starts. You'll get people then." She was dawdling, she realized. She was afraid to go home, afraid that the phone would ring, that Jack would call again and talk to her in that rough voice. And she was afraid that she might say something to make him change his mind about seeing her. Until he called her again, she would be floating in her apartment, and then his call would come and pin her to the wall. If he called at all. Suddenly, she was certain that he wouldn't call back. He would regret what he'd done and decide to withdraw, silently. Or he would tell Laura, and she would give him an ultimatum. If Maisie called him, he would be embarrassed, and he'd apologize brusquely and then hang up.

"I want the blue one and the green one," she told the saleswoman.

The balloons were already beginning to lose their taut buoyancy as she carried them home. Rather than bobbing at the tops of their strings they trailed behind her horizontally, like a pair of well-trained dogs.

As she put her key in the lock she had a flash that something was different: Jack, she thought. Jack's here. The voice, she thought, turning the knob, a man's voice.

But it was Ed she saw when she stepped into the room. He was sitting on the couch with a child on either side, and he was reading to them. Caterina sat on the floor with her back against the couch, her shoulders between Ed's legs. The four of them looked at Maisie, and then Ellie shouted, "Balloons!" and hurled herself at Maisie.

"Hang on, hang on," Maisie said, laughing, as she put one string into Ellie's hand and the other into Evan's. The baby looked solemnly at his balloon and let go of it, and they all watched it float, slowly, to the ceiling.

"That was so sweet of you," Caterina said, getting to her feet.

"Hi," Maisie said to Ed, kissing him.

"Looka my balloon!" Ellie said, and Ed reached up for the string, which she'd released, and put it back into her hand. She immediately let go of it again, and the balloon began its deliberate ascent. "Look!"

Caterina's packed suitcases stood next to the door, flanked by the folded-up stroller and the Port-a-Crib in its gray carrying case. Maisie glanced at the luggage and at Caterina.

"We waited around to thank you," Caterina said. Her smile was big and lazy, and Maisie smiled back at her. Good, you can tell me the whole story sometime.

"And to take you out to dinner," Ed added hastily.

She smiled at him, too, to show him that even though Caterina had been complaining about him for days, she held nothing against him. "No thanks. If you get a shuttle now, you can still get the kids home at a fairly decent hour."

She called a cab for them, and Ed made several trips with the luggage, piling it outside on the curb. Caterina hugged Maisie. "Thank you so much," she whispered.

The driver wouldn't let the balloons in his cab. "Too big. Can't see."

So Maisie held the strings and waved at the two children, screaming at the loss of the balloons, and Ed and Caterina, already beginning to look harassed again. She watched the cab go down the street, a receding box full of howls.

She ate the pineapple yogurt she'd opened that morning. It seemed longer ago than that. Her legs and shoulder blades were beginning to ache from all the aerobics. She wished for a record player or a radio, something to break the silence of the apartment. The phone didn't ring. The balloons were too tired now to make it up to the ceiling; they hung in midair, their strings trailing dispiritedly on the floor. She thought of how Ellie had shrieked with excitement, how Evan had stared and smiled when his balloon went sailing away from him. She went into the bathroom and turned on the bathwater, and while it was running she took a safety pin and made holes in both balloons and threw them away.

Part III

13
A Limited Test

❧

Maisie was like a place he'd lived in once, familiar but different, the same smell, the same view from the windows, but new people living there now, strange furniture, fresh paint on the walls. She looked plainer, in a white T-shirt and jeans, her face at once tired and younger-looking; it took him several minutes to realize that she wasn't wearing any makeup. She'd let her hair grow; it was loose and straight, brushing the hollows of her collarbone. Her apartment, too, was very plain, a single room, neat and bare, with linoleum on the floor and bars on the windows; it was hard not to see her as an inmate of some austere institution, a convent or a white-collar prison.

The drive down had taken longer than he'd remembered, and he'd had trouble finding a parking place, so he was forty-five minutes late. He was able to rely on his apology, and a curmudgeonly account of the delays on the road, to get through the first moments of their meeting.

"I was afraid you weren't coming," she said.

"I knew you'd think that," his voice overly hearty. He thought: This is a sanctioned visit. There was nothing sneaky about it, it was all on the record. Laura knew he was here; he'd told her he was going to try to "wrap things up" with Maisie. "Good. It's probably about time you did." He and Nona had been talking for several weeks now about his coming. With her he'd been a bit more candid, saying he'd begun to recognize that Maisie still had some kind of hold on him, and he wanted to see whether he'd give in to it, or withstand it. He was pretty sure that seeing her would help him get over her. Nona seemed pleased that he was going, and asked what he'd told Laura.

"Laura doesn't demand specifics," he'd said.

"Huh," Nona said with annoying play-dumb innocence, "but shouldn't she?"

They were still standing just inside the apartment door. Maisie asked him if he was hungry and said she'd bought hot dogs.

Two hot dogs in buns with pickles and tomatoes, for years his habitual Saturday lunch. But he hadn't eaten a hot dog in months now, growing leaner and he supposed healthier on Laura's mostly vegetarian diet. "That sounds great," he said.

Her stove was two burners mounted on top of a brown cabinet, which, he realized, was the refrigerator. While she cooked he walked around the room, stooping, although the ceiling was quite high, ten feet, at least. He bent to peer into an orange crate full of books, *Middlemarch*, Tolstoy and Chekhov, paperback copies of *The Golden Bowl* and *What Maisie Knew*, their spines pristine and unbroken. Her books, anyway, were still the same. He pulled out her old copy of *This Is New York*, with its stylized, French-looking illustrations, and flipped through it, reading aloud, " 'Here is Times Square, the biggest drugstore of them all.' "

Maisie smiled, then said, "Oh, no." The plate with the hot dogs had toppled over, into the tiny sink.

"Wash 'em off and serve 'em," Jack said. "I didn't see that." He didn't recognize his own voice.

Over lunch, at the table set in the curve of the barred bow window, he asked about her job. She was temping, she said apologetically.

"What kinds of places have you been?"

"Well, last week a law firm. Just answering phones." She wiped the corner of her mouth with a piece of paper towel and smoothed it back into her lap. "The real pleasure of temping is that you go into these places and see all the people working there, and you're glad you're not one of them. My favorite thing in the law firm was the ladies' room. It was one of those big chrome-and-marble ones, and it was always completely empty except for this giant bottle of Maalox, right in the center of the makeup counter."

He laughed.

"And let's see, I was at a PR firm last month, and the man that ran it told me that if anyone called and asked, I should say they had twenty-two employees."

"Did they?"

"No. Only three."

"I mean, did anyone call and ask?"

"No," she said pertly. That, at least, was a tone and expression he recognized. It made him feel suddenly more guarded, reminded him that this was not just lunch with an old friend.

"So do you think you'll just keep temping?" he asked, more sharply.

"Not forever." She wiped her mouth again. "I'm trying very hard not to think about it."

"Have you checked into publishing here at all?"

"No. There isn't much, and besides, I didn't like it."

"Oh, no?"

"I like reading good books, not bad ones."

"They couldn't have all been bad."

She got up and went to the sink to refill her water glass. "Yes, but you need patience to find the good ones. And you have to fight to keep them. I don't think I'm that competitive."

It pleased him that she was still floundering, analyzing herself. In the same nine months, I've turned a factory around, he thought. "Well," he said, "you'll find something."

"Do you want another beer?"

"Sure." He watched her crouch by the refrigerator, surprised again at how compact she was; he'd remembered her bigger. "There are a lot of things you'd be good at."

"Oh, like what?"

"Well, you're smart—"

"Oh, come on."

"No, you are. Remember the time we bought the car, and the salesman left the room and I was trying to talk to you about how much we could really afford? And you pointed to that intercom thing on his desk and whispered to me that the room was bugged? That would *never* have occurred to me." He was conscious, talking to her, of surreptitiously poking the wound: nope, doesn't hurt anymore. He felt very kind and a little reckless.

"Maybe I should join the CIA," she said, sitting down with his beer.

He laughed.

"So tell me about the factory."

"What do you want to know?" he asked.

"How it's all going."

"Very well."

"Really?"

He thought she sounded skeptical, and he felt his face tighten.

"Yes, actually. I took out a loan for new product introductions, because we were really stagnating with the old stuff. We looked at a couple of options, and we're finally going with a new low-fat line."

"Low-fat french fries? Isn't that a, what do you call it, an oxymoron?"

"Apparently not," he said stiffly.

"Well," she said. "That's wonderful."

Feeling, somehow, that she wasn't impressed enough, he said, "We've done a limited test, and the enthusiam has been tremendous." Wanting her to ask, Who's we?

"A limited test where?"

"Uh, Hartford, Albany, and Providence."

"Too bad. I'd like to try them."

Making him feel as though the testing had been too limited, dinky.

"Well, we'll be marketing them all over New England starting at the end of this month."

"Great," she said. And he remembered she'd once told him that she just didn't think Eldridge French Fries were that good, they tasted soggy no matter how you cooked them.

"How's your mother?" she asked.

"Fine."

"Still on Vinalhaven?"

He nodded, watching someone's bare legs in tennis shoes go by her window.

"And Marion? She's married?"

"How do you know that?"

"Caterina told me."

He remembered telling Caterina, the night he'd brought Laura there. That had been a mistake, an awkward evening, but a necessary declaration, this is who I am now. He wondered if Maisie knew. He thought of Laura chatting easily through Caterina's good dinner, thinking she was meeting friends of his, not knowing they were really friends of Maisie's. How he'd made fierce love to her that night in the hotel, I'm here with *you,* damn it.

"What made her and Barry finally decide to get married? After all those years together?"

He finished his beer. "I have no idea."

Caterina called while Maisie was finishing the dishes. Her wet hand slid on the telephone receiver, and she told Caterina it wasn't a good time.

"You have company?"

"Jack."

"Oh, is this the weekend?"

"Yuh."

"Oh, Maisie. Well, I won't keep you. How is it? Is it incredible to see him again?"

"Uh-huh."

"Oh, well, have a wonderful time. You'll call me when he goes?"

"Sure."

She hung up, shaky from the intrusion.

Jack sat at the table, frowning at her. "Who was that?"

"Caterina."

"You told her I was here?"

"Yes," Maisie said, defensive.

"God, Maisie, can't we just keep this private?"

"I haven't told anyone else."

"Well, don't, all right?"

"I wasn't going to." She turned on the water again and clattered dishes in the small, stained sink. Jack got up and went over to his suitcase, got out a magazine, and sat down on the futon to read. The suitcase was the same old green one he used to bring when he visited her in New York, the one she'd shipped back to him after the company picnic because she didn't want to see him another time. She remembered it lying messily open on her floor in Brooklyn and wished he'd do that here, scatter things. She had a longing to see his clothes, all the old drab shirts and pants she remembered. She thought of a soft green plaid flannel shirt he'd had, with frayed cuffs, but he wouldn't have brought it this weekend, it was much too hot. She tried and failed to remember his summer clothes. The ones he was wearing now, a blue cotton shirt and khaki trousers, were too neutral to be identifiably old or new.

His suitcase was closed, the clasps facing away from her. The magazine he was reading was *Inc.;* there were two men on the cover, one in a suit and one in shirtsleeves, looking pleased with themselves. She'd never seen him reading a business magazine before, and the effect was opaque and intimidating. How could he look the same and yet be so different? The cuffs of his pants had ridden up, and she saw that his socks were not only unfamiliar but, she thought, out of character: red ones, with a pattern of black herringbone. He'd always worn plain blue or black ones before, and she wondered, biting her lip, if these had anything to do with Laura. He hadn't mentioned Laura at all, but the socks seemed to Maisie like a talisman, a symbol of something bigger, the way a priest's white collar, even over casual layman's clothes, could conjure up the entire cassock, the candles, the smell of incense.

"Well," she said brightly, drying her hands. "Should we do something?"

He looked up. "Like what?"

What do people do on a Saturday afternoon? "How about the aquarium?" she said. It would take a while to get there, and it was somewhere neither of them had been.

They took the subway from Harvard Square. The aquarium was dark and noisy, jammed with people, a single ramp that spiraled upward around a great central tank. Jack and Maisie shuffled their way up slowly, trying to find a place to stand looking in; but the glass panels were filled with grown-ups and children staring in at the slowly circling fish. "Where is it?" they heard people saying.

"Up there. Holy shit."

Maisie remembered then that there was supposed to be a shark, and she tensed her shoulders, not knowing where it was, expecting it to swim up behind her somehow. She had the feeling she'd had as a child at Disneyland, when people rode on motorized carts through a model of the human body, screaming when they came suddenly upon the lungs expanding and contracting, the loud beating of the heart.

They came to a place where the outer wall bulged away from them, hung with shark models. She read the labels, SAND SHARK, TIGER SHARK, HAMMERHEAD, GREAT WHITE. They were all, with the exception of the great white, disappointingly small; she wanted them to be monstrous, lethal. The light here was ultraviolet; Jack's shirt and teeth and the ends of her fingernails glowed blue white. The shark models diverted the crowd from the main tank, and she and Jack were able to find a place by the glass.

The world inside the tank was green and slow. Fish swam by, each with its own special bizarreness; luminous stripes, undulating spines, crusty, dirty-looking skin, horizontal burbling mouth. She began to recognize some of the same fish, coming around again. She wondered if their lives would be this boring in the wild, or whether they were stupefied by the smallness of their artificial surroundings, like the lions and polar bears in zoos. Suddenly she was aware, high above her, of a shape that was bigger than the others, a long gray belly with three little vents on either side. The vents looked artificial, like the grille on an air conditioner. The shark swept by and disappeared around the curve of the circle.

"Would these fish all be together, in the real ocean?" she asked Jack. She had to speak loudly in order to be heard, but her voice had an echo.

"I doubt it. I'm sure they researched it carefully, to make sure nothing in here would prey on anything else."

She thought he must be right: it would upset all these children if something in the tank suddenly began to devour something else. But she hoped, climbing up toward the shark, that something would happen; the order of it all, the calm repetition, was getting on her nerves.

Outside, walking toward the subway station, they passed a line of souvenir carts, men in green aprons selling shirts and balloons. "I'm going to get some coffee," Jack said, stopping in front of a snack cart. "You want some?"

She shook her head and wandered over to look at the shirts, flapping on hangers in the breeze from the harbor. She fingered a Red Sox T-shirt and thought of Jack's old one, which he'd worn to greasy shreds at the factory. Maybe he'd replaced it by now, but he could always use another one. She paid for it and went to join him, handing him the paper bag.

"What's this?"

"A birthday present," she said lightly, but already she knew she'd blundered.

"My birthday was weeks ago."

"So just a present, then."

"Maisie."

"It's no big deal."

"Here." He held the bag out to her.

Childishly she put her hands behind her back. She felt scared and relieved: at last something was starting to happen.

"Maisie, take it."

"It's just a T-shirt," she cried.

"I don't care what it is."

She took the bag. "Why are you so mad at me?"

"What do you think?"

"I thought you were here because you wanted to see me."

"I did want to see you!" he shouted.

"But everything I do is wrong." Dunnane used to say that to me, she thought with a pang of belated sympathy for him; she'd felt cold, encased in her own self, when he said it, so that she hadn't heard any real emotion in it. It had just sounded like whining.

"Not *everything.*" He started walking again, and coffee sloshed from the paper cup onto his hand, making him shake it in pain and slosh more. "Fuck."

"Pour some of it out."

"I know what to do, Maisie."

She waited while he poured some out on the cobblestones. Families walked past them, arguing and trailing Mylar balloons, strollers jiggling and bumping over the rough stones.

"I need you not to push it, that's all," he said more quietly.

She took a breath of salt air and fumes from the tour buses idling at the curb. "Just tell me—are you coming back?"

"I knew you'd ask that. Jesus. I knew you wouldn't be able to give it time."

"Yes, but how much time?"

"More. I don't know. Just more than two hours, for God's sake." He was shouting again.

She'd made a resolution to be patient this weekend; she meant to be calm and serene. But she couldn't seem to shut herself up.

"So what should I do with this?" she asked, holding out the bag with the T-shirt in it.

Jack hesitated. Then he said, "What an opening," and laughed. She did, too. She watched him drink some coffee.

"Maybe they'll take it back," she said. Shut up, shut up, just drop the damned thing into the harbor. But she walked back over to the souvenir cart and asked the man behind it if she could return the shirt she'd just bought.

"Sorry, final sale," he said, counting change for a couple eating ice-cream cones. Then he looked at her face. "Oh, sure, why not."

When the couple walked away, he took the shirt from the bag and shook it out. "You don't want another size?"

"No, thank you," Maisie said, her eyes on Jack. He had his back to her, looking out over the harbor. The wind filled his shirt and made the hair stand up on his head. She wondered who cut his hair now; she'd done it herself, all the years they were together. She remembered, suddenly, the feeling of his skull under her hands. The souvenir man put some bills into her open palm and closed her fingers over them, so they wouldn't blow away.

"Wake up," he said to her. He was smiling. A small, handsome black man with a mustache and white teeth. He had an accent, and she wondered what country he was from. But she just said, "Thank you," and walked back over to Jack.

"I'm sorry," she told him. "That was really stupid."

"Did you return it?"

"Yes."

"Oh."

Maisie picked up a half-finished bag of popcorn someone had left on a piling and began throwing it, kernel by kernel, out to the gulls. What am I going to do, if he's so angry? I knew he would be, from his voice on the phone, but I thought it would dissolve when he saw me. She had never seen him like this; even when he got angry, she had always known that in some deep place he wasn't, really, and she could stop the fight at any moment by telling him she loved him, or by crying, or by asking earnestly, "Why are we doing this?"

He dug a fist into the popcorn bag without looking at her and threw a piece of popcorn way out over the water; a gull caught it on the fly.

"They have the meanest faces," she said.

"Who?"

"The gulls. Real thugs."

"That's what they are."

"Really?"

"You've seen them. They'll tear the food right out from under a duck or a cormorant. They even steal from eagles." His old quiet, matter-of-fact tone. Too bad they couldn't talk about birds all weekend.

Maisie was going through Jack's suitcase. He was in Harvard Square, having veered away from her as soon as they'd emerged from the subway, saying he needed to do some errands. She'd stood still for a moment, in the middle of the swirling Saturday crowd, wondering what errands he could possibly have to do, why he couldn't take her with him. Then she'd walked home slowly, stopping to buy chicken for dinner.

The apartment seemed silent and oppressive after she put the few groceries away. She lay on the futon, thinking that she should just go ahead and do the things she would have done on a normal Saturday afternoon, but she couldn't remember what they were. She kept trying to still the voice in her head that was telling her he'd left, he'd gotten into his car and was driving now, back to Maine.

But the suitcase was still here. He wouldn't go and leave it, would he? Full of whatever supplies he'd thought necessary for the weekend. She got up and went to sit before it, undoing the clasps with a loud report that made her jump. Someone in the dorm across the street put on music, "Ruby Tuesday," blaring sourly through Maisie's closed windows. The noise masked the sounds of her rifling, but she realized, nervously, that they would also block the sound of Jack's return. A red polo shirt that she remembered, a single pair of undershorts. He was definitely planning on only one more day, then. More issues of *Inc.* and an old copy of a German book whose name, and even some of the letters in the title, she didn't recognize. His scuffed leather toilet kit, which he'd had as long as Maisie had known him; the sight of it made her sad. She opened it, looking for something private and perhaps wounding, but she saw only a toothbrush and toothpaste, a razor and shaving cream. At the bottom a nearly empty prescription bottle, with her name on the label, of Tylenol with codeine. Left over from the time she'd had her wisdom teeth removed, loaned to him when he'd had a pinched nerve in his back. It pleased her to find it, proof that she was more deeply embedded in his life than he was willing to admit.

The only other item in the suitcase was a pair of white cotton pajamas, with the price tag still attached to the collar by a strip of translucent plastic. Bought just for this weekend, apparently; he'd always slept naked in warm weather and likely still did, with Laura. But couldn't he have gone to bed tonight in his underwear? She sat frowning at these modest, unworn garments.

She was still sitting there when a knock came at the door. Why hadn't he rung the buzzer? she thought, trying frantically to put everything back the way it had been, noisily snapping the suitcase shut. Someone must have let him into the building; but that wasn't surprising, considering how reliable he looked.

He helped Maisie fix dinner, as he always had, as he'd been helping Laura over the past year. The apartment, as evening came on, was lit by a single overhead ceiling fixture; its dimness was harsh and uniform, making him squint, trying to see better. He remembered Maisie listening to music or the news as she cooked, but there was no radio in sight, and they worked in silence. He cut up broccoli on an old wooden board that had been in his apartment in graduate school and before that had belonged to his parents. It had once had a painting on it and a saying, "Oh, God, thy sea is so great and my boat is so small." He had loved to look at it as a child, because the words had seemed so mysterious and terrifying; and only when he got older and the inscription was fading had he thought it an odd thing to have on a cutting board. Now it was gone, just a bare wooden board with the merest ghost of the blue and black and white paint.

He'd bought books in Harvard Square that afternoon, going to new and used and foreign bookstores and buying whatever he wanted, hardcover and paperback. The closest thing to a bookstore in Champs du Soleil was LeMessurier's Stationery, which stocked a smattering of best-sellers and religious texts, so he felt pleasantly guiltless, stocking up for a long stay at home. The fish in the aquarium had made him think of Laura; he went to the Harvard Coop and bought her a coffee-table book called *Fish in Art*. He'd thought of calling her from a phone booth, just to check in, but decided to wait until later. He'd bought a new watchband and sat in a café with a cup of tea and a brownie. He'd looked many times at his watch. All this time counted as time spent with Maisie, even if he wasn't actually with her. It was as if he were logging in hours, which he would write down later on some time card to be accumulated for an unknown end.

Now he was drinking wine. Maisie had bought a bottle of gewürztraminer, he supposed because the name sounded Germanic and difficult and she'd thought he'd like it. He'd recovered his equilibrium after this afternoon's fight; he felt fond of her and vague about details, as though they were both ninety and had been married years and years ago and had run into each other just now and decided to have dinner together.

"You're not smoking," he said to her.

She poured rice into a pot of water. "I quit."

"That's great. When?"

"When I moved here. It's easier in an unfamiliar place."

"I've never seen you not smoking."

His earliest memories of her had to do with smoking. He'd watched her smoke at that first party, before he'd even spoken to her: the way a line appeared between her brows when she inhaled, the way her mouth pursed around the escaping smoke. All those jokes about having a cigarette after sex, and Maisie had really done it, balancing the glass ashtray between her breasts so that it refracted the whiteness of her skin, prism-like. Blowing the smoke in streams at the ceiling. The Indonesian cigarettes she liked smelled of cloves; and since they'd split up, he would sometimes catch a whiff of that smoky clove scent and push his way down a street or a train platform, looking for its source. He wanted to tell her this now; but he had to keep reminding himself that they weren't ninety years old, and too much reminiscing was dangerous.

"It's been surprisingly easy," she went on. "I don't even think about it much anymore. Although I have to admit, I've wanted one all day today."

"Well," he said, smiling at her for the first time all day. He felt immediately disloyal to Laura and decided to call her now, while dinner was cooking. "Can I use your phone?"

"Sure," Maisie said coolly, rinsing a spoon.

He took the phone into the bathroom, shutting the door on the cord.

"So," said Laura. "Are you wrapping things up?" A faint note of sarcasm.

"Working on it," he said.

"It must be weird, seeing her again."

"It is."

"Well. I miss you."

"I miss you, too."

"Egg's been sick."

"What's wrong?"

"I thought he was choking, so I took him to the vet. It was just hairballs."

"Oh, good."

"But I didn't want anything to happen to him, while he was under *my* care."

Slightly irritated by her tone, he said, "Well, I'm glad you took him, anyhow."

"Oh, the vet made me feel like an idiot. Apparently hairballs are very common?"

"I guess so."

"But he's puked a couple of times, and he's just retching and retching—it's really disgusting. I finally just put him in the bathroom."

Jack looked at the tub, the sink, and felt a sudden alliance with Egg. "Well, don't worry about it. I'll brush him when I get back."

"You'll be back tomorrow?"

"Right."

"When?"

"Not sure yet. Sometime in the evening."

"I just wondered if I should make dinner."

"I'll grab a sandwich or something," he told her. "Don't worry about it."

They said good-bye and he hung up. The conversation had cleared the wine from his head. He sat on the edge of the tub and stared at the wall. The tiles were pale yellow, grayed with age, the color of hard-boiled egg yolks. There was a window high up above the tub, just below the ceiling, made of frosted, curlicued, hairy-looking glass; it would open out into the building's main hallway, and he spent a few moments wondering why someone would do that, put a window in the wall between a bathroom and a public space. The sink faucet leaked, and the leak had left an irregular brown stain. Maisie's toothbrush was in the tarnished silver mug he recognized as his own christening cup, and he debated asking to have it back. One of the first times they'd slept together, in his old graduate school apartment, he'd walked by the open door of the bathroom and seen her using his toothbrush. He'd been startled by the sight, but he had gone into the bathroom and stood behind her, watching their two faces in the mirror, and by the time she was finished brushing her teeth he had his arms around her, his hips pressing against the small of her back.

Now he ran his finger over her toothbrush, which was faintly damp. He thought of her brushing her teeth this morning, waiting for him. He felt sad and very tired.

He carried the phone back out to the living room. "What did you tell her?" Maisie asked. She was cutting up parsley, chop chop chop. He didn't feel at all hungry.

"About what?"

"This weekend."

"You mean just now?"

"No. Before."

"I told her I was coming to see you."

"Didn't it bother her?"

"Not especially," he said. He didn't know.

"Well, I bet it did," she said.

"Laura's a pretty secure person."

"Oh," she said. She scraped the parsley over the chicken. Neither of them ate much or said much during dinner.

He'd taken his pajamas and gone into the bathroom to wash up. Maisie was putting away the Scrabble set—they'd played two games, both of which he'd won—and trying to figure out what to do about bed. She could wait until he came out of the bathroom and then ask where he planned to sleep, which would certainly result in another fight: he'd say, Not with you, or, If it's going to be a big deal, maybe I should just go to a hotel. Neither of which she could bear to hear; she thought that if he spoke roughly to her one more time, she'd break.

If she said nothing about sleeping arrangements, there was a chance they'd have the same fight, or that he'd accuse her of trying to manipulate him with her silence; but it was also possible that he would get into her bed without a word. This thought made her pause with her hands full of Scrabble tiles, seized by a dizzying longing to lie next to him, just putting her head down on his chest, tangling her legs with his.

She let the tiles slide into the box, a series of soft little clicks. Then she stood up and put the Scrabble set away in her closet, and she took down an old quilt and spread it out on the floor near the table, at right angles to the bed.

The summer school students in the dorm across the street were having a party. It seemed to be in several rooms at once, on the first and second floors, music blaring from several sets of outward-facing speakers that someone had wired together. In another window someone was showering, a pink body too blurry to be male or female. Down the hall a boy sat at a computer, under a bright study lamp. In a corner room the shade was down; and behind it a pale light flickered, a candle, two eighteen-year-olds naked in bed for the first time.

Jack and Maisie lay in the semidarkness of her apartment, she in bed and he on a quilt spread on the floor. He had emerged from the bathroom to find it all set up, an unexpectedly graceful removal of the question mark about where he would sleep. His new pajamas itched. He was wide awake with the noise from the dorm. He was thinking of Maisie's mouth, the fine new creases that appeared above it now when she said certain words: "who," words that demanded a pursing of the lips. Her white legs, her slightly knock-kneed walk, as though her body were about to collapse in on itself, unable to bear its own small weight. The smell of her skin and her hair, her clothes and all her possessions, pervaded for years by the perfume she wore, so that they smelled the same whether she'd put on the cologne recently or not; a scent he'd loved but forgotten until today.

"It's hot in here," he said.

"It always is," she answered. "I should get a fan."

"I have an extra one, in the house somewhere," he said. Laura's apartment was air-conditioned. "I'll bring it down next time."

"So you are coming again?"

"I'd imagine so. At some point."

"What is going on?" Maisie cried, and he saw her sitting whitely up in bed.

He was pleased at having provoked her, but ashamed of his pleasure. "I don't know. I wish I could tell you, but I just don't know."

"But are we getting back together, or just friends, or what?"

"Maisie."

She flopped down on the bed again. "You like this."

"What. What do I like?" But he knew what she meant.

"Tell me about Laura," she said.

"You really want to hear?"

"No. But tell me."

"Okay," he said warningly. But then he was silent. "She's very athletic," he offered finally.

"What, you mean in bed?"

"Of course not!" he said. "I mean she—she runs every morning, she rides her bike, she—I don't know. She canoes."

"I run," Maisie said, almost to herself.

"I remember," Jack said, and then added idiotically, "But I'm glad to know you've kept it up."

"Yes, well, what else?" Maisie asked.

"About Laura, you mean?" He shaded his eyes with his hand, though the room was so dark. "Maisie, why are you *asking* about her?"

"Because I'm curious. I've been wondering about her for months and months now, building her up in my head. So I figure it can't be as bad just to know."

He turned on his stomach, resting his chin on his closed, stacked fists. "I really don't think Laura is the issue here." The truth was he couldn't think of one thing to say about Laura. He formed words in his head—she is just *there,* in such a private, wordless place that I can't explain her and shouldn't have to—but that was bullshit, a slightly more adult version of "If you don't know, then I'm not going to tell you." What had happened in all his months with Laura? There must be some telling anecdote, something that would shut Maisie up and warn her off without completely devastating her. Laura and I work well together, we cook dinner together, we keep the same hours, she's taught me about gardening. We've never had a fight. One time when she was a teenager she choked on an empanada. . . .

"Well," Maisie said with a reasonableness that struck him as ominous, "she's certainly *one* of the issues."

"Maisie, I don't want to talk about her, okay? I don't want to hurt you."

"What do you want?"

To hurt you, he thought. "You know, you act as though I've come here with some big plan, like I already know where this is all going to come out."

"And you don't?" When he didn't answer, she added, "I'm not being sarcastic, I'm really asking."

"I *said* I didn't." He turned over on his back again and saw that Maisie was lying on her side, looking at him. Her face seemed very large and close, and he rolled slightly away from her. Her could hear her breathing, light, quick.

"What kind of work does Laura do?" she asked.

"She has her own advertising business. Free-lance."

"Oh." Silence. "I thought she was a doctor, for some reason. So is she doing ads for you?"

"Ads, packaging. That's how we met, in fact." So there, Maisie. "She's really helped me figure out the direction of the company."

"Did you ever ask her if they really put things in ice cubes?"

"What?"

"There was that book, years ago. About how they wrote 'sex' in the ice cubes, to make you buy the liquor. And there's supposed to be a naked woman somewhere on the camel, on the Camel cigarettes pack."

"So you think she's hiding things in the crinkles of my crinkle-cuts?" There it was again, that almost forgotten habit of laughing with her. He had to guard himself against it.

"But are you really happy with her?"

"Maisie."

"I know you said I shouldn't push it—"

"Then don't."

"How can I not?" she cried.

"Look," he said. "Laura's there. I live with her, I like being with her. I'm not saying it's like it was with you, I don't know if she's the love of my life, but we make each other happy. I have no intention of hurting her."

"But how do you think it makes me feel, to be told we had this great love that we can't have anymore because you've found something 'healthier'?"

"I didn't say that."

"You make her sound vegetarian."

"She is a vegetarian!" he said loudly.

"I didn't mean *she* was one, I mean she sounds like something a vegetarian would eat."

"What's wrong with vegetarians?" he nearly shouted, wanting to laugh, to leave, to fuck her.

"Nothing, nothing's wrong with them," Maisie said, her voice shaking slightly. After a moment she said, "I'm sorry. I really didn't mean to be a bitch."

"I know," he said, though he was glad she was being bitchy: she wasn't completely helpless and self-abasing, so it was all right for him to be angry at her. "Go to sleep," he said roughly.

Several minutes later she said, "I can't."

He couldn't, either. "Why don't we play a game," he offered.

"Botticelli?"

"Sure." This was something they'd often played, in bed when they couldn't sleep or on long car trips. He hadn't played it since, and they had to spend a few moments reminding each other of the rules. "Okay, my letter's W," he said finally, thinking of Wordsworth.

"Mine's H."

"H. Okay, did Louis B. Mayer once try to buy all the copies of a film about your life, to prevent its being released at all?"

"No, I am not William Randolph Hearst."

He remembered, then, why this game always dragged on long enough to be useful on a car trip, or to lull them both to sleep: they shared all the same references, so they were practically incapable of stumping each other.

On Sunday morning they drank coffee and read. She'd pulled *The Golden Bowl* out of the shelf and sat cross-legged on the floor with it, staring hopelessly at its dense, barely paragraphed pages but holding on to it as a kind of charm that might make him remember whatever it was he'd once loved about her. He was thumbing through her old copy of *Jude the Obscure,* looking at the engravings but not, she thought, reading it. She wished for a Sunday paper, something that catered to restlessness. A crossword puzzle, so she could ask him to help her with it. Reviews of books she would never read. Complicated recipes to tear out and never cook. Obituaries, wedding announcements. Infuriating political stories they could read bits of aloud to each other. She'd heard, lying awake before dawn, the noise of the newspaper truck stopping outside the building, the heavy thud of the subscribers' papers being dropped in the vestibule on the other side of the wall behind her bed. Now she thought enviously of the subscribers themselves, darting out of their apartments in their bathrobes, snatching up their *Globe* or *Times* and shuffling back, yawning, to spend the morning lazily rustling and skimming. She said again, "Are you sure you don't want to go around the corner for the *Times*?"

"No."

"And you don't want to go for a run?"

He shook his head, turning a page. "You can, if you want."

But she didn't want to go out alone, because she was sure he'd take the chance to desert; and he wouldn't go with her, because they might run into someone they knew. It was like one of those sex-obsession movies, she thought, where the two people hold each other prisoner in the sweaty little apartment—except that there was no sex going on.

At around eleven he got up and picked up his pajamas and stuffed them into his suitcase.

"You're leaving?"

"I have to work tomorrow."

"But—but—"

He looked at her coolly.

"But—didn't I *pass?*" she burst out.

He bent over his bag, pushing around the things inside it. "I'll call you."

She backed up against the door. She was aware, blurrily, that he was bustling around some more, with his back to her—snapping the suitcase shut, picking up his keys and sunglasses from the table, going to the sink for a glass of water, gulping it down. Then he banged the glass down in the sink, turned, and looked at her. She had a long moment to wonder what his creased face meant—dismay? disgust? sadness?—and to begin exhaustedly calculating the ramifications of each possibility, and then he came across the room and put his arms around her.

The moment he touched her, a sound started coming out of her, something she felt rather than heard, a rough ugly ripping in the back of her throat. It was the feel of him, the smell of his neck. The knowledge that these things which she had thrown away still existed, still walked around in the world somewhere day after day without her. He held her tightly, so that she was enclosed in a universe made up of the sound of roaring and snuffling—like a zoo, she thought, and realized she must be calming down a little. She began to be embarrassed at the noise she was making, yet if she quieted, he'd let her go. But it was a sound that couldn't be manufactured: once she became self-conscious about it, it stopped. She pulled her face away and saw that she'd soaked the front of his red shirt, and she heard footsteps in the hallway outside the apartment door and hoped it was just people passing deafly by, not curious neighbors who would now point out her door to each other and say, "Domestic trouble."

She looked at Jack and his face was sad, but not, she thought, disapproving: his arms held her loosely, and he was looking down at her, and she felt guilty, suddenly, for having forced a tender gesture from him. She pushed him away and lifted a hand to smooth back her hair.

"But this doesn't count," she said hoarsely. "It's like the German and Allied soldiers sending Christmas cookies back and forth between the trenches. Right?"

"Oh, Maisie," he said, in the gentle voice she remembered but hadn't heard all weekend.

"What."

"I don't know." And then he left.

14

The Underground City

❧

The next night Jack and Laura were in the supermarket, doing their weekly shopping. Every Sunday afternoon Laura mapped out menus for the week, checking the ingredients they would need against the contents of her cabinets and refrigerator, to come up with their Monday-night shopping list. He had never seen her buy anything that wasn't on the list.

"No, not those," she said of the bag of pinto beans he was tossing into the cart.

"They're not the right kind?"

"I like the Spanish ones. Plus they're cheaper."

He watched her put them back and pick out the kind she wanted. He was waiting for her to bring up Maisie, ask him how the weekend had gone. She hadn't said anything last night or this morning, and although her tact had at first relieved him and made him grateful, he was beginning to feel annoyed. She must want to know, so why didn't she ask?

"We're out of olive oil," he said.

"I know. I wrote it down."

"Any preference?"

"The kind with the green label."

"They all have green labels."

"*This* kind," she said, pulling down a bottle. "I would think you'd know what brand by now."

He thought, So she *is* upset; and he wondered if he ought to be the one to bring up Maisie, but he couldn't figure out how.

Then they were walking down the freezer aisle, and suddenly, behind the misted glass, there were SunLights, a neat little display of green-and-gold boxes.

He'd been overseeing their evolution for months, from sketches to dummies to printed prototypes to actual packaging, stacked high in the freezer rooms at the factory; but it was strange to see them out here alone, debuting without fanfare or witnesses.

"Yay," Laura cheered softly, holding on to his arm. He smiled stiffly. "Aren't you excited?"

"I guess so," he said slowly.

She shook his arm. "Hey, come on."

"Yeah." He couldn't figure out why he was feeling so strange. Ashamed, almost. People were actually going to pay money for his product—his, not his father's or great-grandfather's. One dollar and nineteen cents. They were going to take it home, cook it, eat it, feed it to their children. Supermarket managers were buying twelve cases and getting two free. They were displaying the shelf talkers Laura had designed, which had "The Skinny French Fry" lettered in gold on a green background. They were running ads and coupons in their Sunday circulars, splitting the costs half and half with Eldridge. Over the next few weeks ladies in green-and-gold aprons would be standing in the aisles with toaster ovens and stacks of tiny paper plates, offering customers free samples. He'd done everything right, yet he felt as though the effort and intelligence involved had been not much more than that necessary to pull off a junior high school science project, like building a papier-mâché volcano that exploded with a mixture of vinegar and baking soda, or making a telephone from an old cigar box.

"Let's buy one," Laura said, reaching for the handle of the freezer door.

He put out a hand to stop her. "No."

"Eldridge," she said. "You're pooping your own party." She rubbed the back of his neck. "Look at that packaging. It really stands out, don't you think? Though I still think that sun logo should have been bigger." She laughed. "I feel like we're standing by the nursery window, admiring our baby."

"It does look good," he said, trying to muster up some enthusiasm. She took his diffidence for modesty, laughed, and let go of his arm, first giving him a little snap-out-of-it push.

"Well, should we keep worshiping, or get on with the shopping?" she asked.

"You go ahead. I just need to check something." He opened the door and began straightening the piles, which were already straight. He watched, from the corner of his eye, as her tall strong figure glided away with the supermarket cart full of vegetables and pastas and yogurt. No one was in the freezer aisle.

He waited, staring in at the Sara Lee section, while several people strolled by and added frozen things to their carts: waffles, tortellini, fish cakes, diet TV dinners. A woman with a toddler in the bottom of her cart, groceries piled on top of his legs, swept by and grabbed a bag of Ore-Ida hash browns almost without stopping. Then a middle-aged woman in huge tight blue jeans and a gray cabled sweater, not at all resembling his target audience (affluent singles ages twenty-five to forty-four and health-conscious parents of children ages two to eighteen), wandered over, opened the door of the french fry compartment, and stood for nearly a minute, so that the glass clouded and Jack, frowning at the back panel of a foil bag of garlic bread which was thawing in his hands, couldn't see anything. The door shut, the sound of a box tossed into the basket she held over her arm, and he saw a blur of green and gold, the sun logo. He smiled at her, and she looked startled but smiled slightly back.

Still holding the garlic bread, he went off to find Laura, striding in time to the music coming down from the ceiling speakers, a slow rendition of some song that had been on the radio a few years back, a melody he recognized but couldn't name.

"How did things go with Maisie?" Nona asked, settling herself on the couch and fanning her loose cotton shirt around her. He caught a glimpse of her thighs, pink underpants.

"I'm not sure, actually. We fought a couple of times, which I guess didn't surprise me."

"About what?"

He told Nona about the Red Sox T-shirt, the conversation about Laura. He said, "I was pretty rough on her all weekend."

"Does that bother you?"

He thought. "Well, no, in a way I think I was proud of it."

"Proud?"

"Well, you and I talked about how I was damned if I'd let her push me around at all. And I didn't. But I don't know. It also made me feel kind of embarrassed, that I needed to prove I had all this power over her. Because it wasn't as though she was contesting it. She was so anxious to please me. I was beating up on someone who'd already said 'Uncle.' "

"But you're not sure you can trust her 'Uncle' at this point?"

He smiled at the idea of Maisie and her untrustworthy uncle, and Nona, seeing his face, smiled, too, her fingertips pressed together over her mouth.

Then he was saying, sober again, "I want to trust her," and to his horror his voice was shaking, his nose and eyes were running, he was sobbing in her office, through what was left of their hour.

He drove from Nona's office to the factory, feeling cold and capable after his complete loss of control. He shut the door of his office, picked up the phone, and called Warren Phinney, the broker who'd been working, desultorily, on the sale of the business.

He'd met Phinney once, over a year ago, in Boston, having gotten his name from an item in the Exeter alumni magazine: *After eleven years at Bear, Stearns, Warren Phinney, '64, has started Dutton & Phinney, a Boston investment bank. Last summer he cruised in Newfoundland with his wife, Margaret, and their three daughters on their 49-foot ketch,* Caveat. *Warren says he'd be happy to hear from any Exonians interested in buying or selling companies.*

Jack had expected to find someone rumpled, windblown, friendly, possibly a bit desperate for business: someone with whom he could roll his eyes a little over the prospects of selling an ailing company, someone with whom he could roll up his sleeves and concoct boyishly energetic strategies. Now, now, Jack, he'd imagined Phinney saying, let's not get discouraged here. . . .

But Phinney had been a taut, military-looking man about whom everything was restrained—his suit, his striped tie, his faint scent of soap or after-shave. Graying black hair clipped close to his pale head. Ship models and computer software on the shelves behind him, a gold clock on his immaculate desk, a no-small-talk air that had Jack in and out of his office in twenty minutes.

"I just wanted to double-check," Jack said now, "that we're still in your active file."

"Oh, sure you are, sure." A pause, chuff-chuff, Phinney lighting up a cigarette or a pipe.

"But you haven't got anyone definite at the moment?"

"It's a tough time in the french fry business," Phinney said. "I don't have to tell you that."

"You know, we've been doing some interesting things here lately," Jack said slowly. He told Phinney about the results of the limited testing, the orders that were already coming in on SunLights. He imagined Phinney's pen scratching on yellow paper, recording this new ammunition.

"Well, then now is probably not the best time for you to sell," Phinney said finally. "You've got this new product, why not stick with it and help it along, and then when you've really got some numbers to show for yourself, I'll be able to get you a much better price."

"No, no, I really want to try selling now," Jack said. "I'm just asking whether you think that knowing this, I mean that we've got this good thing coming up, whether that will help make it more attractive."

"Well, sure, it won't hurt."

"I guess what I'm really saying is, I'd like you to get much more aggressive now."

"There's only so aggressive I can be, without a retainer. I've got a lot of deals going on right now, so I'm not able to do it for you on the come."

On the come. It made Jack think of sex, and of the fish he and Maisie had seen in the aquarium, circling slowly with their mouths open, waiting for anything that swam in. Phinney had raised this question of the retainer a year ago: he could work with one or without one. Without one, Jack had told him, with an inner shrug: why pay when he wasn't even sure how he felt about selling?

Now he said, "Okay, how much?"

He didn't tell Laura he'd made the phone call. But that evening he was clingy with her, wistful. After dinner they sat in her living room, Jack reading while Laura paid bills. He looked around the big orderly room, with its high clean windows, the soft pinks and browns of the rug, the framed watercolors on the walls. He thought of her wry comment about how neat it had been before he'd moved in. It was still neat. It would be neat if he moved out. Maybe she wouldn't be hurt too much, if it came to that. She'd had a life before him, and she'd have one after him.

"I love your apartment," he said suddenly.

"Yeah, I do, too," said Laura, perfectly mimicking the wistful note of apology in his voice, but smiling sideways at him.

He wondered what Maisie was doing now, in her ugly little room.

The next night, Friday, Laura stood at the stove, sautéeing onions, pouring in curry powder. Her face, as she cooked, was calm; he kept superimposing on it Maisie's anxious frown, her small, quick motions.

"The table all set?" Laura asked. He'd gotten home just a little while ago, she'd kissed him and given him a quick light shove, setting him right to work.

"Yes." He glanced at it through the kitchen doorway: white plates, dark blue placemats, big white napkins in wooden angelfish napkin rings. Above the table, a hanging lamp with a blue cloth shade; it made a soft igloo-spaced shape of light. Laura's sister was coming for the night, with her husband and child; they were on their way back to Providence from a week in Montreal.

Her sister's name was Beth, but for some reason he couldn't remember the husband's name or the child's, though Laura had told him several times. He asked her again. "Todd," she said with an air of humorous impatience, "and my niece is Linden." Linden, of course. Some of her drawings were up on Laura's refrigerator, with her name written in big ragged capitals. "And she's five?" he asked.

"Four." She went to the refrigerator and got out a bowl of vegetables she'd been marinating in yogurt. "Four and a half, really."

"You think she'll eat curry?"

"She eats everything," Laura said, stirring. "You know what her favorite food is? Olives." She put the spoon down on the counter. "It's too bad they can only stay a night, because otherwise we could have gone to the camp."

"Has Linden ever been there?"

"Only once. Beth doesn't love it the way I do. She gets bored. But next summer I'm going to see if she'll give me Linden for a week. She'll be old enough for me to teach her to swim, and she can help me in the garden. Oh, Jack, that reminds me, next weekend we'll have to do something about the tomatoes."

"The tomatoes?"

"Those stakes we're using aren't strong enough. They're all flopping over, I suppose because it's been a wet summer. Will you try to remind me this week to get something stronger?"

He gripped the edge of the counter and then let go. "Sure," he said. "That's fine. But, Laura, the weekend after that, I just thought I should tell you, I'm going to have to be in Boston again."

"Oh. On business?"

"No," he said.

He watched while she filled a small pot with water and measured rice into a cup. The overhead lights made the edge of her black head white; loose little strands of hair stood up, curling, glowing, disappearing as she moved. She poured the rice into the pot. Then she said, "Again?"

"I'm sorry. It's just a lot more complicated than I thought."

Laura sighed. "Well. I suppose I should scream, or throw plates at the wall."

"You wouldn't do that."

"No." She smiled sourly at him. "Maybe that's my problem."

"Laura. I just can't say to Maisie, Okay, let's get a divorce. I'm just not ready to say it."

"And you really think going down there for more weekends will help you get to that point?"

"I don't know."

"Oh, God," said Laura. Then: "My sister will be here any minute. Let's not get into it now." She looked at the clock. It had a catfish painted on it; the hands were the catfish's whiskers. "Should I actually cook the rice, do you think, or wait till they get here?"

"Wait." This was all so calm. He hadn't expected screaming or plate throwing, but this calm was unnerving.

"I'd better put clean towels in the bathroom," said Laura, and she disappeared.

He lifted the lid off the curry pot; hot, spicy steam bathed his face. The windows were clouded over. What was he setting in motion, so casually, with so few words?—a phone call to Warren Phinney, a muted confession to Laura. He had to be careful, he had to be responsible; but he'd always been careful, so careful he could barely move. And now something inside him was cracking, breaking apart, screaming at him to be reckless. Wait, he said to it, just wait a little more. Be sure.

When Laura came back into the room he smiled at her, and to his relief she smiled back. He went to her and put his cheek against her hair.

"You know what I wanted to ask you," he began.

"What." She was stiff in his arms, not turning to face him.

"Have you ever done those subliminal-image things, in any of your ads?"

She laughed and relaxed against him. "What, you mean write 'sex' in the ice cubes?"

How peculiar, the same words Maisie had used. But he supposed it was the classic example, the one everyone would think of first.

"Have you?" he pressed.

She moved away from him across the kitchen, a seductive, self-important little sidle that made him feel sad for her: oh, Laura, you think I'm flirting with you, but it's really Maisie I'm thinking of.

"You should know me better than that," Laura drawled over her shoulder. "I'd never stoop that low. Why should I, when I can just use regular pictures to get people to pay too much for things they don't even know they want."

"I don't like this," Linden said suddenly at dinner.

"What?" said her mother. "Sssh."

"It's too spicy," Linden said.

"What about plain rice?" Laura said to her. "Would you just like some plain rice?"

"No," Linden said, rubbing her eyes with her hands.

"She slept in the car," Beth said. "It always takes her a while to wake up."

"Oh, me too," said Laura. "I know exactly how that feels, Linden. Really crabby, right?"

"No," said Linden.

"What about peanut butter, Linden? Should I make you a peanut-butter sandwich?" Laura stood up and held out her hand. "Let's go see if Aunt Laura was smart enough to buy peanut butter."

They went into the kitchen. Beth sighed and looked at Jack. She was younger than Laura, lighter, warmer. The same low voice, but different inflections, more hesitant. She asked him shyly for more wine. Todd was talking about Montreal. "It's really a strange city," he said, "because most of the development in the past twenty years has been underground."

"I've read about that," Jack said.

"There's a whole second city down there, really," Todd said. "All connected by the subway stops. You go down, and you can walk for miles without ever coming up. Linden and I got lost one day. We had to keep popping up into the street, just to orient ourselves."

"It's because of the climate," Laura's sister added softly. "It gets so cold there in the winters, people don't want to be aboveground."

"That's a good idea," Jack said. He liked them; except for the slight edge of introductory shyness, they might have been people he'd known for a long time. But he felt no urge to ask them questions, to have more than a pleasant social conversation.

"Well, good and bad," Todd said. "It's actually been fairly damaging for the city at street level. There's just not enough going on up there. On St. Catherine Street, which is the equivalent of Fifth Avenue, say, you'll find a fancy department store right next to a strip club."

"I got a little snappish with Todd when we were walking around," Beth said. "It's very uncomfortable in a city, when you have no sense of where you are."

"Yes," said Jack. He knew from Laura that Todd and Beth were both city planners. This was how they spent their vacations, going to different cities and just walking around. He served them more curry and checked the level of the wine. Better open another bottle. Todd talked about how the underground city had its own neighborhoods, ritzy sections and slums. Laura came back from the kitchen with Linden, holding a dish of ice cream. "She ate most of a peanut-butter sandwich, so I thought this would be okay," Laura told Beth, who shrugged.

"If your aunt Laura won't spoil you, who will?"

"That's right," Laura said, pulling the child up to sit on her lap. Linden held up her spoon, feeding Laura her ice cream, and when Laura lunged forward to take the spoon into her mouth, Linden pulled it away and laughed. "You're my doggy," Linden said.

"I am? Woof, woof."

Todd asked Jack about the factory. "And it was a family business?"

Jack answered him, defensive at first, but then relaxing as it became clear that Todd's interest was genuine. Laura took Linden over to see where she would sleep: a bed of cushions from the big chair, covered with an old green-and-white quilt. Jack thought of his bed on the floor at Maisie's.

"You want to feed the fish?" Laura murmured, and she held Linden over the tank and let her sprinkle in some flakes from the can.

"Why doesn't the cat eat them?" he heard Linden ask.

"He'd like to," Laura told her. "He sits here day after day on the arm of the couch, looking bored, but what he's really thinking is, Someday those silly people will get careless and leave the lid off, and then I'll have myself a real feast."

Jack cleared away the dinner plates and put up water for tea. When he came out of the kitchen, Todd and Beth were sitting on the couch with Laura and Linden.

"You know what the cat's name is?" Laura was asking Linden. "Egg. Isn't that a funny name?"

Linden smiled obligingly, and then she asked, "Why does he have such a funny name?"

"I don't know," Laura murmured, "maybe because his coat's the color of egg yolks."

"Maybe because he's scrambled," Linden said, and laughed.

"Maybe he's hard-boiled," Laura said. "Maybe he was poached."

"Because he was little, and he seemed like he might break," Jack told them shyly, sitting down on the floor beside the couch. The minute he said it he wished he hadn't—it made him think of the night he'd met Maisie, walking her up the stairs of her building and hearing frantic scrabbling behind her locked apartment door. It was only the kitten, she'd said. She'd just gotten him a few days ago. A friend who worked at the medical school had smuggled him out of a lab where they were doing experiments on cats' brains; he'd been born there, and the staff had kept him hidden until he was old enough to leave his mother. When she'd gotten him, Maisie said, his fur had been matted with shit because he'd been living in a small cage and his mother had been too upset to clean him much. He spent his days running around bumping into walls, because he hadn't yet adjusted to being out of the cage, and he was still afraid of people. But that night, when Jack and Maisie had stayed up talking for hours, sitting on her floor in their stockinged feet, the kitten had crept closer and finally gone to sleep in one of Jack's shoes.

"He's not little anymore," Linden said.

"No," said Jack, stroking the thick yellow fur, "he's a big guy now."

Lying in bed next to Laura later, he waited with trepidation for her to bring up the subject of Maisie again. But she was talking about the evening, how it had gone. "Beth looks tired," she said. "Don't you think? Or maybe you wouldn't notice, since you've never met her before."

"She reminds me of you," Jack said.

"We'll let them sleep late tomorrow. Maybe we can take Linden out to breakfast, before Beth and Todd wake up."

"That would be nice."

"You know," Laura continued, "even with the second bedroom, this apartment would really be too small for a kid."

"Well," Jack answered after a minute, "but you weren't planning to stay here forever, anyway."

"What about the farmhouse?" Laura asked in the same casual tone. "Would you ever want to fix that up?"

"It's just a rental."

"You could probably buy it, if you wanted to. Or you could look for another house."

"I suppose."

"But another one with a barn," she continued immediately, yawning. "I always wanted a horse, when I was growing up."

"It's fun."

"You had one, didn't you?"

He nodded, in the dark. Thank you, Laura, for changing the subject. "His name was Scout. We got him from a friend of Marion's, who told us he was thirty years old. Then we found out she'd gotten him a few years before from another girl, who'd said he was thirty, and the owner before *that* got him when he was thirty—"

"So he was really about fifty," Laura finished.

"Marion and I always fought over him—whose turn it was to ride him, and who was supposed to feed him. We'd alternate giving him breakfast, and she used to come into my room at six in the morning and say, 'It's your turn to do Scout.' She'd be up and dressed, but it wouldn't occur to her to just go out and do him herself."

"Beth and I fought a lot, but I thought it was because we were both girls. I always wanted to be an only child. I don't mean in that momentary way that all kids want it, I mean really. It was my big dream. But now that I don't get to see Beth much, I miss her. What do you think of Linden?"

"She seems great."

"Isn't she? She's so complete. Some kids, when you meet them they don't seem to have all the pieces yet. But with Linden, you feel like oh: there's another person in the room."

She waited for an answer, but Jack was ashamed to admit he hadn't been paying much attention to Linden.

"It's funny," Laura went on, "when I said that about wanting to be an only child: I wouldn't want to *have* an only child. I think it makes it harder for them to be kids, if they're the only one."

Now there was a long silence, and Jack wondered why she'd brought up this subject, which was one they'd never discussed before. Was it her way of trying to ascertain where they stood, now that he'd thrown the question mark of Maisie between them, or was it simply seeing her niece that made her talk about kids?

"Well," he said finally. "That's a ways off."

"Not that far," Laura said. "Especially if I want a bunch. I need to get going."

"How many is a bunch?" Jack asked.

"Oh, six," Laura said lightly. "Nine."

"Fourteen," said Jack, but she didn't laugh.

"What's that?" she asked suddenly.

"What?" A thin wail, from outside their room somewhere. He let his arm trail down the side of the bed, feeling for Egg.

"It's Linden," Laura said.

The comforter made a crackling noise as she pushed it back. Jack put on his bathrobe and followed her into the living room. Linden was sitting up in her bed, crying. Laura knelt beside her. The room was dark except for the humming glow of the fish tank.

"What is it, Linden?"

"I want my mommy," Linden said, her eyes closed.

"Your mommy's sleeping. What is it? Can you tell me?"

Linden opened her eyes, still crying, and pointed to the fish tank. In its light, her face was green.

"What? My fish? They're all sleeping, too, Linden. See? And they're nice fish. They won't hurt you." Laura put her hand on Linden's back, rubbing it gently up and down.

Linden shook her head and pointed. "They're monsters."

Jack looked, and saw on the wall the magnified black images of the tails and fins beneath the overhead light, the huge wavering plants. "It's the shadows," he said.

"Is that it?" Laura asked. "The shadows? Is that what's bothering you?"

Linden nodded.

"Well, that's no big deal, Linden. See? I'll just turn out the little light in the fish tank. See? There."

"They're still there," Linden said.

"No, they're not. I can't see them, Jack. Can you?"

Jack said, "Would you like a light on, Linden? I can turn on this lamp right here. Or I could put on the light in the kitchen."

"Take the fish out."

"We can't, sweetheart," Laura told her. "The tank is too heavy. See all that water inside? It's much too heavy." She glanced at Jack, then spoke to Linden again. "Would you like to sleep with us, Linden? For a special treat?"

Linden nodded, and Laura picked her up. Her legs went around Laura's waist. "Oh. That's right. You're so big, Linden."

He kept his bathrobe on and got carefully into the bed with them. Linden's head sank down into the crack between the pillows. He felt her small leg against his side.

"Should we tell you a story?" Laura asked.

Linden was crying again. "I don't want you. I want my mama."

"But she's asleep. She's very tired. Let's let her sleep, Linden."

"I want her."

"Okay." Laura got out of bed again, carried Linden out. She was gone for a minute or two. When she got back into bed, Jack groped under the covers for her hand. She let him take it, but when he squeezed it, she didn't squeeze back.

15

Floating and Falling

❧

Jack didn't call for two weeks. Maisie viewed the lapse as punishment, something she must bow her head to and bear without flinching. She tried not to think about it in terms of what she might have done wrong.

Kris called her from the temp agency one afternoon and asked if she could come in the next morning to talk to Bert Little, the owner. Sure, Maisie said. She'd met Bert once or twice when she'd been in to pick up checks. He seemed to spend very little time in the office, and when he was there he sat with his feet up on his desk, drinking coffee, reading magazines, and ignoring what went on around him. Once he had played for Kris and Maisie a tape of himself singing and playing the piano. He was writing a musical version of *The Great Gatsby*.

> *In the air*
> *There's something crazy,*
> *A scent, a laugh*
> *That whispers: Daisy. . . .*

Maisie had listened politely to the song and told him she liked it. Kris had rolled her eyes behind Bert's back and later told Maisie that he'd been writing these musicals for years, always unproduced, always convinced he had a hit on his hands.

Maisie couldn't imagine why he would want to see her, unless to play her more songs because she had seemed an appreciative audience. You couldn't get fired from temping, could you? She knew she'd been doing a good job, and besides, if they did want to fire her, Kris would be the one to tell her: as far as Maisie could tell, Kris did everything.

She walked over to the agency on a white, hot morning, yesterday's heat still boiling up from the sidewalks. Bert stood up when she came in and shook her hand, then sat down again. Kristine smiled at her and then went out to get a cup of coffee.

Bert had an aging boy's face—she guessed he was close to sixty—red and eager, moon-shaped creases under the eyes, and skin that was beginning to sag from the jawbone. An olive tweed jacket, a maroon bow tie, stained old Top-Sider sneakers in which his feet, crossed at the ankles and resting on his desktop, rotated slowly as he asked Maisie about her background. When she told him she'd gone to Concord, he mentioned he'd been at St. Paul's; when she said Harvard, he said Amherst. He let her know that he'd spent childhood summers on a lake in Wisconsin and that he summered now in Woods Hole; she countered with a wistful reference to Vinalhaven, although she didn't mention exactly whose house it was and how little time she'd actually spent there. This exchange of credentials made her feel disappointed in Bert—he seemed to grow warmer and more respectful with every word she uttered—and yet pleased that she actually did possess the credentials with which to reassure and impress him. She knew, sheepishly, that this was one of the things she missed about Jack: the fact that he'd been born to these schools and summer places and could shrug them off, while she could only pretend to shrug; really it still gave her a small thrill whenever she said "Harvard."

Bert's conversation continued to meander through such subjects as book publishing—he had an old college roommate who was a senior editor at the house where Maisie had worked—Broadway musicals, and primogeniture, which he'd been thinking about a lot lately, how the economy and in fact the whole history of a country was affected by the presence or absence of primogeniture as an organizing principle. Maisie nodded and looked serious and wondered whether he did this with all his temps, used them as sounding boards for whatever was on his mind. He spoke like a man starved for listeners, and she was surprised when she noticed that he was wearing a wedding ring.

"So," he said finally. "Next Monday, nine o'clock. Be here."

Maisie was confused. "Excuse me?"

"Jesus. Do you mean Kristine didn't even tell you?"

"Tell me what?"

"That noodlehead. She's leaving. Kristine is leaving, and I'd like you to take her place." He sounded annoyed; Maisie knew it was because she had failed to pick up on his telegraphic Bogart-like offer of employment. He'd wanted her to stand, say, "Right," and walk out. She was annoyed, too, at the way he'd spoken of Kristine, and at herself for being too weak to object to it.

"But what exactly will I be doing?" she asked.

"You'll be running the damn place," Bert said, raking his hair with his fingers. "Answering the phone. Testing would-be temps. Matchmaking. Don't ask me. Ask Kristine."

"Will she be back soon?" Maisie asked.

"How should I know?" said Bert, opening a sailing magazine and beginning to read.

She took the elevator down and found Kris in the lobby, leaning against the wall, sipping coffee from a paper cup. "I hung out down here because I figured you'd want to talk," Kris said. "So, did you take the job?"

"I don't know. He seems to think I did."

Kris shook her head. "Yeah, that's one of his problems. He hears what he wants to hear."

"What's he like?"

"A jerk. Very snobby, very sexist, but harmless. He'll treat you like dirt when he's there, but he's never there. You basically get to make all your own decisions, you have all the contact with the temps and the employers. Every now and then he'll come in and second-guess you, mess up everything you've been doing, and then leave. You make pretty good money, but when you ask for a raise he'll squirm and tell you his wife only makes blabbedy-blah."

"Does his wife run a temp agency?"

"No, she's a bank examiner. She makes five times as much as you could ever hope to see. But the point is, Bert thinks she's grossly underpaid, and if *she's* underpaid, then *you* should be underpaid."

"Why are you leaving?"

Kris wiped coffee from her mouth and smiled. "Oh, we're moving to New Mexico. Arturo grew up there, and he's starting a business with an old friend."

"That's great!" Maisie said. "What kind of business?"

"Selling paper towels and stuff. But it's better than it sounds, he'll be kind of an independent franchiser, recruiting other distributors."

Maisie bit her lip. "It sounds exciting," she said.

That afternoon she called Jack at the office. She'd been looking at the telephone for an hour, cleaning her apartment with the kind of fervor that seized her only when she was considering something difficult, or expecting guests. She genuinely wanted to get his opinion on this job offer, but she also wanted so badly to talk to him that she doubted her own sincerity and was afraid that he might doubt it even more readily. She couldn't afford to lose any ground she might have gained over the weekend, but she couldn't pass up a legitimate excuse to talk to him. "Oh, screw it," she said aloud finally, dropping the vacuum cleaner and reaching for the phone.

She spoke to a strange secretary, and spent only a moment on hold before Jack took her call.

"Is Mary all right?" she asked him.

"Mary? She's on vacation."

"Oh, I was worried for a minute."

"No, she's fine. She had a checkup a couple of weeks ago, in fact, and everything was clean."

"That's wonderful."

"So what's up?" His voice was surprisingly friendly.

She told him about her job offer, and he listened without interrupting. "So what do you think?" she finished.

"It's a permanent job?"

"Well, permanent. It's not as though I have to sign on for life."

"But it's not just short-term."

"No, I'd have to stick with it a while."

"It sounds to me like you really want to take it."

"I do," she said, sounding surprised. "I think I'd be good at it, and I feel like I could really understand the people who come in looking for temp work."

"But you're worried about this guy?"

"Well, but he's never there, Kris says. I think the business is a sort of toy for him. He owns it, and he picks it up and drops it when he feels like it, but mostly Kris says he's at his weekend house, or sucking up to famous people. She says he's the world's biggest name dropper."

"Uh-huh."

"He's a jerk, but I liked him. Sort of. Do you know what I mean?"

"Sort of."

"So I guess I will take it, then."

"But something's still bothering you."

"No," she said slowly.

"Yes, there is."

He was being so soft with her, so attentive. It made her feel breakable, sad. Why was he being so careful?

"Oh, well, I guess it's just not what I expected to end up doing, that's all."

"But you're not ending up. As you say, you're not signing on for life."

"Right."

"I've decided there aren't many people who have really passionate vocations. Or anyway, people whose vocations really coincide with their abilities."

"Well, but I always thought I would. Have something like that, I mean."

"I know," he said gently.

There was a long silence, during which she wondered what that smell was that always seemed to hang in the air of a just vacuumed room. Was it the vacuum cleaner bag? The exhaust from the motor? It seemed odd that a machine that sucked things in should also put out something as distinct as this strange stuffy odor. Then she said, almost absently, "So will we see each other again soon?"

"Next weekend?" he said, and she felt a quiet small throb of anticipation: a tryst.

"Not tomorrow, you mean, but the weekend at the end of next week?"

"That's right."

"Okay," she said pleasantly, and wondered when he would have called to suggest this, if she hadn't called first.

Kris was in the office Monday when Maisie showed up, and she said she'd be there for the next two weeks to teach Maisie the job. "Not that there's two weeks' worth of teaching," she said. "But I have to serve out my notice."

"You mean you'd just given notice when I was in here last week?" Maisie asked.

"Oh, yes. Bert didn't wait till the body was cold. I quit, he told me he was sorry to lose me, and then he started looking through our résumé file."

"God," Maisie said. "I'm really sorry."

"Don't be. I'm not kidding, I can't wait to get out of here. It hasn't been a bad job," Kris added hastily. "I just think, No more Boston winters. No more subway. No more asshole boss. Not that you'll necessarily think that."

"You're scaring me!" Maisie said, smiling. But for some reason she wasn't scared; it was the first job she'd ever had where she hadn't walked into the office and thought, instantly, I shouldn't have taken this. Much as she liked Kris, she couldn't wait for her to leave. Kris was showing her how to get through a day—check the answering machine first thing, then flip open the "Week Ending" chart and pull out your orders for the day, look at your starts, make your phone calls, call to see if each temp has arrived safely, fill out your quality-control conduct reports, set aside time for client recruiting, try to bunch all your interviews in either the morning or the afternoon, even though it won't work out that way because people can never come in when you want them to, grade the applicants on appearance, manner, and skills. Maisie said, "Uh-huh, uh-huh, uh-huh," but she was itching to start talking to the people.

At the end of the week Bert came in and took her to lunch. She told him, a bit hesitantly, that she thought they could distinguish themselves from all the other Harvard Square temp agencies by recruiting temps who had special skills: languages, tutoring, carpentry, graphic design, instead of just secretaries and clerical workers. He laughed and said he thought finding jobs for those people would be like finding needles in haystacks. She said, "I know it's probably just beginner's fervor, but do you mind if I try mentioning these services to our clients? I've been going through the files a little this week, and it's amazing what some of the people we've sent out to type and file have listed on their applications under 'Other Skills and Hobbies.' "

He shrugged. "It's not a very practical notion. But go ahead and do it as a sideline. There are fifty million temp agencies in Harvard Square alone, and if you can manage to distinguish us from the other guys, then more power to you." He smiled. "Sure, go ahead. As long as you get all the basic shit done, I don't give a fig what else you spend your time on."

In Jack's piece of fish, something moved. A brownish-pink slow flutter. He poked at it with his fork. "There's a worm in here."

Maisie put down her fork and bowed her head but kept her eyes raised to his. The frightened, guilty look irritated him.

"Well, don't eat any more, that's all," he said. "We should take this back. Where did you get it?"

"Fish and Fowl," she said.

"Foul is right."

She didn't smile.

"Is it just my piece, or is yours wormy, too?"

"It was one big piece," she said, not looking at her plate. "I cut it in half."

"Here, give me your plate."

She passed it over, hesitantly. He found three more worms. "How late are they open?"

"Let's just throw it out, Jack."

"No, they shouldn't get away with this. I'll go, if you want."

She put her head down on her empty placemat and burst into tears.

He watched her. "Oh, come on, Maisie, it's not that big a deal." Then, "You're right. We won't even bother returning it. Here." He got up and scraped the plates into the garbage, sealed up the plastic bag, and carried it out of the apartment to the garbage room across the hall.

"There," he said, letting the apartment door fall shut behind him. He bolted it and put on the chain.

"Don't forget the police lock," Maisie sniffed.

"We'll get one of those stickers that says you're protected by an alarm system, even though you're not," said Jack. "One of the ones with pictures of German shepherds on it."

"Are worms scared of German shepherds? I think we should find a sticker that has a giant robin on it."

She was smiling now, and he found himself smiling back at her.

"I thought I was going to die when I saw that first worm," she said. "But I thought, No, no, shut up, just pick around it."

"You mean you saw worms in your half? You knew before I said anything?"

Now she looked scared again. "Well, but I thought—"

"What? That I'd walk out for good if you took away my plate? Jesus, Maisie. Next time, *tell* me, all right?"

"All right," she said shakily. "Should I cook something else?"

He grimaced.

They finished up the wine while they washed the dishes, and then Maisie suddenly said, "Let's go out."

"Where?"

"Let's look at the stars. We can go to the field in front of the high school."

"You mean identify the constellations? Do you know how to do that?"

"I know the Big Dipper, and the lady who's shaped like a 'W.' "

"We could buy a book, I suppose."

"Oh, Jack. What difference does it make which is which? They never correspond to the pictures anyway. We'll just make up our own."

They lay on their backs on the prickly grass. Jack said, "If you close your eyes and count to one hundred, your eyes will adjust to the darkness and you'll actually be able to see more stars."

They closed their eyes and he let her count, slowly, aloud. They were lying at right angles to one another, with their heads close together, and he had a drunken feeling of simultaneous floating and falling. Once he gasped and fumbled at the dirt with both hands, as though grabbing for an invisible railing.

"What?" said Maisie.

"Nothing. I just almost rolled off the edge."

"Fifty-seven," she said, "fifty-eight . . ."

At one hundred he opened his eyes and blinked. The sky looked just the same, peppered with white, haloed with pale orange night glow.

"You're right," Maisie said. "I can definitely see more."

"You can?"

"Well, not in the foreground, maybe. Not more big stars. But it's like the background has filled out and gotten more dimensional, you know?" She took a swallow from the brandy bottle she'd brought along and passed it to him.

He sat up and drank, gazing at the high school, a looming sprawl of concrete surrounded by bright streetlights. When he looked up again, only the brightest stars were still visible. "But there's Pegasus," he said slowly, "and the Dragon, and the Swan."

"How do you know all that?"

"I don't know. Boy Scout camp, I guess," he said, lying down again and tucking an arm beneath his head.

"I didn't know you were a Boy Scout."

"I had twenty-three merit badges."

"You're kidding. For what?"

"I have no idea. Birding, I suppose. Lifesaving. I don't know. Making fires."

"And you spent a summer at Boy Scout camp?"

"A week. It was supposed to be two, but I walked out."

"You did?"

"Those kids had no interest in being out in the woods. We'd go on nature walks, and they'd have these BB guns hidden in their shorts, and they'd try to get squirrels when the counselors weren't looking."

"So that's why you left?"

He shook his head and reached for the brandy bottle. "One night we went on an overnight. We hiked all this way into the woods, and it started to rain. And we had to pitch our tents in the mud, and try to light a campfire with wet wood in the pouring rain. We put down some tarps that were supposed to keep our sleeping bags dry, only they leaked, and I was just lying there with a wet back listening to these other kids snoring and telling dirty jokes, and I suddenly thought, I don't have to do this, and I got up and walked out."

"But didn't you get lost?"

"It was a state park I'd done a lot of bird-watching in, and I knew exactly where we were. We were only about a mile and a half from the highway. I just followed the trail and then hitched a ride home, and told my mother I was quitting Boy Scouts."

"What did she say?"

"She said, 'All right, dear.' "

They both laughed.

Maisie drank more brandy. "But that's a great story. What a little rebel. I didn't know you'd ever done anything that rebellious in your life."

"I'd forgotten all about it till just now," Jack said. "Isn't that weird? I didn't even remember that I knew those constellations."

"I tried to walk out on the Brownies once, but my mother wouldn't let me. I giggled during some flag ceremony, and one of the leaders yelled at me. So that night I told my mother I wanted to quit."

"Why wouldn't she let you?"

"She was the other leader."

He laughed softly for a moment and then tried to stop, but the laughter kept coming, shaking him like hiccups. He rolled onto his stomach and pressed his forehead into his cold, dusty hands. He felt a soft, tentative hand patting him between the shoulder blades, and immediately he rolled over onto his back, coughing. Maisie was kneeling beside him, her knees touching his rib cage.

He blinked at the sky. "And that's the Milky Way."

"What is?"

"That thick white streak."

"But how can it be? We're *in* the Milky Way. How can we see it?"

She was still pressing against him, her head thrown back. He looked at the long pale line of her throat.

"You can be in a crowd and still see that it's a crowd."

"But the crowd doesn't look far away if you're in it. This looks so distant. How can it look that way if we're actually part of it?"

He didn't know.

When they got back to the apartment Maisie turned on the lights and started to laugh. "Look at us."

Her hands and face were smeared with dirt, and bits of leaves and grass clippings and grit clung to the front of her green sweater.

"*And* I'm cold," she said. "You want some more wine? Brandy? I can open another bottle."

"Do you have any aspirin?" He sank down on the futon.

"Poor Jack." She passed a light hand over his temples on her way into the bathroom, and he shifted his weight uncomfortably. She came out with the pills, and he watched her gliding around the room, getting him water, taking down clean towels from the closet, pouring herself more wine. It was her old, confident way of moving. This was the first time she'd moved that way since they'd been seeing each other. In this apartment she huddled, she crept.

Now she threw a towel over her shoulder, smiled at him, and turned to carry her wine into the bathroom, and he thought she almost seemed to be dancing.

He read the sports section, checking every now and then to see where his headache was—yes, it was fading, still there if he shook his head, but definitely receding. He was vaguely aware of the shower stopping, the bathroom door opening, Maisie coming back into the room. He glanced up from a picture of Michael Jordan and saw, for an instant, his wife, naked: oh, of course, a sight that was at once exciting and familiar. Then he looked again. She was so pretty, he'd forgotten; but it was more than that: when he looked at her body, he could feel it, the soft give of her breasts, the curve of her waist, the fit of her legs around his. He closed his eyes against the memory, then opened them again. He was hard, uncomfortably twisted beneath the metal fly of his jeans. She stared at him, and he stared back, angry and aroused, admiring her nerve, embarrassed that he'd pushed her this far, to a gesture neither of them could retreat from.

Finally she put a freckled forearm across her belly, grasping the opposite wrist, shifting her weight with a jerk, a lift of one white hip. "You won't."

"No."

"Why?"

"Because I think it would cloud the issue."

"Isn't it part of the package?"

He looked at her questioningly.

"If you're weighing all the factors, trying to decide whether you want me or not, isn't it part of—"

"That's disgusting," he said.

"Why?"

"It just is."

"But why?"

"Because you're not some—some—"

"Some what?"

She stared at him, her eyebrows lifted.

"Fine," he said. "Here." He stood up, threw down the paper. He pushed her down on the rug, on her stomach, lay on top of her. His hands were under her, one soft breast mashed flat against his palm. Her thighs and the small patch of hair, still damp from the shower, but dry inside, closing herself against his finger. He pressed his neck down against her moist, hot face and began squirming out of his jeans. She brought her hand around to help him, pushing at the stiff denim. Her pliancy inflamed him further, and he shoved himself against it, inside her; but when he felt her clench beneath him, gasping—he was hurting her—he slowed down and finally just pulled out and rolled away. She stayed on her stomach, her face turned away from him. After a moment he reached up for the quilt from the futon, tossing it awkwardly over her.

"Maisie."

She didn't answer, and when he put a hand on her leg she didn't move. He got up and pulled his jeans back on.

"I'm going out."

He walked down to the river, across the bridge, and through the dark quadrangles of the business school. Every window of every building was lit with the same bright yellow light, as though no one dared not to be studying, or dared to deviate from the regulation desk lamp. The night had turned chilly, with a restless scraping wind that reminded him of the night last fall when he'd gone out and harvested his vegetable garden; and he thought of Laura, in bed now, sleeping, or maybe lying awake wondering about him and Maisie. His hands felt coated, smooth; he raised one to his face and smelled Maisie's bath powder.

When he was too tired to walk anymore, he headed up to Harvard Square and drank a cup of coffee in a brightly lit bakery. There was a big clock on the wall above the counter: it was almost eleven.

"You want to know the exact moment when I realized Zach was different from you and me?" a ponytailed boy at the next table was saying to two girls in black. "The exact moment? We're in this pizza place, and Zach looks across the room and says, 'That's Jacques Derrida.' Don't ask me how he knew it was him, but anyway, he says, 'I'm just going to go and say hello to him.' And when he comes back I say, 'Boy, do you have guts. I wouldn't have even been sure he spoke English.' And you know what Zach says?"

"What?" asked one of the girls.

"He says, 'Oh, I spoke to him in French.' "

"Zach meets Jacques," said the girl.

The three of them glanced at Jack simultaneously, waiting for his reaction. He pushed back his chair and left his half-drunk cup of coffee and crumpled napkin beneath a big sign, in red letters, that read PLEASE HAVE CONSIDERATION FOR OUR PATRONS AND STAFF. BUS YOUR OWN TABLE.

When he knocked softly on the apartment door Maisie opened it, in her nightgown. She had taken out her contact lenses and was wearing the heavy brown glasses he remembered. The bed was made up and the covers thrown back, with a book lying facedown near the pillow.

"I'm sorry," she said as soon as she'd shut the door.

"Maisie, I'm sorry," he said, as if she hadn't spoken.

"I pushed you."

"Still."

She went to sit on the bed, her back against the wall and her knees drawn up with the nightgown covering them tightly. He sat on the floor with his back to her.

"I don't know if I can do this," she said. "I knew it was going to be hard, I knew that, but it's like we're just wallowing. I can't see how we're ever going to get *out*." Her face was white. She gripped her knees.

"I just wanted to break with you," he said. "I think that's honestly why I called you in the first place. I wanted to prove that I was immune to you. But I'm not."

"Well, that's good, then, isn't it?"

"But look what I did to you tonight."

"It's all right," Maisie said.

"It is not."

"Let's cut this out," she said suddenly.

"What?"

"This 'you're the saint, no *you're* the saint' business. All right? You're mad at me because I treated you like dirt, well, fine. I'm not treating you like dirt anymore. And I'm not going to keep apologizing."

"I never asked you to."

"Yes, you did. You're making all the rules and it's my job to play by them. Like the worms in the fish. Why was that all my fault?"

"You were the one who got hysterical about the worms. Not me."

"Yeah, because you've made it very clear if I say or do the wrong thing, you'll walk out and not come back. Well, fuck you. I'm sick of being tested."

"You're making things up."

"What, that this is all a test? I am not."

He looked at the cracked ceiling, the slanting orange crates laden with books and clothes, the hissing silver radiator. Moving his eyes downward quickly made him dizzy. "All right. You say whatever you want."

"And you won't walk out?"

"No." He felt tired, immediately after he spoke, and straightened up to try to snap himself awake. "So? What is it you want to say?" His voice came out so sharp, so wary, that he repeated it in order not to scare her off. "What?"

She drew back and her face flushed, with embarrassment, he thought. But then she said, her mouth contorting, "You see? That's how you talk to me. All the time. Who made you the judge?"

"I'm not the judge," he said wearily.

"Well, you're the one who's deciding when we see each other, and whether or not we're going to get back together. This isn't how real people live. We're not shopping together, or seeing movies together, or sleeping together, for God's sake. We're not doing ordinary boring stuff together, and finding out whether it *is* boring. So all you have to base your decision on, as far as I can tell, is how nice I am now, or how grown-up I am now, or how much I love you. Well, I do love you, but there's nothing in these weekends that could possibly prove that to you."

"Maisie, if you're suggesting we try living together again, I ought to tell you that's impossible at the moment."

"What. Because of Laura?"

"Partly."

"I can't believe you're still seeing her."

"I'm *living* with her."

"I *know* that," said Maisie. She lay down on the bed with her back to him.

Then they were silent, and they must have fallen asleep. He woke up some time later to feel the radiator's steel ribs mashed against his back, his legs sticking out stiffly in front of him. The clock at the back of Maisie's old stove said quarter to four. She was asleep on top of the covers, her glasses still on her face but askew, one stem down along her cheek and nearly touching her mouth. He moved on his knees over to the bed, and gently he took her glasses off, folded them, and set them on the stool that served as her bedside table. Her nightgown was draped smoothly over her knees, and her small feet were crossed at the ankles, as though she were a tomb effigy. He'd forgotten how neatly she slept. Even her breathing was pretty: soft little exhalations of the lips and nostrils, hushed and controlled, like the sounds she'd made when she smoked. Her eyelids were shiny and faintly pink, trembling with whatever dreams went on beneath them. He put a hand on her face, his fingertips tracing the cheekbone, and without increasing the pressure of that hand, he used the other arm to push himself up onto the bed beside her. There was hardly any room, and he lay on his side with his left arm beneath him, the right hand still resting lightly on her face.

"Unnnh," she said softly, and then she opened her eyes and looked at him.

He turned away, reached up over their heads and switched off the light. He began to kiss her, gently at first, but then harder: she'd got him after all. But he didn't want to think, he wanted her nightgown off, her knees open, her arms stretched over her head. And after a while he felt her shaking beneath him and knew that she was coming, or crying; he didn't care which.

He let himself into the old Grosvenor School building at one o'clock on Monday morning; the purply fluorescent light pulsed in the long silent hallways, dimming and then joltingly brighter, like eyes trying hard to stay awake. Inside the apartment the lights were on, a murmur of music from the kitchen. Laura, the sleeves of her terrycloth bathrobe pushed above her elbows, was rolling out dough on the wooden tabletop. He kissed her hair, and she rubbed his shoulder once with her cheek, leaving a smudge of flour.

"What are you making?"

"Croissants."

The room smelled of butter and faint pine floor cleaner. The radio was tuned to some late night jazz station: soporific bass and saxophone, nervous trumpet.

"It was stupid of me," Laura said, leaning hard on the rolling pin. "I started after lunch, but I forgot how many times you need to roll out the dough."

"How many?" asked Jack, rubbing his palm between her shoulder blades. He was feeling very calm, very safe: you see, I'm back, don't worry.

"The book says thirteen."

"What happens if you cheat?"

"I've never dared to." She turned the dough; it slapped down on the table with a heavy, fleshy sound. "You get this far and you don't want to risk ending up with so much wasted effort."

Jack kept rubbing. "What number is this?"

"I don't know. I've lost count."

"Laura."

He sat up with her all night, through five more rollings and the baking. The croissants were ready in time for breakfast. He ate two, though he could hardly taste them. Laura sat across from him and gulped coffee and watched him, and he told her again and again how good they were.

Maisie was alone in the office a few days later when the phone rang, and it was Jack.

He said, "Next weekend I have something I have to do, but what about the weekend after that?"

"No."

"No?"

"I can't do any more weekends."

He didn't answer.

"I can't just sit there and be a punching bag. I think we either have to say all right, we're going to try being married again, I mean really try; or we should just stop seeing each other and think about a divorce."

"I don't want a divorce," said Jack.

"I don't, either."

"Well, so that's all, then."

"I don't mean it to be an ultimatum," she said. "I mean, this isn't a calculated—I'm not thinking, Gee, why don't I put my foot down and see what he does. I'm just telling you: I can't stand this."

"Well, it may not be an ultimatum, but let me ask you, is there a time limit on it?"

"You see? That's what I mean. That's what I can't stand."

He apologized; then he said, "But Maisie, say I do want to be with you, how would we manage it? Would you be willing to move to Champs du Soleil?"

"You still haven't broken up with Laura."

"No."

"Then asking me that question is like getting me to lay my head on the block, and then you'll tell me whether or not you're planning to chop it off."

He laughed shortly.

Maisie went on: "I've told you what I want, and that I'm willing to try, but you're the one who's still dancing around."

"Why can't you understand that the logistics of this—"

"Jack, the real problem is that you can't go on sleeping with two women." Or maybe you can, she thought. It scared her to think that he was capable now of being a cad. I've ruined him. I treated him horribly, and now he's hardened.

But he took a deep breath and said, "Okay. I am trying to sell the company. I've called the broker who's handling it and told him to get really aggressive about finding a buyer, and he called me this week to tell me he's got someone who's interested. He thinks that with the product improvements and the new projections there's a good chance we can work something out. Okay? But I have no idea if it'll happen, or how long it might take."

"And what about Laura?"

"I don't know. I don't want to hurt her."

"Jack!"

"She got into the middle of this without—she had every reason to suppose my marriage was over."

"And it's her tough luck that it isn't. Come on, Jack. She knew this might happen, or she should have known."

"Well, you can't put me on a timetable about breaking up with her."

"Fine. One more thing." She felt as though they were negotiating a business contract.

"What?"

"I would move to Champs du Soleil. I mean, if things don't work out with your selling the business. I like my job here, and it sounds to me like you do want to get out of the factory. But if it makes a difference, I'll come live there."

"Okay, well, you've given me a lot to think about," Jack said.

"I know," Maisie said. "But I love you."

"I love you," he said in the same solemn tone, and they hung up. Maisie sat for a moment with clenched fists. I'm right, I know I'm right. But she was just going to have to wait, and see what he decided.

16
Vandals

❧

On a cool Friday afternoon in mid-September, almost exactly a year after their first weekend at Laura's camp, Jack and Laura paddled across the lake in near silence.

The subject of Maisie had not come up between them since he'd returned from his last Cambridge weekend a month before. They talked about work, and what was in the newspaper, what they saw on television, and what they were going to cook for dinner. They ran out of shampoo and debated whether to buy the same brand again or try a different one. Someone offered Laura a kitten, and they thought of taking it but decided it would probably upset Egg. Had they always talked this way, Jack wondered, or had they just reached a point where there was nothing else, nothing safe to talk about beside the merits of solid white versus chunk light tuna?

He had not told her that for the past few weeks he'd been negotiating through Warren Phinney to sell the company. Jack had been a bit suspicious of Phinney for turning up a prospect so fast—he works fruitlessly for a year with no retainer, and then the minute I give him one and agree to a minimum fee of $30,000 for the sale he suddenly conjures up a buyer? But if Phinney were really a crook, he'd have let a few months go by on retainer before finding a prospect.

The buyer was a man from New Jersey who was prepared to put down half the purchase price in cash and come up with the rest over four years. He had seen the statements Jack's lawyer and accountant had prepared on the company's past performance, the year-to-date and projections for the rest of the year, the clients, the payroll, the physical plant, the owner's take-home. Jack felt all of it could be read two ways—either as the portrait of a perpetually struggling company that happened to have had a slight upswing recently, or of a formerly troubled company that had now been turned around. The buyer, according to Phinney, saw it as the latter, and was anxious to come for a visit. They were negotiating now about when that would be; Jack preferred a Saturday, since the factory would be closed and nobody would be there to become alarmed or suspicious, but the buyer wanted to see everything on a typical workday.

He had not told Laura because she would know what a sale would mean: he was preparing to get out of Champs du Soleil. He was afraid she'd say, "I'll go with you."

He hadn't told Maisie yet, either. He had not spoken to her since their last, terse phone call. He knew that what she'd said was true: they couldn't experiment with each other in little self-contained chunks. Either they were married, or they weren't.

The surface of the lake was clear and perfectly flat. He swung his paddle, and the bow of the canoe sent out two diagonal white lines, which writhed on the water for a moment and then disappeared. Laura sat behind him, and he sweated, sensing her eyes on him.

There was something strange and dark about the house. Laura ran past him, stumbling up the beach, and he realized the glass in the windows was gone. The padlock was missing from the door; the wooden panel hung loose on its hinges, half-open. He sprinted to get there before her. "Wait," he said. "Someone might be inside."

She shouldered by him, into the living room. The heavy wooden chairs were upside down with their thick legs splayed in the air. The cushions on the couch were slit open, hairy stuffing springing out. "Oh, God, oh, God," Laura said softly. And he saw that the old chalk landscape drawing that had hung over the fireplace and the eighteenth-century map of Maine were gone. Books spilled out of the shelf at the foot of the stairs.

"The pots, they took the pots," she said from the kitchen, and he remembered the battered tin kettle, the tarnished copper saucepans. "Jesus, Jack, the *fat* jar!" her voice rising, and he said stupidly, looking at the sink full of potato chip bags, and rib bones, rotting orange peels, a broken wine jug:

"What fat jar?"

"It was earthenware," she screamed, "you remember, gray with a blue deer on it, that's *hot* now, it's an *antique*. That was my *grand*mother's *fat* jar."

He looked at the corner of the stove where it had always sat, full of whitened drippings, and opened his mouth to puzzle with her, console her, but she ran out of the room toward the back of the house. He followed, expecting to find her in the bedroom, but she was standing outside the bathroom, weeping, her mouth a straight line and her eyes wrinkled shut. He held her shoulder and looked past her and saw that the marble sink had been wrenched from its base; the weathered oak planks were split around the edges of the hole, exposing the new-looking white inside of the wood.

"They must have used a crowbar," he said wonderingly, and Laura cried:

"Why did they have to steal my *sink?*"

They were outside the cabin, Laura sitting on the big rock and Jack standing in front of her. She said finally, tiredly, "They knew exactly what they were doing."

"You mean because they took things like that jar and the sink?"

"They knew exactly what everything was worth. They weren't just some dumb vandals."

"Well, if they took the stuff to sell, you might be able to trace some of it. Get it back."

"They took the poetry from the bookshelf. Just because it was in old bindings. They took the bird log. It wasn't even worth anything, but it *looked* fancy and old."

"Well," said Jack. "We'd better call the police."

She shook her head.

"You have to report it." But there was no telephone in the house, no neighbors for miles around.

"It can wait. I mean, this obviously didn't just happen. They were living here, Jack. You saw all that crap in the sink. The *beds* were slept in. They took their time, figuring out exactly what was worth stealing."

He wondered how long they had stayed: not more than a day or two, certainly, in the middle of the week. They must have known that the camp was being used just for weekends. But she had said "living here" as though the thieves had taken full possession, sensing her absence, her distraction; and he realized that they hadn't been here for nearly a month now, although he knew that in previous summers Laura had been here every weekend and sometimes stayed for weeks at a time.

"Did they have a boat, do you think?"

She shrugged. "It could have been a truck. There's an old road, we can check it for tracks. Nobody's used it for years."

She'd never mentioned a road before. He'd always assumed, without ever asking, that the camp was on an island, with a long unexplored shoreline, reachable only by water.

The sun was moving down behind the pines at the far end of the lake, lighting their tops with silver.

"Do you want to go home?" he asked. It was six o'clock; if they left now, they could make it almost across the lake before it got dark.

She said coldly, "We have to clean up."

"We could come back next weekend. When it won't seem so raw."

She didn't answer.

"We could bring the Jeep."

"No," she said. "You have to drive nearly into Canada to pick up that road."

"Or I could come alone, if you give me directions." It seemed, suddenly, terribly important to get her away from this place. He looked at her pale, swollen face, the deep undereye creases and the bulging flesh beneath them.

"My stuff is probably in Canada by now."

"Wouldn't they get stopped, going over the border with a truckful of—whatever," he said.

"I don't know," she answered shortly. "But anyway, it's not your mess, it's my mess. I'll clean it up."

But in the end, she did let him help. He righted the chairs and covered the cushions with old towels from the missing linen cupboard. He stripped the beds and tied the sheets in bundles to be laundered in town. He washed the remaining dishes and put them away in the sagging wall cupboard, lined up the books in the shelf. He went out back to the outhouse and scrubbed the privy's oak toilet seat with disinfectant—why not the toilet seat? he wondered, throwing lime down over the stinking soil. Didn't they realize how collectable wooden seats are these days?

Laura made a list of what was missing. The thieves had burned all the visible candles down to pools of wax, but she had brought some in her bag, and when it got dark Jack rummaged for them and set them in empty saucers. He dug into the cooler for a bottle of wine and opened it with his Swiss Army knife; Laura's corkscrew was gone.

"Let me see," he said, holding out his hand, and Laura passed him her list.

Telescope
Binoculars—(2)
Bird log
Poetry books
Tom Jones *(red cover)*
Cranford *(")*
Scarlet Letter
Radio
Fat jar
Chess set—1 black knight missing
Ivory dominoes
Barometer
Photographs—frames?
Landscape drawing
Map
Audubon wood ducks
" pileated woodpeckers
Sink
Linen cupboard
Woven blankets—(5)
Kettle
Copper pots
Delft pitcher
" platter
" sugar bowl
Blue Willow plates—(7)

"What do you mean, 'photographs—frames'?" he asked.

"I mean they must have taken them for the frames. The pictures themselves weren't worth anything."

"And they stole a knight from the chess set?"

"No. The knight was already missing. They stole an incomplete chess set."

He passed the list back to her. "I never knew half this stuff was here."

"Well, it was."

"It always seemed like a house full of odds and ends, or as though there weren't many things here at all."

"I hate thinking of it as Delft this and Audubon that." Her voice was calm now, but the jelly glass of wine in her hand was shaking. "And that list isn't even counting all the dopey little gadgety things they took."

"What kills me," he said, pouring more wine for both of them, "is the malice. The stuff in the kitchen sink, and slashing the cushions. The sheets and towels all over the floor. They were really out to wreck the place."

"Don't say it kills you, Jack. It doesn't kill you." She walked over to the front window. "Besides, what do you expect? You thought they'd fold up the linen after they stole the cupboard?"

"No."

"You thought they'd carry water from the lake to wash the dishes they used? It can't be very comfortable, robbing a house with no running water."

"I'm just trying to say, I understand why you're so upset. It's more than just the robbery."

She continued in a lower voice, "And I guess they slashed the cushions because they thought something might be hidden inside. Or maybe just for fun." She was running a finger lightly over the edge of broken glass in the window frame; he winced, watching her. "Next weekend I'll come back with some glass and putty. And a how-to book. I don't know anything about repairing windows, but I'm sure Time-Life has a book about it. Or *Reader's Digest*. I could never get a real glazier to come out here, it's much too far. I don't know. Or maybe I should just board them up, and fix them in the spring."

He noticed her saying "I" instead of "we."

"Did you check the garden?" he asked.

"No. Why?"

"Because I just wondered if there was any damage there."

"Jack. It was *people,* not a hurricane. Not *woodchucks.*"

"I know that."

"You check, if you care so much."

She went out on the porch and stood there, her arms folded over her chest. He followed.

"Laura," he began. He looked at his watch: nearly midnight. "Where do you want to sleep tonight?"

"In bed."

"No, I mean—I don't know. I thought maybe we'd want to sleep in one of the upstairs rooms."

"Why?" She sat down on the porch step, resting her chin in her hands.

He put a light hand on her head, stroking her rough, dusty hair.

She said, "It's not even my things I mind about. I wouldn't have cared so much if they'd broken into my *apartment* and trashed it. It's this place." She jerked her head out from under his hand. "I brought *you* here. You should know. I told you, that first weekend. I told you I never brought anyone else here."

He held very still, his hand still poised in the air above her. "So who are you mad at, me or the guys who did this?"

"You jerk." She was crying now. "Why are you making me *ask* you? Why don't you just tell me?"

He didn't pretend not to understand what she meant. He sat down next to her. "I didn't know how."

"You say: Laura, you've been a wonderful nurse to me all these months—"

"Stop it," said Jack.

"Are you saying I'm wrong?"

"That you've been my nurse? My God, Laura—"

"Am I wrong that you're going back to her?"

"No," he said flatly. "No, you're not wrong."

She looked at him for a long, cold moment. "Well, you should have told me in town. Not here."

"But I wouldn't have wanted you to come out here alone and find all this—" He turned and waved his hand at the three bulging plastic garbage bags on the porch behind them, filled with broken dishes, torn sheets, slit lamp shades.

"So what are you saying? That you came to protect me? Gee, I'd really like to break up with Laura, but maybe I should go out to the camp with her one more time, just in case it's been vandalized?" She stood up, running her hands over her face. "I'm going for a swim."

"Don't be ridiculous," said Jack, not moving. "It's freezing."

"I've swum here in September before. Lots of times. Without you here telling me what I can and can't do."

He stood up and held out his hands to her. "Come into the house. Come on, baby."

She snorted: "Baby!"

"I'm sorry." He didn't know how that had slipped out; he'd never called anyone "baby" before. She was heading away from him, over the stones that separated the house from the lake.

"Come back," he called, following her onto the rocks.

"No."

"Well, then let's go for a walk."

"They took the flashlights."

"Canoeing, then. We'll take out the canoe." He didn't know if this would be safe, canoeing at night, but at least it would keep her from swimming. He wasn't going to let her go anywhere alone, and being with her on top of the black water seemed safer than being in it.

The canoe's belly rasped along the stony beach, made a soft plushy sound entering the water. The lake, nearly up to his knees where he held the bow, was very cold, colder than the air; a warm mist draped its surface like a spiderweb. It occurred to him after a moment that he should have climbed into the canoe already; it would be more difficult now that he'd pulled it out this far. Laura hadn't said anything; usually when they took the boat out she murmured a constant gentle stream of instructions. He waded back to the center of the boat, swung one leg over the gunwale, and pulled himself in; the boat rocked uneasily. Laura, holding the stern, wasn't doing anything to steady it. He turned but couldn't see her face, just her dark shape. When he'd made his way to the rush seat in the bow, she gave the boat a shove and got in so smoothly that there was no rocking motion, just her sudden weight and then the sound of her paddle breaking the water.

They paddled in silence, he didn't know how far. He couldn't see the shore, only knew where it was by a few blurred dots of light from scattered camps. One of them must have been Laura's house; the others were neighbors', although the word seemed wrong considering the distance between the lights. He wondered if the other camps were full of people who'd arrived that day to find their houses vandalized, or perhaps he was seeing the lights of the thieves themselves, in some other deserted cabin, working their leisurely way up the lake. The more he thought about it, the more convinced he became: they were there, somewhere along that jagged shore, he was looking right at them. It was an effort for him not to mention this possibility to Laura.

Behind him he heard a light splash, a soft smack of something hitting the water, and then the boat rocked and he turned his head to see Laura tumbling sideways into the lake.

He shouted her name, but then he was quiet, steadying the boat, and he heard the receding small splashes of her hands and feet as she swam away from him. He couldn't see anything but his own hands, gripping the pale wood of the paddle, and the luminous dial of his watch: Twenty minutes before one. He leaned down and put a careful hand into the water: the chill was numbing. Would it feel any warmer to her, with the exertion of swimming; or would she not realize how cold it was until it drained her strength? She knew the lake, he told himself, she had swum in all kinds of weathers before, and at night, too. He had been the one who'd worried, old ladyish, that the water was too cold. But still, he felt frightened, sitting in the mist and silence, not knowing how far she'd gone. She could die out here, and he wouldn't know. Three minutes had gone by. He opened his mouth and called her name.

To his relief, she answered. "What."

"Where are you?" he shouted.

"Keep calling. I'll swim back." Her voice sounded strong and clear. He put his paddle in the water and tried to strike out in the direction of her voice.

"Stop it," she said. "Stop that splashing. I can't tell where you are."

"Here!" he called.

"Just stay there."

Her voice sounded no closer than it had. He gripped the gunwales until he heard the oncoming sounds of her swimming. "Right here," he said again.

"Where?"

"Here."

"Again?"

"Here."

A sudden shudder of the boat, her hands slapping at the side. He stowed his paddle under the seat and scrambled, crouching, to the center. He saw her white hands making their way along the gunwale, end over end, to the starboard stern. He leaned the other way, to steady the boat. They had done this before, in the summer, playing, one of them jumping off and climbing back in while the other one held steady, trying not to tip over, but laughing, not able to concentrate, so that the boat would tip over, and they would roll under it and come up on the other side. Once he'd gone under and caught his foot in one of the struts, a long moment fighting weightlessness to reach it with his hands and free it.

He felt her pulling at the boat, heard her panting.

"I can't," she said.

"Come back to the center," he told her. Her hands came back; he could see her white face just below him. He took hold of her hands and pulled; the boat rolled. "Wait," he said. "Give me your foot." He ran his hand down the cold sodden calf of her blue jeans and managed finally to wrestle and hoist her, heavy and dripping, into the boat.

She lay in the bottom for several moments, and he crouched above her, getting his breath.

"Well," he said finally. "You had your swim."

"Yes," she said. Her teeth were chattering. She sat up.

"I lost my paddle," she said.

"I know," he said, thinking of the small splash he'd heard right before she went in. "I'll get us back, if you can tell me how. I have no idea where we are."

She sat with her legs crossed, her arms wrapped around her body. He laid down his paddle and said, "Take off your shirt. I'll give you mine."

"That's all right."

"You'd better take it." He unbuttoned it and was startled at how soft the air felt on his torso, clean and cold.

He persuaded her to go upstairs to one of the guest bedrooms. She got undressed and lay under a ragged, dirty quilt, shivering and shivering. "I'm sorry," she kept saying through clattering teeth. Her face was yellow in the candlelight.

He'd been sitting on the edge of the mattress, but he finally stretched out on top of her, trying to warm her up.

"That was a stupid thing to do," she said. "I don't know what was the matter with me." Then she sat up, pushing him away. "I don't like this. I don't like the way I'm acting."

He turned his head away from her and took a deep breath that bent the candle flame, fluttering, toward him. "Look," he said. "Let me tell you this one thing. It's not you. It's Maisie."

She said nothing.

"It's not a choice between you and her. It's a choice between her and anyone else."

"All right, Jack. I get it." Then she rolled over on her stomach and said something he couldn't understand.

"I'm sorry, what?"

"Nothing. Get out of here."

He tried hesitantly to get up from the bed.

But she reached for him and pulled him to her. Her face was wet. "No," she was saying. "No. Stay."

In the morning, half-awake, they made love. Laura held his face with both hands, but when it was over she turned away from him. "What was that for?" she said into the pillow.

They drank coffee, stowed their things in the canoe, and left. Back in town, he stayed in the Jeep while she carried the plastic garbage bags to the Dumpster behind the building and took her duffel bag and the laundry upstairs. Then she came back and motioned him to roll down his window.

"Will an hour be enough?" she asked.

"Sure."

He got out, and she swung herself up into the Jeep and drove off. He went upstairs to pack his things. He found Egg just inside the door of the apartment; Laura had put him into his travel carrier, lined up beside his empty food dishes and litter tray.

17
The Offer

❧

The buyer appeared, blond and sleek. He'd flown to Portland from New Jersey and driven up from the airport in a rented car; he emerged in a suede-collared parka, lizard shoes. His name was Dick Coburn.

"You've heard of Coburn Foods?" Warren Phinney asked, while Dick Coburn stared modestly at the carpet in Jack's office. "Well, that was Dick's grandfather."

"Oh, so you know the frozen food business, then," Jack said.

"Dick has no direct experience in the business," Phinney said. "But you know, it's in the blood."

Coburn had been a fighter pilot, worked in PR, sold sails and jet planes. He was itching, he said, to get into another business of his own, something low ticket and high volume. "With jets, you sell three, you have a great year," he said with a disarming buck-toothed smile. "Those same three deals fall through, and you're up the creek."

Jack showed them around the plant. Dick kept his hands behind his back and asked questions, a prince touring a flood site.

"Local people, I imagine," his murmur nearly lost in the clatter of the manufacturing room.

On their way upstairs to Jack's office, they ran into Dave LaPalme in the hall. It seemed rude not to introduce him.

"Dick Coburn—Dave LaPalme, our head of sales."

"Dick Coburn!" Dave shifted folders to shake hands. "Coburn Foods, I bet. Man, you guys made a real killing last year on those microwave omelets."

Dick lowered his eyes. Dave looked at Jack, his eyebrows raised: Hey, *this* is interesting.

Later that afternoon, when they ran into each other in the men's room, Dave said, "What was that all about?"

"Dick and his wife are thinking of buying a summer house around here, and I invited him to stop in for lunch," Jack said, trying to create the impression that he and Coburn were old friends.

Dave threw his piece of paper towel into the trash. "Are you selling?"

"What makes you think that?"

"No shit, Jack. Are you?"

He had made no prior decision to equivocate, but faced with Dave's direct question he answered automatically. "Coburn was just interested in taking a look at how we operate." Damn Coburn anyway, this was why Jack had wanted him to visit on a Saturday. Phinney had told Jack of a company whose sale had been scuttled at the last minute, after the initial agreements had been signed. Word of the impending sale had gotten out, and the employees had taken advantage of the owner's vulnerability to press for higher pay and flextime, both of which the buyer had immediately rejected as changing the terms of the sale. When the owner had conveyed the buyer's firm stand to the employees, they'd responded by going on strike. Sorry, said the buyer, I have no interest in taking on a troubled business.

"Because if you are thinking of it," Dave said quietly, "I would've hoped you'd tell me." His big face was red, shiny.

"If I ever did get serious about selling, I would tell you."

"I mean, I wouldn't blame you," Dave said. "A couple of years ago, me and a couple of other guys went in together on a triple-decker down in Portland. As an investment, you understand. To turn it into condos. There was some little old lady on the ground floor who'd lived there forever, paying like no rent. We offered her the chance to buy her apartment, but when she couldn't come up with the money, you think we let her stay there?" He shook his head. "I'm saying I understand your position. I'm just asking to know."

Jack didn't answer. He remembered himself, that long-ago weekend of the company picnic, telling Maisie his conditions for selling: I wouldn't want anyone who was going to automate, or use the property for real estate.

And now he was being accused of duplicity by a man who threw old ladies out onto the street?

He and Nona had talked about the sale in their final sessions together. Her view was that no one could be loyal to everyone; Jack had to decide where his first loyalty lay and then do whatever was necessary to abide by it. No, she didn't think he was a skunk. Look at where the company had been two years ago; look at where it might be today if he'd sold immediately after his father's death. He'd done everyone a lot of good by taking it over, and humbling as it might be for him to believe, she'd said, smiling, they would all survive his leaving. Even Laura would survive.

"I haven't seen her in a while," he told Nona. "I keep trying to think of some legitimate reason to call her, some project for her to work on, but there isn't anything. Why am I so anxious to prove to her that we can still be friends?"

"Don't expect miracles," Nona said.

"Didn't I do the same thing with her I did with the factory: taking on something that wasn't going to go anywhere, and then having to extricate myself after entangling other people?"

"No, because you didn't know at the time that things weren't going anywhere. Did you? Honestly."

He shook his head, relieved. Somehow Nona had changed from a judge to an advocate. But he was running out of things to say to her. The prospect of not seeing Nona any longer frightened him, yet he was growing convinced that she was waiting for him to make the break.

In the middle of the next session he announced suddenly, "I think I'm done."

He'd been secretly hoping for a response—pleasure at how much progress he'd made, or dismay that he was leaving her—but she just nodded and said that they should schedule a couple more sessions, to wrap things up, as she put it.

At the end of the last session, he shook her hand. It was warm and firm, and he realized he'd never touched her before and would never see her again.

Now Dave came a few steps closer and put his hands on the edge of Jack's sink. "A guy like Coburn could come in with his own people and screw us all. Not you. The rest of us, I mean."

"I wouldn't let that happen," Jack said, who had already talked to Coburn about keeping on the top executives.

"Yeah, you'd be fine. You'd get your money and get out of here."

Jack turned on the faucet and began washing his hands. When he was done, he shook off the water and raised his eyes to find Dave still watching him in the mirror. "At the moment I have no plans to sell," he said.

On the third Monday in October, Warren Phinney called with an offer that made Jack blink: he knew that on paper the company was worth that much, but he had trouble believing that someone would really be prepared to pay it.

That Thursday he took the ferry from Rockland and sat at a steamy window, looking out at the churning sapphire water. His mother was waiting for him on the Vinalhaven dock, the ends of her gray hair lifting in the wind. She was wrapped in an old camel's-hair coat, and her colors were the colors of the wintry island: brown and silver. She put her cold cheek against his.

"Darling, it's so good to see you. And Marion's coming for the weekend, too, you know."

"I know." He needed to tell both of them about the impending sale, so that they could sign the papers; and he dreaded it. Marion was capable of being stubborn just for the sake of stubbornness; and his mother—well, who knew what she really felt about anything?

The house had a dry smell; the new electric baseboards clicked. He'd been coming here for summers since he was eight, but it felt different now that his mother was living here full-time.

When Jack's father died, his mother had done a quick, emphatic sorting, redirecting his magazine subscriptions to friends who had shared his interests, mailing his monogrammed silver cuff links to a nephew who had the same initials, calling Goodwill to come that week to pick up his clothes. She'd given to Marion the William and Mary highboy that had been handed down in the family; to Jack she'd offered the writing desk bought in Paris on their honeymoon. And your father's awful wing chair, do you want that? I've always hated it.

Me too.

Ah, well, then I'll put it into the auction.

No, no, I'll take it.

Her paring down and moving was so unsentimental, so decisive, that he thought she must have been envisioning it for years. He would have understood it better if his father had been sick for a long time, how the death then would have been a release from worry and bondage, a sudden lightening. But his father had died instantly, and instantly his mother had shed her old life.

"Take some lunch," she told him now, picking up her eyeglass case from the kitchen table. "I'll just go and practice for a bit." She had taken up the flute, which she hadn't played since high school.

"Aren't you eating?"

"I had a late breakfast. Cats? Lucius? Norm? Nectar? Coming to listen?"

"Would it make you too self-conscious if I listened, too?" Jack asked.

"Oh, darling, I'm awful. I butcher the Bach, it's all starts and stops, you wouldn't want to hear."

"No, really."

"No, no, you have your lunch. And then read a paper. I'll be back in just a few minutes." She scooped up a cat, and the other two followed her, tails pluming, from the room.

She'd left him a plate of cold chicken and potato salad on the old wooden counter, and he took a forkful of food and then wandered around the rooms, going back occasionally for more. He had the idea that he would find just the right thing to read and then would sit down to eat properly, but he couldn't quite figure out what he wanted, or where it might be in the shelves his mother had had built in the living room and dining room. An expedition story, he thought, Scott or Shackleton or Hillary. He knew exactly where they'd be in the old Champs du Soleil house: the shelves in the space between the door frames leading into his parents' bedroom.

But here he didn't know; the new shelves seemed stuffed with things he'd never seen before: gardening and knitting books, sheet music, anthologies of poems about cats. He went back for another mouthful of salad, feeling dissatisfied at what had become of this house—he missed its old summer bareness, ancient damp chintz furniture—and at the way the old Champs du Soleil furniture looked out of place, the rugs too rich, the tables too polished, too many books, as though the house had eaten too much and grown sleepy.

He looked down at his plate in surprise: he'd just finished the last of the chicken. He rinsed his dishes and put them into the dishwasher his mother had installed, then stood looking out through the thick rippled window glass at the browning lawns, the tangle of bushes on the bluff, the sharp blue gleam of the ocean.

He put on his coat and took his binoculars, just in case—the one other time he'd been here in October, he'd seen a dovekie. As he rounded the sun porch, his feet sinking into the soggy grass, he heard from somewhere deep in the house the halting quaver of the flute.

They had finished their dinner—or rather, he had; his mother had drunk several glasses of wine and barely eaten anything—when he told her he'd had an offer on the company.

"Yes," she said, waiting for him to go on.

"But would you mind, if I sold it?"

"Of course not, darling," Janet said. "You do whatever you want." Her tone was distracted and cooing; she seemed to be addressing the big tabby cat lying in her lap.

"You're sure?"

"Oh, sweetheart. I know you never wanted to go into that business in the first place. You've been just wonderful, taking it over the way you did."

"At the time it didn't seem like I had much choice."

"Of course, it is a little sad." She stood the cat up in her lap and put her nose against its head. "Of course we are a *little* sad, right, Nectar? Not *terribly* sad. But a little sad." She rested her chin on the cat's head and sniffed. "But we always thought it was a stupid company anyway, didn't we."

"But it's not, Mom. That's not why I'm getting out. I like the company, I've actually enjoyed working there."

"Oh, darling, not really."

"Yes," he insisted. He told her how much the buyer was paying, and how much money would come to her and to Marion.

"Do you mean it's actually profitable now?" she asked, seeming to pick up on this for the first time, though he'd told her about it several times over the phone. "That's extraordinary. Oh, well. Poor Daddy."

"Why poor Daddy?"

She kissed the cat between the ears. "He tried so hard." After a moment she said, "Do you know what he was doing when I met him? He was a senior at Yale, and he wanted to go to law school. He wanted to be an international lawyer. He would have been brilliant."

"You've told me this."

"But instead," his mother continued, "he decided to go into the business. He was utterly unsuited, but he couldn't see that. He couldn't admit it. Do you remember a few years ago when he wanted to take me on the Greek cruise for our anniversary?"

"No."

"It would have cost twenty thousand dollars. At least. I said, Are you sure we can afford it? And he kept answering, Will you please stop? That was what—our thirty-fifth anniversary. Four years ago. And when he died, I asked the lawyer, just out of curiosity, to tell me how much Daddy had been taking out of the company then, and you know what the answer was?"

"Nothing."

"Nothing," his mother repeated. "He'd put money *in* that year." She ran her fingers over the cat's spine and sighed. "Oh, well. I suppose he thought I'd hit the roof if I knew. Oh, well."

"And you would have."

"Probably," Janet said lightly. "But I wouldn't have *left* him. Do you think he thought I would have left him?"

He didn't answer. His mother drank more wine.

"No, darling," she said. "You do whatever. Sell it, keep it. Whatever you want."

"Well," said Jack, plucking a grape from the bowl at the center of the table and putting it absently in his mouth, "I'm actually planning to move back to Boston."

"Oh, really? You're going back to school?"

"No, I'm going back to Maisie."

"Maisie," his mother said, her eyes widening. "Oh. Well, why would you want to do that?"

"Because—" he started to say, but she cut him off.

"Oh, dear, I'm sorry. It's really none of my business. It's wonderful, of course."

He ate another grape.

"I'm just so *surprised,*" she said. "What about Laura? Have you told her?"

"We broke up about six weeks ago."

"That's too bad," his mother said, finishing the wine in her glass. "I liked her." She stood up, still holding the cat, which hung passively in her arms, blinking. "Well, I'm off to bed. There's ice cream in the freezer.

Turn off the lights when you come up, all right? And run the dishwasher?"

"Mom?"

"Good night, dear." She kissed the top of his head—he heard, rather than felt it—and went out.

Marion and Barry arrived the next evening, with three of their dogs. Janet's voice grew high and frantic when she saw them: she insisted that the dogs be locked in one of the bedrooms so they wouldn't disturb the cats. "They're not going to like that," Barry drawled, one of his rare remarks.

"I'll bring them in some steak," Marion said.

"You're spoiling them," said Janet, but she ate dinner surrounded by a ring of cats, like a little court; she dropped furtive scraps from the dining room table.

Saturday morning was colder, with a heavy gray fog that left only a circular strip of lawn around the house. Beyond this strip the opaque air swirled and boiled, as though straining against an invisible barrier that just barely managed to keep it from enveloping the house altogether. Janet had gone into town, Barry was asleep, and Jack and Marion were hanging the storm windows. The windows were old and heavy, dusty and cobwebbed from their season in the cellar. Marion squirted them with Windex, and Jack wiped them with a rag, laying them in rows on the frozen lawn. He told her, in short gasps, about the offer from Dick Coburn. She listened, aiming her bottle and standing between shots with the bottle held between her booted feet, her hands in the pockets of her down jacket.

"Well," she said. "You're certainly giving me a lot to think about."

He crumpled a cold, filthy piece of paper towel and let it fall on the grass. "Right, but we have to decide this week."

"This week? What's the hurry?"

He stood another window on its edge while she sprayed it. "The offer's only good till the twenty-second."

"That doesn't seem fair."

"Well, it's like buying a house. You make an offer, and it's only good for forty-eight hours or whatever. It's just how these things work."

"But this is a much bigger decision than buying a house," Marion said sharply. "I mean, selling the company—this affects the welfare of dozens of people. How do the employees feel about it?"

He wiped. "I haven't told them. It's not their decision, Marion." His hands were red and numb, and his feet ached with cold. He still had the habit of packing carelessly to come home; whatever he forgot, whatever a change in the weather made necessary, he expected to borrow. He wished again that his mother hadn't given away all his father's clothes.

"You haven't told anyone? You're just going to spring it on them?"

"Well, of course if the deal goes through I'll make some sort of announcement. I know Coburn will want me to stay on for a few months, to make a smooth transition."

"It seems pretty sneaky to me. What would be the harm of telling people, asking how *they* feel about the whole thing?"

"Because frankly at this stage I'm not changing my mind, however they feel." They'd cleaned the last of the windows; he stood up.

"Well, all right. I guess I just feel as though a company, especially a smallish company, is a community."

"Pick up the other end of this, will you?" Together they circled the house with the heavy storms, laying each on the ground below the space where it would hang, the three narrow ones for the dining room bay, the tall ones for the front porch, the squares that went on either side of the living room fireplace, the heavy oblongs to block off the French doors along the back of the house. When they finished it looked as though all the windows had been blown onto the grass by some precise, gentle bomb.

"I'll get the ladder," Jack said. "Anyhow, think about it for a day or two, and then let me know." He said it with an air of finality, but when he came back carrying the damp, splintery stepladder, she continued, as he'd known she would.

"And what about job security? Will the new owner guarantee to keep people on?"

"We discussed it," he said, opening the ladder. "But you know these things often backfire. He may want to do some restructuring, bring in people he's worked with before. I think he should be free to do that." He pushed the ladder close to the house, motioned her to stand on it. He handed her the first storm window, helped her to steady it, and then climbed up on the ladder beside her. "Okay, one, two, three." They lowered the tilted window heavily onto its hooks, slowly let it sink against the window frame. "Besides," he continued, climbing down, shaking out his arms, "who knows, *my* people may hate working with him, and want to leave a month after he comes in. About the line workers I don't think you have to worry—I see no reason why he'd let people go."

Marion stayed on the ladder. "What's to stop him from turning around tomorrow and selling out to a big corporation?"

"Nothing."

"Well," she said. "I'll think about it. But you can't pressure me to accept so quickly just because—"

"I don't understand what your problem is. You've never shown the slightest interest in this"—the foghorn blared out suddenly below them, and he raised his voice to be heard above it—"and I've been in there for two years busting my ass—"

"Well, but I knew you were ethical. I knew the business was in good hands."

"Don't give me that. Ethical had nothing to do with it. You were too squeamish, or too lazy—"

She drew her pale brows together and said flatly, "I don't have to let you talk to me that way."

"Then sign the papers," Jack said, a little surprised by his own vehemence. "Because I'll tell you something: I'm prepared to just walk the hell out of there and let the company rot."

He walked around the corner of the house to where the next storm window lay, and after a moment she came after him, struggling to carry the ladder.

"God," she said. "You sound just like Daddy. You're the aristocrat and they're the peasants. Only Daddy would never have sold them out like this."

"Right," he said. "You spend years trashing him, and now all of a sudden he's a model of loyalty."

"You and Mom always talk like he was this poor martyr. Well, he liked being the president of a company, even if he was crummy at it."

He closed his eyes for an instant. "What's your point?"

Marion looked puzzled, then she shrugged. "Who knows. Sell. Do what you want."

They worked in silence along the back of the house, covering the dining room windows and the French doors while the sound of the foghorn faded and swelled and faded in the invisible bay below. After a while he wasn't angry at her anymore, and he saw by her face that the fight had been left behind, as all their fights always were, without any real understanding but without a grudge.

She held a window for him and tilted her head. "Mom says you're getting back together with Maisie."

"So?"

"Nothing. I just wondered if that's why you're in such a hurry to get out."

He folded up the ladder. "What if it is?"

"Don't get mad again. I only mean you might not be thinking all that clearly."

"I just don't want to end up like Dad," he said, not knowing whether he meant it or was only saying it because he knew it would mean something to Marion.

He'd been vague about how long he planned to stay in Vinalhaven, so that when he asked his mother to drive him to the pier that afternoon she appeared neither surprised nor disappointed. She kissed him goodbye, and he smelled her old scent of sandalwood soap. "Thanks for doing the windows, darling," she said. "That was a tremendous help."

The ferry was slow, slow. It began to snow lightly; he stood at the railing and watched the flakes fall down by the lit windows and disappear on the black water below. The sky grew dark; he didn't see the lights of the land until the boat was almost upon it, and when they hit the landing with a deep silent bump he was already holding on to the gangplank chain, waiting for them to unlock it. He was the first person off the boat.

On the road the snow was heavier, a white swirl that sucked him southward. He kept the car at nearly seventy, but still he had the feeling he wasn't driving fast enough: a disaster had happened, one of those dreams where a gigantic wave was looming over the beach, looming endlessly, while he scrambled to choose one among all the people he loved, drag her safely out of its reach.

He arrived in Cambridge shortly after midnight. He rang Maisie's buzzer, waited a few moments, and rang again. Oh, God, maybe she'd gone away for the weekend. Maybe she'd moved away, maybe he'd waited too long.

But she appeared finally on the other side of the glass door, wearing an old cotton kimono and her brown glasses. Her face, as she reached for the lock, was at once cautious and trusting. He stepped into the hall, dropped his bag, and wrapped his arms around her. They made it into her apartment somehow. The lights were all out, but he knew where the bed was. He sat on it and held her in his lap. She had her arms around his neck and she was talking, breathless sentences strung together: she'd been asleep when the buzzer rang, she'd thought it was part of her dream, and if she'd been more awake she probably wouldn't have come to the door because she wasn't expecting anyone, she'd practically sleepwalked down the hall. But she'd known he would come soon, she probably shouldn't tell him that, but she'd known it. And oh, Jack, you want to hear the most incredible thing, my mother called tonight and told me she's getting married, this man she's been seeing for years just got widowed, I know it seems wrong to be so gleeful about it, but they've been waiting so long and she sounded so happy, isn't it strange?

Nothing she said meant anything to him. He was holding her, kissing her neck and her hair, the plastic stems of her glasses.

She wound down finally and was silent. They sat there for a long time.

18

The Greatest Little Life

❧

"My husband likes them really thin," Maisie said to the butcher who pounded her veal scallops. "I'll have to come back with my husband," she told the saleswoman who was trying to talk her into a purple suede skirt. "I can't work late tonight, my husband's coming down," she said to Bert in the office. My husband, my husband. At first when she said it, it sounded arrogant, an invitation to the gods to come after her again; but after a while the words sounded natural; and after that they began to seem silly with so much repetition. She would catch herself about to say them and then say them anyway.

"Who is this husband of yours?" Bert asked. "When can I meet him?"

"Whenever you want," Maisie said lightly. He was spending every weekend with her now, she could make plans without asking him. He drove down on Thursday nights, usually, taking Fridays off from the factory.

"Next Saturday, then? For dinner?"

"That sounds great."

"Gosh," he said, puckering his face above his dotted bow tie. "You haven't even met Jenny yet, have you?"

"No." Bert talked about his wife all the time. Jenny's just as cute as a button. She's smart as a whip. She was a cheerleader at Ohio State, that was before I met her, but I swear she's still got that same sweet little body. You would not believe her breasts.

Now he said, flipping through the pages of his sailing magazine, "I was watching *Bus Stop* the other night, and in the middle of it I thought, Jenny's breasts are every bit as terrific as Marilyn's. More so, because Jenny doesn't have that fat butt."

Maisie nodded and went on sorting Kris's old "Grade D" folders (these were the less employable temps, the unkempt ones who couldn't type or who'd gotten bad conduct reports because they'd daydreamed when they were sent out to dip pizza plates in Teflon coating) into new categories. "Russian teacher," she wrote on one man's card. "Kennedy School of Gov't? State House (translation)? Publishers? Museums?"

This idea of hers, recruiting temps with special skills and matching them up with interesting employers, was turning out, as Bert had predicted, to be a somewhat quixotic enterprise. But she was handling the mainstream part of the business, the secretaries and clerical and factory workers, efficiently; so he let her do what she wanted. She liked interviewing the would-be temps who walked in, the ones who had a complicated explanation for why they were temping. They wanted to be painters, writers, singers. Some of them had been temping for years and had an apologetic or bitter air when they revealed their other vocation.

"I'm an actor," they said, and they waited for Maisie to call their bluff.

"That's wonderful," said Maisie.

There was one man who'd spent his life helping to build church organs, but the organ builder he'd worked for had died, and he couldn't find anyone else to work for. She'd spent a whole morning talking to him about the variables that went into designing each organ—the acoustics, the architecture of the church, the preferred repertoire of the choirmaster. And even with that, he said, the sound of each instrument when it was finished came as a complete surprise to him.

"Do you play the organ?" she had asked.

No, he said. He could do the rudimentary playing that was necessary for fine-tuning, but he'd never wanted to learn any real organ music. I like having that as part of the mystery, he said.

She asked if he'd be insulted to be offered carpentry work, and he said absolutely not, he'd consider himself lucky. She sent him to the Ritz to help on a team that was restoring moldings and mantelpieces, but she told him she'd start calling furniture makers and antique restorers to see if she could find him some finer work.

"You don't have to do that," he said.

"Oh, listen, we've got a bunch of them that call us all the time," she lied, "and I never have anyone skilled enough to send them."

Sure enough, the fifth furniture maker she called had had an outbreak of flu in his shop that week, and he was trying frantically to get ready for a show down in New York. The organ guy sounded great, he said, and could she find him two more guys?

When she'd told Bert about it, he'd said, "Well, that's great, dear heart, but it does seem to be a big expenditure of energy to find someone a couple of weeks' work."

"Well, what I'm thinking is that maybe we should look into finding people permanent jobs as well," she said. "I could fool around a little with it, and if it goes anywhere, you could hire someone else to do the temp stuff and I could work on that side of the business."

Bert threw his magazine on the desk, leaned over, and punched her in the arm. "*God,* you're fertile!" he said.

Bert and Jenny lived on the top floor of a row house on Beacon Hill. Inside, everything was cream-colored: the walls, the rugs, the furniture. "The color scheme is one of the advantages of having grown kids," Bert said, showing Jack and Maisie around. They had drinks in their hands, heavy crystal glasses that felt in constant danger of dropping to the floor. Bert stopped in front of each painting, each piece of furniture, so that they could admire it, and he told them where he and Jenny had bought it or from whom it had been inherited. His hair was wet, combed back, and his face was pink and shiny.

"*Damn* it, I wish you could see the view," he said, standing with them by the dark window in the bedroom, at the back of the apartment. "Jenny and I gave a brunch last Sunday, and we pulled the table back in here and had grapefruit and champagne overlooking the river and the boats, and the light was just so fucking amazing. And I looked around the table and I thought, Here we have this Harvard professor, and this incredible photographer, and this guy who's just won the Pulitzer, and his wife who's just so fuckin' gorgeous you could die, I mean, she's like something out of a fuckin' Botticelli, and I just thought, *Jesus,* I'm lucky. You know? I've got the greatest apartment, and the greatest little wife, and the greatest friends, and the greatest business. I mean, it is just the greatest little *life*." His face was purple, apoplectic with joy. Maisie looked away.

"We think of moving," Jenny murmured. "We actually found a dear place in Back Bay, which I was all set to buy. But Bert wouldn't give up his river full of boats."

She was sharper than Maisie had imagined, with a narrow face and body and very short, almost crew-cut gray hair. Bert had talked so much about her breasts that Maisie found herself, surreptitiously, glancing at Jenny's midsection, but it was swathed in a beltless gray flannel jumper worn over a cream silk blouse, like the uniform of some expensive archaic girls' school.

"I love your shoes," she said abruptly to Maisie.

"Oh, thanks," Maisie answered, surprised. They were yellow with turquoise heels, and she glanced at Jenny's feet, in black patent-leather flats. Something made her add, "They hurt like hell, though. Jack and I were walking around Boston last weekend, and they just scraped my feet raw. I mean, literally, I was bleeding."

Jenny made a grimace of cool distaste, but whether at the thought of such discomfort or the fact that it had been described so graphically, Maisie wasn't sure.

"Now how long have you two been married?" Jenny asked.

Maisie shot Jack a look: it was the first time since they'd gotten back together that someone had asked this.

"Almost three years," he said pleasantly.

Maisie reached for his hand and felt his fingers squeeze hers. "And what about you and Bert?" she asked. Immediately it seemed too personal a question.

"Thirty-three."

"You're kidding! You must have been really young." What was it about Jenny that made everything one said to her sound wrong? Maisie tried not to look behind her, at their bed, which was large and covered with a white silk comforter. It had a truncated canopy sticking out from the wall high above the pillows, a wispy white veil gathered into a huge knot at the center.

"No, actually we weren't. I guess we look younger than we are, dearie," Bert said, squeezing Jenny's shoulder.

"Yes, well some of us do," Jenny replied without looking at him.

"I was speaking of you, of course."

"All right," she said dismissively. "Have you asked these people if they'd like more to drink?"

"Sweetener?" Bert said immediately to Maisie, and it took her a minute to realize that he was offering her more gin.

"So you guys are babies!" Jenny said, peering at Maisie.

"Well," said Maisie.

"It's just so nice to see bright young women going into business," Jenny continued, and Maisie couldn't think of an answer.

"Bert says you're a bank examiner," she offered finally, and realized that it sounded as though she didn't quite believe Bert.

"That's right."

"Well," Maisie said after a moment. "Your ceiling is just wonderful." They all looked up: it was pale blue, painted with ragged white clouds.

"The artist is a friend of ours, from New York," Bert said. "He was in a group show at the Whitney a few years ago. If you come back in the living room, I'll show you the catalog."

"Oh, don't bore them with that, sweetheart," said Jenny.

"They want to see it!" He took Maisie's arm. "You do want to see it, dear girl, don't you?"

Maisie looked uncertainly at Jenny. "Sure."

For dinner Jenny served artichokes, with the centers scraped out and filled with hollandaise, and then stuffed sole. She got into an animated discussion with Jack about the end of monarchism in the first quarter of the twentieth century.

"The end of dynastic rule is a fascinating subject," Jenny said. "I remember when we saw *The Last Emperor*—"

"The Last Empire," Bert corrected.

"Oh, that's right, *The Last Empire,* I remember thinking about the fall of the Romanovs, and wondering—" She stopped.

"Were the situations really comparable?" Maisie asked. "Because in Russia, you know, World War One had really—"

"No," Jenny interrupted in a thoughtful voice. "It *was The Last Emperor.*"

"No," said Bert. They had both assumed the same still air of concentration.

"Yes. You're thinking of *Empire of the Sun.* That was the one about the little boy in Shanghai, the Steven Spielberg."

"Are you sure?"

"I'm sure. It was *The Last Emperor.*"

"Well, fine. For argument's sake, let's assume—"

"No, not for argument's sake." Jenny turned her gaze to Jack. "It was *The Last Emperor,* right?"

He cleared his throat. "I think it was."

"See? He thinks I'm right."

"But it's easy to see how someone could get it confused with *Empire of the Sun,*" Maisie put in. "The two movies came out around the same time."

"You see," Jenny told Bert, "I am capable of being right sometimes."

"I never doubted it."

"Though you may not think so."

"I apologize."

Jenny shook her head.

"One thing about Jenny," Bert said, "she always laughs when she's angry."

"What?" said Jenny, her blue eyes opening wide.

"She does. That's how I can tell when she's really cross. She wrinkles up her whole face and does the cutest little chuckle."

"I do not."

"Sweetheart. You do."

But now Jenny's head was thrown back, her teeth showing: Ha, ha, ha, ha, ha.

"Oh, my God," Maisie said.

She took Jack's arm and they walked down the street, away from Bert and Jenny's building, leaning forward against the cold.

"So that *was* really strange, right?" Jack said. "It wasn't just me."

"Do you think they're like that when they're alone, or do they need an audience?"

"Oh, an audience," Jack said. "When they're alone, they don't talk at all. He sits on one of those little gold chairs and she whacks him over the head with *The New York Times.*"

"But we were never like that, Jack, were we?" It was the first time since they'd been back together that either of them had dared, joking or in earnest, to tread on such dangerous ground.

"No," he said, a caricature of horror, "not like *that.*"

"*We* never *bickered,*" said Maisie.

"Never," Jack agreed solemnly.

They rented a bigger apartment, with two bedrooms and a real kitchen; when Jack got his money from the sale of the factory, they might think about buying something. The original sales figure had seemed to Maisie enormous, but when Jack had calculated the shares he was paying out to his mother and Marion, and the reserve he was keeping back so that he could give everybody extra-large Christmas bonuses (a farewell gesture meant to counter any bitterness or anxiety the employees might feel about his selling—Maisie agreed it was a good idea), the amount had shrunk disappointingly. They would invest what was left and use it as a cushion, they decided—to make a down payment on a house, to travel, or to tide them over while Jack looked for a new job, or if they had a baby and Maisie wanted to stop working for a few months.

They were lying on their bed one Friday evening after dinner, reading, when Maisie suddenly said, "What's that smell?"

"What smell?"

"It smells like"—sniff, sniff—"perfume."

"I don't smell anything."

"Jack, I'm not kidding. What is that?" She sat up. "It's not *my* perfume." It was a sweet, light scent. She inhaled once more and it was gone, and then it seemed to be back again.

Jack kept reading his book. Maisie looked at her own book without seeing it, and then she said again, "No, really, what is it?"

"I don't know what you're talking about," Jack said stiffly, not looking at her.

"Don't tell me you can't smell it."

"I don't smell anything," he said, sounding annoyed now. Or guilty. She pushed his book down and stared into his face. She knew she was being silly, that there was no perfume scent, but a little part of her had already made the full descent into terror and uncertainty. She wanted him to acknowledge that she had the right to worry; she wanted him to roar at her that he loved her and would never again do anything to hurt her.

But he stared back at her and said, "This isn't funny."

She waited a moment, then asked, "What did you do today?"

"What do you mean?"

"I mean, what did you do?"

He said coldly, "I met with Warren Phinney in the morning. In the afternoon I made phone calls. I walked to the post office and mailed out résumés."

"Oh, well, that must be it," she said. "Maybe someone in the post office line with you was wearing perfume." He nodded and looked at his book again. But still Maisie waited. "But you're sure," she said in a small voice, "that you weren't with someone?"

Why couldn't he just hug her and tell her he would never touch anyone else?

"Is that what you really think?"

"No," she said hastily. "Not really. But—"

"But what?" His voice was low, ominous.

"Well, don't you understand why I might worry? I mean, I know it's crazy. But don't you understand why I might be a little crazy, about this particular point?"

He didn't answer. Maisie sniffed again, audibly. "You're right, anyway. I don't smell it," she said. She didn't, and she suddenly knew she never had. "I must have been imagining it."

She didn't bring it up again, but she watched him surreptitiously as they both read their books. After a long time she began to kiss his jaw, his neck, the hollow just above his shirt collar. He ignored her and kept reading. She got up and finished the dishes, brushed her teeth, turned off the lights in the living room. She came back into the bedroom and put on her nightgown. Jack was still reading. She sat on the bed and took the book away from him, and finally he rolled to face her, pulling her down beside him. She kept her eyes open the whole time, and then she held him between her knees, her hands folded in the small of his back, long after they'd both stopped moving.

Another Friday she was at her desk at work, feeling badly because she'd just sent a woman with an incredible résumé—master's in art history, curatorial course at the Courtauld, internship at Winterthur—to do word processing at a law firm, when the phone on her desk rang. It was Jack, and he began by saying, "I don't want you to worry. I'm all right." He'd been turning left at an intersection, and a car had been coming in the opposite direction, also with its turn signal on; but the other car hadn't turned, it had kept on coming and had run into the passenger side of Jack's car. He was calling from the hospital. I'm all right, he kept saying, just shaken up. I just wanted them to have a look at my back.

Maisie said she would leave work immediately for the hospital, but he talked her out of it. I'll be gone by the time you get here, he said, I'm leaving now, in fact. My back doesn't hurt at all anymore, and they didn't find anything wrong. The car's a little banged up, but it runs fine. I'm going to shop for dinner, and then I'll go home and clean.

"We'll cancel tonight," Maisie said; they were having people over to dinner.

"No, don't cancel," Jack said. "I told you, I'm fine."

She thought of him all afternoon, unable to concentrate on anything at the office. What if the other car had been going faster, what if it had run into him head on? She wanted to lock up and go home, but she was alone at work, it wasn't one of Bert's regular days. She called the apartment, but Jack didn't answer; she knew he was probably still out doing the shopping, but she thought: What if he had a delayed reaction to the accident? What if he collapsed in the supermarket, and they didn't know where to call me? What if he fainted behind the wheel of the car? She called again, a half hour later, and this time he did answer; he was unpacking groceries, about to start vacuuming. His voice sounded a little faded, she thought, and she hung up, still convinced that he was secretly, seriously hurt.

When she got home he was lying on the couch, looking at a magazine. She ran to him and was afraid to hug all of him; she hugged his arm, kissing the blue stripes of his shirt. He was all right, he told her over and over, but she kept telling him all the things she'd been thinking this afternoon, how worried she'd been. Finally she realized that he *was* all right, none of the bad things she'd imagined had happened. She looked at her watch: it was quarter to six, and their friends were coming at six-thirty. She stood up and looked around the living room.

"But you *said* you would *vacuum.*"

He looked startled, but then he laughed at her, and she laughed, too. He vacuumed, and she dusted and put things away, throwing clean laundry recklessly into drawers without folding it. See, she thought, we really are married again; there are no scars.

Thanksgiving weekend they flew down to see Maisie's mother in Virginia, where it was unseasonably warm. They took a picnic to a state park, and they hiked into the woods and spread out a blanket near a creek, far off the path. They were kissing, and she undid his belt and slid her hand into his undershorts, holding him, and she whispered into his ear, "Fuck me."

His eyes closed. "Not here."

"There's no one around. Come on."

"Let's go back to your mother's."

"No." She slid her hand lower.

"It's not safe," he said.

"So what?" she murmured, rubbing with her hand. "We can take a chance, one time. And even if I did, so what? I want a baby with you."

"It's too soon," he said, sitting up.

She took her hand away, a momentary chill. But he was right; it was one of the things she loved about him, that she was free to be reckless, teetering on the edge, because she could always trust him to pull her back. "Okay," she said, pushing gently on his chest, unzipping her own jeans, moving down on him, "then let's do everything but."

On Saturday they went to dinner with Maisie's mother and her fiancé, Ralph Levinsky. He was enormously tall and heavy, going bald, with a beard and one eye that wandered off to the side while the other looked right at you. He had a soft voice and chain-smoked Camels. He took them out to a seafood restaurant, and when Maisie asked him shyly what kind of urology he did, he said, "Please. Not while we're eating." She laughed.

He talked about growing up in the poor part of town, in a house that gave out onto a narrow brick alley. "It was only about eight feet wide, marvelous for learning to drive. My parents had a big old Pontiac, and we used to go zooming up that alley in forward and reverse. The car was a mess, but we all became very precise drivers. In fact, one of my brothers raced for a living."

They all shared a platter of mussels. Alice was talking about her own family, her great-aunt Nedra.

"Whenever I visited her, she would take me out to the dime store and buy me a tropical fish, in a little plastic bag. I used to say, But Aunt Nedra, I don't have a fish tank. And she'd go like this"—Alice flapped a hand dismissively—"and say, Don't worry, darling, you'll find a place for it. So I would go home, and my mother would flush it down the toilet."

They all laughed.

"And she kept her windows open all year round, and she spread peanut butter on the sills for the squirrels. Oh, and the biggest thing in her life was that she went down to Florida every winter to collect seashells. So in the fall she would start growing her fingernail—this one," Alice said, holding up the pinkie of her right hand, "and by November, it would be out to here, it *curved,* like a little shovel, and she'd walk down the beach all hunched over running that fingernail through the mounds of shells. She liked the miniatures, the perfect ones. When she died—I don't know if you remember this, Maisie, you were very young—her guest bedroom was full of shopping bags, you could barely get into the room, and the bags were full of these shells. Oh, and here's what else we found. A Lord and Taylor bag full of turkey bones. Wishbones. She must have saved the wishbone from every turkey she ever ate in her life."

Maisie had never heard her mother talk so much. In the ladies' room she said, "I like him."

"Oh, good," Alice said, clearly relieved. She wiped lipstick from the corner of her mouth and smiled quickly at Maisie in the mirror. "And I'm so happy that Jack came down with you. It's all right between you? Really all right?"

"I think so," Maisie said carefully. It made her nervous when other people seemed so amazed that she and Jack had gotten back together; she could think it to herself, how miraculous it was, what a narrow escape they'd had, but when her mother or Caterina said it she always heard a dubious note in their voices, as though they were waiting for the other shoe to drop.

Alice pulled a compact from her purse. "Now, we haven't figured out yet about the wedding. It'll probably be very quiet, we'll just go to City Hall. But I'll let you know."

"No orchestra?" Maisie said. "No photographer? No displaying the presents?"

Alice slapped her, lightly, on the top of her head. "Don't be fresh."

19

The Announcement

Two days before Christmas, Maisie and Jack drove up to the farmhouse in Champs du Soleil. He'd been spending a few days a week there, but the house looked as though it had been uninhabited for months: everything coated in cold, thick dust. They swept and made a fire, and Jack went out to cut a tree while Maisie made ornaments out of gold and silver paper. They'd spent their only other married Christmas with Jack's mother, so this would be their first Christmas alone together, their first tree, their first little roast beef.

His deal had gone through. The papers were signed, and all that remained now was to announce the sale to the employees. He was planning to do that at the company Christmas party tonight. He had not invited Maisie to come, and she had not suggested it, knowing that Laura might be there and, besides, feeling that it would be awkward and arrogant to sweep in at the last moment as Jack's wife after such a long absence, only to say good-bye to people she had never known. She planned to spend the evening packing; the lease on the farmhouse would be up on the thirty-first.

Jack was distant and clumsy, helping her hang the rickety little ornaments on the tree.

"Weren't we supposed to put the lights up first?" she asked, pausing with a gold angel lifted high in her hand before the half-decorated tree.

It was a tall, bushy spruce, and even with all the decorations it had an empty look.

"Were we?"

She put on a record of Christmas carols, so that they wouldn't feel they had to talk. Now that he'd actually sold the company, she was sorry. Not sorry enough to wish the deal undone, but aware of her role as the catalyst for the sale, afraid of her own influence. Now she thought: I could have lived here, in Champs du Soleil. I could have found some sort of job, made friends. But she knew she was only thinking these wistful thoughts because there was no longer any danger that she'd actually have to abide by them. She could have lived here for his sake, but she would have hated it; he'd known that, and he loved her; and that was the true and final reason for his decision to sell.

Jack crouched over the box of green and blue lights, sliding the little clasp down from the neck of each bulb. She went and put her hand on the back of his neck and then took it away again.

"Are you worried about tonight?"

He shook his head, untangling wire. "But I'll be glad when it's over."

At five-thirty he left her to finish the tree and went up to get dressed. He was moving slowly, but she felt as though he were rushing around, and she had an urge to flatten herself against the wall and stay there until he left the house.

The Christmas party was held in the King's Inn, just off the highway. It had begun to snow by the time Jack arrived, great white needly gusts that tumbled across the parking lot and made the garlanded doorway of the motel seem farther from his car than it actually was.

The King's Imperial Ballroom, as it was called, was a long, low room with an acoustic tile ceiling. White lights outlined the doorways and ringed the warped parquet dance floor. The band Mary had hired blared out Christmas carols and pop songs. Jack hung his coat on a metal hanger and stuffed it onto an already crowded rack, and went to find Mary, to congratulate her on the arrangements.

"I don't know," she said breathlessly, "they could've done a better job with the centerpieces. I told them 'festive.' Do you think these are festive?"

He glanced at the round tables, wreaths made of red carnations and evergreen, threaded with small white lights. "I think they're pretty festive," he said.

"They're so flat. Don't you think they're flat? I thought they'd stick up, somehow."

She was wearing a glittery gold dress and over it a black cardigan, pilled with gray lint. Her face was shiny, her cheeks painted with red circles of blush.

"I like your pin," said Jack.

She looked down at it—it was a wreath on her left breast with a plastic Santa Claus head in the center—and touched it with a finger. The wreath lit up like a movie marquee, a wave of lights flashing on and off in sequence, and Santa's nose glowed red. "Screw you, tumah," she said, and laughed.

"But it's gone, though," Jack said, smiling uncertainly.

"Oh, yes. I just like to remind it to stay gone." She kissed him suddenly, on the mouth, and then pulled back, giggling. "Drunk as a skunk."

"Will you dance with me, later?"

"You kidding? 'Course I will. You've got to dip me, though. Your father always used to. Get ready, he'd say, and lay me out flat. I'd stick a leg up in the air. It was a riot."

"I'm not that good a dancer."

"Oh, don't give me that." She kissed him again, and whispered in his ear: "It's in the genes."

"Well," he said. He caught sight of Laura, over Mary's shoulder, standing alone in a dark blue dress with gold buttons. Maisie referred to such dresses, when they passed them in store windows, as "Republican first-lady clothes." Laura's black hair was up, coiled on the back of her head. He was surprised she had come. She was looking at him, but when he caught her eye she turned and walked over to Bernadette Duchaise, from accounting.

"Well," he said again to Mary. "I'd better go—"

"Mingle," she finished, giggling.

He listened as Dave LaPalme told a string of dirty jokes to two of the sales reps. He heard one of the reps saying to the new receptionist, "I have a tattoo, you know."

"Really?" she asked. She had soft, silvery-blond hair. She was very young.

"I bet you can't guess where it is."

"Where?" She was still smiling, but she began, slowly, to back away from him.

"No, you have to guess."

Jack asked her to dance. When they were out of earshot of the reps, he said, "Don't let him bother you."

"Who?"

"That guy. If someone says something coarse to you like that, just feel free to walk away."

"You mean Marco?" She squinted up at him. "Oh, he's so fun."

"You know him?"

"He's my *step*father." She shook her head slightly and gripped Jack's fingers. "Now spin me around."

He spun her and saw in the dimness a small flash of light: Mary, demonstrating her Santa pin for someone. "Screw you, tumah," came her harsh laughing voice, floating to him over the music.

He danced with Mary, and with a soft plump woman named Jeannine who ran the Eldridge Outlet Store that was attached to the factory. She told him about her vacation to Disney World, her anecdotes rushed and incoherent, and she said she had pictures in her purse. He went back to her table with her and looked at the pictures: Jeannine with Pluto, three fat little girls with Mickey, all four of them standing in line for the Pirates of the Caribbean. He looked at his watch and wondered where Dick Coburn was; he and his wife were flying their own plane up from New Jersey. He hoped the weather wouldn't stop them from coming. He thought of Maisie, alone in the farmhouse, and missed her with a sudden acuteness that was almost luxurious. After tonight they'd be off on something new together, all alone. But for some reason he found himself thinking of a day a few weeks ago when he'd done the shopping and had brought home, among other things, a box of fabric softener sheets to be used in the dryer. Maisie had laughed, picking it up. How do you even know about fabric softener, Jack? It's so un-Jack! And he hadn't answered, and she'd watched him for a moment and then put the box down, and he could see her figuring it out: Laura used this stuff, didn't she? But she had not asked the question aloud.

"And here we are with Snow White and two of the dwarves," Jeannine said. "The kids know which ones, but I keep forgetting."

"It must have been fun," Jack said, getting up. "Thanks for showing me." He went over to Laura, sitting alone at the next table with an untouched plate of salad in front of her. He squatted beside her chair. "How are you?"

"Okay," she said, with an accent on the second syllable, as though this answer surprised her as it came out of her mouth. "I hope you don't mind that I came."

"Not at all. I'm glad." It was a relief to see her, to have her speak to him in her old, cool, friendly way. He didn't quite trust the friendliness, though.

"There were some people I wanted to say good-bye to," she said. "You included. It seemed unprofessional just to leave without telling anyone."

"Leave?" He flinched at the word *unprofessional.*

"I'm moving back to Chicago. I've got a buyer for the apartment, I think, and the camp's on the market. If you know anyone who might be interested, let me know."

"I will," he said, trying to match her coolness. "When are you going?"

"Next month sometime. I've got some other clients to finish up with here."

So she was selling the camp, the place she loved best in the world. Because of him? Then he ought to tell her he was leaving Champs du Soleil. But there were other people sitting at the table; he didn't want to talk here. He asked Laura to dance.

He held her loosely, and they rocked back and forth to the music, keeping a polite, dancing-school distance. The band was very loud. He said, "You look good."

"Thank you."

"Really."

"Well, that's flattering," Laura said. "Especially since I'm almost four months pregnant."

He pulled back his head and smiled at her, thinking she'd made a joke. But he saw on her face a look of impervious radiance, so that he knew she'd spoken the truth, and he felt his own face change and go still.

She was the one who laughed. "Don't look like that. It's all right."

A terrible relief. "You mean you're going to— When?"

She drew her dark brows together. "Oh, no. God. I didn't mean that."

"Oh."

"It's too late, anyway. And how could you think I would—you know how much I want a baby."

"No," he said quickly, honestly. But a series of long-forgotten images went clicking, revolving into a neat new line. Laura watching Little League, Laura wistfully taking his arm in front of the glass case in the supermarket, Laura carrying Linden to bed.

"Of course you do. We must have talked about it."

"We didn't," he said stubbornly. Suddenly he remembered: the night of her sister's visit. If I want a bunch, I'd better get started.

"Well, then that was because I didn't want to pressure you," she said.

"So you just went ahead and got pregnant."

"Not on purpose. It's not like I had this great silent craving that sucked a baby out of you."

But he felt that was exactly what had happened. He pulled her out of the party, through the dancing couples, and out the door into a brightly lit hallway lined with numbered guestrooms.

"Were you ever going to tell me about it?"

"I just did."

"But what if I hadn't come over to your table at all—would you just have gone away and never let me know?"

"No, I would have told you. But I had a lot of things I had to figure out myself first. I didn't even know, right away, that I would keep it. And I couldn't just call you up or come barging into your office. You know I don't like big dramas."

Yes, you do, he thought. You just cover it up with your manners and a face that doesn't show what's going on inside you. But you run your hands along the broken window glass, you jump out of canoes, and you tell me this, on the dance floor at a Christmas party.

She was talking: the sales of the camp and the apartment would generate enough money for her to live on for a while. She really did intend to move back to Chicago, so he'd never have to see the baby. It would be awkward for her to stay around here, but that wasn't why she was doing it: she had friends out there still, and the free-lance business would be better. Besides, she wanted to be near her parents. She hadn't told them yet. They would be shocked at first, but then they'd come around, and—

"What do you mean, I can't see it?" the sleeping thing inside him suddenly waking and roaring.

"Well, of course you *can,* I wouldn't stop you, but I'll be in Chicago, as I said. It might be confusing if you just walk in twice a year with a bunch of presents."

"I'll walk in whenever I fucking feel like it."

"Listen," Laura said. "Can you listen? Just for a minute?"

He crossed his arms and looked back at her.

"I did think a lot about whether or not to tell you at all. And I finally decided I had to, because otherwise it would be like stealing something from you." He started to speak, but she cut him off. "But the point wasn't to throw it in your face, or try to make you feel guilty. I'm not mad at you, okay? I was, but I'm not now."

"When did it happen?" Jack asked.

"It must have been that morning."

"But—"

"And don't quiz me about that morning, what I did or didn't remember to put in, whether I did it on purpose or not. It was an accident, but it's nothing I should ever have to explain, to you or to anyone else. And don't you ever tell anyone, either, don't you ever say that word *accident*. I don't want my kid to ever hear that word."

He made motions at her to keep her voice down; people were passing in the halls, wandering in search of bathrooms.

She went on, suddenly calm and reasonable, as though he'd been the one who had been almost shrieking just now: "You're mad because I want to go off by myself and have the baby. Well, how would you feel if I was clinging to you instead, and whining for money, and saying you had to marry me or at least help me raise it? Wouldn't that be worse?"

He didn't answer.

She said with some of her old dryness, "It would be worse for me, Jack. I'm a little old for a shotgun wedding."

He said dully, "I won't even *be* around here. I'm selling the company."

"*Are* you?" Gracious and pleasant, her child-of-the-Foreign-Service voice. "To whom?"

"A guy named Dick Coburn." He looked at his watch unseeingly. "He should be here soon. We're making the announcement tonight."

"So you're leaving Champs du Soleil?"

"I'm moving to Cambridge. Maisie has a job there she likes."

"Well, that's wonderful," Laura said, and he thought that she was making this so civilized, she had it all figured out, she was slipping away and taking his child (his child!) with her. And there was a deep ache somewhere in his head and chest and belly, a sense of hopeless, killing pressure, that had begun the instant he said the word *Maisie*.

Dick Coburn arrived twenty minutes later with his wife. She was blond, wearing a fur coat. They were both tanned and had an air of furtive glamour, walking in as though they hoped not to be noticed but knew their hopes were unrealistic. They found Jack at the bar.

"Sorry we're late," said Dick. "We ran into some bad weather over Hartford, and it was a little hairy after that."

His wife's name was Callie. She asked Jack about amenities.

"Amenities?"

"Shopping, restaurants, country club. Water-skiing."

"Callie was former Florida champion," Dick put in, with his aw-shucks grin.

"Ah," said Jack. "Well." He gave a vague answer, making Portland sound nearer than it was. He said he didn't know about water-skiing; he had a wild impulse to introduce them to Laura: I found some customers for your camp! He could see her, talking to Dave LaPalme near the dance floor. He knew he should make more small talk with Dick and Callie, but he wanted to get out of there.

"Let's do it," he said, and he took Dick by the arm and went to ask the bandleader for the use of his microphone. There was a wooden podium on wheels at the back of the dance floor; Jack wheeled it to the front, for something to lean on, and this action quieted the crowd, so that when he leaned into the microphone to ask for their attention, he saw a mass of waiting faces. He cleared his throat.

"The Eldridge Potato Company has been in my family for nearly eighty years." The microphone whined, and he stopped until it subsided. "My great-grandfather started it, at a time when commercially canned food—because that was what he started out doing, canning potatoes—was viewed the way cars had been viewed just a decade before. He moved to Champs du Soleil, and everyone shouted at him, 'Get a horse!' " Jack stopped; this had seemed such a clever analogy when he had written it down the night before, but nobody laughed, and he thought, What am I talking about? He put the piece of paper on the wooden podium and smoothed it; the paper crackled into the microphone. He went on, not reading now, just talking:

"When I was growing up, the company was something I took for granted. It was just always there. Our freezer at home was always full of Eldridge fries, my father smelled of them, I always thought that smell was part of his after-shave." *It was the smell of this company: I still can't separate the smell of the office from the smell of my home or my father or myself or my town.*

"When I first got here, I hid out in my office, watching the clock, thinking if I could just make it till five, I could go home and forget about work till the next morning." *I was scared of all of you, I didn't know what I was doing. I missed my father, and I didn't even know that. He must have done this. He must have stood up at Christmas parties, in years when there were no profits, no bonuses. He must have had to do pep talks when there was nothing to be peppy about, when he felt ashamed to be standing up here at all. Oh, Dad. I hate when Mom and Marion talk about you as "Daddy," always with that condescending tone, as though your dignity was foolish, and your stubbornness, but I know how hard you tried. I'm sorry that I've done this, when you never could. I'm sorry the company's making money, I'm sorry I've found this arrogant hot-shot buyer. It wasn't anything I did, really. It was luck.*

"But what I found out is that the company wasn't this big impersonal thing that we could all take for granted. I appreciated for the first time how hard my father worked all his life, how hard all of you work. Machines break and need to be fixed. Trucks don't show up. Clients walk away and you have to replace their accounts. The company wouldn't just always be there; we had to fight to keep it there.

"So I couldn't hide out in my office like a kid. I started to pay attention to how good all of you were at your jobs. How Lizzie Tursky ran the fryer day after day and never burned a batch. How Charlie Santore came in to negotiate last year's contract with me, and sat in my office for seven straight hours until I agreed to his figures, without ever once playing dirty or raising his voice. How when the supermarkets got more and more competitive, Dave LaPalme spent weeks on the road calling on airlines and schools and hospitals, expanding the institutional side of our business. How when we bought the curly fry machine last year, the four people who would be responsible for running it came in on a Saturday to learn, so we could get going on Monday with no down time.

"Now I know you're all thinking, Why doesn't he shut up already and give us our Christmas bonus"—laughter here, so that he sped up the rest of his speech—"but I did want to thank you, for teaching me so much, and for realizing what I know was my father's hope, and I'm sure you've all hoped it, too, of turning this into a strong and profitable business.

"I do have the bonus checks here, but first I need to make an announcement. I know some of you have probably already guessed this, and I hope whatever rumors may have been floating around haven't upset anyone too much. For personal reasons, I've decided to sell the company."

He paused, expecting what? Applause? Booing? There was nothing, silence, and the faces he could see looked politely interested, no more.

"It's one of the hardest things I've ever done. But I've been lucky enough to find a wonderful buyer, Dick Coburn, who wants to work with all of you"—pause, pause, pause, don't worry, you're not going to lose your jobs—"to continue the success and growth we've started."

His announcement was greeted with polite clapping. Dick took the microphone and said how pleased he was, how excited. He talked about Coburn Foods, how frozen food was in his blood. He said his two children were heroes now in their school, since they'd told everyone their dad was buying a french fry factory. And we've all been enjoying SunLights, he said, patting his flat stomach. Everyone laughed. He introduced his wife and said that anyone who knew where the good water-skiing was up here should speak now or forever hold his peace. More laughter. All right, then, Jack thought, and stopped listening.

There was a look you would sometimes get. Hurt, but closed in, so I knew you didn't know it was showing, as though your fly were unzipped. You looked like that when you came home from the factory, when Mom would ask how your day had been and then say, coolly, Don't you ever *have a good day? I saw that look all through my childhood and didn't know, ever, what it was; but now I do. You tried so hard to be good, to be clever, to be responsible, but you weren't smart enough, not in the right way, and it just kept caving in on you. Mom was right when she said that this was the wrong thing for you to have spent your life on; but she said it with such a bitter sense of your utter wrongness that you couldn't ever just agree with her and ask her, So what do we do now?*

For months after you died I tried to remember your face, and I couldn't. Why are you here so suddenly? I wanted you terribly right after you died, and when things were so bad with Maisie, but you never came then. I wish you weren't here now, pressing down on me. But I can't look at Dick's back or the bandleader's face to distract myself, because that would erase you and I might never get you back again. I can't bear it, I can't; but don't go.

I've fucked up with Maisie, I've fucked up with Laura. What am I going to do?

I've fucked up, he thought, but it was a conscious thought now, something spoken nearly aloud, like trying to force his way back into a dream. He found that he was looking at the bandleader's face and Dick's back, and that he was worrying about whether his speech had sounded maudlin.

". . . and I'll try real hard not to let you down," Dick finished. More clapping, and then Jack stood at the edge of the dance floor, handing out bonus checks from a shoebox, thanking each person, and introducing Dick Coburn again and again. Too bad you're leaving, people said. Where are you going? What'll you do? Deserting us, huh?

Mary came and kissed him; she was crying, she said over and over again, "Oh, I can't believe it." Someone else grabbed his arm, and the next time he saw Mary she was talking to Laura; he watched until he saw Mary leave. People were going home. Laura had her coat over her arm. He went over to her and said, his voice cracking, "I've been thinking about what you said. And you can't."

"Can't what?"

"Have this kid."

She put her arms into her coat; he watched, without reaching to help her, and she looked back at him. "Well, I'm gonna."

Maisie had spent most of the evening on her knees in the upstairs bedroom Jack had been using for storage, surrounded by cardboard boxes that contained the detritus of their old life together. The remnants of her thrift-shop college wardrobe—fifties jet-spangled cardigans, a tattered blue sari shot with gold threads which she'd worn sometimes to parties. Cowboy boots, clogs, gladiator sandals. A black scarf she used to wrap around her head, turban style, and wear with gold hoop earrings. A box of her old college papers. "*Paradise Lost* and Genesis: Milton's Variations from the Text," "Please, Sir, I Want Some More: *Oliver Twist* and the Poor Laws," "Did Jane Austen Confuse Morals with Manners?" A journal she'd kept sporadically in high school, in which every entry seemed to begin with the words "Oh God, oh God . . ." Wedding presents, some still in their original gift wrap, slit open just enough to identify the contents and write thank-you notes. Electric coffeemakers, wooden and crystal and pewter candlesticks, a tarnishing silver wine rack, a brass mirror made to look like a ship's porthole. A few pieces from the china pattern she'd chosen, the yellow-and-blue design Monet had used at Giverny; her mother had warned her that it was too expensive, people wouldn't buy it for her; and in fact Maisie had gotten only three place settings.

None of this stuff seemed to belong to her, but it was all in cardboard cartons labeled MAISIE in Jack's handwriting, piled on one side of the room. On the other side, across a clear aisle of floor, were stacks of cartons labeled JACK; and she thought of him in the cold little beach cottage near Portland, separating her things from his.

She sat paralyzed in the mess for a long time; then she began to sort it into three categories: Trash, Goodwill, and Keep. Keep was the smallest pile: the china, one set of candlesticks, a few odds and ends. She was sitting on the floor with the cowboy boots in her lap—they were beat-up and a little affected-looking, but they'd been expensive, even second-hand, and she might go through a stage where she'd want to wear them again—when she heard Jack's footsteps on the stairs. She looked at her watch: it was after one.

"How was it?" she called, and then he stood in the doorway and she saw his face. The deal fell through, she thought.

He sat down on the floor, still in his gray overcoat. "Laura's having a baby."

"What?" asked Maisie, although she'd heard and understood and believed it, instantly.

He repeated it. "She's moving to Chicago. To get out of our way, I think. She doesn't want me to see it."

"Uh-huh," said Maisie. But this will ruin our Christmas. We have a tree. What about the presents? "So where were you?" she asked.

"Hmm?" He ran his hands along the side of his head, stretching the skin back.

"It's one o'clock. I assume the party didn't just break up."

"I drove around for a while."

"Alone?"

"Yes."

"Oh." She put the boots down, softly, beside her. "Were the roads bad?"

"I guess so," Jack said.

"Well," she said slowly. "Anyway, I'm glad it didn't happen when you were still with her."

"Why?"

"Because then you would have stayed with her." He didn't answer. "Wouldn't you?"

"I don't know," he said dully.

"You would have dumped her to come back to me?" Was it or was it not the mere chance of timing that had saved them.

"I don't know, Maisie!"

After a moment she asked, "Did she do it on purpose?"

"No."

"She told you that?"

"It was the last morning we were together. She was very upset. She slipped up. All right?"

"Don't yell at me." She looked at him, still in his overcoat, sitting with his head bowed, his legs sticking straight out in front of him. The little she could see of his face, lit by the bare overhead bulb, was all bones and cavernous shadows. She made her voice gentle. "What are we going to do?"

"What are you talking about? There's nothing to do."

He's thinking how this wouldn't have happened if I'd just stayed with him in the first place. "Why would anyone want to have a baby without a husband?" she said almost to herself.

"I don't think she wants to have it alone, but she *does* want to have it, and she *is* alone."

He sounded sorry for Laura, which hit Maisie as more of a betrayal than the fact that he'd gotten Laura pregnant.

"Maybe she's doing it just to spite you," she said with menacing brightness.

"Maybe," he mumbled.

She wanted to get up and run, down the stairs and across the fields. Instead she crawled over to the cartons she'd emptied earlier in the evening and began refilling them, methodically, according to her new categories: Trash, Goodwill, Keep. She hated everything she touched, even the Keep things; she wanted to throw it all out and never see any of it again.

Jack was sitting perfectly still, his head drooping down. She felt she should say something to comfort him, but if she spoke, she would scream. She picked up a scuffed vinyl jewelry box and held it for a moment. She'd looked inside it earlier and found, amid a jumble of broken fake gold chains and Brownie pins and single earrings, a half-empty pack of cigarettes. She wanted desperately to smoke one now, but she knew that Jack would take it as a reproach: see what you've made me do? The box, as she lifted it, let out a few soft notes of music. It had a wind-up key in the back, and it had once played a tune that she had loved; her mother had told her that the name of the song was "Fascination," and sometimes when Maisie wound the key her mother would come into her room and sing the words to her. There had been a ballerina in the box, who popped up when the lid was open and spun slowly before a small oval mirror. The mirror was gone now, and all that was left of the ballerina was the small coiled spring on which she'd stood.

The jewelry box had been placed in the Keep pile, hours ago. Now Maisie didn't know what to do with it.

What she wanted now, more than anything, was to take their marriage for granted, to know that they could be buffeted by anything and still stay together. And she *was* taking it for granted: even though he had told her this terrible thing, it had not crossed her mind that she might leave him for it, or that he might leave her. It was more as though they were both huddled together under a weak but heavy roof; the roof might fall and crush them, but it would crush them together.

But maybe it had crossed his mind. Maybe he was sitting there so quietly now because he couldn't figure out how to tell her that he was leaving her to be with Laura. It wasn't that he loved Laura more; but now, with the baby coming, it was his responsibility to go make a family with her. Or maybe he did love Laura more. Maybe Maisie was the bad, beautiful first wife who would always haunt him a little, but who was hopeless to live with. She'd made him laugh, she'd made him feel protective, she was great in bed, but when it came right down to it, she was flighty. She'd left him once, and he could never trust her after that. Yeah, we tried getting back together for a while, she imagined him saying, years from now (maybe to his child? Explaining who was the lady in those pictures in the old shoebox at the back of the closet—well, you see, Daddy was married before. But no, he'd never be that frank with his own kid. It would be a friend, someone who was embarking on his own second marriage to someone boring and safe. The sparks just aren't there, he would say to Jack. But I *like* her so much. Do you think I'm crazy? And Jack would say, Let me tell you about my first marriage).

She passed a hand over her face and looked at her watch. It was one-thirty. "Well," she said, "we should probably try to get some sleep."

She started to get up, but Jack was still talking.

"Maisie, how will you feel if I want to see it?"

"See what?" she asked.

"The baby."

"You mean if we're still married?" She'd traveled so far down that other road in her head that she couldn't take in what he was saying. He wasn't going back to Laura? Was that what he was saying?

The dark blur of his body hurtling toward her, his face pressing into her stomach. "Don't," he was saying, "oh, don't."

She cupped his head and held him against her. Underneath her confusion a dim little sense of elation was beginning to dawn.

"You mean you thought *I* would leave?"

"You said, if we were still married . . ." he gulped out.

"Because I thought you were going to leave."

He turned his face up to look at her. "Oh, God, Maisie, I just got you back."

She couldn't speak. She kept holding him; they were staring at each other. His face was red, with white patches under the eyes. She was filled for a long moment with the sense of her own great fortune: how had this come about, Jack in her lap crying out that he loved her?

Well, his former girlfriend was having his baby, that's how it had come about.

Slowly she took her hands away from him, resting her palms on the bare wood floor on either side of her. She knelt in silence. She knew he needed more reassurance, but some ugly part of her made her say, "But what do you mean, you'd want to see it?"

He said miserably, "It'll be mine, part me. I can't not be part of its life."

"Jack." Can't we just pretend none of this ever happened? Where is all that passionate happiness that was in the room just a minute ago?

"I'm its *father,*" he said firmly, and she felt as though she'd been slapped.

She answered instantly. "It will kill me if you see it, I can't be married to you if you do."

He looked at her, and his face frightened her. "Do you mean that?"

Yes, she thought, yes. She wanted to say it and see how he answered. If he said "All right, then, I won't see it," she would know he loved her; and if he said "Tough," she would know he didn't. But she looked back into his still, serious face and thought, No, that's not right. Always before when they'd fought, she'd said whatever came into her head, trying to goad him into a response. The worst that could happen was that he would get so angry he'd leave her; and she had not been afraid of that. She'd never believed it would happen and never realized how unbearable it would be until it did. She couldn't go through it again. She had to look at this unforgivable thing and decide, gazing past the weeks of pain and tension that were certain to come, now, whether or not she could stand it.

She said, speaking quickly after the long silence, "No. No, I don't mean it."

The next morning, Christmas Eve, she went outside early and smoked a cigarette. It was from the pack she'd found in the jewelry box the night before, and she dragged on it now with a sense of sneaky entitlement. She wasn't going to become a smoker again, she'd never buy another pack; but these were hers from a long time ago. If she hadn't absent-mindedly stuck them in that jewelry box, she'd have smoked them already. They didn't count. Besides, she deserved to smoke them. Laura was having a baby.

The smoke pierced her lungs and curled out dramatically into the cold morning air, mixed with the white stream she made just by breathing. Inside, Jack was still asleep. Their presents to each other lay in bright wrappings under the tree. Tomorrow they would open them, dutifully. They would kiss each other and act pleased. He would put on the new green sweater and thumb through the books, and later they might go for a walk and look at birds through the telescope she'd bought him. She had no curiosity about what he was giving her.

Once, when she was working as a secretary at the Harvard natural history museum, she'd been standing at the Xerox machine and she'd felt a sudden sensation of the floor rocking under her, as though she were standing on the deck of a boat. It was so slight that she thought she'd imagined it, but then a colleague had come running into the Xerox room, wide-eyed: Did you feel that? What *was* it?

Maybe a bomb, Maisie had suggested, giddy with pretend horror-movie fear. Maybe an earthquake.

That was an earthquake! someone else had shouted, running by in the hall.

They'd all rushed, then, to check on the glass flowers, cabinet after cabinet of meticulously detailed crystal: glittering orchids, peach blossoms. But nothing had broken; the specimens lay serene and unmoved in the late afternoon sunlight. When Maisie walked to the subway stop that evening, her legs were still trembling, but the streets looked as they always did: no crumbling buildings, no strangers searching her face to see if she'd felt it, too. She began to think again that she'd imagined it —when she got home and told Jack, he looked astonished and said he'd been in his carrel at Widener all afternoon and hadn't felt a thing—but then on the news that night there was a short report: a tremor, they called it, the faint aftershock of a larger quake in the Midwest somewhere. She felt vindicated—it was an earthquake, I felt an earthquake—but nothing changed. So she'd been in an earthquake, so her legs were shaking, so what?

Now she thought: There will be a baby out there. Jack will be its father. She kept saying these things to herself, waiting for something to move or change. But everything was still, the pale pink sky and the fields of frozen grass, as she stood there bringing the cigarette to her mouth and taking it away again.

20
The Rescue

❧

One Sunday afternoon near the end of January, the phone rang in the Cambridge apartment, and Maisie picked it up. "Hello?"

No response.

"Hello," she repeated sternly.

After a slight hesitation, a woman's voice asked for Jack.

"He's not here," Maisie said.

"Is there any way I can reach him?" the woman asked.

It's Laura, she thought. She made her voice friendly. "I'm afraid he's out doing errands right now. He should be back in a couple of hours."

"Oh," said the woman. "Well then, never mind."

"Can I take a message?" Maisie asked. "Or can I help you?"

"No," said the woman. She was calling from someplace noisy.

There was a silence. "Is this Laura?" Maisie asked, and she waited for the woman to hang up.

No answer, and Maisie took a deep breath, trying to remember all the things she'd meant to say to Laura if she got the chance. But what she said was, "Are you all right?"

"I don't know. I don't know what to do."

"What is it?"

"I'm bleeding."

"Oh, God."

"The book I have says to go to bed right away, but I'm on the road, I don't know where I am—"

"Shouldn't you call a doctor?"

"I don't know."

"Where are you calling from?"

"A restaurant."

"But where?"

"Near Boston. I'm on Route 128. I don't know where."

"Ask someone," Maisie told her.

A clunky noise of the phone being put down. Then Laura's voice again. "It's just past the junction of Route 2, on 128 North. A Roy Rogers."

Maisie took a deep breath. "I'll come get you."

"When?" said Laura, and Maisie thought that she really must be frightened, to have stayed on the phone like this, to accept this offer.

"I think it'll take about twenty minutes."

Laura hung up.

In the car she thought of all the things she could have done instead. Asked to speak to the manager of the restaurant, told him to call a local doctor. Found a doctor herself in the Yellow Pages, or an ambulance service. But no, she'd wanted to prove to herself and to Jack and Laura what a magnanimous person she was. She hoped her heroism wouldn't cost Laura the baby. Yet already a small part of her was beginning to think, Ah, but if she loses it . . . But not because of anything I do or don't do, she thought. Don't let her lose it because of me.

In the weeks since Jack had told her about the baby, they had barely spoken of it. She had not wavered from her realization, that first night, that she wanted to be married to him no matter what, but her sense that their reunion had been a giddy, miraculous thing (they had walked bent to the wind, their arms wrapped around each other, down the dark street outside Bert and Jenny's apartment) was gone, replaced by grim determination that they would stay together. She went to work, she watched Jack sending out his résumé and making phone calls to consulting firms. She told Caterina about the baby, no one else; there was a long silence in the receiver, and then Caterina said, "Oh, Maisie. Oh, my God. I couldn't stand that," and Maisie, who had hoped for comfort, actually felt grateful that Caterina hadn't come back with a series of wise platitudes. Instead she wound up supplying the platitudes herself: Don't worry, it'll be all right, it's terrible, but we'll get through it. She hung up feeling that the bottom had fallen out of everything: if Caterina couldn't stand it, how could she? But she could, apparently.

They bought furniture for their new apartment: a couch, an old rug for the bedroom, a glass coffee table. They vacuumed the floor and went to the movies, they spoke to their mothers on the phone. Jack went to bed early and slept late, napped in the afternoons. She looked at him, curled in the bed, and tried to imagine what he was feeling. They no longer talked about having children of their own.

She saw the restaurant to her right, just off the highway. She was squinting ahead, trying to see the turnoff, passing an exit, when she suddenly realized that the exit itself was the turnoff; and she had to brake and back up a hundred feet to make it.

The restaurant was beige and green, bustling with old people from the tour bus she'd seen parked outside. She looked around for a dark woman sitting alone, and was at once relieved and frightened when she didn't see anyone who could be Laura. She must have thought to call a doctor, or maybe she'd felt better and kept going. Still, Maisie stood in the middle of the restaurant, scanning the room. She caught sight of a sign with an arrow that read RESTROOMS, and after a moment she followed it into the ladies' room.

The room was empty, but the door on the last stall was closed. "Laura?" Maisie said to it.

"Yes."

Maisie put her hands lightly on the door. "Are you all right? Can we leave?"

There was a click and the door swung inward: Laura on the toilet, her chest resting on her knees. Her jeans were down around her ankles; Maisie caught a glimpse of bright white underpants, red stains. She averted her eyes. "Should I try to call a doctor?"

Laura raised her head and looked at Maisie; her eyes were very dark, and her face was damp. Maisie thought of Caterina, with her head between her knees in the hot kitchen.

"Does it hurt, or is it just the bleeding?" Maisie asked, and wondered why she was asking: the answer wouldn't help her know what to do.

"It hurts," Laura said, and Maisie knew by her voice that she was too sick to think or move.

She put a hand on Laura's arm, just below the shoulder; she was surprised at how taut and muscular it was, and she thought, Jack touched it too. "Come on," she said. "Stand up." She knelt to help Laura pull up her jeans, aware and unaware, nurselike, of the brown legs, the matted darkness at the crotch. She backed out of the stall and pulled Laura after her, unhooking Laura's leather handbag from the back of the door. She put the bag over her shoulder and looked down at it involuntarily. It was gaping softly open; she saw a book with pregnant women on the cover. Laura was at the door of the ladies' room, walking very slowly, holding herself.

When they reached the car Maisie asked, "Would the back or front seat be better?"

"Back," Laura said. Maisie held the door open for her, and she fell in, lying with her long legs doubled, her knees in the air.

"I'm sorry," Laura said as they pulled out of the parking lot.

"What are you doing out here, anyway?" Maisie asked.

"I was in Providence for the weekend. Visiting my sister."

"Did the bleeding just start?"

"Yes," Laura said shortly, "or I would have stayed where I was."

"Well, listen," Maisie said, her eyes on the road—she'd had to get back in the northbound lane and was looking for signs for the next exit, so she could turn around; why the hell did they put the exits so far apart? "There's a really good hospital right down the street from us, so I'll just take you right to the emergency room. Just to be safe," she added, glancing in the rearview mirror, seeing Laura's knees.

"I've lost it, anyhow."

"What? You mean already? Are you sure?"

"You can't bleed this much and still be 'safe' as you call it."

Maisie pressed her lips together and saw, finally, the green exit sign looming larger and larger. She swung off the road and through what must have seemed to Laura a sickening series of loops and then back on again, going south.

She'd driven several miles when Laura said: "I wouldn't have bothered you with this."

"Oh, no."

"But I didn't know anyone else in Boston."

"I'm just sorry Jack wasn't around," Maisie said. "But he was out—the hardware store, drugstore, groceries. I honestly didn't know where to find him."

"Well, you shouldn't have to do this," Laura said firmly. Her voice sounded stronger than it had. Maybe everything would still be all right, Maisie thought, and then wondered what she could possibly mean.

At the hospital the nurses took Laura right away, ahead of all the other people waiting in Emergency. Maisie sat in an orange room full of screaming children and ancient men. There was a TV high up on the wall, tuned to a basketball game. She tried calling Jack, but there was still no answer. She looked at her watch: ten of four. Laura's call had come at around two-thirty, she thought. She picked up a finger-dented copy of *People* and read a story about Fergie. A doctor came out and said to the room at large, "Maisie?"

When she and Laura got home, Jack was there. His eyes widened at the sight of them, and his face went tight, but Maisie was thankful that he didn't say anything. Neither did Laura. She held Maisie's arm, a wounded soldier leaning on a comrade, and allowed herself to be led into the bedroom. She was silent while Maisie, gratuitously, pointed out the bed, the door to the bathroom. The bed was unmade, rumpled: Maisie looked at it and thought of this morning, ages ago now, sitting on top of Jack, rocking, one hand behind her back rubbing between his thighs. Would the sheets smell? she wondered. Would Laura smell them and cry? But she couldn't take time to change them; Laura clearly was going to cry and wanted her out of there.

She shut the door behind her and beckoned Jack to follow her into the kitchen. He still had that blank, stunned look, and she spoke quickly, trying to erase it.

"It's all right," she told him. "She was having some bleeding, but it's stopped now and the doctor said it's probably going to be all right. They did an ultrasound, and the baby looks fine. She saw it moving, on the screen." She went over and squeezed his hands briefly; his knuckles cracked.

He cleared his throat. "But why is she here? With you?"

"She called me. Well, you, actually, but you weren't here. She was on the road from Providence, and she started bleeding. I went and got her." She paused, waiting (she recognized, ashamed) to be commended for heroism.

"Did you see it?"

"See what?"

"The ultrasound."

"She didn't ask me to come in. So I stayed in the hall."

She put up the kettle and told Jack everything that had happened at the hospital. She felt slow and utterly calm, as though she were walking on a layer of cloud that kept her from falling to the earth below. "So all they can do now is wait and see."

"Shouldn't she be in the hospital?" he asked, his voice cracking.

"They didn't seem to think it was necessary. But they did say she should rest, so I asked her back here. I hope that's all right."

"Of course."

"She couldn't drive back to Maine by herself."

"No, you were right."

"This must be so humiliating, needing help from us."

"She wants kids so badly," he said. "You should have seen her with her niece. They both had ice cream all over their faces, and I thought, Oh, but Laura cares so much about being neat."

"You're making it sound like she died," Maisie said with some sharpness. "Or like she's this ancient spinster. She's still going to have the baby."

"I know." He drank some tea, making a fist around the handle. "How long is she staying here?"

"We didn't discuss it. I mean, as long as she needs to, right? Listen, Jack—do you think I should maybe go stay with a friend?"

He looked at her. "Why?"

"Because I was thinking maybe it's going to be uncomfortable for her, having both of us here."

"Well, in that case maybe I should be the one to go."

"You?"

"She let you help her. Not me."

"Oh, come on. She asked for you when she called." What is this, she thought, now we're fighting over who Laura likes best?

"Or we could let her go to a hotel."

"Alone? She's sick, Jack."

"I know that," he snapped. "I just didn't think *you'd* be comfortable with her around."

Maisie poured boiling water over a tea bag and handed him the mug. He looked down at it. "Do you want to take it in to her?" she prodded.

He pushed open the bedroom door. The room was dark, the shades down. Laura was in the bed, lying on her side with her knees sticking out over the edge. Her eyes were open, turned toward him, watching him cross the room. He stumbled over something soft and tangled on the floor, felt hot tea running over his wrists, hitting his ankle. He looked down. Her clothes. He sat on the edge of the bed and held the mug out to her. When she didn't reach for it, he put it on the floor. Her large flat hands gripped the sheet beneath her chin. Her chestnut-colored shoulders were bare.

"Would you rather I left you alone?" he asked finally.

"No, stay." Her hands relaxed slightly. "I know there's nothing I can do, but I feel like I have to be vigilant."

"But everything looks all right, they said."

"*They* said."

Egg sprang onto the bed, purring loudly, stepping with elaborate delicacy across the rumpled bedclothes to mold his body against Laura's.

"Can you get him out of here?" she asked, her voice trembling.

He picked up the cat and dumped him outside the room, catching a glimpse of Maisie's curious face from the living room couch. He shut the door.

"Thank you," said Laura. She had turned on her back, with her knees up. Jack sat on the edge of the bed. "I'm sorry to be cluttering up your house like this."

"You're not."

"Your wife was very nice to me." After a moment she said, "She must love having me here."

"I don't think she minds."

"Oh, Jack, you're so dumb sometimes." She took a breath. "But maybe you're right. I do feel a little like one of those teenage unwed mothers, being fussed over by the rich couple that's going to adopt my baby."

He stood up.

"I'm sorry," said Laura. "Don't tell her I said that, will you?"

"All right," he said after a moment.

"It's hormones. They really do get you. I have times when I cry and cry, and other times when I can't stop laughing. This weekend, Todd and Beth were driving me around the Rhode Island seashore. I was sitting in the backseat with Linden. Beth had her window open a crack, and she said, 'Is it too blowy for you back there?' I said, 'Yes, close it!' And then she asked me if I'd be more comfortable in front, and I said, 'Yes!' and made Todd stop the car so I could change places with her. I was laughing and laughing at the way I'd sounded. Like some fat pregnant monster." She laughed now, then sat up and rubbed her fingers under her eyes. "Beth was quite shocked, about the baby. I hadn't told her before. She kept asking me if I knew how much work it was going to be." She wrapped her arms around her knees. "Do you think I'm crazy, to have it? But I guess you're the wrong person to ask. And it's a little late to be asking."

"Yes."

"Don't look at me like that. I'm just babbling. You know how much I want it, really. And I may never get another chance."

"You're only thirty-seven."

"Only!"

"Lots of women thirty-seven haven't started their families yet. Maisie says—"

"Oh, *Maisie* says. Tell me what she says."

He bent to pick up her clothes, tossing them onto a chair, and then walked to the door. "Let me know if you need anything else."

She was running her fingers through her hair, raking it forward over her shoulder. She began to braid it. "When I was in the emergency room this afternoon, they were all so neutral. The nurses, and the doctor. Do they think you're going to sue for malpractice if they show the slightest sign of optimism before they're sure? Or maybe they just weren't sure, I don't know. But I was thinking about this old wrought-iron bassinet that's in our family. My father and his brothers all slept in it when they were little. So did we. It came with us in all those moves, all over the world. Beth had it, for Linden. I got her to give it to me, this weekend. It's in the trunk of my car. And I was thinking, lying there, that if I lost the baby I couldn't bear to open that trunk when I got back to Maine. I'd have to get someone to do it for me."

Who? he thought.

Echoing his thoughts, she said, "I don't know who. I haven't made many friends up there."

"That's because you spent so much time with me."

"No, it was that way before you. I don't make friends easily."

She smiled at him, surprisingly, and went on:

"People say you make friends when you have a baby. You sit around the playground and talk about diapers and pacifiers. We'll see how *that* goes." She lay down again, pulled up the covers, and said sleepily, "I'm actually looking forward to that."

Maisie was sitting on the couch, looking at a book full of pictures. He sat down next to her. "It was sticking out of her purse," she said. He looked down at it and saw a series of drawings of women at different stages of pregnancy. He was astonished and fascinated by the enlargement, the darkening of breasts and belly, as though they had painted themselves for some tribal rite. Maisie looked at him and began slowly turning the pages. The book was a hardcover, as scuffed and worn as a school textbook; he could imagine Laura in her white armchair in Maine, reading and rereading, absently stroking Egg—but no, he'd taken Egg, Egg was here.

They looked at drawings of the baby itself—even at sixteen weeks (counting backward to when he'd been with Laura in Maine), it already looked like a baby, fragile but there, an enormous head with eyes, nose, and mouth on a tiny bloated body. The drawings made the baby look alert and aware, somehow, even though the text denied this.

He thought of Laura poring over the book, allying herself with all the details of pregnancy described there. He glanced sideways at Maisie and saw on her face an expression of wistful fascination. He put his hand on the back of her neck, and they looked at a picture of how the pregnant woman should sleep, on her side with a pillow under her knees; diagrams of exercises she could do if her back hurt, pictures of a bearded, gentle-looking man rubbing her back and lifting her hips, as she lay with her eyes closed, in a bulging T-shirt. Pictures of women sipping tea, explaining the new baby to a toddler, soaking in a bathtub, looking up at a screen during an ultrasound test. A naked couple making love, different positions to try. The book made pregnancy seem all-consuming yet somehow contained, cozy, and, with a certain degree of study and intelligence, controllable.

Around midnight they unfolded the futon and put sheets on it. He kept glancing at the bedroom door, expecting Laura to emerge; but there was no light in the crack beneath the door. He lay on his side waiting for sleep, and Maisie sat up next to him, reading the pregnancy book in a bright pool of light.

In the morning Jack and Maisie got up early and folded the futon back into a couch, as if to conceal the fact that they'd slept there. They made coffee and debated whether or not to bring Laura some, but Jack said he thought it was too pushy. She'd come out when she was ready.

"Should I go to work, do you think?" Maisie asked, looking at her watch. It was eight-thirty.

"Oh, yes, I think so." They were speaking in low voices, sitting at the kitchen table with sections of the Sunday paper. They'd barely looked at it the day before, and it lay between them piled neatly: to scatter it over the apartment as they usually did would have implied a disrespectful sense of abandon. Maisie was reading the magazine section, wanting to do the puzzle but reading instead a long piece on the West Bank, photographs of Palestinians with bloodied faces and their hands tied behind their backs, before and after pictures of a house being blown up.

Laura came in just as Maisie was getting up to leave. She was wearing Jack's plaid flannel bathrobe, and Maisie's fists tightened momentarily at the sight of her; but a glance at Laura's flushed, dazed face, her hair limp and tangled, made Maisie absolve her instantly from any ulterior motive. She offered coffee, but Laura said she'd prefer tea. Maisie put up the kettle, and Jack went over to the glass canister where they kept the tea bags, and she saw him plunge his hand deep into the jumble of different kinds and brands to come up with a very specific one, a Twinings China Black, which he unwrapped and put into a mug without consulting Laura. I do have to go to work, Maisie thought, I have to get out of here or I'll go crazy; but she leaned against the counter and watched Laura sitting with her elbow on the table, the side of her tilted head resting in her open palm.

"Are you hungry?" she asked Laura. "Would you like some breakfast?"

Laura ate a toasted bagel, and Jack asked her, not quite looking at her, how she was feeling.

"Okay," said Laura. "I slept surprisingly well. Are there any more bagels?"

"That was the last one," Maisie said apologetically.

"Oh."

"But there's bread, and cereal—well, listen, help yourself." She moved aside to let Laura go past her to the refrigerator. "Whatever's in there is fine," Maisie continued cheerfully, and Jack frowned: to warn her to curb her effusiveness, she supposed. She went out of the kitchen and put on her makeup; she had to do her lipstick twice, wiping off her first, shaky attempt. When she came back Jack was sitting at the table and

Laura was sitting with the remnants of a bowl of Cheerios. Maisie wondered what they'd talked about.

"I don't know what's the matter with me," said Laura. "I'm starving." She sat with her feet tucked up on her chair, the backs of her thighs showing, and ate a piece of leftover lasagna. "I'm really sorry," she kept saying. "I hope this is okay."

"It's fine," said Maisie. She'd been planning to serve the lasagna for supper that night, but it wouldn't have been enough for the three of them anyway.

"But this is great," Laura said. "How do you make it?"

"I just follow the recipe on the box, pretty much."

"Do you cook the noodles first?"

"Yes."

"Because you don't have to, you know. You can just lay the noodles on dry, and then pour a cup of water around the edges of the pan."

"Into the pan, you mean?" She glanced at Jack, drinking his coffee over by the window, and saw that he was mesmerized by this conversation.

Laura nodded, her mouth full. "The noodles boil and bake at the same time. It's much easier." She held out her plate. "Is there more?"

"Sure," said Maisie, reaching into the refrigerator again.

"I'm really sorry, I don't usually eat like this. I don't know what's the matter with me."

"You probably didn't eat much yesterday," Maisie said. She put another piece of lasagna onto Laura's plate and left the pan on the table.

"And good tomato sauce. Do you make it yourself?"

"From tomatoes, you mean? No, I use paste. From cans."

"It doesn't taste like it."

"I once served it to a friend, my tomato sauce," said Maisie, "and literally just as I was dishing it out, he launched into this big monologue about how his mother made it from scratch and spent three days simmering the tomatoes. Simmering, he said, not boiling, and all the while I'm trying to scoop my little Contadina cans into the garbage."

"Well, that's ridiculous," said Laura. "I make it from scratch, and it does not take three days."

Her tone was so vehement that Maisie was snapped into silence. "Well," she said finally, as Laura finished what was on her plate, "I'd better go."

"You have a lot of books," Laura said, standing in the living room in front of the shelves with her hands in the pockets of Jack's robe.

"I guess so," he said.

"Are they mostly Maisie's?"

"No, I just never unpacked them in Maine."

She nodded and kept staring at the books.

"Are you sure it's okay for you to be walking around?" Jack asked. "Didn't they say you should stay in bed?"

She shrugged. "If you have plans for the day, go ahead. Don't hang around because of me." She pulled out Maisie's biography of Isak Dinesen and flipped the pages. She put it back in, beginning with one hand but then raising the other to help, jamming it.

He sat on the arm of the couch. "You know," he said, "I really wish you'd let me do something to help."

"You mean money?"

"Well, certainly that, for a start."

"No, Jack."

"Why not?"

She lowered herself into an armchair. "Because I can't take money from you, and nothing else. And I can't take anything else."

"I think that's selfish. And not very realistic."

They sat in silence; then he asked, "Did they ever catch the robbers?"

She shook her head. "I knew they wouldn't. I can't stand the place now. I went back once, and boarded up the windows and doors for the winter."

"Will it sell, looking like that?"

"Someone might fall in love with the land. I don't know. I can't think about it."

Egg came and stretched out on the floor between them, his yellow eyes blinking sleepily. Just like in Maine, Jack thought, but something was different, Laura looked bigger. Was it the pregnancy? But no, that hardly showed yet. It was the ceiling, he decided, the scale of the room; the twenty-foot ceilings in her schoolhouse apartment had dwarfed them.

"When are you moving to Chicago?" he asked.

"Friday."

"This Friday?"

She nodded. "My apartment's a mess. I have so much packing to do."

"Shouldn't you be resting, still?"

She plucked at the flannel of his bathrobe. "I'm going to call Beth. She'll drive me up there, and help me pack."

"I'll do it."

"No!" she almost shouted. "I said I'll get Beth."

"Where is she?" Maisie whispered that evening, her arms full of groceries. Jack was sitting in the living room, doing nothing. The bedroom door was open.

"She went to a hotel."

"Jack!"

"I didn't suggest it. She wanted to. She wanted to be alone."

"She couldn't take any more of us."

He shrugged.

"But is she all right?"

"I guess so. She called the hospital before she left. The doctor said as long as she isn't bleeding anymore, things should be fine."

"But what if it starts again?" Maisie put the grocery bag on the floor. "You shouldn't have let her go."

"She's a grown-up, Maisie. And as you say, she was pretty fucking sick of us."

"But you know which hotel she's in? You'll check up on her?"

"Yes."

He lay down, crossed his arms behind his head, and closed his eyes. She picked up the groceries and went into the kitchen. It felt strange not to have Laura here. She'd bought more of the China black tea, a bag of thin sugar wafers. She'd imagined sitting up late with Laura tonight, after Jack had gone to bed. She'd thought about her all day as though she were a friend, someone she'd known at college but not very well, visiting for a few days from out of town. "You jerk," she said aloud, "you asshole, Maisie."

She put the groceries away and set about making a salad with the barbecued chicken she'd bought in Harvard Square. "Jack," she called, bending into the refrigerator, "where did you put the celery?"

He didn't answer, and she went into the living room. He was still on the couch.

"There was a full package in there, I thought." She imagined Laura eating celery, standing by the refrigerator in Jack's bathrobe, her white teeth chewing in her sad brown face. She went and stood over Jack. "Are you not feeling hungry?"

"No," he said.

"Me either." She sat down on the floor. "I feel so weird," she said finally. "Do you?"

"I'm just tired," Jack said.

"Do you think she's all right?"

"I don't know."

"I'm glad she's gone. I might have gotten very tangled up with her, if she'd stuck around."

He turned on his side to face her. "You were incredible."

"Well, but it was a little sick. I had this urge to find out all about her, where she'd grown up and what kind of music she liked. Who her old boyfriends were."

Jack, who presumably knew the answers to all these questions, said nothing. Maisie sat down on the floor and leaned her head against his waist. She felt his knuckles stroking her hair.

She asked, "Why do I have this urge to bend over backward to show her there are no hard feelings when there are?"

"I don't know."

"But did you feel it too?"

"I didn't feel anything."

"You're just saying that, because of me."

"No, it's true."

"Did you see her stomach, this morning when she was in your bathrobe? It does show. You could see it, a little swelling."

"I didn't notice."

"Jack. Come on. You must be interested, it's your kid."

"No, it's her kid. She won't take anything from me, not money, not even a ride back to Champs du Soleil. Whenever I offer, she makes me feel as though the *offer* is selfish, like I'm trying to atone but I don't really care."

"She's still in love with you," Maisie said.

"I don't think so."

"That's why she can't take these little bits and pieces you're offering." She took hold of his hand and told him to be patient, by the time the baby was born Laura would let him see it, and he'd be able to help. She listened to the wise, serene words that were coming out of her, and inside her another voice was screaming, as it had screamed for the last month, but she'd never sat still enough to listen to it before: This will taint us. This will be here forever. When we have our first child it won't be your first.

Jack took his hand away and she turned to look at him, certain he'd read her thoughts. She saw his face crumple, and he began to weep, soundlessly.

"What," she said, climbing up on the couch and putting her arms around him. "What. It's all right," she kept saying. "Ssssh. It's okay." After a while it started to sound forced, so she stopped saying it.

In a hotel room a mile away, the baby floated in darkness, growing safely, they hoped, in a way they could now imagine though they would never fully grasp or believe it.

Outside their open windows, the noises of evening traffic rose and fell, lone cars sweeping by on their way in and out of Boston. The bare tree branches creaked in the wind, a calm eternal sound that would go on night after night no matter who slept in this building, or whether the building was here or not.

Part IV

21
The Crooked Thing

Maisie had always imagined that there would be a definitive Lucy-and-Ricky-Ricardo moment when she would turn to Jack and say, "It's time," and they would make a dash for the hospital. But it took weeks; all the things that the books said meant impending labor happened to her, and no labor. Dr. Burkholder poked at her and said, "Well. This baby sure ain't going to wait around for its due date."

"Really?"

"Nope. You're three centimeters dilated and seventy percent effaced. What I'd do now is go home and put away all the Oriental carpets."

"Why?"

"Because when your water breaks, it's going to *break.*"

Jack drove with one hand going home; he held Maisie's hand with the other. It was the end of October; the baby wasn't due for another month. She looked out and thought that this would be a wonderful day for the baby to be born: a sky full of swollen dark clouds edged in gold, flashes of gold in the river, yellow leaves blowing everywhere.

Laura's daughter Jane was nearly two now. Jack had seen her twice, the first time when she was just ten weeks old. He'd flown out to Chicago alone one afternoon and followed the rising crescendo of a baby's screams up three flights of stairs in an Evanston apartment building. Jane had colic, Laura said into his ear, holding the baby; she screamed like this every afternoon. He'd held the baby, a hand supporting her crotch, leaning her over his forearm and bouncing her gently up and down. Laura looked tired, her body still swollen, her eyes small and dark-rimmed; Jack told her to go rest for a while, and she went without the slightest hesitation.

He walked Jane around the apartment and showed her the pictures on the walls; she stared at each one, and her crying abated to a gaspy sniffle for a moment before she lost interest and began screaming again. He put her against his shoulder and stroked her small, hot back. The screams filled him with pity, made him feel helpless and at the same time infinitely patient. "It's all right," he said to her over and over, "sweet Janie, it's all right." When she finally fell asleep in his arms, he looked down at her and tried to think, This is my daughter. But the thought didn't seem to hold, it kept slipping off somewhere. She didn't look like him, or like Laura. But then, he'd never been able to see any resemblance between a baby face and an adult face.

He had stayed for two days, cleaning the apartment, changing diapers, taking Laura and the baby out for dinner. Jane didn't cry at all in the restaurant, though Laura sat tensely waiting for her to start. Jane held her head up on Laura's shoulder and smiled at the people at the next table. Jack thought that maybe Laura should take her out more, because she seemed to cry less when there were distractions; but he felt he couldn't suggest or criticize her in any way, so he just said, "Jane seems very social." "Oh, she's a little flirt," Laura said, kissing Jane's leg.

Laura's camp hadn't sold, and she admitted she was glad about it now; she wanted Jane to grow up knowing that place. As Jack was leaving he offered again to give her money; and this time, coolly, but clearly pleased, she took it.

When he got home Maisie hugged him, said she'd missed him, and asked all sorts of questions about the baby. Who did she look like, how did it feel to hold her, how long would the colic go on, wasn't there any way to relieve it? Later in bed she started to cry, and he held her and they talked about having a baby of their own.

When he'd flown out again, a year later, Maisie was pregnant though they didn't know it yet. Laura was working, back to her thin brown self, and he went with her to pick up Jane at the baby-sitter's house. Jane didn't pay any attention to him at first and cried when he tried to hold her; but after dinner he made up a game with her, hiding a stuffed turtle in the hem of his shirt and bringing it up through the collar; she laughed at him, and he saw that her smile was like his. Otherwise she looked like Laura, with olive skin and dark eyes and hair. Laura was seeing a man named Roger, whom she thought she would marry. He came by on Saturday morning to help her shop for a new car. Jack and Roger watched Jane have her breakfast while Laura showered; they agreed she was a beautiful child. "And artistic," Roger said, flipping on the overhead light in the dining room; Jane raised a hand to it and said dramatically, "Ah!" Roger laughed, and echoed her tone perfectly: "Ah!"

The night before her due date, still pregnant, Maisie had her first dream about the baby. She had delivered it without paying much attention, then wandered out of the delivery room for a while. When she came back, the baby was in a little metal tray, like a roasting pan, with a paper sheet pulled up to its chin. She asked the nurse what it was, a boy or a girl. The nurse said, "I think it's a pig, and it's not coming around." So Maisie went out of the delivery room again, because she couldn't face it. When she came back Jack was lying on the delivery table holding the baby, and Maisie could see that it was a perfectly normal baby boy.

There were photographs of Jane, in an envelope in the drawer of Jack's desk. Maisie looked at them sometimes, when he was out. Jane in her plastic crib in the hospital, Jane propped against pillows, Jane sitting on the floor at eight months, an open copy of a Dr. Seuss book on the floor in front of her. Laura had carefully stayed out of all the pictures, except the last ones: a twin set of Jane at the beach, sitting on Laura's shoulders and posed identically on the shoulders of a blond man Maisie assumed must be Roger, Laura's husband. These last pictures seemed to convey a sense of finality: You see? This is our family now.

Jack showed her the pictures when they came, wordlessly. They couldn't exclaim proudly over them the way they would have if Jane had been a niece, or the child of friends. Laura's notes, which he also passed to Maisie, always said the same thing: You wouldn't believe how fast she's changing. She doesn't even look like these pictures anymore.

As Jane got older the pictures somehow grew more opaque, her face more elusive. You couldn't pretend anymore that you knew all about her. She was a child with a life; the snapshots were impatient moments of stillness. They made Jack sad, Maisie knew, they chronicled the receding of a child who'd been far away to begin with. She tried to sympathize with him, even though for her Jane's receding was something of a relief, making a void into which her own child would be born, unencumbered.

But still, Jane seemed to her like the real child. Her own pregnancy seemed like an imposture. It was so uneventful that she had trouble believing in it at all, even when the baby started to move. She had lain in bed balancing a glass with a spoon in it on her stomach; when the baby kicked, the spoon clinked against the glass. We're playing a game together, she said aloud to it, tentatively.

On the afternoon of her due date, she began to feel sad. Even if she went into labor right now, the baby would be late. But it wasn't supposed to be late, it was supposed to be early. Now what? She lay in bed, feeling panicky. She must put this reprieve to good use. Get out while there was still time. If she called a cab and went to the airport, she could buy a ticket to London and hop on the plane, get away.

But no, all that would happen was that the baby would be born in London.

The next day she said to Jack: "Oh, well, no baby. It missed its chance. Maybe we'll have one next time."

He looked at her in amazement: "That's exactly how I feel."

She went back to work, for the rest of that week and part of the next. She was going to take three months off after the baby was born and then go back part-time. Jack was working for a Cambridge consulting firm, helping German clients who manufactured fancy stoves and cooling equipment figure out how to market them in America. He went in at six in the morning to make phone calls to Europe; he was home by four, and would be able to care for the baby in the afternoons and evenings.

They kept going out to dinner, because their friends with children were warning them to savor these last days. Strangers waiting in line with her at the bank and at the layette counter told her stories: babies born brain-damaged, babies born dead. She went to get her hair cut, and the shampoo girl swathed her in a sheet and handed her over to Lenny, who cut her hair. "Hey," he said, "weren't you due at the beginning of the month? What did you have?"

"I'm still pregnant," she said, pressing the sheet against her front.

Dr. Burkholder was having contractions. Ah, thought Maisie, that's nice of her, this way I'll know what they feel like when I start having them. Then she woke up. It was Friday morning. Jack, next to her, was still asleep, his flushed face half-buried in the pillow. They were what the books said: a tightening and loosening, and she lay there feeling them with some amazement. In the spaces between them, she decided she'd imagined them, but then another one would come. She thought she'd let Jack sleep, and then when he woke up she would smile at him and tell him serenely that she'd been having contractions, and he'd say, "Why didn't you wake me?" But she had another one and he still didn't wake up, so she poked him.

He wanted to time them; they were seven minutes apart. They looked at each other in alarm—that was pretty close. He made her call the doctor. "I think I'm in labor," she said timidly to the receptionist.

"I'll have the doctor call you back," the receptionist told her.

While she was waiting, Maisie didn't have any contractions. Would the doctor believe her when she said she was in labor? What if they thought she was a hypochondriac, someone who cried wolf, and then when she really went into labor no one would believe her? Jack sat in a chair by the side of the bed, reading *The New Yorker*. How could he read? But she recognized the pinched, still look of his face, the way she thought a turtle must look when it's retracted as far into the shell as it can go, waiting for a safe time to come out.

The doctor said it was common for labor to stop the minute you called the doctor. Call back when they're every five minutes, she said.

After another half hour Maisie said, "This is stupid," and got out of bed. The contractions still hadn't come back.

Jack closed his magazine slowly, his eyes still focused on the page. He finally shut it altogether and tossed it on the floor. "Well, you want breakfast?"

She was annoyed with him for being so calm and distracted. "The doctor said I should only eat lightly."

"So . . . applesauce, or something."

"I'm not hungry."

He shrugged and cracked his knuckles. She got dressed, and they went out for a walk. Her coat didn't button, but it didn't matter. It was a strange day for December, a soupy sense of humidity even though it was cold. They walked very slowly, for a long time. She had felt wonderful all the way through the pregnancy, but now suddenly her belly was a heavy thing that had to be pushed, making her feel she was walking uphill even when she wasn't.

In the evening Jack made her macaroni with vegetables, and she thought: Is this what I'll throw up in the delivery room? She watched part of *Holiday* on TV, and then realized she'd been feeling contractions again, wearying and familiar, as though she'd always had them. She ignored them; she'd been jilted one time too many. At the end of the movie she told Jack, and he timed them: thirteen minutes. He got into bed with her and turned out the light. Some of them hurt now, a fist digging deep inside her. "Talk to me," she said.

He hesitated, then came out with long rhythmic lines of German. She let it go on for a while—it sounded like lots of things bumping up against each other in a rough but orderly way, pieces moving inside a clock. "What is this?" she asked finally.

"Faust."

"Do something in English." He had memorized lots of poems as a teenager.

So he told her "Ode to a Nightingale" and some Robert Frost poems, and then he was quiet. She had another contraction.

"Here's one," said Jack.

> *I whispered, "I am too young."*
> *And then, "I am old enough";*
> *Wherefore I threw a penny*
> *To find out if I might love.*
> *"Go and love, go and love, young man,*
> *If the lady be young and fair."*
> *Ah, penny, brown penny, brown penny,*
> *I am looped in the loops of her hair.*

O love is the crooked thing,
There is nobody wise enough
To find out all that is in it,
For he would be thinking of love
Till the stars had run away
And the shadows eaten the moon.
Ah, penny, brown penny, brown penny,
One cannot begin it too soon.

They lay in bed holding hands. She kept having to go to the bathroom, and after each time she got undressed and took a shower: she wanted to be perfectly clean in the delivery room. The contractions were coming every five minutes, every four, every six. It was one in the morning. We'd better call, they agreed. They dialed the answering service and set things irrevocably in motion. The doctor called back and said it sounded like the real thing: they should come right over to the hospital. This is it.

They don't panic. Nobody puts pants on backward. Maisie gets into her blue trousers, black sweater. She lies on her back on the bed with her feet hanging over the edge, so Jack can put on her socks and sneakers. She goes down to the bathroom one last time, and after all those showers doesn't quite dare take time for another one: she doesn't want the baby born in the car because she was so vain about her own cleanliness. Everyone says you don't care about these things when you go into labor; you throw up and shit all over the delivery room, and you don't care. But she cares. On the back of the toilet is a box of baby wipes, bought because the books told them to stock up before bringing the baby home. She says, "Is it okay if I borrow one of these, baby?" and she uses it and wraps it in tissue and throws it away. Her eyes fill with tears: the baby has let her use one of its things.

Driving to the hospital by night: the same route they took for eight Tuesday nights, going to their childbirth classes. Quiet, empty streets, piles of old bluish snow on some of the curbs. Every now and then another car or a truck: Who are these people? Why are they out in the middle of the night?

"Doesn't everything look beautiful now?" Maisie asks. "So quiet and still. Wouldn't it be nice if we could live in the nighttime all the time? Maybe someday the world will be so crowded that they'll have to divide everybody into two shifts, the way they do at big regional high schools.

There'll be a day shift and a night shift, and I'll take the night shift. Which shift would you take?"

Jack has been quiet, watching the road. "The day shift, I guess."

"Well, so we'll have to get divorced after all," Maisie says, the joke not funny, but a barometer of how well she's doing, how calm she is.

She announces herself to the old lady on duty in the hospital lobby, who blinks back sleep and asks if Maisie wants a private room. Jack stands in the doorway looking foolish and worried, clutching Maisie's bag and the cassette player and an old orange-and-green pillow from his parents' house in Champs du Soleil. The admitting lady clamps a plastic bracelet on Maisie's wrist and asks Maisie to sign a form that has another bracelet attached to it, for the baby. The bracelets won't come off unless you cut them off. When she does that, she and the baby will be home.

The contractions have stopped, and when the admitting lady asks if Maisie wants to walk or take a wheelchair, Maisie says, "I'll walk."

The lady nods, and shuffles slowly toward the elevator. She is wearing slippers, and Maisie wonders, following her, whether these are the "paper slippers" the childbirth teacher has said the hospital will supply. Somehow she is having more trouble conjuring up a mental picture of what "paper slippers" might be like than of any of the other things that might happen to her in childbirth.

"Cathy will take you," says the girl behind the maternity reception desk, and they follow Cathy to one of the hospital's new birthing rooms. The birthing rooms are supposed to be cozy and homelike, but they are just windowless hospital rooms with cutesy American Country wallpaper. There is a narrow bed, a sink, a supply cupboard, a fetal monitor. And a tiny raised plastic bassinet under big heat lamps: that is where they will put the baby. When Maisie and Jack leave this room they will have had the baby.

Cathy tells Maisie to get undressed, does her temperature and blood pressure and all the routine bustling little tests. Jack sits on a chair near the bed, staring at Maisie and giving her smiles that are meant to be reassuring. She doesn't need reassurance, she doesn't need all this fussy attention; she feels as though she's accidentally tripped an alarm, or as though they're all mistaking her for someone else. She wishes the contractions would start again; at least they make her feel legitimate. Cathy puts a belt around Maisie's belly, hooks her up to the fetal monitor.

"Okay, now let's check your dilation." Cathy prods gently, frowns.

Maisie calculates: she was three centimeters before the contractions started, and she's been in labor on and off for twenty-four hours. She's probably at about six, and at ten she can begin to push.

"Three centimeters!" Cathy announces. She looks at Maisie's face. "Maybe a hair more," she adds quickly.

"But I've been at three for a month," Maisie tells her.

"Well, listen, let me call Dr. Burkholder at home and see what she wants to do," Cathy says cheerfully. Maisie is sure Dr. Burkholder will swear and tell Cathy to send her home.

The minute Cathy goes out, the contractions start again. The numbers on the fetal monitor screen dart from nine to twenty-four to twenty-six and then gradually down again. Maisie looks at Jack, and he comes over and takes her hand. He smiles at her.

"But don't say 'Honey, you're doing great,' okay?" she reminds him. The night the childbirth teacher showed them videos of babies being born, all the husbands in the films were so patronizingly encouraging to their wives that Maisie said to Jack, "Your job is just to be there, okay? Don't coach me."

"How're you doing?" he asks, stroking her wrist.

"I feel like an idiot," Maisie says.

"I love you."

"You do?"

Cathy comes back in and unhooks Maisie from the monitor. "Now I'm going to have you guys walk around for an hour or two. That usually does the trick. Dr. Burkholder will be in around six-thirty, and if things aren't moving faster by then, we'll induce you with Pitocin."

She takes them out into the hall, shows them where the ice chips machine is, and leaves them to walk. Jack gets some ice chips in a cup and hands it to Maisie, and again she feels ridiculous: ice chips is one of the clichés of labor, mentioned in all the books, and what the hell is she doing here actually sucking *ice chips?* She's read too many books, that's the problem, the whole thing is one big cliché checklist: walk the halls, check, lean on husband during contractions, check, ice chips, check.

They walk slowly up and down, up and down. On one end the terminus of the walk is a little lounge where three people doze in front of a television set: a Fred Astaire movie, but the woman he's dancing with isn't Ginger Rogers. One of the dozers is in a hospital employee smock, but two are in civilian clothes, a man and a woman. Waiting for someone else in labor? But why are they allowed beyond the regular visitors' waiting room? A complicated emergency labor? But then why are they asleep? On the other end of the walk, down several corridors, they pass a bin of laundry, blood on the floor. They stop and turn around at the sign for the neonatal intensive care nursery: they don't want to go down there.

Dr. Burkholder comes in, looking shockingly of the outside world, Saturday casual in jeans and a beige cashmere turtleneck, her blond hair pulled back in a ponytail. "Let's see what's going on here," she says, examining Maisie. "Three centimeters."

"Oh, and a hair more," says Cathy.

"Maybe," the doctor says doubtfully. She peels off her gloves. "Okay, we're going to start you on Pitocin."

"Will the contractions get a lot more painful?" Maisie asks.

The doctor shrugs. "Listen, you can continue forever with these stinky little contractions"—she holds out the monitor tape as evidence, but Maisie hasn't the least idea what the monitor tape shows—"or we can get serious and start Pitocin and have the baby in a few hours."

"Okay," Maisie says weakly—stinky little contractions, she hasn't been doing it right, then—"but will it hurt?"

"How badly is it hurting now, on a scale of one to ten?"

She tries to be stoical. "Oh, fives, maybe some sevens."

"Well, these will probably feel like your sevens."

"I can stand that."

"All right. Now I'm going to break your water"—a gush of sudden warmth, and Cathy taking wads of wet gauze sheeting out from under her, putting down dry—"and I'll see you later!"

Cathy sets up the IVs, one for fluids and one for Pitocin. The Pitocin one has a meter like a gasoline pump, which shows how much is being pumped in. She flips a switch. "See, we start you slow, then gradually up it." Flip, flip, flip. Maisie breathes, smiles at Jack. He looks frightened and sleepy.

"Well, that's the end of my shift," Cathy says. "See you."

Another nurse comes in: Gail. Cold, lashless gray eyes. She flips up the Pitocin. The contractions hurt more. Dr. Burkholder comes back: five and a half centimeters. "*That's* an improvement," she says, grinning, and she stays to chat a bit. Her husband is doing his first grand rounds at nine, and she wonders whether it would make her more nervous to go watch him or not to go watch him.

"What kind of doctor is he?" Maisie asks.

"A vascular surgeon." She laughs. "Maybe I will go—I brought rotten tomatoes to throw at him."

Maisie laughs and has a contraction. Breathe, breathe, only now there's a sharp little gasp in her throat and she's going too fast. Gail waits for her to finish and flips up the Pitocin some more. Bitch. They leave, and Maisie looks at Jack.

"I don't know if I can do this. Do you mind if I start thinking about an anesthetic?"

"Of course not!" He holds her hand. He doesn't try to coach her with the breathing, and she doesn't ask him to; they look at each other sadly; they know they're both in over their heads.

Gail comes back and flips, flips up again. The pains are hard, hot, twisting things that make Maisie want to get up and flee, but she can't; they pin her to the bed. If she could scream and thrash around, the way she's read many women do, the pain might be bearable, but she's too embarrassed. She's panting and gasping; the carefully practiced breathing is like a glass that's shattered on the floor, exploding in different directions.

Dr. Burkholder comes back in. "How soon can we consider an epidural?" Maisie asks her politely.

"Right away." She pats Maisie on the leg. "Smart girl."

They bustle around and do things to her between contractions, which are coming every three minutes. The anesthesiologist comes in and introduces herself: she is young, with dark hair and rich brown eyes; she locks eyes with Maisie and smiles at her. She looks like Caterina, Maisie has time to think before another contraction takes hold. They turn her on her side, swab her with something cold, give her a shot of novocaine.

"When do I drink the terrible antacid?" she asks; the childbirth teacher mentioned this in class.

There is an appalled silence; then someone says, "That's right, we forgot." A laugh. "She's on top of things, this one." Somehow this little lapse, instead of unnerving her, reassures her: so they don't know everything, we're all equals here, collaborating on this labor.

"Okay, curl yourself up around your baby. You're going to feel kind of a shock in your legs, okay, and now here's the anesthetic going in."

A crackling buzz that jerks her legs uncontrollably, a cold snaky feeling down her back.

"All done," they say.

"All done? But I thought it was supposed to take fifteen minutes."

"That was fifteen minutes."

They turn her on her back, but with a pillow propping her a little to one side, so that she won't lie on the catheter. Another bad contraction.

"Let's change your breathing," Gail says, and she breathes and Maisie breathes with her, gratefully.

"That's one happy baby," Dr. Burkholder says, looking at the monitor. Maisie doesn't know how she can tell, but she drinks it in. She makes it through the next contraction without gasping. "Could I be feeling better already?" she asks, and they laugh at her. By the next one she's sure: definitely better. They dim the lights and smile at her; she smiles back at the anesthesiologist: "Thank you."

"What a wonderful invention," she tells Dr. Burkholder.

"I know. If I ever have a kid myself, I'm definitely having an epidural. Okay, you're dilated some more. You'll have a baby by early afternoon."

She and Jack are alone. No pain, no reason to breathe. Just a slight, detached sensation of pressure when a contraction comes. She smiles at him. "Go to sleep."

"Are you sure?" His face is white.

"Yeah."

He puts on *The Marriage of Figaro* for her and falls asleep in the chair. She reads about Anna and Vronsky visiting the artist, but she's forgotten each sentence by the time she reaches the next. She's aware sometimes that music is playing, but she can't listen to it. She looks at the clock, at the fetal monitor, at Jack. She loves him, but she's sorry for him: he's very small and far away. She wonders about the women who go on and on about how wonderful their husbands were during labor, coaching them and standing up to the doctors on their behalf, climbing into bed with them and holding them, rubbing their backs and feet. There is no room in this little bed, surrounded by machines, for Jack; she doesn't want him to touch her or tell her that everything will be all right. How would he know? Nothing he could say, no tenderness in his voice, could make this hurt less; only the anesthetic snaking into her back can do that. Do the other women have stronger, more fearless husbands, who can somehow fight off pain? Or do they endow their husbands with more power, so that all the coaching and foot rubbing is genuinely comforting to them?

"Eight centimeters," says Gail. She wakes Jack and sends him into the bathroom, to change into what she coyly calls the "paternity suit": blue surgical scrubs and a hat that makes him look like the Flying Nun.

"No," she says, laughing, "it ties in the back."

He looks sheepish and fixes it. Gail goes out to get the doctor, and Jack stands by the fetal monitor, which is thumping and rollicking along. "It sounds just like a train," he says.

Now she feels perfectly peaceful, and aware of how much she loves him.

"How were the grand rounds?" Maisie asks as the doctor puts on her rubber gloves. "Did you go?"

"Yes, and he was wonderful. Well, guess what? It's time to push."

When the contraction comes, they tell her to take a deep breath, let it out, draw up her thighs and hold them, take another deep breath, put her chin on her chest, hold her breath, and push. She should be able to do three pushes with each contraction. She does, and Gail says: "It's amazing you have so much muscle control left even with the epidural."

Maisie feels smug: at last she is doing something right.

Dr. Burkholder looks inside her. "I can see the baby's head. Could be blond, like her mom."

Another anesthesiologist comes to give her more: she hates him on sight. Arrogant young man, who doesn't look at her but makes her feel, for the first time, the grotesqueness of her position, her nakedness. When he leaves, he looks at Jack. "Hey, good luck. My wife just had our first kid three weeks ago."

Everyone who comes in looks at the monitor and says, "Baby's doing great," or "What a happy baby." Maisie is glad to hear it, although she is beginning to suspect that it's standard hospital patter, like when her hairdresser tells her she has such great hair.

"Push," Gail chants. "Come on. Push him right on out your bottom. Push. Push."

Gail is holding one leg, Jack the other. She can't look at him; she just has to push. If he left now, she would be frantic, but he's there only to be taken for granted. "Push," Gail says. "Come on, push."

"You're not pushing hard enough," says Dr. Burkholder, coming in to check her.

Screw her, Maisie is pushing as hard as she can; besides, Gail has already told her she's doing a good job, how dare the doctor say she isn't? Why doesn't Jack tell the doctor not to talk to her like that? But she pushes harder, trying to be a model patient. She's had so little to do since the epidural; at least she must do this one thing right.

They put an oxygen mask over her face. It makes her feel as though she's getting less oxygen, a stifling plastic smell, and it's hot, and it keeps slipping off, ruining her concentration. She is gasping through the contractions again. They want her to push four times with each, but she can't, she ends up gagging. The first push is okay, the second the deep grinding efficient one, the third okay again, and the fourth a washout, a token effort, with Maisie gagging away into her oxygen mask and the nurse and doctor looking at each other in what she imagines is disgust and disappointment. It doesn't occur to her to say: Wouldn't it be better to just stick to three pushes? but it does occur to her to wonder why Jack doesn't say this.

They keep taking her temperature; it is going up. Finally Dr. Burkholder tells her that the baby is in distress. Maisie looks at the monitor and sees that its heart rate, which has been comfortably steady at around 140, is now up in the low 170s.

"The baby isn't getting enough oxygen," the doctor says. "We may want to do a cesarean."

"Push," says Gail, on the other side of the bed.

She pushes harder than she knew she could. Now all she can think about is the baby, how it's up to her to make sure he's all right. Between pushes she looks at the galloping monitor. She thinks of children falling through the ice, deprived of oxygen. Ten minutes, they say, you have to get them out in ten minutes.

"Does this mean he'll have brain damage?" she asks the doctor.

The doctor looks at her sternly. "Maisie, if there were any chance of that, do you think I'd be standing here discussing the possibility of a C-section? Don't you think I'd be in the delivery room, doing one?"

Rebuked, she doesn't ask any more questions. She pushes, pushes. They decide to take some blood from the baby's scalp to test something, Maisie doesn't understand what, but it will show if the baby can stand more labor. She hears them arranging for equipment, technicians to stand by. It sounds as though they're going to run the blood down the hall. She thinks of the Olympic torch. Jack holds her leg up and she pushes, no time to be tired, no time to gag, just push. They take the blood, and word comes back that the baby's okay. But what does that mean? Okay for how long? Still there are those ominous numbers on the monitor. But how ominous? How much worse is 170 than 160? What does it mean, the baby's in distress? How much distress? But she hasn't the energy or the mind to formulate any of these questions, and anyway she's afraid of the answers. All she can do is push.

She thinks of Caterina and Laura. They did it, they had babies. They are real. But she is a fake, she always has been. She's learned to hide it better lately; her husband doesn't know it anymore. But the labor knows it. The labor has put her in her true place: strapped to machines, to drugs, to oxygen, yet still, with all this help, unable to do it. She thought she could get through without being caught, but she is caught, her essential weakness exposed; and the baby will pay.

They decide to do the scalp sampling again, but they have to wait for the equipment; someone else is using it. She is looking into Jack's face now, pushing. They're still waiting for the equipment. Finally she bursts out: "What's taking so long?"

"It's all right," Dr. Burkholder tells her. "Someone else is using the equipment, we just have to wait for them to finish."

She already knows that. What she wants to know is: if there's any chance the baby's in danger, why *aren't* they in there doing a cesarean? Why are they waiting around for a piece of fucking equipment?

Finally the equipment rolls in again, and Dr. Burkholder tries to get more blood out of the baby's scalp, but she can't. Maisie keeps pushing. The doctor gets some blood but worries that it might not be enough. Word comes back from the lab that they haven't been able to read the blood; it clotted too fast. All of this may mean something, but Maisie doesn't know; she keeps pushing.

"All right," says the doctor. "How about if we go down to the delivery room and have this baby, okay? Let's go get this little pumpkin out."

They transfer Maisie from one bed to another, and say again how much muscle control she has left. She thinks: Why are they *chatting?* Hurry up and get me down there.

"Okay," says Dr. Burkholder in the delivery room. "Let's give a try with forceps." No more cashmere turtleneck and jeans; she is dressed like a surgeon, in scrubs and mask. No more cutesy wallpaper. Maisie doesn't want to see anything that's going on. There is a mirror, but she doesn't look. Jack, his face masked, sits next to her head. The forceps are in a huge jar, like a Chinese egg jar, full of fluid. Dr. Burkholder stands over it like a witch doctor, pulls something out, fits pieces together. She seats herself between Maisie's legs. Maisie's feet are up in stirrups, her legs are draped. She is grinding away, pushing. "Can you feel this?" the doctor keeps asking.

Maisie doesn't know. She does feel something, but it's not unbearable. She keeps trying to do the breathing, to relax, but her breath comes in gasps, and each time the doctor stops. "If you breathe like that, I assume I'm hurting you." Then she says, "The baby's come way down. You pushed him down. Now let me see if I can turn him and get him out of there."

The anesthesiologist, the arrogant one, is pumping in more cold anesthetic. "Can you feel this?" he asks, pricking Maisie's belly.

"Yes."

The doctor stands up. "I don't know. I'm going to do a C-section."

They start to get Maisie ready, but again it seems too leisurely, swabbing her with things, shooting more drugs into her. How badly off is the baby? Why don't they just knock her out and get him? The anesthesiologist is worried because she's still feeling his pinpricks as sharp, and she's confusing him with her answers. But she doesn't know what she's supposed to feel: little or nothing? She doesn't want the baby to die because she's being fussy about how much pain she's feeling. On the other hand, she doesn't want to find out while they're cutting her open that there's not enough anesthetic.

"We'd better do a spinal," the anesthesiologist says finally.

Maisie ignores him and pushes, grinding down with her whole body.

"I'll try once more with the forceps while you set up," Dr. Burkholder says. Then she says, sadly: "I'm going to have to give you an episiotomy."

"Fine," Maisie says, thinking: What about the cesarean? And how come she sounds sorrier about this than about that? She is pushing, pushing, pushing. She hears the doctor say that the head is out. This means nothing to her; she is thinking about the cesarean, and pushing. Then the doctor says, "It's a little boy," and she hears Jack, beside her head, burst into tears. She looks down and sees a white blob and an umbilical cord, dead white. The doctor's clothes are covered with blood and brown smears: shit? Maisie's? The baby's? They've taken the baby into a corner. Jack cries at her side. Maisie waits for them to come back and say what's wrong with the baby. She doesn't care that he's been born, she can't afford to care. All she can think of is that now she won't need a cesarean, and that she's thirsty, and that her legs hurt from being up in the stirrups.

They bring the baby over, wrapped up and wearing an absurd little cap. They hand him to Jack. Jack talks to him and starts singing, softly, a sea chantey. Maisie doesn't care. She glances over: a big red squinty head. She's still waiting to hear what's wrong with him.

"And here's the placenta," Dr. Burkholder says. That Maisie is interested in. She asks to see it: a big piece of liver. Maisie talks about different cultural attitudes toward the placenta: some cultures revere it, bury it, make a ceremony of it. See, I'm a civilized person. I'm sorry I got so upset during labor.

She gasps out her thanks to everyone: the nurses, the arrogant anesthesiologist. The doctor sews her up. Next to her Jack sings to the baby. "My stomach is flat!" Maisie exclaims. That's what she's interested in, the placenta and her stomach. Not the baby. She's still afraid to look at him.

They wheel her into the recovery room, and they take the baby to the intensive care nursery: he has a split lip from the forceps, and they want to make sure it doesn't need stitches. She doesn't care that they've taken him away. All she cares about is that they've taken her legs out of the stirrups and given her a cup of cold water.

They bring the baby back, in a little plastic bassinet. He's just bruised, he won't need stitches. Still she can't look at him much, just shyly, out of the corner of her eye. Jack picks him up and holds him against his chest. They don't talk. She's always imagined that she'd comfort her baby right away, hold it, talk to it, but she's still waiting to hear what's wrong with him. Gail brings more water and says good-bye; Dr. Burkholder smiles down at them and then leaves; Maisie thanks them both fervently. Someone has mentioned the baby's Apgar scores: nine and nine. That's very high: does that mean he's okay? No one pays any attention to them in the recovery room: does that mean they're all okay?

The man in the cubicle across the way tells his wife he's going to call the kids, that he'll ask the nurse to give her some antinausea medication, that he'll see her later. Maisie wonders why he doesn't just stay with her, and she thinks how lucky she is to have Jack, who would stay with her no matter what, who sings to the baby when she can't.

A young guy comes and wheels them upstairs: Maisie's bed and the baby's crib in tandem, a little flotilla. He puts them in a room that looks like a hospital room: such a relief to be someplace that looks like what it is, after those hypocritical little birthing rooms. The sky outside the window is purple, almost black; somehow a whole day has gone by.

Jack moves to help her transfer to the bed, but the orderly stops him: she's got to do it herself. At last, something she can do herself, the first step toward recovery.

Then they are left alone. Jack in a chair, Maisie in bed, and the baby's crib pulled up tightly against the bed. Jack falls asleep. And Maisie lies there looking at him and then gazing, finally, into the baby's face, so small, so bashed up, and slowly she realizes that she loves him passionately, that she's always loved him passionately, that he's the same creature she's known for months only now he's here and he got here, somehow, safely.

She raises herself on her elbows and sits up, painfully, reaching her hands down between the plastic walls of the bassinet. The baby is a frighteningly floppy bundle; she is certain he'll cry when she picks him up. But he doesn't cry. He lies on her knees, his liquid pewter eyes blinking at her. She is too shy to talk to him, but she begins to sing, very low, the same song Jack sang in the delivery room. She is uncertain of both the words and the tune, but she thinks of the soft sound of Jack's voice, and tries to recall it with her own.

Printed in the United States
26258LVS00001B/379